Wallace Family
Affairs
Volume I
Tracy's Complications

Carey Anderson

DEDICATION

This story is dedicated to my loved ones who indulged in my imagination with me. I appreciate your time; I could never thank you enough

Cover design: Cover Couture

Join me on Facebook –
www.facebook.com/careythewriteranderson

Twitter - @CareyTheWriter

Blog - http://careyanderson.blogspot.com

Website – http://www.careythewriteranderson.com

Carey Anderson's work of fiction.

Here's the first story from within my head!

ACKNOWLEDGMENTS

I would like to thank my baby-girl who is my life's ultimate expression of a dream realized. Thank you for sacrificing mommy time so that I could have the time to work some things out on paper.

I would like to thank my Soul Sistah #1 who has been my captivated audience since middle school. Without your love, support, encouragement, and FIRE I never would've completed Volume I or II, etc. Thank you for bringing me laughter when I couldn't get outside of my head.

I would like to thank my Sister-In-Law for taking time out of your busy family life to humor me with a read through of my latest thoughts and expressions. (SS1 & SIL THANK YOU for the trip to St. Helena where we spent the day lost in my imagination. I will never forget it, and it was exactly what I needed. THANK YOU!)

I would like to thank my dear cousin for reassuring me that my little hobby was relatable and entertaining. You are definitely a speed-reader, thank you for taking time out of your busy life to be entertained by my imagination.

I would like to thank last but not least Mrs. Laverne Dyes! Mrs. Dyes the day that you read my short story to my class changed my life. Thank you for giving me a positive outlet for all the angst going on in my life. You have forever changed my life, I am so thankful to have ever known you.

And so it begins!

CHAPTER 1

I know Richmond California has this reputation all of a sudden for being just as bad if not worse than Oakland. But I grew up there. It's not the most pristine environment, but at least when I was growing up it didn't feel like this horrible place to live. Richmond is situated right on the bay, next door to Berkeley, and on a light traffic day in less than twenty minutes you could be in San Francisco. I'd say my family was your typical religious family. My dad worked hard to provide for our family, and my mom worked until I was in high school. For a while it was just me and my brother Terrence. Terrence was always my rock and favorite person. One day mom and dad sat us down and explained that they were gonna have a baby. At first we were happy, oh how exciting a new baby was gonna be. The day they found out it was gonna be twins my life drastically changed forever. Everything became about the twins, Terrence and I got lost in the shuffle. Well maybe not so much Terrence cause he was still the only boy. My little identical sisters although I loved them dearly seem to steal the show whenever we went anywhere. People would go on and on about how cute and pretty they were, and even though I was standing right there the compliments would stop there. That's when I began to feel invisible and useless. Since both my parents worked and tried very hard to keep our family in the middle of the congregation, it didn't leave them much time to realize how neglected I felt. My mom would get irritated with me when I made references to being ugly about myself. She didn't understand that I was only reflecting the way people made me feel.

My parents used to rave over my good grades. When my grades slipped they said nothing; I quickly learned that I needed to get my grades for me and not to make them happy. In high school I got a job just so I could be away from home as much as possible. Working in the movie theater was so much fun. I got to meet new people; it always felt more like hanging out than it did work. In addition to being the invisible daughter I was the plain Jane or sometimes the ugly friend. So naturally I thought I was going to die when a boy actually liked me. Or let me make the correction, I thought he liked me turns out he only really had physical concerns in regards to me. I was crushed, and I quickly learned that most guys had the same agenda. For a girl being raised in a Christian household awareness of this fact felt quite troubling to me. Suddenly I felt like the entire world was sexually active and I was amongst the last of the virgins standing in the world. My brother seemed to easily stay on the straight and narrow, where I daydreamed about the broad and spacious. Terrence met Amy when he was sixteen and he was immediately smitten. They properly dated until Terrence was twenty and could afford a wife. Where I just about lost my mind when I went to college. I met a guy who convinced me that he loved me. Out of obligation I gave in and gave him my most prized possession. I still mourn the loss of my virginity to this day. I was fortunate to find a job while in college that allowed me to afford an apartment and a car. Although I didn't move far away, since my life took an alternate path I didn't see my family much. I kept in contact with the girls mostly and they would pop by from time to time. Once they were off to school I really didn't see family too much. I often felt guilty about my lifestyle but I never felt worthy to go back especially if I was still sinning.

****

Oh my goodness! Is that me? Marie was proudly showing off our vacation pictures. I smiled trying to act like I was ok with the reflection of myself in the picture. How did I let my weight get so out of hand? There's nothing like looking at yourself for who you actually are and not liking what you see.

Talking with our little group a while later we decided to make it a group effort to get healthy. I never thought of myself as a competitive person, but since I am the heaviest person in our group

I felt like I stood out like a sore thumb. Some of them only needed to tone up where I needed that and to lose. I didn't want to get left behind. Plus talking to my doctor, she really put fear in me about the possible side affects on my body if I continued to carry this weight.

After searching the Internet I found a plan that I could manage, nine days raw fruits and veggies and a few other items. I put myself in a zone and I did it. The weight didn't melt off like it was moving on the rest of my friends. I had to work a little harder at it than everyone else, slow but steady my journey began.

At night I thought about Steve, my on again off again ex. When we got together I wasn't in my most confident space, but I knew I looked good naked. My previous relationship was a devastating disaster. That idiot left me feeling broken and confused. Steve glided in as if he was heaven sent. Everything felt right with Steve even when it was wrong. I loved Steve with all my heart; my passive aggressive nature caused me to internalize all the wrongs in our relationship. Not really knowing how to ask for what I wanted or how to get it, I internalized the demise of our relationship.

In the end Steve complained a lot about my weight, now he didn't exactly do this to my face. He complained to my friends and family. Once we sat down at the table and he started lecturing me about my portions. He even took his fork and divided the food on my plate. Of course I said nothing to voice my disgust. Communication was definitely an issue in our relationship. We argued but it never really resolved anything because both of us were holding back. Steve convinced me that the one area where we did communicate best in was the bedroom. I called him on his half efforts to please me, and I did my best to reciprocate the effort. Steve loved how I responded to him and even though he tried to hide it his body craved my touch.

So many things had gone wrong between us but we never had the chance to officially say goodbye. So we kind of hung on by a thread, we kept in contact. But lately Steve had become distant which only meant he was in a new relationship. So I gave him space to explore his relationship while I kept my head in the game. In one month people noticed my hard work. The difference was showing and I was on the road to seeing myself in a different light. I started caring about my appearance again, and doing things that made me feel good about being me.

CHAPTER 2

Steve was calling again, and sure enough it was a relationship that had pulled him away. But now that they were on the verge of breaking up he was calling on a regular basis. I haven't seen him in months so he had no idea about the progress I had made in my weight loss journey. I didn't mention anything about my journey to him. I've lost 40 pounds but I still had 60 to go to meet my goal. My goal was to surpass my body shape when we initially hooked up. But at 40 pounds down I was already looking AMAZING!

My good friend Nicole is getting married, and she asked me to be her maid of honor. I was truly honored, and looked forward to being there for one of my dearest friends. She threw an engagement party to celebrate, and she asked me to greet the guest as they entered the party. The old me would've been intimidated by her request. But I sucked in my stomach and I told myself I could do it. There were so many people I didn't devote any of them to memory. Once the arrivals slowed down, Nicole asked me to join the party. She introduced me to a few people, but she got pulled away.

I went outside to talk to Nicole's mom for a bit. Then someone came to talk to her mom, as I started to walk away he was approaching. "I'm Andrew"

"Hello Andrew, Tracy" I said with a big smile.

"Nice to meet you Tracy, who do you know here?" He said swiveling around to look around the party.

"Nicole is one of my good friends. I'm one of her bridesmaids." I said as nonchalantly as I could.

"I'm a groomsman. Maybe I'll be able to escort you down the aisle." He said with a smile.

Who is this gorgeous man talking to me? And why of all people did he come to talk to me? "Maybe" I said, nothing this perfect could ever happen in my life.

I loved that night I wasn't shy and awkward. Probably because I couldn't really convince myself that someone this fine could ever be into me. We conversed all night even when the events of the

7

night separated us, I could see Andrew search for me and then come for me. What's wrong with this guy I thought to myself? Is he one of those guys who need to feel like they're a gift to the woman they're with, so they purposely look for someone a lot less attractive than they are to keep the upper hand in their relationship? Maybe he's just a good guy, which is what I was hoping. Something so perfect couldn't ever happen in my life.

"So can I get your number there may be a wedding emergency that we need to handle together."? We both laughed, "I know that wasn't smooth. But I know I would regret letting you leave without at least asking for your number."

Does this mean he likes me? I was flattered and happily gave Andrew my number.

Four days later Andrew called, we talked for hours. It felt so good to have this experience, a nice guy calling me up and then asking me out on a date. We went over the basics, no children, later aspirations for a family, etc. I liked talking to him; he was serious with the perfect amount of silliness at appropriate times. I waited for him to bring up sex. I braced myself for it actually. To my delight he wanted to know me. He asked me questions about myself and actually listened to the answers. That made me nervous, but I loved how it made me feel.

****

Frustrated I went through my closet looking for something to wear. I had pieces of outfits, but nothing date worthy. I didn't want to look like I had nothing to offer but sex. But I wanted to at least look nice. Frustrated I hopped in my car and went to the mall. While I was in the mall looking for something to wear Steve called me. "I saw your car in the parking lot where are you?"

"Macy's, in the women's department by the escalator." I said "I'm on my way..."

Suddenly I was nervous. I hadn't seen Steve in months and he was going to see me for the first time since I started losing weight. I turned my back to the escalators and nervously shifted through the racks. I knew he'd like what he saw, but I didn't want any problems either. Then I found an awesome turquoise blouse; I became distracted, caught up in the idea of the possibilities of the blouse time passed. When I looked up to see where Steve was, Steve was almost passing me looking lost. Our eyes met, I smiled and his mouth dropped open. "WHAT DID YOU DO?????" he screamed as he rushed me and picked me up off the ground. This was the best reaction yet. As he squeezed me he kissed my neck, I never told him how much I loved that. "Look at you girl!"

"How you been?" I said trying to grab my composure.

His mouth was talking but his eyes were dancing all over my body. His breathing got heavier and suddenly he was mister conversational and energetic. After thirty minutes he finally asked, "What's the shirt for?"

"I have a date Saturday so I came to get an outfit. What do you think?" I held the blouse up to my chest.

He tried to hide the annoyance on his face, "I guess that's cool. What were you gonna put it with?"

"I have jeans and heels already. I was thinking a new blouse and maybe a jacket if I could find one. "

He rolled his eyes, "I guess that will work".

"Hater" I said as I took my shirt to the register.

Right on my heels Steve followed me to the register. "So who is this guy?" he tried to sound as unthreatened as an ex-boyfriend could sound.

"You remember my friend Nicole?"

"Yea" he said as he pretended to be uninterested in the explanation.

"She's finally getting married. We met at the engagement party."

"So you met this guy and just like that you're going out?"

"I guess so."

Steve changed the subject; meanwhile he continued to drool over my new form. He followed me to the coat department, and he rolled his eyes when I picked up some more perfume. Although he tried very hard to convince me to stay out for a nightcap, I declined and told him I was going over Marie's. So he stayed on my line the entire drive to Marie's. The rest of the night he sent me text messages, exclaiming his approval of all my progress. Marie greeted me at the door with a huge smile and hug. I showed her what I bought, and then I told her all about my encounter with Steve at the mall. We laughed about how good it felt to have that experience. I told her how nervous I was about my date with Andrew. I could tell this experience with Andrew was going to be unlike any other experience I've ever had. It was already unique in how it started and even where it stands to date. I said a prayer asking for a sign if Andrew was supposed to be the one for me. After I went home to prepare, I soaked in my bathtub trying to imagine what our date would even be like. I went to sleep that night with a huge smile.

CHAPTER 3

My heart screamed and I almost ran, but there was nowhere to run to. Andrew was here for our first date and his knock at the door sent my heart into a panic. What if he took one look at me and felt disappointed because he remembered me differently. When I opened the door he smiled really big at me. I on the other hand was liable to pass-out; he was finer than I remembered. He initiated the hello hug, and oh my goodness! He smelled so good! I invited him in for a minute. He said he liked my place. I liked the look of him in my apartment. Andrew was tall cinnamon brown, with dark brown hair, beautiful dimples, and brown eyes that seem to glow. He carried himself like he was aware of who he was, but he didn't make a big deal out of it, I liked that. He took me to a small restaurant in Pinole not too far from my house. I thought I was definitely going to be shy and awkward this time around, but with Andrew our conversation flowed. There weren't any awkward pauses, or loss for words. He naturally talked, listened, and asked me questions. We finished dinner, and hours later we were still sitting at the table and laughing and really enjoying each other's company. A couple of times I pinched myself under the table just to make sure this wasn't a dream. When the restaurant was closing he very slowly drove me home. We sat in the car talking for a while and then we slowly made our way to my door. When he didn't try to kiss me goodnight, I thought he wasn't interested. But he called me the next day to ask me out again. We ended up talking for hours. He even acknowledged that our conversation flowed real easy. I still wondered if he was really attracted to me or if he only saw me as a friend, especially since he didn't try to kiss me after our second and third date. Before our fourth date we were talking on the phone as usual. I made a reference to not feeling so attractive in my current body image. He paid me the biggest compliment by telling me that I was beautiful. Our fourth date began with a kiss, and ended with a knock your socks off kiss. It was very hard not to invite him in. He called me from the car, and sat outside my apartment for an hour. Even though he went home we stayed on the phone until almost morning. During that conversation we made a date to work out together. Things were going really well with us, so well that I lost count of how many dates we had gone on. Sometimes we would end one date, to start another an hour or so later. Sometimes he'd come over and we'd watch TV all cuddled up and lost in each other's limbs. Kissing him was my new favorite hobby. We haven't gone much further than that for now. Which hasn't been easy, cause quite naturally I want to give him everything, but I could see Andrew and I actually having a future and I don't want to rush things.

It wasn't alarming that Andrew popped up at my door. We were now at the point where he popped up whenever he felt like it. But he looked sad which put me on alarm. Instead of freaking out outwardly like I was on the inside I chose to be calm. He asked me to take a walk with him, so I did. We walked in silence for a few minutes. Then I stopped walking, "What's up?" I asked

He started rambling; my heart sank more and more with every word. "I don't want to lose your friendship. I need some time to get my head together." He said
Friendship? I thought we were a lot closer than just friends, but I guess that's what I get for thinking. "Believe it or not I understand. If you have unresolved feelings for your ex its best that you figure that out before you move on to someone new. Friends?" I guess he thought I was gonna be all choked up and broken by this. Well I was, but I wasn't gonna show that to him. Steve is on my line every day and every night, trying his hardest to get in my head. I guess losing another thirty pounds helped a little. Steve keeps trying to convince me that I've lost enough weight. But I really want to reach my goal I'm more than half way there. By the time I reach my goal I should be bikini ready. Not that I'd ever wear one in public, but at least the option is still there. Who knows one day I might be feeling myself and BAM! I'll have the body to do it.

"Friends. I really appreciate you taking this so well Tracy. Are you sure there are no hard feelings?"

If he only knew, "I'm sure. Andrew we weren't even serious yet. Everything's fine. I'll see you at rehearsal in a few months."

"Ok, are you sure you're ok?"

"Andrew? Why wouldn't I be ok?"

"I don't know, I don't want you to hate me." He said

"Why would I hate you?"

"Um I don't know probably because I want to get back with my ex girlfriend. You're great Tracy, sweet, warm, intelligent, affectionate, and sexy.... I mean I could go on and on."

"Ok, so it sounds like you're the one torn up about this whole thing."

"I feel like I'm making a HUGE mistake. I know it's not fair to say this but I really care about you."

Yea right! But I didn't want to throw the tantrum I was feeling inside. "You know what, it shows."

"How?" He asked

"By the fact that you care enough about my feelings to let me know that you want to go back to your ex. It's rare that a guy would do that. Andrew, I'm gonna miss you. But trust I will be ok. I will be ok because you cared enough about me to end things before I was devastated."

"I feel like I'm making a mistake. Tracy, am I making a mistake?"

"Andrew, you owe it to yourself to have closure. And if it turns out that you fall back madly in love and you marry her then you'll know you made the right decision. But if it turns out that you go back and it doesn't work out you won't have any regrets. And if I'm available then hit me up. Either way we are ok. One thing for sure you're a standup guy, and very few of you exist today. Don't worry, you will be ok."

"Please don't think less of me, but I need a hug. I'm getting emotional."

"Oh Andrew" I opened my arms to hug him. We embraced for a long time ten minutes maybe then we had a LONG PASSIONATE kiss. Then I walked away. I could tell when we saw his ex the other day at the movies that she was gonna call him or that they'd be getting back together soon. For one she looked like she wanted to die. Andrew and I looked good together and she was looking a hot mess. I bet she makes him bring her to the wedding as an opportunity to redeem herself. Oh well, I could tell she's pretty and even if she wasn't it doesn't matter. He wants to go back to her so she wins. Steve will be happy to hear about this. He was hating on my relationship so badly it wasn't even funny.

I wasn't in the door ten minutes when Steve was at my door. "You're home early"

"Ok" then I thought about it and suddenly I felt sad. Then realizing that I felt sad made my eyes water up and before I knew it tears we're pouring out of my eyes. I walked into the kitchen and started unloading the dishwasher.

"Are you on your way out. "

"I... No" I tried my best to make my voice sound normal, but it cracked anyways.

He walked into the kitchen and I could see that he was startled by my emotional state. "What's wrong?"

"Nothing"

He grabbed my hand an pulled me into him, "what's wrong"

I said a very low "we broke up" as I let all the tears out. His grip got tighter. Then he tried to lean in for a kiss. I backed away, "what are you doing?"

"I'm sorry"

"Ok" I said frowning at him.

"Do you want me to leave?"

"No but don't try that right now. I don't need that from you right now." I said through tears.

"Ok"

CHAPTER 4

"I don't understand why you've been so distant lately."

"Oh I'm sorry, didn't I breakup with my boyfriend?"

"Yea but that was over a month ago."

"Oh excuse me if I actually care about the men I date. Everyone can't be cold hearted like you."

"I'm not cold hearted"

"Yes you are even when you're done with a person you make them believe you care until you suddenly have someone else to move on to. But then again you don't really breakup with anyone. You keep adding on more females and since you're not technically committed to any of them you act as if you're not obligated to any of them. Excuse me if I've gotten a taste of being número UNO and I don't wanna take 15 million steps backwards." I said

"So you're gonna sulk around because you got dumped. I guessed that's why he dumped you. All I was trying to do was cheer you up." Steve said shrugging

"No, you just wanna get in my pants. I don't know why you didn't appreciate me when you had me. And even then as soon as I give in to you, you move on. For all I know you're still seeing everybody else. You're not even offering me anything. If I didn't sleep with Andrew, why would I sleep with you?"

I could see the irritation all over his face. But I had nothing to lose so why hold back. He's been sweet as pie every time I seen him. I really appreciated that and needed that. Truth was I cared about Andrew more than I had allowed myself to understand. Whatever the case I liked the way Steve acted when he was trying to get in good with me.

"Yea right you didn't sleep with him. You guys went out for months."

"Just because things jumped off with us doesn't mean I'm like that with everyone. Andrew was different, he didn't pressure me, and honestly he could be the one who got away."

Steve's face dropped. "Well it sounds like he was passing time with you, using you to make his ex jealous. He wasn't really into you. I don't know how he could talk to you, kiss you, look at you, and not try to sleep with you. Doesn't sound like a real man to me. "

"I never said he didn't try, I said he didn't pressure me. But thank you for the compliment." There was silence. "Steve, will you be my date for Nicole's wedding?"

"Is this about making him jealous?"

"No, I know they'll be there and I don't want to be at the wedding alone."

"What are we doing here?"

"I'm not following you." I said

"I'll go but I want us to be a couple."

"Steve, is this a competition thing?"

"Real talk?"

"Yes, real talk."

He took me by the hand and led me to the couch. "I'm gonna be honest with you. It's been bothering me that you were ever with old boy and then you appear to be putting him up higher and higher on a pedestal. I should be your man; I want us to get back together. And no I'm not saying this just to sleep with you. Don't get me wrong I want to, but he's not the only one who will wait for you." I wrapped my arms around his neck started kissing his cheek. "Does this mean yes?" then we kissed a deep and long kiss. It was a good kiss but still didn't compare to Andrew.

"Yes, but please be patient. I want our first time to be memorable." I said

"Ok"

The rest of the evening we kissed the night away no words were expressed.

CHAPTER 5

Although I know tomorrow is Nicole's day. I was a glow with a sense of accomplishment. I was at my goal weight, and I hadn't slept with Steve and it had been MONTHS. I don't think he could believe I was able to resist him. But little did he know I couldn't stand it any longer. I had a plan, I just needed to get through the rehearsal and dinner and then through the wedding tomorrow.

We were at the ceremony site of course I was one of the first people there. The wedding party was slowly arriving Nicole and I told everyone to be there a hour and a half earlier than they needed to be so that everyone would end up being on time. I agreed to get there first to greet everyone. It had been so long ago that the entire wedding party was together that most people didn't even recognize me. That was fun and I really hoped they'd all get it out of their systems before Nicole and Hubby showed so that all the attention was on them.

I expected Andrew to be there. I didn't expect him to bring his girlfriend. The moment he laid eyes on me his whole soul lit up. Everyone noticed even his girlfriend. I could tell it annoyed her as he made a beeline over to me. He had the biggest smile on his face and his arms were already stretched out before he got close. Looking at his girlfriend I tried to extend my hand for a handshake but he ignored that and continued in for his hug. He squeezed me so tight and he lifted me off the floor and spun me around. Can you say he was making a scene? I had forgotten how good it felt to be in his arms and how no matter what he always smelled good. "Oh my goodness Andrew! It's good to see you." I said as he put me down.

He stared at me with the biggest grin, and then his smile slightly dropped. "Let me introduce you to Toya" her smile was fake. And although she made sure she looked nice, I could see her sizing me up. And that it was killing her inside. "Toya this is Tracy".

"Hello, nice to finally meet you."

"Same here" she said as she was continuing to size me up.

Andrew gave her a disapproving look and then turned his attention back to me. "I'm sorry I'm late, Toya insisted on coming but she always runs late."

Toya then gave him the look of death; "we discussed this in the car. I apologized for that already. Could you not throw me under the bus right now?"

"Well it's ok. They knew people would run late so they moved the start time ahead. You're actually early. Everyone's kind of hanging out until they get here." Everyone was watching us. They all knew that Andrew and I dated, and a lot of them knew that they were back together. Andrew was making it known to everyone that he was still feeling me; it made me kind of sad. I mean, if he liked me so much, and was feeling me all like this.... Why did he leave me to go back to her? Would he do this to me if we would've stayed together? Honestly I didn't get it.

"So do you guys know the marching order yet? Who's walking with who?" Toya asked

Andrew's eyes moved around the room, "yea they told us that a long time ago. Tracy's walking with me."

Toya turned purple, "I asked you, and you said you didn't know."

Andrew had sad eyes as he motioned for the livid Toya to walk with him. Neither of them looked back at me and from the looks of it Toya was on a major tangent. They walked back outside. Nicole's friend Sonya came over with a very annoyed look on her face. "You ok sweetheart?"

"Me? Yea, I'm cool. I guess I don't understand what just happened."

She smiled, "let's get a drink after this and I'll give you the dets"

"Works for me"

Last to arrive were the happy couple. Nicole looked beautiful and so happy. Toya sat in the back corner of the room pouting and staring at me. I tried one more time to go over and be friendly. But she wasn't having it; she acted like I didn't exist. She completely ignored me. Which is confusing, she won right. He left me to go back to her, so I didn't get why she was acting this way. We practiced the wedding march a few times for the last run through they had us exit the auditorium and enter as we would the next day. Andrew and I were the last two to enter before the bride.

"I miss you!" Andrew said in a guilty confession just above a whisper. I squeezed his hand. "Are you seeing anyone?"

"Yes actually. It's the season of getting back with Ex's." we both kind of laughed.

"Figures, something told me it was a mistake to go backwards. But sometimes"

Nicole cleared her throat, "you're up"

"Come on" I kind of nudge him to move forward. If looks could kill! Toya was staring us down when we walked in. She was pissed and didn't care who saw. Most of the wedding party was looking at her, some even pitied her.

Once rehearsal was over we all went to the Old Pasta Factory for the rehearsal dinner. Sonya and I sat in a booth in the corner in the bar area. I told Nicole we would join them shortly.

"Gurl, don't pay Toya no attention. She's a mess, and has always been a mess. I was surprised he went back to her in the first place."

"He told me his last relationship was an off again on again relationship."

"To say the least. She's one of those beat a brother down sisters. There's always some drama and some way he's gotta prove that he loves her. The cold piece was that she broke his heart, she broke up with him cause she met someone else. Don't know who the guy was but he did a number on her a dose of her own medicine. She guilted poor Andrew into getting back with her if you ask me. You can still tell how much he cares for you."

"But if she was so problematic why would he leave me to go back to her?"

"From what I can tell she probably guilted him about something. He doesn't look happy with her, and they fight more than anything these days. The thought never occurred to her that he could be happy with someone else. Now the shoe is on the other foot, now she gets to be the crazy jealous and insecure person. Yep, I'm surprised she's lasted this long. I know it's none of my business but you two will be back together." She said

"But I have a boyfriend." I said

"Oh yea, your male version of Toya," then she chuckled. I didn't. "I'm just telling you what I see."

"I get it, but who wants to hear that?"

"I dig you darling, Steve ain't the one either. He may be a good time, but you don't marry him. Guys like him don't wise up until they're way older slowing down and realize they need someone to take care of them."

"Oh my God Sonya!"

She laughed. Then Toya walked to our table. She was startled when she saw me.

"Looking for somebody?"

"Have you seen Andrew?" She asked Sonya, she pretended like I wasn't there.

"I saw some of the groomsmen walking towards the parking lot. I didn't look for individual faces."

"Thanks" she said and then she slowly walked back to the private room where all the family and friends were eating.

"See what I'm saying. She's trying to hold on too tightly. Give that man some space."

In two big swallows my Long Island was done and another one was set on the table for me. The waiter pointed to the opposite corner and there were the groomsmen. Andrew waved. I waved back. Then Sonya and I drank it. When we asked for our tab the waiter told us Andrew paid it. We went back in the room and ate with the family. The rest of the night Toya was like a hawk and I was her prey. Every move I made she saw it. After awhile it wasn't even annoying anymore it was just pathetic. When we got back to the hotel I talked to Steve for a little bit, and confirmed what time he would get to the ceremony.

Slowly one by one everyone started falling asleep. Soon only Sonya, Nicole, and I were awake.

"Are you nervous?" Sonya asked

"No, tomorrow I marry my love what's to be nervous about?" Nicole said blissfully

"I don't know I just imagine being nervous." I said

"Well when you marry Andrew you let me know." Nicole said

"Nicole, not you too." Sonya and Nicole laughed. "He's here with his girlfriend for crying out loud."

"Oh whatever! I heard what he said to you. " Nicole said

"Ooh! What did I miss?" Sonya said

"Nothing! He told me he missed me."

"See! And she keeps trying to act like she don't know it." Sonya said

"But I have a boyfriend, so there's nothing that I could do about that even if I wanted to." I said frustrated

Nicole and Sonya exchange looks. "So you're saying that you and Steve are in love?"

The question made me uncomfortable, "I love Steve".

"But that's not the same as being in love is it."

"Steve loves me!"

"Not saying he doesn't, but you aren't answering the question."

"What is the point of this? You guys want me to be over here waiting for someone who may never come back to me? And Andrew and I weren't in love."

"Please! Gurl maybe you guys hadn't gotten to that point yet where you told each other. But Andrew told my man he loved you."

Then it happened against my will tears forced their way out of my eyes. My sudden eruption startled them. "This isn't fair! Please stop telling me this. He's with her! He left me for her! He chose her when he had me! None of this makes me feel good. I don't wanna think about him. He belongs to someone else." then my cry became harder more painful and I ran to the bathroom. I put a towel over my mouth and I laid in the tub crying my eyes out. It was so unfair for them to tell me any of this. After awhile I got up and looked in the mirror. My eyes were swollen; I put cold water on a face towel. Then I went to my bedroom and found a space on the edge of the bed that had two other bridesmaids fast asleep in it. Nicole and Sonya tip toed into the bedroom, they each kissed me on my forehead. "We're sorry, we thought you should know"

"Thanks" I said keeping my eyes closed.

CHAPTER 6

After my short catnap I found myself laying restlessly. I figured I might as well get up and exercise. Since I wasn't all that familiar with our location I decided to run on the treadmill. About a mile and a half into my run Andrew and Gerard walked into the gym. I nodded in their direction and focused on my breathing and form. I could see Andrew watching me in the mirror. I closed my eyes and focused on the music blasting thru my ear buds. I got a cramp in my side, which also served as my sign that I was over my five-mile requirement. I hit the slow down button. When I got off the treadmill I stretched for five minutes and then I waved goodbye. Andrew's eye stayed glued to me.

When I got back to the suite it was hopping. Breakfast was in propane-heated dishes. The photographer was taking candid photos of everything. I liked the idea of having everything photographed. And then all over the suite people had make shift styling stations. The girl who was doing my hair was working on another girl. So I hopped in the shower and ate breakfast. Then I snuck downstairs and checked into my room. I moved almost all my things into my new room so there wouldn't be any confusion later. Or put people in the middle of my business. Then I quietly came back to the room. No one noticed I was gone. Once my hair was done, I sat in the makeup chair. I loved the way Rosalind did my makeup. She knew I didn't want overly dramatic makeup. I wanted to look like me only more polished. We chatted about my weight loss and the wedding. When she was done we both admired her work. Never in a million years did I ever think I could be so beautiful! We both kind of sat back and said Wow! The photographer snapped pictures of us while we weren't paying attention. I became the photographer's pet once I had my dress on. He followed me everywhere snapping pics of everything. Nicole's mother and grandmothers were in tears when they saw her all dressed and ready. Steve texted me and told me he was at the ceremony site. It was time to go. Although Nicole put on her strong face she grabbed Sonya and I's hands and squeezed them. Her way of saying she was now nervous. We waited inside the limo bus until it was time to start the grooms men waited outside in the order of the wedding march. One by one the bridesmaids descended off the bus to their escort and into the hall. As the last two on the bus I looked at Nicole, she was beautiful! She gave me her million-dollar smile and I walked towards the front. Andrew just about stopped breathing when he saw me. And I'll be honest he looked GOOD; his tux looked like it was made for him. He had a fresh haircut, and I could see the love in his eyes. He put his hand out to help me off the bus and we stepped in front of the doors. When they opened all eyes were on us. It felt like millions of eyes were on us. Of course I found Toya even in the crowd. Her mouth literally fell open. When she saw me and then the laser beams shot from her eyes. Then I found Steve, his eyes got big as well but then I saw his chest swell with pride. He looked good too. I was relieved that he looked so nice. When we reached the front we took our places and everyone stood in anticipation of Nicole's entrance. Toya kept her eyes on us. And Steve focused on me. He mouthed hi and I mouthed hello. Then Toya's head snapped to see who I was talking to. I could see the recognition on her face; Steve didn't take his eyes off me. Nicole's Hubby got choked up when he finally saw her, she was an exquisite bride. The ceremony was beautiful and quick. The wedding party quickly boarded the limo bus headed to our picture location while the guest headed to the reception. Everyone was excited and celebrating! Champagne bottles started popping. When we arrived at the Marina Nicole and Hubby started taking pictures. Andrew kept staring at me.

"You look BEAUTIFUL!"

"Thank you, you look good as well." his continued stare made me a little uncomfortable, so I found Sonya and busied myself talking to her. We took pictures and then they dropped the bomb on us. They wanted bridesmaids to take pictures with their escorts. Sonya and her escort were up first and they posed for a passionate embrace.

"I like that! Everybody try something similar." Nicole said

I rolled my eyes and then I downed my glass of champagne. They snapped four more poses. Andrew stalled until we were last up. After four glasses I was no longer tense about our turn. For our first pose Andrew walked up behind me and put his arms around me. EVERYBODY immediately went crazy! I keep forgetting how good it feels to be in his arms. I know I keep saying that, but you have no idea how good it feels to be in this man's arms, nothing compares to the feeling. Instantly I fell back into old feelings. After four snaps it was time for our next pose. He loosened his grip just enough for me to turn around and face him. I put my arms around his neck and as we both seemed to lean in for the kiss the camera clicked and we both snapped out of it. Andrew let go of me and the photographer directed our final three poses. They were nice but I knew the first two would be my favorites. When we were boarding the bus again I shot Nicole a look and she had a guilty smile. When we arrived at the hotel for the reception we entered the reception hall the same way we entered the ceremony location. And like before Toya had eyes full of hate, but this time she and Steve were sitting next to each other. As soon as the new couple entered they had their first dance. At the bridge of the song the wedding party joined in. At first the space between Andrew and I resembled a junior high school dance. But the longer he looked at me the shorter and shorter the space got. We weren't pressed up against each other in the end but we were definitely touching. Then he said, " I messed up. I miss you so much." I smiled to make it seem like he was telling me something funny. "He better never let you go!" then the music stopped and he rushed out. When we sat down I started fanning myself I needed to cool down. Toya rushed out the door following him. People made their way to the newlyweds. Steve came straight to me like my tractor-beam-of-hotness pulled him in. The first thing he did was kiss me. "Hello Gorgeous!"

"Hello Handsome!"

"You look AMAZING!"

"Thank you, your looking good yourself."

"Thank you, so after we eat they're gonna play music. I can't wait to get you out there."

"Ditto" he kissed me again and then he made his way back to his seat. He didn't mention Andrew nor did he seem concerned. When the food was being served to our table Andrew & Toya came back in the room. She rushed to her seat and he sat next to me. She seemed calm and no longer concerned with me and Andrew was more relaxed as well. Rashad walked over and high fived Andrew. "You's a wild boy!"

Eeewwllll! I looked at Andrew but he wouldn't look at me. But he was no longer pent up. I didn't say anything to him. If they wanted to stop the ice sculpture from melting all they had to do was place it by us. It suddenly became cold on our end of the table. Toya was no longer concerned with me; she didn't look at me once. But she was overly conversational with Steve who kept looking at me and shrugging. Andrew sat quietly and ate his meal. As soon as they started the music Steve popped up out of his seat. I don't think he even noticed that Toya was talking to him. In his defense she was talking to everyone at the table, but she couldn't hide her irritation when he got up and took off like that. As he glided to the table Andrew had pure jealousy all over his face. He nodded at Andrew and Andrew returned the nod then he held his hand for me to place mine in his. Steve took me to the middle of the floor. He kissed me and people started cheering, and then he pulled my body into his as we slow danced. It seemed like forever before others joined us on the dance floor. But I didn't care, my man was not afraid, ashamed, or embarrassed to be labeled as such.... My man! Nor was he professing feelings for someone else. Every once in awhile I glanced over and Andrew was still sitting. Most times looking directly at me or other times he'd turn his head as I looked. I told myself I didn't care. And regardless of how good I thought Andrew was to me, who's to say he wasn't doing this same thing with Toya while he was supposed to be with me? I didn't wanna sit and try to figure this puzzle out. It was an open bar, and I had the room upstairs. Steve and I stayed on the dance floor, the only time we came off was to drink or pee. The bass from the music was pumping like a heartbeat thru my body, I was drunk, and I was with Steve. Say whatever you want about him, but tonight he made me feel special. I felt beautiful, and I felt loved. The Bride and Groom stopped the music to say their thank you's and good nights' cause they were retiring for the evening. Steve held me in his arms like Andrew did earlier. Did I put a memo across my forehead that told everyone I liked to be held this way? After they exited a lot of people started to leave and the music started slowing down again. Steve pulled me into his arms and kissed me again as we danced slowly. Then he lifted my chin "honey you are wasted, should I get a room?"

I smiled, "no need I have one already."

Then he kissed me deep and strong, "you are too much". Not too many couples away from us Andrew and Toya were dancing, he'd been drinking but I couldn't tell with Toya. She looked bitter and tired. As our last song of the night came to a close he lifted me up in his arms, "are you ready?" I laid my head on his chest and shook my head yes. "Let's go" As he carried me out I saw Andrew standing and looking helpless. I liked being carried around, I liked that it appeared to be effortless for him to lift me. He had to put me down at the door because in our drunken state neither one of us could manage the stupid card key. We barely got in the door good. There was so much passion, lust, and desire in each kiss, touch, and caress. In my mind I thought I would take a shower to freshen up before we got this far. But every time I pulled away it provoked him to make things more passionate. I couldn't believe how easily and readily my body responded to him. It had been so many years. "Steve" I stroked his head. "Baby, I wanna take a shower"

"Now?"

"Yes, I want this to be right."

He huffed a big puff, "fine"

I hopped off the bed. "Can you unzip me!"?

He unzipped my dress and then he started kissing my back. It felt so good. But I moved away from him anyways. I pulled my

bag into the bathroom I put my dress on the hanger I turned on the shower water and then I looked at my body in the mirror as it began to fog up from the steam. It was like I was looking at someone else. Then he opened the bathroom door, I tried to pretend I wasn't uncomfortable with him looking at me. "I need to wash up too."
I smiled and stepped into the shower. He stripped down in no time flat. He stepped into the shower behind me.

CHAPTER 7

I laid there not understanding my feelings. Last night was beautiful and satisfying, but there was a part of me that wanted to get up and run away. I didn't understand it. After wrestling with my thoughts I decided to go to the gym and try and run a bit. I sat up on the edge of the bed, "where you going?"

"I'm gonna try to go to the gym for a little bit."

"You should focus on hydrating yourself first. All those drinks last night will put too much strain on your muscles."

Now if he said that in a kind caring manner maybe I wouldn't naturally want to disregard him. It felt like he didn't want me to go. But instead of telling me he doesn't want me to leave he makes it seem like there's something wrong with me for wanting to go. "I'll be fine." I got dressed in a hurry while Steve laid there huffing and puffing. I couldn't understand why it would bother him that I wanted to go workout. My weight was the pink elephant in the room that he wouldn't talk to me about directly. I would think my dedication to going to the gym even when I feel a little hung over was pretty awesome. I started to feel a sinking feeling and it wasn't the elevator falling to the first floor. The elevator doors open and who is it? Dag Nabit! Toya is standing in the lobby with two Starbucks cups in her hands. Her whole body tensed when she saw me. Not in the mood for her I tossed a smile her way as I grabbed my hair to put it in a messy ponytail on the top of my head. I walked past her without acknowledging her. I didn't look back to see if she was watching me walk into the gym. But I knew she was. Why are they still here? I don't understand Andrew. Why would he breakup with me just to regret me? And why did he regret losing me so much? Yes I would agree, clearly his relationship with Toya is way more maintenance than he and I together. But he had to know what he was going back to, right? There was so much that I didn't understand. But really did I even want to understand it all? No! Let me have a moment to say HE BROKE UP with me! I did the right thing, told him it was ok for him to go back. I don't understand what I was supposed to do. As I sighed I walk into the gym and who's on the bench sitting there looking sick?????? I didn't feel like seeing him, I was halfway feeling sick and seeing him wasn't helping me feel better. I was tired of being nice. Andrew looked at me and I turned on my heels and walked out the gym. I walked into the gift shop and paid four dollars for a bottle of overpriced Gatorade. As I walked out of the store Andrew was walking towards the elevator. I wanted to run out of the hotel instead of walk.

"Tracy" I pretended like I didn't hear him I was almost to the door. "Tracy!" I kept walking. "Tracy!" as soon as I hit the corner outside the hotel I took off running towards the beach. I was almost to the sand when I realized Andrew was on my heels! How could I forget how fast he was? He was the one who showed me how to run in the first place. Of course the master would out speed the student. I wasn't gonna give up that easily PLUS I didn't know he was chasing me before. With all my mite I prepared my mind and body to shift into fifth gear and blow the doors open. Leaving Andrew and whatever drama he was about to bring me in the dust. My feet hit the sand and I probably got six good strides in when my legs reminded me that I was working on NO WATER and yea the Gatorade was still in my hand. I got the worst cramp, and instead of running I was now falling. And it wasn't a pretty commercially prepared fall like you might see in the movies when the chick falls because she's so emotional. No mine was real, and not pretty. My face hit the sand and all I could think is "my hair". Andrew chased my Gatorade, which flew, across the beach. If I had any strength I would've hopped up and ran in the other direction. But instead I laid where I fell laughing and slightly crying my behind off. Andrew had tears flying out of his eyes he was laughing so hard at me. "That's what you get for running from me."

"Why are you chasing me?" I asked as I sat up on the sand and dusted the sand off my face and body.

"I called you, but you acted like you didn't hear me."

"I didn't"

"Then why did you run?"

"I was coming out here to run in the first place."

"Un huh keep it up and you'll fall flat on your face again."

We both laughed. "What do you want?"

"I don't know. I guess I wanted to talk to you."

Instantly my anger was back. "About what Andrew? What do we have to talk about? There's no unfinished business between us. You wanted to go back to your ex and I stepped aside. No questions, no guilt, NO DRAMA! But yet here you are.... Why?"

He sat next to me on the sand. "I miss you. I miss our friendship. I miss having you in my life. There's been so many times I've wanted to call you for an all night phone session like we used to do."

"Well why didn't you call?"

"Because.... I didn't know if you'd stay on the line once you realized it was me."

"Right, why would I stay on the phone with you when we weren't together." instantly I felt a little guilty for all the times I was on the phone with Steve even while we were together.

"I've never had with anyone what I had with you."

I sucked my teeth, "you have some nerve telling me that now. Regardless you have a girlfriend we have nothing to talk about."

"Why could you and Steve remain friends, but we can't?"

I didn't know he knew about that. "What do you mean?"

"So it turns out that Toya knows Steve. He used to date a friend of hers."

"Ick Andrew! I don't want to hear anymore. Steve and I were together a lot longer than a couple months."

"Almost seven months means nothing?"

"Almost seven? We were together longer than that."

"I'm talking about the time that we were about each other. But maybe I should count it all."

"Do whatever you want it's not like it'll make a difference. In the end you dumped me."

"I didn't know what to do. When Toya dumped me for the umpteenth time I really thought it was over. I took the love I had for her and tucked it away. Yea I tried to get her back but she seemed to mean it that time. I moped around for a while but it wasn't doing me any good. I always knew it was unfinished business, but man. Then we met started hanging out and then dating. For once I wasn't waiting like her faithful puppy. At first she didn't seem to notice but as time went by she started calling. After awhile I broke down and I would talk to her, but only when you were busy. You were always my first priority. I guess she didn't believe that I was dating you until she saw us at the movies that time. The next thing I know she's popping up at my house. It was nothing at first but it became too much. I cheated on you. I hated myself for it. I felt you deserved better. I couldn't bring myself to tell you, so I figured it was better to go back. Toya was acting so different; I really believed she changed.... I"

"Andrew!" he stopped, "you don't have to explain all this to me. Yes! I didn't understand, but in all of this you had choices. And call it whatever you want, you chose her over me. I know men have needs and maybe I had you waiting too long. I don't know, but whatever the deal it's your business. I wish you well with Toya."

"Tracy, I know I hurt you. You were good to me, all the sudden out the blue I broke up with you. I know you're mad at me."

"You wanna know what makes me mad?" he looked at me and then back at the sand. "I don't like this. Why can't we say hello. Be here for our friends and be done with it. Yea we used to date, but that's not what's happening now. We both moved on it's what happens. But, no you gotta keep making every interaction this emotional scene like a movie or something. How many times are you gonna keep apologizing for something that can't be changed? You're here with Toya; I'm here with Steve. We've both moved on. You keep making this too complicated and it's pissing me off."

"Because it is complicated"

"It's not COMPLICATED! Stop saying that!"

"It is complicated," he said

"Is NOT!"

"Yes it is," he said

"ISN'T!"

"Why are you saying that?"

"I thought I explained it to you. It's not complicated! It's not!"

"It is" he exhaled deeply

"Why do you keep saying that?"

"We were in love" he said matter of factly.

Without even thinking about it, I said, "no we weren't"

And then out of nowhere he grabbed my face and kissed me. I refused to give him my tongue even though I wanted to. His lips were so kissable; I could've stayed like this all day. My body betrayed me and melted while he kissed me. Then I pushed him away, "stop it!" I tried to wipe his kiss off my lips. "I HAVE A BOYFRIEND!!!!"

"I know and I'm here with someone. I wanna be with you."

"Andrew! I can't even deal with you why can't you hear me STOP IT!"

"Fine! I'm trying to pour my heart out to you. I'm trying to be real with you like I always have."

"No you're asking me to cheat on my boyfriend."

He scoffed at me, "no I was asking you to give me another chance."

"Oh so my life is supposed to pause because you want me back. Ok! Ok! You wanna know. I put on a BRAVE face for you. Said all the right stuff, but it hurt me that you chose someone over me. Now you're upset because you should've never left me. Maybe you should've been honest with me from the beginning. Told me about Toya!" then I stood up and started dusting my pants. "Here I was hoping that at some point we could be friends, but if this weekend is any indication I don't wanna be your friend. We didn't have sex! We should be able to be friends and move on with our lives. But no you gotta make EVERYTHING"

He stood up and walked away. Um hello I was in the middle of my speech and he walked away. Ugh! That's something Steve would've done. I opened my Gatorade and gulped it down with the quickness. Seems like it went straight to my bladder I instantly had to pee. I did the fancy pee-pee walk back to the hotel never catching up with Andrew but four people behind him. Of course when I step into the lobby there's Toya. Looks like she's been crying. When she sees me she about loses it and starts yelling at Andrew. I go in the bathroom. I could hear her all the way in my stall. I couldn't hear what she was saying but I could hear her. I wasn't in the mood for any of this especially her screaming like a crazy person when I had a headache coming on. I washed my hands a little slower hoping she'd be gone by the time I walked out the bathroom. But no her voice wasn't going away and some point I'd have to leave this bathroom. I dried my hands and then checked my face in the mirror. I put my "I don't care posture" on and then I walked out the bathroom. It looked like the hotel manager was trying to calm her; Andrew wasn't even there anymore. She was facing me when I came out the bathroom. Then she started screaming, "I KNOW YOURE TRYING TO STEAL MY MAN! BUT ANDREW IS MY MAN HO!"

Now I had a choice, I could stoop to her level or ignore her. Well since I was already limping from a body that was not ready for anything fast and heavy I chose to keep walking to the elevator.

"YOU KNOW YOU HEAR ME! STAY AWAY FROM MY MAN!"
The elevator doors closed and I exhaled. That gurl looked crazy. Her eyes were red from crying, and she was mad as all get out. When I walked into the room Steve was sitting on the edge of the bed popping a Aspirin and downing some water. "That was fast" he smiled a knowing smile.

"You were right it was too soon to try and workout."
"Well I got something that will make you feel better."
I looked at him in disbelief, "you're kidding???"

"Woman if you don't get over here."

I felt conflicted, part of me wanted to say OH YES! But the other part of me wasn't feeling it. "Steve can we eat first? I need something to soak up all the alcohol in my system."

He agreed but he looked disappointed. I wanted to be impressed, but there was a voice in the back of my head telling me not to get used to it.

He wanted to eat in the restaurant in the hotel but I convinced him that I wanted pancakes from Pancake House. Breakfast was fine but our conversations kept going in the wrong direction. I could see him getting irritated with me, but I couldn't understand why. Then he said, "I need to slow down on my drinking. I feel hostile right now and I don't know why."

I reached across the table and I rubbed his hand, "thank you for telling me."

"Telling you what?"

"That it's not me you're mad at. I was starting to wonder. I was thinking didn't I rock your world last night? Shouldn't you still be in happy bliss?" I smiled real big.

He smiled too, "um yea, but wait until we get back to that room. I'm gonna blow your mind."

We exchanged smiles and then the waiter was at the table. Now I know I was supposed to order from the slim & fit menu but the buttermilk pancakes were calling me. So I ordered egg whites, turkey bacon, and buttermilk pancakes. I figured one splurge wouldn't hurt me. Although I'd been splurging all weekend. Even though I told myself I would only eat only one pancake. I found myself staring at the empty plate that used to hold three pancakes. "It's ok, I'll work really hard this week." I told myself. When we got in the car I looked at the clock it was just after eleven am. "We gotta checkout in less than an hour. We should get our stuff and I'll follow you to your place." I said

"Why can't we go to your place?"

"We're always at my place. Let's go to yours." I said

"Yea, but I have a roommate."

"It doesn't matter to me."

"Besides I wanna give that body another run through. I don't want to embarrass anybody." He said

Now call me crazy, but one of my complaints before was his seemingly lack of stamina. So why is it bothering me that all he wants to do is hop back in the bed? Maybe I'm paranoid; he did wait how many months "faithfully"? Maybe he was being faithful like he said; he was never like this before. And he's not in any hurry to get away from me, so let me stop complaining and be happy about this new corner we just turned in our relationship.

CHAPTER 8

"Honey ten pounds are not the end of the world."

I kept a straight face but sweat instantly poured from each pore. "I know, I'm upset because it's happening and I.... I don't know."

"Women's weight always moves up and down."

"I wouldn't feel so bad about the ten if I hadn't gained fifteen before this. It's like it's coming back as fast as it can." my eyes started welling up.

"Could you be getting ready for that time of the month?"

"No, I just..." suddenly heat flashed over me. Then suddenly all I could see was white and then black. I felt like I was napping but everyone sounded panicked around me.

"Tracy! Tracy! Are you ok honey?"

"What was that?" I said as I sat up.

"Honey please go to the doctor. Make sure you're ok." My mouth was completely dry. I stood up and my legs were still a little wobbly. "Come on honey, I'll drive you. Let me go get my purse." I nodded ok. I couldn't remember when my last period was. I can't be pregnant! I've made sure we stayed protected every time! It has to be stress. Lately Steve and I argue about everything. So much I sometimes turn off my phone and live in silence. Just this morning I was trying to convince myself that I didn't need him in my life. It has to be stress. It has to be. Shirley came back into the bathroom with both of our purses.

"Thank you Shirley, I'm ok though. I don't need to go to the doctor. I think I need to go home and rest."

Shirley was my friend at work. She looked concerned, and call me crazy but it felt good to feel like someone cared. I convinced Shirley that I needed to go home. But she would only agree as long as she could follow me home. Once I was inside my apartment I watched as she drove away. Then I went straight to the drug store. I bought a three pack of pregnancy tests, a gallon of water, and the impulse purchase was a snickers. As soon as I got home I regretted seeing the candy bar in my bag. It kept calling me, begging me to pay it attention. So I threw it in the freezer. I don't like frozen snickers so that felt like a good fix. The thought of trying to figure out an approach to these test was driving me crazy. Steve and I seem to argue about everything. We didn't seem like friends anymore. I couldn't understand why we were having so many problems. Unfortunately I had a LONG conversation with myself. I was honest about how much I loved this man. How huge he'd been in my adult life. I wished I could hit the off button and be done with him. But my heart clung to the good times, and suffered through the bad. What if I was pregnant, I don't have a clue at how Steve would respond. My dream was to have a loving husband who adored me. I'd find out I was preggers and consumed with joy I'd give my husband the news and he'd be elated to know I was carrying his child. He'd be so happy he'd tell anyone who'd listen. Not this scene! I didn't even want to see Steve right now. If I was pregnant I can pretty much count on him flipping out. Being a single parent and staring at a miniature version of him. Then suddenly Andrew flashed across my mind. Seemed like every time things became unbearable with Steve, Andrew would flash across my mind. Although it had been a year since I'd talked to him, I thought about him all the time. I thought about how different things could be for me right now. I wondered how he'd take the news once he found out. I wondered if he would even care anymore. I guess that's the problem with a dreamer like me. I'm always dreaming things different than they are, I do it so much that I miss t he mark in the here and now because of my jaded eyesight.

Condoms and a diaphragm should be enough protection. But honestly I didn't always use the diaphragm. Laziness and spontaneity may have worked against me here. I don't want to be on hormones unless I absolutely have to be. Steve didn't care, half the time he seemed annoyed that I wanted him to use condoms. He was always trying to get around them. No matter what I was never that dru...nk! CRAP! But there was that one time. Marie picked me up for Happy hour to wallow in our pain together at the bar in

Chase's. I remember begging Steve to pick us up, he dropped
Marie off. She thought he was so nice, etc. then I got a lecture the
whole way home. He spent the night, but I was so sick the next
morning he cleaned up and I didn't take out the trash to even notice
the used condoms or lack there of. PLEASE!!! NO!!!!!!! How long
ago was that? I couldn't remember it all seemed like black and
white fuzz. Please don't link me to this guy for the rest of my life.
If I'm not willing to have his baby, why am I sleeping with him?
And after all we've been through cutting him off wouldn't go over
well. Regardless of what happened when I peed on that stick, Steve
and I are over. I mean it this time, no second-guessing myself etc. I
opened the box and read the instructions. I remembered someone
saying first thing in the morning was the best time to take these
things. I opened the freezer and as my hand reached for the
snickers I grabbed the frozen yogurt chips I made instead. As I sat
on the couch my cell phone began to ring. It was Steve, he
probably was checking to see where I was and if I was gong to
make dinner. I turned my phone off and put my feet up on the
couch.

I hope I'm not pregnant, but I can't remember my last period.
I guess I relaxed some because in the beginning or at the restart of
our relationship, once I got over the shock of Steve's newfound
stamina, we were like rabbits. All over each other, once I called
him in the morning and told him to meet me at my place for lunch.
When he called and said he couldn't get away I went to his job. We
went to an empty office on the empty side of his office floor. The
excitement and the pure shock on his face was almost pleasure
enough. But as time went on he started slowing down on me again.
I'd come home and I'd wait for him. He'd say he was tired or
whatever, and once I was completely turned off here he'd come.
There were times that I didn't want to, but I didn't wanna leave him
hanging. I would start off so dry, that I'd start thinking about how
much it would hurt later. Thank goodness for the lubrication in
condoms and my spermicide, oh and the fact that no matter what
he was not large. Sometimes he'd bring Magnums talking about

they fit him better. I mean, who was he kidding.... More than once they came right off. If I saw that package I'd have to get my diaphragm I was not playing with him. I knew he was sensitive about his size so I wouldn't say anything. Knowing it was his weak spot, I would remain quiet or talk around it when he'd steer our conversation towards asking me what I thought. To me it was like the woman with small breast, if her man made her feel insecure about them...well what kind of man was he? Steve was good, when he wanted to be. Outside of some positions, and times I allowed him inside when I wasn't feeling it I didn't really notice. But I knew it was his main insecurity, I guess if he slept with more women it was supposed to erase the fact. I don't know how that wasn't revealing his secret. But I guess as long as it worked in his mind it didn't stop his behavior. Not that I had confirmation that he was cheating on me, but I could feel it. That had to be the reason why we were arguing all the time.

I must've forgotten to turn the house ringer on cause the message indicator light began to flash. I had five missed calls on the house phone. I called the answering machine, "Tracy, call me as soon as you get this message. Your cell is going straight to voicemail. My grandmother's in the hospital, I don't feel like dealing with my mother but I need to see my grandmother. Call me!" his voice was pleading. How did he know I was home? He probably called my line at work and heard my voicemail. Shoot! So much for relaxing and building courage to breakup. I called him back; he was pulling up to my apartment as I called. I ran and threw the box and evidence under my bathroom sink behind my big conditioner bottle. The whole ride to the hospital he complained about his mother. He hated his mother, but only because she hated him and he didn't really understand why. She had her own set of issues and instead of working to instill better in her son, not only did she pass on her nonsense, but also she did things to make it worse. I didn't say too much on the car ride to the hospital. But he filled the silence with nervous conversation. When we got there we were relieved to find out that she had heartburn and was not having a heart attack. THE DRAMA! Of course then the whole way home he fussed about how dramatic the women in his family were as if this gene had passed him. I tried to hint that I wanted to be alone, but he acted like he couldn't get the clue. And then of course I couldn't relax on my couch, no this fool wanted some and I was not in the mood. I played dumb with all his hints, which only meant that when I laid down to sleep he was gonna come full force. Knowing that my bed would be squeaking eventually I debated whether it was even worth it to put on my diaphragm. I had a sinking feeling in my gut. But I decided to put it in just in case it was a false alarm.

"Baby I'm tired and not feeling all that well." I said as he came to bed.

"I want to cuddle. I've had a crazy day. I just need to feel loved."

I rolled my eyes knowing he didn't mean it. He hadn't asked me what was wrong or why I left work early. He didn't even act like he cared to know. And of course cuddling turned into caressing and the next thing I knew he was hard and it was happening. His kisses were gentle but strong; I could tell he was going to take his time. At least that meant there'd be something in it for me. So an hour and a half later I rolled over satisfied and REALLY tired.

I decided I would call in sick since it was Friday. But I was waiting for Steve to get up so I could pee on this stick in peace. He informed me as he rolled over that he wasn't going in to the office. So got I up to use the bathroom. I was really nervous but the urge to pee was more important. I grabbed a plastic cup from the kitchen and I went in the bathroom and locked the door. I peed in the cup and then I stuck the stick in the liquid. If I didn't like the first result I'd use the other two as confirmation. As I sat there waiting for the second line to confirm the rest of my life Andrew popped into my mind again. I remembered talking about children with him. He was excited about one day being a father. He was adamant about being married before impregnating the mother of his child. Steve said he wanted to have kids, but I knew it wasn't gonna be with me in his mind. He would get jealous if anyone had my attention for longer than three seconds. I didn't see him sticking around if this other line shows up. What the heck might as well use all three test, I'm not doing this again. The first test only showed one line. YES! The second one had a faint second line. WHAT????? It was there but barely there like the test could've been defective. THE SAME THING WITH THE THIRD!!! I let out a loud grunt forgetting that I was sneaking to take this. I poured out the cup in the toilet rinsed it and put it in the garbage with the sticks. I decided I would get a blood test and be done with it. Steve was still in the bed, "what's wrong?"

"Nothing" I said as I got back in the bed. He watched me with a weird look on his face. A little while later he went to the bathroom. I didn't think anything of it. When I woke up he was watching me with a blank look on his face. "Stop staring at me."

"Tracy you know I don't want any kids right now right?"

I sucked my teeth, "yes".

"So when we're you going to tell me about the test?"

"What test?" then I turned my back to him as I freaked out.

"I Thought I could at least trust you to be on the same page as me."

"What?"

"Are you trying to trap me?"

"What?"

He got mad, and started huffing. "Why every time you take a chance and try to trust someone stuff like this gotta happen. I will not marry you!"

His words punched me. My eyes welled up with tears. "What are you talking about?"

"I don't have time for this. I saw your test in the garbage. I wondered why you were making so much noise in there. I'm not ready to be a father, so let's be clear on how we're gonna proceed. "

I guess he thought he was putting me in my place. "Trapping you???? You????" I couldn't get over his ice-cold tone. Of course I could tell this wasn't his first time having this kind of a conversation. And did he forget he was talking to me? How could he be so cruel? Tears flew out of my eyes like fire. I wanted to fire back and put him in his place. But my mind went blank; all I could feel was rejected. It was clear to me that it was all about the challenge of getting me back. Fact of the matter is I'm the best thing going on in his life. He has a job he hates; he needs a roommate to afford his life. Where I live quite comfortably over here on my own. Matter of fact I had been considering buying a home instead of renting. I didn't discuss it with Steve because... Well because of all of this. But now I'm trapping him. He kept going on with his speech, acting like he was doing me a favor by being with me. I sat there with tears running my face as he went on and on while he put his clothes on to leave. I was a scheming, plotting, evil female like all the rest, I was stupid for even trying to trap him, my momma should've taught me how to catch a real man by cooking and cleaning and being a supportive partner. Um! I thought I was doing all of that. I couldn't believe he went all the way there on me. He could see the effect his words were having on me, but he didn't stop. He went up and down the list of why I wasn't worthy to be with him. I sat there crying and silently praying I wasn't pregnant. As soon as he left I emailed my doctor. Explained I didn't write down my last period. And how I was afraid I could be pregnant. She responded right away that she sent orders to the lab to have me tested right away. Crying all the way to the lab, I kept trying to think of a next move, to make a plan. All my mind could focus on was how much he didn't want me. And yes so I was gonna breakup with him, but it hurt when it came the other way around. I watched as the technician labeled my vile of blood. He didn't realize how much of my life's stability laid in his job. As I walked back to the parking structure Steve was calling. I hoped he was calling to apologize or something, anything would be better than the way he left things. But he continued to go off on my voicemail. He was barking so much I wondered if he was foaming at the mouth.

When I got home the feeling became more real. I stood in front of the mirror staring at my stomach trying to use mind control. "There's nothing in there" I kept telling myself. My cellphone kept vibrating on the table. I figured it would only be a matter of time before he came back over. I hopped back in the shower, washed my hair and then decided where I was going. I got dressed up and packed and overnight bag. I decided to wear my hair curly. Really it was because I didn't want to fuss with it today. And it was as if my hair understood my emotional state and decided to give me a break. My curls dried so beautiful and shiny. I put on my green maxi dress gold hoops, sandals, and bangles. No makeup, but I put on shiny lip-gloss. I packed a dress for tomorrow, etc. and headed out the door. When I got in my car Steve blocked me in my stall. Pissed I sat there and waited for him to walk over I wasn't getting out the car. He took his time about walking up to my window. "Where you going?"

"You're kidding me right?"

"Do I look like I'm kidding!" I sat there silent and fuming. "We need to talk."

"Really Steve? I think you said everything you needed to say this morning."

"Forget what I said this morning, we need...."

"I can never forget that you said it. Now please move your car. " I didn't want to give him the satisfaction of another tear from me.

"Tracy we need to talk."

"Maybe you should've thought of that before you started barking accusations at me. No one has ever made me feel as low as you made me feel this morning. I'm not some one-night stand, or just a booty call. I thought I was your woman, I thought we'd be able to calmly discuss this. You don't care what I feel or what I'm going through. All you can ever do is think about yourself. Even last night I didn't wanna have sex. I told you I was tired, but what happened? It's always about what you want. I'm the one making sure we always stay strapped. And the one time my defenses are down look at what you do. I was the drunk one remember. You knew exactly what you were doing, but now it's my fault????? There's nothing to talk about. You have ruined my life either way, and now I have to figure out how I'm going to deal with this. Please move out the way before I call the police and tell them that an ANGRY black man is holding me against my will!"

He threw his hands in the air and walked back to his car. He made sure he drove as violently as he could as he drove away. I called Marie and she told me to come by her job. I sat in her cubicle and whispered my whole sad story. She literally had to close her mouth. She only knew the nice Steve, the kind Steve, the Steve everybody raved about. Yes, he seemed like a little bit of a playboy to her, but a good guy nonetheless. I kept checking my voicemail at home. Every time I heard Steve's Voice I deleted the message. When Marie got off work we went out to dinner, but I couldn't eat. I was too upset to eat. I hadn't eaten all day, but I didn't have an appetite. I sat there moving the food around my plate. I reached for my phone to check my messages when....

"Tracy?"

My heart sank when I heard his voice. How could this day be anymore cruel? "Andrew!"

I stood up to give him a hug. Not only did he look GOOD he smelled good too. "You look good girl! How have you been?"

"Thank you Andrew you've always been kind. This is Marie, Marie this is Andrew. As they said their hellos I looked to see if I could tell who he was with. I don't think he would've bothered to come over if he was with Toya tonight. "So how have you been?"

He started shaking his head before he answered. "I've been well. You know going through the motions. Well I don't want to keep you guys. I wanted to say hello."

I wanted to tell him to call me. I wanted to tell him all about my horrid mistake. I should've chose him that day on the beach. At least I would know by now how much he loved me. He didn't seem affected by me at all. Maybe that was his point to come over and show me that he was over me. Maybe he and Toya turned a corner and they were in a good place. Maybe they were in love now and possibly planning their wedding. Maybe they're already married. Or worse what if he met someone else, and then all the above. I have to let the idea of him go ESPECIALLY in my situation now. Who would want me now? A single mother with a CRAZY and INSECURE baby daddy. Yea, it's pretty much a wrap for me. I could feel myself sink in my chair.

"Is that THE ANDREW?"

"Yep"

"Oh my! That man is FINE! Why did you guys breakup again?"

"He wanted to go back to his ex."

"I can't believe you let him go."

"Gurl most days me neither." I sighed and reached for my phone again. There was one new message. "Ms. Thomas please call your doctors office we have your lab results."

When I called, the doctor was with a patient but she authorized the receptionist to talk to me. "Ms. Thomas your test was positive. According to our calculations you're about nine weeks. We will need to schedule a follow up appointment to discuss your options. You still have time to choose but we need to go over everything with you."

Tears streamed down my face like a river. I can't believe this!

CHAPTER 9

Ok so for the first time in a long time I've prayed. I don't know how I'm gonna do this. Steve has done nothing but show his butt. Especially when I told him abortion is not an option. I will NEVER put myself through that kind of pain for anyone. Although I blame him I have to take responsibility for my actions in all this. I guess I always kind of knew it would end up this way. He'd run away and I'd end up manning up for the both of us. Steve is so torn; part of him wants to be with me. The other part is tortured and horrible. I don't exactly get it, but I tell you I feel so trapped. I've cried myself to sleep almost every night. Forget about dieting my lack of an appetite has fixed everything. I know I gotta snap out of this but I can't seem to get it together. I cry all day at work, I come straight home and cry some more. The only time I try to sound fine is when I talk to Steve so he won't have the pleasure of knowing how devastating his words are to me. I answer the phone hoping he's had a change of heart or something, but NOPE he's screaming, accusing, and belittling me. Every time he does it I start cramping.

Tonight I was fed up and tired of him acting like I was responsible for this whole thing. I got real calm although inside I was RAGING! For everything he said everything he accused me of I had a calm and sarcastic answer. Although inside I wanted to SCREAM!

I started feeling that cramping feeling but they said at the labor and delivery ER that it was probably just the feeling of my stomach stretching. In two weeks I've been there three times. There was one nurse I saw every time I went that was so sweet to me. The last time she told me to rest and she talked to me while she did office work in and out the room. She had me feeling up to telling my parents about the baby. Every time I thought Steve and I were close enough to introduce him, something would go wrong. Not that my parents would've been excited about meeting him. I was living in sin, and until I fixed that nothing was gonna fix that. But nurse Sandra had that whole bedside manner thing down. She had me so calm and relaxed I'd forget why I was there. She did tell me that my blood count was seriously low. I made an appointment with my doctor to discuss. Leaving the hospital she had me so relaxed and excited about my baby.

I was so happy to finally put right back on him everything he was shoving on me. Every time he said something horrible I swallowed the anger and said something worse. In the end I told him to lose my number and to NEVER call me again. When I slammed the phone on the charger I was fuming. I was cramping so I got in the bath to soothe my aching muscles although this time the ache was sharper. I laid back and tried to relax, "tomorrow I'm changing my number. And I'm moving!" I told myself. I started figuring everything out in my head. I'd work from home until I figured out where I was going. Then I'd take time off work to move. Once I was set up then I'd figure out my next move. One day my baby's gonna ask about their dad. At this point I was willing to say I got inseminated. Steve is not a part of this picture. The cramps finally started to calm I opened my eyes to look for my sponge and the water was red. My mind went numb. I called my doctor and told her I was on my way. I told her what happened and she said she'd call the hospital to let them know I was coming.

I couldn't bare to call Marie again. So I put on a pad, drove myself to the hospital. Nurse Sandra was there and she had sadness in her face for me. She held my hand during the exam. I saw a few tears roll down her cheeks for me. She kept telling me it was ok to cry. When I Finally let go and let out a few sobs her grip got a little tighter. This woman has no idea how much her caring for me helps. Steve, the man I created this situation with, is somewhere cursing the day I was born like I did this to him. His reaction to this whole thing has me in a state of suspension. The past month has been unreal. The sound of that machine blocks anything I could feel except the huge lump in my throat. When I try to swallow the lump just to be ok tears pour of my eyes like blood. Whenever the doctors talked to me it was like they were speaking another language. I couldn't really comprehend everything and then I started feeling really tired. I could hear feet rushing around me and someone was trying to talk to me about some forms, but I couldn't open my eyes, I was really tired.

"You know I really do love you Tracy." Steve was sitting on my couch wrestling with his hands like he does when he's fighting to speak from the heart and he can't find the words. "This whole thing really scares me. I don't know how to be a father. I'm afraid I'll mess the baby up. I don't want to be the reason why another person is messed up in this world." he looks like he's gonna cry but he doesn't. He keeps wrestling with his hands. "I don't want you to hate me too. I can't handle you walking away from me especially when I tell you how much I need you." I try to say something but no words come out. He looks at me, "where are you going?" then he jumps off the couch and rushes towards me. "I just told you I love you" he grabs my wrists and his grip burns my wrists as he moves his hands before my face. "This is why I don't try to tell people how I feel. You're going to leave me now!" his face turns red and he's so angry it almost seems like he's foaming at the mouth, "I won't let you leave me!" he reaches back and with all his might he strikes my face. In shock I can't even scream I look at him. He's crying as he reaches back a second and a third time. My face feels warm. Suddenly I'm free and I try to run but I'm moving in slow motion, but he's moving full speed. As he catches me we start falling to the ground. The feeling of falling jars me and I wake up. I'm sweating profusely and my room is dark. As I try to focus I see the heart monitor, and IV. I must've woke Marie and my mother up because they're both staring at me with sleep in their eyes.

"You ok?" Marie said

"Nightmare" I said, suddenly with the realization that my mother was in the room I was extremely embarrassed. How much did she know? How angry was she? Although her eyes only showed love and concern for me.

"I'm gonna get you some juice." Marie got out of that room so fast. I couldn't blame her if the shoe was on the other foot I would've done the same thing.
My mother walked over to the sink and wet a paper towel. She wiped my forehead with it, it felt cool and refreshing. That lump was back in my throat, and tears flowed from my eyes. My mother was crying too, "they said you're anemic, and that you lost a lot of blood." then she kissed my forehead. I didn't feel worthy of her kindness. She grabbed my hand like nurse Saundra did. "You're gonna be ok baby".

CHAPTER 10

It had been a long time since I had been around my immediate family just hanging out. Without any question my mom brought me to her home from the hospital. My dad gave me the biggest hug, but the amazing part was that they didn't ask any questions or even talk about it.

My mom kept making big pots of greens. Omelets with spinach, monster green smoothies with spinach and kale, grape juice. Basically anything with iron to build my blood count. When I looked in the mirror I could see how pale I was.

At night the nightmares kept happening, I'd wake up and cry, then I'd cry myself to sleep. My doctor took me off work on disability for six weeks. Meanwhile I talked to my boss about switching to the Oakland office. I liked working in the city, but honestly I could do without the commute.

Baby or no baby I still needed to buy a house. Working on this process with my mom helped me fill my mind with something. My brother Terrence and Sister in-law Amy helped me pack up my apartment and put just about everything in storage. My mom insisted that I stay with them until I found a house. I changed my cellphone number and since Steve and I didn't really have friends in common I didn't have to worry about anyone giving him my number. As I prepared to send out my text blast with my new number I came across Andrew's number. A feeling of drama washed over me. I had to listen to my heart, I deleted the number. It felt good to wipe my slate clean.

I even agreed to go to service with my parents. There were a lot of people who were genuinely happy to see me, but then there were others. It's a shame how just a couple can spoil the experience. But regardless I felt good about being there. Some didn't recognize me because I had lost so much weight. It had been years since I even thought of attending service. I think the last time everyone there saw me I was almost at my biggest. Completely forgettable nothing like the woman I am today. Just before I started gaining weight I started coming into my look, but I couldn't see past my weight so I really grunge down. There are plenty of heavyset women who are beautiful, I couldn't see past my weight when it was me. I wanted to be Vesta Williams or Monique, I guess it was the way I grew up, cause all I could see was my weight. And I assumed that when people looked at me all they could see was my weight as well. I guess when I think about it attitude is everything, when I met Andrew I had lost some weight but I was still relatively a big girl.

Andrew, I hate that I keep thinking about him. I guess it's the wondering that eats me up about him. Wondering if he's still with that crazy girl. Wondering what would've happened if I would've went for him at Nicole's wedding. Wondering if he felt affected by me when he saw me that night. I wondered if he thought about calling me? I wondered if he hated me now? I could go on and on. Oh well, no use crying over spilled milk. As I always tell myself even though it didn't turn out for the best with Steve I did the right thing. If I would've gave in how do I know it wouldn't have been an issue between Andrew and I. Ugh! But any who, I enjoyed going to service with my parents. It seemed to make my parents really happy that I was there with them. Then the matchmakers... Sister Harris tells my mom and I that her son is coming to visit. The way she raised her eyebrows at me made me laugh. I remained silent, as my mom knew I wasn't ready for a relationship right now, but did nothing to make light of the situation. Then Sister Harris invites us to a gathering at her house the following Saturday. My mom started raving about my desserts when I asked what I could bring. So she asked me to bring a dessert and my mom to bring a salad.

CHAPTER 11

I wasn't expecting much when we arrived at sister Harris' house. Little kids were running around in the backyard. Most of the people there were my parent's age. But then Joy and her husband Anthony arrived. They have the cutest little boy, and for some reason he seems to be drawn to me. He's almost walking, but if you put him down to crawl who does he come to? Joy and I grew up together, but when I started going my own way we lost touch. She didn't even recognize me when her baby boy made a B-line to me. Lil man always has the biggest smile whenever he sees me. Its like this baby could sense my loss and his smiles were sent to help me. Joy was holding Lil man and as soon as he saw me he got really happy and he started flapping his arms and legs. He looked like he wanted to leap across the room to me. As soon as Joy gave him to me he laid his head on my shoulder and started playing with my necklace. Oh how I needed this hug. My eyes watered up and before I could stop it tears started pouring out of my eyes. I couldn't escape the thought. What if with my track record and how things normally go with me.... What if I never get to have this? What if there's something wrong with me and I can't have a baby ever? Would any serious minded man want me if I couldn't have his baby? Going to service is nice, and good for the soul, but they're all looking for virgins. Good girls who've always done the right thing. I always have to learn things the hard way it seems.

Joy was talking to someone when she noticed my tears. She kept talking and when the person was called away she motioned to me to join her as she walked out back. The baby had fallen asleep in my arms. Every time I looked at him my heart would pound like it was trying to beat out of my chest. That would make the tears come.

I thought Joy was gonna start drilling me with fifty million questions. Questions I wasn't willing to answer. But she didn't, she told me how she met Anthony. Their courtship, it's like she was filling me in on the gap since the last time I talked to her. Joy was a real person. Yes, she turned her life over to God, but she still had struggles. Not like me, but still struggles all the same. Listening to her made me relax and feel like I didn't have to be as uptight as I walked into this afternoon feeling.

Literally as I opened my mouth to share sister Harris walks up, "Tracy this is my son Cameron. Cameron this is Tracy." we shook hands, Cameron wasn't ugly, but I could tell he thought a lot more of himself than he should've. Like he was doing me a favor by saying hello. "You remember Joy."

"Of course. Where's Anthony?" Cameron said

"He's inside, a lot of the men were in Brother Harris' sports room."

"Oh right, let me go say hi to pops. I'll catch up with you guys later."

I guess Sister Harris was pleased with our interaction; she had the biggest smile plastered on her face. She stayed for a little, chatting with us. I could tell she liked me, which was a nice feeling. Steve's mother didn't like me, but she didn't like her own son so it's not like I paid her too much attention. But you could tell she was hoping for something to happen here. Unfortunately her son isn't the guy for me. There's a such thing as confidence and there's another thing when you think you're God's gift. I got major Gift vibes from Cameron. Besides I'm not ready for a relationship. I smiled and nodded.

As the day and evening progressed Cameron would pop his head out, play mister smooth and then retreat. I guess this kind of behavior is attractive wherever he's living at, but it's not working for me.

I did my best to ignore Cameron and I decided to share that I was looking for a house with Joy instead of the rest. She asked me some good questions like was I looking for a new home or a older home or a fixer-upper? Since I'm single and have yet to tap into my handiness I told her I'd prefer a new home with minimal to no handiwork required. But I liked the idea of a house with character. She said she'd keep an eye out for something. I told her I wanted to be in the Berkeley area. Joy got excited about the idea of helping me decorate. We spent the rest of the evening looking at decorating ideas online on our phones. Little Anthony never left my side. He kept giving me hugs and kisses and speaking his baby language to me.

The next morning after service Cameron made a beeline to me. "Hey I didn't get a chance to invite you to go skating with a group of friends tonight."

I could feel eyes on me so I searched the room until I found them. BINGO! Karen was staring from across the room. Karen was a little younger than me and apparently insecure. I don't know what this story is but already my caution signals are going off. He asked like he knew I was looking for an excuse to be in his presence. "Thanks for the invite, but I won't be able to make it tonight." I tried not to sound disgusted.

"Aw, come on. You know you haven't gotten a chance to meet everybody. There's gonna be people there from other congregations as well. Besides we haven't gotten a chance to get to know each other."

Gag me with a spoon! "What do you mean by that?" I tried to take as much disgust out of my voice as possible.

"I mean we haven't seen each other in years. Mom's seems to be so excited that you're here. I wanna know what you've been up to."

"Oh I see, well I won't be able to make it. But it looks like Karen definitely wants to talk to you." I motioned her over with my hands. She looked like she wanted to try to pretend she wasn't staring in my mouth. But then again she looked eager to come over. "How you doing?"

"Fine, and you?" she said

"I'm good, Cameron was just saying that he's getting a group together tonight to go skating. I can't make it, but"

Cameron kept his oh so cool demeanor and chimed right in, "hey Karen how you doing?" he said as he went in for a hug.

"I'm fine, wondering why I'm just now finding out about you being out here? I've been missing you."

That was my cue to walk away. "Ok, I'm gonna see you guys later."

As I walked away I caught eyes with Sean. He was quietly watching the scene. He smiled and I raised and eyebrow. Why was he smiling at me?

"The Smith's and Hawkins families are coming over for dinner. Could you do me the hugest favor and make the dessert?" my mom asked as we walked out.

"Of course, any specific request?"

"Hhmmmm" my mom smacked her lips together mimicking a check on her taste buds. "Ooh! What about those pies u make with the cheesecake, lemon curd, and whipped cream topping? Ooh yea that sounds good."

"Done, but I'll need the kitchen first."

"Ok, but I'll need you to hurry up. I'll prep while I wait for you to comeback."

On the way to the store I decided I would make five pies. Enough for everyone to have some tonight and then take one home.

I was so focused on my mental recipes that I didn't hear my name until Nicole was standing in front of me. "Hey girl how are you?"

"Hi!" I gave her a big hug. "I'm ok how are you?"

"I'm good. I got your text a couple of weeks ago. I've been meaning to call you or just stop by."

"Oh well I gave up my apartment, and I'm temporarily back at my parent's."

Her eyes dropped to my stomach, "that's good. When are you due again?"

I could feel the lump come back. I said a very pained, "I'm not anymore".

Nicole turned red as she gasped. "I'm sorry! Are you ok?"

"I will be."

"How's Steve holding up?"

"Fine I guess."

She hesitated, I could tell she had fifty million questions, but she hesitated to ask. "We're gonna have people over next month. I want you to come by."

"Ok, text me the details." we said a few more things but we went our separate ways. After that all I could think about was Andrew. Was he gonna be there? Did he hear about my pregnancy as well? I couldn't help but feel a little embarrassed.

Feeling a little deflated I returned home and poured my heart into making the pies. I was concentrating so hard that I guess my hands were making like lightning. I finished those pies so fast. They were beautiful when I was done. As I was taking a picture of my creations my mom walked in the kitchen. I could see the surprise of so many pies and then the sadness she was reflecting when she looked into my eyes. She gave me a big hug. Which I really needed, but at that moment I found myself wishing she was Steve.

I wondered if he felt bad yet for how much he was stressing me. I wondered what his reaction was when he tried to call me and the number was changed. Or how he felt when he finally decided to pop up at my place and found that I didn't live there anymore. Maybe all the violent dreams were my guilt for leaving him like I did. The part that kills me is that he doesn't know the baby isn't anymore. He still thinks there's a baby. Running from things like this only backfire in the end. But for now I gotta take care of me because he doesn't love me, that much is clear.

I told my mom I was gonna go lay down. I felt depressed and defeated. No matter how good of a front I tried to put up, I was heartbroken. Suspended in a whole world of numbness, but when the numbness broke I'd bleed all over again. As soon as my head hit the pillow I was back in my apartment. I was sitting on the couch reading a book. Then a key begins to unlock the door. My heart flutters as Steve walks in with a beautiful lily bouquet. I hopped off the couch and wrapped my legs around him. I kept kissing him and kissing him. He was laughing trying to take his key out the door. I got down and put the flowers in a vase and set them in the center of my table. They were so big and beautiful. He sat on the couch as he tried to tell me about his day I guess. I wasn't listening; I wanted love from the only person that mattered to me in the world. I sat up under him on the couch. My hands were metal and his body was the magnet. I couldn't stop touching him. Then I heard the apology my heart has been waiting for over the past few months. That did it I was all over him. We kept telling each other how much we loved each other, and each time he sincerely told me he loved me I melted a little more. His touch felt wonderful, I was born to love him. As we laid on the couch completely satisfied he slid a diamond and sapphire ring on my finger. He told me that he couldn't live without me. As happy as I was I couldn't let a heart felt yes come out my mouth. I kept kissing him until he stopped me and demanded and answer. Feeling like a deer caught in headlights I paused, and then I saw the personality switch happen before my eyes. He became angry, and of course the thought to run always happened too late. As he tackled me the feeling of falling jarred me awake. My pillow was full of tears. I laid there as I continued to cry, I wanted this to be over. I decided to send him a letter to his job.

Dear Steve,
I'm sorry for being such a source of pain in your life. I thought you should know that I lost the baby. I didn't want you to think I was keeping the child that never was, away from you.
Have a good life,
Tracy

I wanted to say so much more. But I couldn't find the words to express it. I placed it in a white envelope no return address. I put more than enough postage on the envelope. I drove to the Richmond Post office just in case he decided to be a detective. I know Oakland is huge, and that I never brought him out here to meet my parents but I didn't want to chance anything.

When I got back to my parents house there were extra cars outside. The houseguest had arrived. When I walked in the door the first person I saw was Cameron, Ugh!

"Hey?" I said as I then noticed Sean sitting in a chair in the living room. Karen walked out the bathroom. "Hello."

I walked into the family room and my parents had the card table set up. The men were playing dominos, while the women were at the kitchen table playing cards. "She's back". Sister Harris said

"Oh good. Sweetheart we were waiting for you to eat. Ladies let's pause our game here." my mom said.

Now if I remembered correctly my mom didn't say anything about the Harris' coming over and weren't we at their house yesterday? Oh well, I can't worry about it is what I told myself. We had just enough seats at the dining room table for everyone. Dinner was actually quite nice. Everyone was sharing stories and it was just enough to take the edge off of my mood. Even though I was sitting in the middle of Sean and Cameron. Sean's demeanor was different than Cameron's and Steve's for that matter. Sean didn't have anything to prove to anyone he was laid back and cool. Cameron on the other hand spent the night attempting to speak as an authority on everything. He was funny at times, but little did he know the more he opened his mouth the more unattracted I became. Karen was definitely digging him, and once she saw I wasn't interested she calmed down a lot. She even became conversational. Sister Harris on the other hand noticed the shift and she kept trying to redirect Cameron's attention towards me.

"I thought you guys were going skating." I said

"Well once you said you couldn't make it, I let go of the idea. There's some folks who's still going but when moms told me about this, I switched my plans."
Sean along with the rest of the table watched my face for a reaction. "That was nice but you didn't have to do that."

He put his hand on my thigh under the table. "Well since I'm visiting for a short period of time I figured I had to make each moment count."

OH NO THIS FOOL DIDN'T!!!!!! I pinched his hand as painfully as I could. "You and Karen should've went like I told you earlier."

Not liking what she was hearing Sister Harris changed the subject. Sean seemed to be taking it all in. He was definitely a part of the evening but he wasn't too much. It was a nice change of pace. Everyone went back to their games once everyone agreed that dinner was over. Sean and I cleared the table and set three of the pies on the table.

"Where did you buy these?"

"I made them."

"What?" then he looked me up and down. "Wait a minute these ain't none of those skinny pies, half the fat none of the taste?"

I playfully scoffed at him. "I guess you have to taste it and let me know."

"Oh see, you ain't right." Sean said as he smiled really big.

Sean helped me clean the kitchen while everyone was involved in their games. Sister Harris was clearly annoyed that Sean and I were talking while I ignored her son. But hey Cameron is not my type of guy. He isn't ugly just not the guy for me. He was clearly looking for someone who would fall at his feet and that just wasn't me. AND let's not forget the inappropriate touching under the table where we were having dinner with both of our parents. I still owe him a fat lip for that. After the coffee finished brewing we served everyone coffee and pie. Everyone was singing my praises and I could tell Sean's curiosity was peaked. When we got back in the kitchen I gave him a slice and then I watched him take his first bite. His eyes crossed and then he dramatically threw his head back. "You didn't make this!!!!!"

I smiled "yes I did".

He stopped talking while he enjoyed the rest of his slice. I was so tickled. The rest of the night he begged for the recipe. I told him I didn't have a recipe written down and that it was created by taste. My mom called it the gift of taste. I would taste something and come home and duplicate it by taste. Steve enjoyed this talent at first, but after I started losing weight he wouldn't ask for desserts anymore. He wouldn't really ask about food much. I guess he thought his not asking was helping me. I never shared this aspect of myself with Andrew. I was in lose weight mode during our relationship, so everything was an experiment.

"You're not gonna eat any?"

"Naw, eating that will put all my weight back. Watching everyone else enjoy is good enough for me."

"hmmmm. Well I think I need to eat your piece so it won't go to waste."

"Help yourself." I said as I sat and watched his process all over.

By the end of the night I expected to have Sean's number or give him mine. But he never mentioned it, and he didn't appear to be looking for my number. He and Karen left first. And once they left I made sure to stay by my mother's hip. I could see that fool Cameron following me to my room claiming he was looking for the bathroom. Cameron left when the Smiths and his parents left. Finally! I retreated to my bedroom; Steve was all over my brain. Afraid to fall asleep finally I couldn't fight it anymore. Here I go to be disappointed again.

CHAPTER 12

When Nicole called me two days later I told her the whole story. She cried with me and tried her best to assure me that I made the best decision to drop Steve like a bad habit. She told me that she saw him out with friends, it looked like they had just come from playing b-ball. She said he kept looking at her like he was trying to put his finger on where he knew her from. She said he seemed pretty normal. Which was pretty disappointing. I know it's stupid but I was hoping that he looked pretty messed up. Like he was missing me and couldn't function without me. Oh well right.

I told her about Sean when she asked me if I had met anyone at service. I told her he wasn't necessarily a someone, but that he was "interesting" to me. Part of me wondered if he would be so interesting if I wasn't comparing him to Steve or Cameron. Cameron in my eyes was the poster guy for who you should avoid at service. Unfortunately for his mom she couldn't see who her son really is. If she did she wouldn't encourage anyone to talk to him. Now I don't remember giving that fool my number but somehow he was calling me every day. Acting like we had some kind of a connection when we've barely spoken. But I'm a nice person so when he called me I answered the phone. Nicole was telling me to watch out for him cause he sounds like the stereotypical bad news guy. I asked Nicole if she and Hubby had decided to start a family yet. She said not just yet, they had plenty of time to begin that Chapter of their lives, but for now she was perfectly fine with things the way they were.

"So who's gonna be at your house next month?"

I could hear the smile in Nicole's voice. "I was really thinking of keeping everything low key. It won't be a bunch of people for sure. Probably just our wedding party and maybe a person or two sprinkled in here or there. Anyone in particular you looking forward to seeing?"

"No, I'm not sure that I'm exactly ready to see anyone at this point. But I was curious."

"What makes you not ready?"

"The fact that every waking minute I'm thinking about Steve. That wouldn't be fair to anyone."

"But didn't you just say that you were disappointed that the guy didn't ask for your number?"

"But that's what I'm trying to tell you. Sean doesn't give a majorly interested vibe. I think he's curious, but I don't take him for interested. It would be nice to have someone to talk to especially a non-threatening male female relationship. I don't know, I could use a good hug too. Who knows what I'm saying."

"All I'm gonna say is remain open to whatever may come up. You never know nothing could happen and you would have yourself all pumped up for nothing. Or everything could be wonderful. Just stay open minded."

That night I started thinking about the men two and a half years ago there was no one, well there was Steve. But he wasn't an option, not a real option anyways. Now there's Andrew, but for all I know he's not a real option, Cameron, who I might as well have stuck with Steve for that kind of drama, so I guess he's not a real option either. Sean, but he's not really an option either. Ugh! What's happening to me? Can't I meet someone make a new friend without it having to be a relationship. Well that's where I plan on putting Cameron straight in the friend's zone.

So basically Andrew's gonna be at Nicole's and I don't really know how I feel about that. Of course I wanna see him, but it would be devastating if he was as nonchalant as he was last time.

CHAPTER 13

Sean and I exchanged numbers, but everything between us has been awkward. Our conversation doesn't flow, and he acts as if he's interested but when I slow up enough to see what he's talking about he acts like he's not interested. When Shirley called me to check on me I gave her an update on everything that has been happening. She kept alluding to him batting for the other team and/or being extremely confused. As much as I didn't want to hear that, the seed of doubt had been planted. The past two weeks have been interesting to say the least.

I was ready to go back to work next week. I was a little disappointed that I hadn't found a place before going back to work. I had hoped to at least be in contract for a place. But nothing I liked was in the price range that I wanted to pay. I was pre - approved for a lot more than I wanted to spend. I didn't want a condo, or townhouse. I wanted an actual single-family residence. But lately it seems that houses aren't really built this way in the Berkeley area. I will hold out for what I like.

My parents have been great in all of this. My mom finally broke down and asked about Steve. She didn't want all the details, but of course she was upset that he wasn't at the hospital with me. As usual I protected him by telling her I didn't tell him I was in the hospital, which was true. But I didn't tell her how he had been treating me, which is why he wasn't there.

Getting back into work mode seems to make the nightmares less. As long as I went to bed thinking about work I hadn't had a dream about Steve in three nights. Even the dreams stopped being as violent once I sent him the letter. It was kind of like I stopped kicking myself over it.

Part of me thought about calling Nicole and canceling. I was afraid of the reaction I'd get from Andrew, and if his girlfriend was there acting like she did at the wedding... Ugh! Anxiety about the gathering was driving me crazy. So I told myself to stop thinking about it and any time the thought of it started to stress me I'd switch the channel sort of speak. But YES I did spend almost every day shopping for the perfect casual outfit. After over a year in this size you would think I would be used to shopping for this body. I always second-guessed myself when I picked up that size six anything. I'd take and eight and ten just in case. Depending on the store would determine whether the six or eight would fit. Then as I looked at myself in the mirror in amazement, I would suddenly break out into a dance solo. And then of course the butt check, if my butt looked good then I had to buy it. In the end I decided on black jeans, a ivory lace tank with an ivory cami, sapphire blue blazer, sapphire heels, silver and pearl dangly earrings. My hair curly, and makeup barely there. Just eyeliner and gloss. Yes the outfit in my brain sounds perfect. Now the day needed to hurry up and come. Butterflies from the unknown kept flooding my stomach. I literally fought with myself several times; as I would pick up my phone to cancel and tell Nicole I couldn't make it. So what if Andrew showed up, I'm not interested right? Right? The debate I kept having with myself. Your honor please let the record reflect that I did have deep feelings for him while we were together one could even label it as slight love. Truly not love in its deepest form but I was definitely happy to be with him. I definitely couldn't wait to see him, spend time with him, and talk to him. At one point you could even refer to him as my trainer. Once he found out about my lifestyle changes, he did what he could to help me. He was the one who got me running. He showed me how, how to run, how to breathe, how to push myself, how to relax my aching muscles. He didn't ride me about my weight either, he acknowledged my progress but it wasn't his primary focus of our relationship. He was a great guy and I'll give him props for being that. But he broke up with me, could it have been because I held out too long? Maybe I held out because I sensed something wasn't quite right. Naw, cause if that was the case Steve never would've gotten that far with me. Ok, ok maybe it was easier to go back to what I knew than to try something new. I am actually terrified of being with someone new. Maybe that's why I settled on being with Steve that old shoe. But the way he acted at the wedding was confusing. Andrew was kind of intense and the whole scene was wrong no matter how you paint it. Even if Andrew was the better man, I still did the right thing right? Andrew was there with his "girlfriend" and I was there with my boyfriend. To ask, no pressure me to suddenly switch up like he wanted wasn't right. I would have all kinds of regrets if I would've gave in. Right? Oh well, when he walked away he was MAD at me. So there's no point right. Calm down. He either won't show, won't care that I'm there, show up with that girl, or spend the evening ignoring me.

CHAPTER 14

I liked the layout of this office already. The cubicle walls were high and the actual spaces were good size. I had room for my dual monitors, file cabinets, and desk knick-knacks. The office Admin Danielle showed me around the floor. She gave me my card for the building garage, ID badge. As the IT technician brought my station up to speed I talked to Shirley about all the things that happened over the past six weeks since I'd been out. She decided to work from the Oakland office on Friday to bring me up to speed on my projects. The next few days would be spent clearing my outlook inbox sorting emails and then reading them.

Around noon I could no longer ignore the rumble in my tummy. As I sat in my guess chair I tried to decide what I wanted for lunch. To keep it simple and not end up with something I didn't want I decided to go across the street to subway. By the time I started heading towards the elevator it was after 1pm. As I waited for the elevator I checked out my reflection in the mirrored panel in between the elevators. I looked fine, I knew Oakland wasn't as formal as San Francisco but I didn't know how casual the office got. So I wore black slacks, a taupe blouse, a black headband, Taupe shoes, black earrings, and a black and taupe purse. I was retouching my gloss when the elevator arrived. It was empty and on the next floor the doors opened butterflies filled my stomach when Nicole stepped on the elevator. We both screamed in excitement.

"What are u doing here?"

"I transferred to this office for a change of environment. You work in this building?"

"A few days a month. Had I known you were here I would've asked you to lunch."

"Oh well I'm on my way to get a sandwich. Trying to get my station setup. It's taken a little longer than I thought it would."

"Well is it ok if I join you? I haven't had lunch yet either. I was trying to think of where to go real quick. "

"OF COURSE!" I was happy to have someone to have lunch with.

We talked about miscellaneous things but she could tell I was beating around the bush. So she paused and smiled at me. "You know I'm so nervous about Saturday."

Her smile dropped a little. "There have been some updates. I didn't know if I should call you or not."

My heart dropped, "what?"

"Please promise you won't say anything? Hubby let it slip on accident." she swallowed hard, "I don't know if it's such a big deal really. Andrew and Toya have a son."

My heart sank again, "he's married?"

"No, but they have a son."

"How old is he?"

"He's almost a year."

My brain quickly did the math. She had to have gotten pregnant around the wedding. Remembering all that he told me about having children I couldn't believe he didn't marry her. I guess what people say and what they do is two different things. I sat there not knowing how to feel. "Why didn't he marry her?"

"Toya? Are you kidding me? Can you blame him?"

"I know he was adamant about no children before marriage. I figured he'd be on top of his job to make sure it didn't happen. Maybe he wanted to have a baby with her and all that he said was just talk."

"I don't know about all that. But please don't let on that you know about this. Be surprised."

"Trust! I am completely surprised, but it doesn't matter especially now." I couldn't help but show my disappointment. Honestly I was hoping that we'd talk this weekend. I was hoping that we'd get back together. But now he's forever bonded to that crazy woman. That's a lot for anyone to take on. Crazy as she may be she could be a wonderful mother.

"Look Tracy don't jump to conclusions. You don't know the situation. Just wait until you talk to him."

I said a very defeated, "yea sure".

Nicole changed the subject. She gave me a huge hug probably regretting that she said anything at all. When I got back to my cubicle the tech was still working on my station. Now completely irritated. I packed up my computer. I calmly told the tech that I needed to go home and log on. I told him to send me an email when the station was set up and ready. He was very apologetic about the delay. I needed to focus on something else. I kept seeing Andrew's face in my mind. I was trying to imagine his reaction to her news. I couldn't gauge it. As I drove on autopilot my cell phone rang. The car called out that it was Samantha Brooks my realtor.

"Answer call" I commanded "Hello"

"Hello Tracy, this is Sam is this a bad time?"

"No, I'm hands free in the car."

"I just got a listing that I think you NEED to check out. How soon can u meet with me?"

"I'm in the car right now. I could be there in fifteen minutes."

"Oh! That's great! I'm really excited for you to see this one. I really think we have a winner here."

"Ok, sounds good I could use some good news today. I'm on my way to your office right now. See you then."

When I got to Sam's office she was standing outside doing her happy dance of excitement. Seeing that wide grin on her face made me laugh.

When we got in her car she was full of positive energy. She was talking very fast and gesturing while driving. She explained the house we were going to see was put on the market this morning. The owners bought it as a fixer upper. And they were working towards making it their dream home. She explained that everything in the house was brand new, but following the original integrity of the house. Even the plumbing was brand new. The couple's relationship did not make it to the end of the renovation. The wife who was a stay at home wife cheated. As part of their divorce settlement the husband had to sell the house. Well we know what the markets like, but he's listing the house for even lower than that. He's almost giving the house away.

When we turned onto the street I knew I was home. My eyes almost bulged out of my face when she pulled into the driveway. Now I understood her excitement. I instantly got the biggest smile on my face. Sam kept looking at me and smiling and raising her eyebrows up and down up and down. Looking at the front yard I thought about the work I'd have to do to keep it up. But ask me if I cared. The driveway led to the two-car garage. There was a red paver walkway from the driveway to the front door. And the same pavers led from the sidewalk to the front door. The house was a mocha color with dark chocolate trim. It had a stucco finish. The front door was red with a mail slot in it. When she opened the door the smell of fresh paint hit my nose immediately. The floors where dark cherry wood and shining. The walls were a smoky grey with white trim. The living room was huge with a huge fireplace and mantle. The crown moldings were beautiful. The dining room, which was right off the kitchen, was huge just like my parents dining room. I could easily fit a twelve chair dinette set in there and there would still be plenty of room. I envisioned dinner parties with my family and friends at least once a month. The kitchen was huge! It had a center island with the stovetops; there were four burners and a grill in the middle. The entire kitchen had granite countertops and stainless steel appliances. There was a beautiful bay window above the sink. Then there was space for an average family size dinette set. And the windows next to this area were huge. The family room was good size. I could fit two couches, a pool table, ping pong table, and still have a bunch of folks over without being crowded. Right off the family room there was a bedroom and the downstairs bathroom. It was a average sized room and it had a full bathroom with a shower. The linen closet was in the bathroom. Sam followed me around with that same grin plastered on her face. I hadn't seen the rest of the house and I knew I wanted this house. The stairway was nice and not too steep. The banister was the same wood as the floors. The first bedroom off the stairs was a average good-sized room with a small but nice sized walk in closet. This room shared a bathroom with the bedroom next to it. The bathroom had double sinks a good-sized tub/shower combination. It was a basic bathroom but still wonderful. The room on the other side of the bathroom was identical to the other it was just on the other side. Next there was another bedroom, but it was small compared to the others it had a standard closet with sliding mirrored doors. The end of the hallway led to the double-doored piece of resistance. I couldn't wait to see the master suite. When we opened the doors the first thing I noticed was the fireplace in the master suite. The bedroom was huge. There were double doors that led to a small deck. There was a nice view of trees, the Berkeley Hotel was just below and you could see a lot of the grounds from the balcony. There was an area off to the right that could be used as an office, nursery, or lounge area. There was a walk in closet that was so huge it could've been another bedroom. The master bathroom had double vanity sinks. A huge sunken tub that I instantly started dreaming about as my personal haven. A separate shower with one of those shower heads that poured out as rain. A separate toilet area. There was a vanity next to the sinks. I looked at Sam and she still had a wide grin. Then she showed me the garage. It had a double door garage door but it was deep enough to fit four cars with extra space. There was a basement that was being converted into a wine cellar, and it had a sauna in the far corner. In the backyard, which was also huge, there was a grass area tall trees that lined each side of the property. There was a gazebo, which also had a hot tub. Closer to the house there was a patio area that had pavement and a basketball hoop. There was a old school brick BBQ pit. On the garage side of the house there was still enough space to park a RV and still have enough room to walk comfortably.

When the tour was finally over I looked at her and I said, "How in the world can I afford this place"?

So then Sam broke down the whole deal. It was too much house for just me, but with that SWEET deal how could I pass it up? We went back to her office and I made and offer right away. She called the seller who accepted my offer on the spot. I couldn't believe it. I gave Sam my check for my earnest money deposit. As soon as I got home I called my lender and asked for a list of inspectors. I connected them with Sam, as I wanted an inspection for my own peace of mind. A couple hours later I took my parents by to see the place and their eyes lit up with proudness. But my mom insisted that I have an alarm installed before I moved in since it was such a huge place. When I got home I logged on my computer and worked a good four hours working purely off of adrenalin from the day. I needed this to fill the void that settled in my stomach. That night I laid there wondering how big my stomach would've been by now. I wondered if I would look different. I wondered if I would've been the woman who blew up or would I have been all stomach. I know most women hope for the latter when in all actuality most women were like the first. I couldn't believe Andrew was a father. I couldn't believe he wasn't married. Even though they weren't married he was still tied to a crazy woman for the rest of his life. I told my crying heart to get over it and to let him go. I wasn't gonna allow myself to linger on it any longer. So I decided to change the thought process and think about my new house. I told myself to take my time about decorating and to do it like I wanted to do it.

CHAPTER 15

Friday night I had insomnia. I was up until three a.m., when I finally fell asleep I fell asleep really hard. I was dead to the world. I woke up and it was after two and the gathering started at three. At first I panicked I hated arriving late anywhere and having people look at me when I walked in the door. But then again I didn't care. I felt so rested and at peace with myself. I finally got myself to go to sleep by telling myself I didn't care whether I saw Andrew today or not. I was having a pep talk with my heart really. I didn't want to feel one way or another about Andrew showing up with Toya today. I didn't want her to start any mess with me.

I found myself moving slowly. At the last minute in the shower I decided to wash my hair for extra popping curls. As I slowly got ready in the room I realized the clock said it was after four and I was only halfway ready. My mom came in the room excitedly chatting about the house. She was so excited about the house she couldn't talk about anything else. I smiled, as her excitement was refreshing. When I got in my car the clock said it was five seventeen. Then my phone rang, the car called out Nicole.

"Answer" and then I said, "Hello sweetheart I'm moving slow I'm coming"

"Ok because I was about to say, it's not like you to be so late."

I laughed, "I know I'm on my way now"

"Ok, I'll see you in a minute"

As if the radio knew I needed a major distraction hit after hit came on. This car ride was too short; I was at my destination too fast. Nicole was looking out the window when I pulled up. She came and met me at my car. "You look nice"

"Thank you" I gave her a tight lipped smile.
She led me around the side of the house instead of going inside. There were card tables set up randomly around the yard, there were people at each one. Some were playing cards and others were playing dominos. Some were inside watching TV. Others were in

their own conversations. Nicole led me to a table in the far corner. "We got winners," she said standing real proud.

Then Hubby said, "You sure you want that whooping just yet? You might wanna go slow and start with another table."

"Ha! Ha! Remember that when we send you scurrying away"

Nicole and her husband continued to talk mess to each other for the rest of his game. I dared not look around again for fear that I might see Andrew, or worse Toya. When the losers exited the table Hubby kept talking trash the entire time. Their trash talking did put me more at ease and focusing on the board and dominos in my hand helped me stay distracted. Each time I played I was scoring and at first it was funny how much trash Hubby was talking and I said nothing. Once we hit our third house and they were on their first Hubby started getting quieter and quieter. So eventually Nicole called him on it. We were a "ten-ny shoe" away from victory and Hubby was real quiet. Hubby was staring real hard at the dominos he had in hand. It was like he was mentally trying to change them into something else. "Study long! Study wrong!"

"See that's it right there! You are using your womanly powers on me. That's why you're winning. "

"WHAT??"

Everyone fell out in laughter as Hubby tried his best to keep a straight face. "You heard me. Y'all over here cheating."

"Right!!!" Nicole said mocking him.

"Yes you are, why's Tracy being so quiet??? NO WOMAN IS EVER THAT QUIET!!!"

Everyone erupted into laughter!

I replied with as much sass as I could muster, "I'm just sitting here wondering what game you're playing. Cause if it were bones, you wouldn't have given over the game so easily."

The crowd Oohed!

"Oh ok! We playing again and I ain't taking it easy on y'all this time! Bring yo A game."

"A! Man! I gotta get going I gotta go to work.," his partner said with an embarrassed smile.

"How you gon let these girls scare you away from the table!"

"He's a smart man, he ain't following you down that hole!"

Nicole said, "Doubt you find anybody crazy enough to partner up wit you."

So of course, as soon as the words came out her mouth I knew who was gonna step up. "I got your back brah!" out of nowhere there he was. When he glided past me his cologne danced in my nose. It had been months and still that smell instantly told me who was coming. "How you doing?" he said to me as he confidently took his seat. I saw his eyes quickly dance over my face, hair, hands with appreciation and approval.

"I'm good! How about you?"

"Yea I'm good, real good." he said as he and Hubby fist bumped. "Let the games begin!"

Nicole washed the dominos with a wide grin on her face. "I don't know why you smiling, my boy's here! You bout to get whooped!" Hubby said

As Nicole and Hubby went back and forth I kept telling myself to be cool. Just because he looked at me like that doesn't mean nothing. We used to date so yea he might still see something he likes. But it doesn't mean anything. Then as I picked my dominos, that fast, did he just wink at me? Instantly a blushing smile came over my face. But I stopped it right away. Just be cool girl! Don't let him see you sweat! I decided to focus on my dominos and stop looking around. He's trying to distract me with his charm and good looks. I got to keep my cool.

"Ssshhhh! Woman! Its time for your spanking!" Hubby said in a dramatic outburst!

There was now a crowd of spectators to our game. Hubby and Andrew talked trash the whole time. Again! When we made our first house before them the conversation slowed a little. But they had a whole celebration when they made their first house. But as soon as they sat down we then made our second house. Hubby started complaining that whoever washed the dominos last wasn't doing a thorough job. But what was funny is that it was him.

Five points to go, and they were down by fifteen the tension was so tight you could've cut it with a knife. I smiled a huge smile when I dominoed.

"NNNNNNNNNOOOOOOOO!!!!!!!" Hubby fell on the ground like he was wounded. "This woman you gave me God! She has made me weak. She sitting ova der using her womanly charms knocking me off my game Lord!" he laid there with his hand over his heart like he was doing a would Red Fox impersonation.

"Get up fool!" Nicole said as she playfully hit him.

I could see Andrew checking me out in my panoramic view. I couldn't help myself; I got up to go get some punch. I was thirsty, plus I wanted him to watch me walk away from him. What did Tupac say? Put a Lil twist in your hips cause he's watching. I didn't go overboard but just enough to show him I still had it. When I got to the sliding glass door, he was still sitting there. And YES he was watching. I held back my smile of satisfaction. After I entered the house the thought crossed my mind, Toya could be anywhere in this house. Check yourself girl, that's somebody else's man. I went in the kitchen grabbed a can out the sink full of sodas and ice.

As I popped the can Sonya walked in the kitchen "Hey girl!"

"Hey!" we hugged "how you been haven't seen or heard from you since the wedding? I see you're still holding your weight down."

"Girl, I'm trying. You know how it is we start shuffling, taking care of business. What's new with you?"

"Let me think, oh let me see." then I realized all the gestures she was making with her left hand. She had and engagement ring on.

"Shut up!" I did the excited and happy dance with her. "Congratulations!"

"Thank you! Thank you! His name is Philip he'll be here a little later. I gotta introduce you."

"Ok! So ok! How did you meet? How did you fall in love? Tell me the whole story."

"It's too hot in this house. Let's go outside.," she said as she grabbed me by the hand and led me outside. Andrew and Hubby were playing another duo, but Andrew raised his eyes to see where we were going. I acted as though I didn't notice him watching us.

Sonya told me her whole story. How she was supposed to be going out with another friend and all dressed with nowhere to go she called Nicole. Nicole and Hubby were going to hear some music and they invited her to tag along. She said she bumped into Philip at the bar literally and he spilled his drink. She said she didn't even understand why she lost her balance right at that moment. But she apologized and bought him another drink. She said he was appreciative and they went their separate ways. She said after the show they went out for a bite to eat and who did she bump into in the waiting area? You guessed it. She said they started talking as they waited and then he told his friends that he'd catch up to them later and he joined them. She said they've been drawn to each other ever since. Kind of made me think of Andrew and how we met that night and things just seemed to workout for us. Kind of like had Toya not happened could we be engaged as well? She said their engagement happened fairly recently. She said their families mixed well.

"Girl sometimes I feel like this is the man who was made for me. We seem to compliment each other in every way."

I sat there nodding and imagining the feeling. I had my back to Andrew so I couldn't tell if he was watching me or not. But then the reality of what happened between us came surging back and all the sudden my blazer was too hot. I took it off and hung it on the back of my chair. Nicole came over and the conversation took on more life. Both of my friends were gushing with love for the men in their lives. I had no one so I did my best to imagine how good it felt to know who loves you. Who's willing to stand besides you and say YES! I put you before all others! I guess I drifted too far cause they were both looking at me. "What happened?"

"Girl, where did you go?"

"Oh you know me. My mind races at 50 miles per hour."

"I see, we asked if you wanted to come inside and see my ideas?"

"Sure!" we went inside into the master suite away from everybody. Nicole brought a bottle of wine and three glasses. Sonya sat in front of the computer gliding from site to site. She had definitely put a lot of thought into the whole affair. She had almost everything planned except the actual date. After awhile I told them about my house. Once again we were on the Internet this time looking at furniture and inspirational sites.

As I swallowed the last drop of my Moscato I was sad that the bottle only held just over three glasses. "We should go wine tasting. We could hire a limo to drive us there and back."

"That sounds like a plan. I'm so in!" Sonya said extremely excited.

"Let's pick a date." Nicole said

As she launched a new browser to search the web we heard yelling. We all looked at each other and said in unison, "Toya!" We ran to the backyard. There she was screaming in Andrew's face with the baby screaming as well on her hip. Andrew was livid but just standing there. Although her back was to us I could tell she hadn't lost all her baby weight. But she looked good in form all the same. The baby was screaming and reaching for his daddy. When Andrew reached for the baby, Toya snatched her hip away. That made everyone moan. She had her finger in his face she was extremely mad. She kept telling him he was crazy to think she would sit at home with a baby while he was out hooking up. Andrew didn't say anything he just stood there MAD as all get out taking it all in. Then she started crying accusing him of making her out to be the crazy one. The baby was still screaming and she seemed oblivious to it. Finally he said, "I don't have to make you look like anything you're doing it all by yourself. Leave my son or take him with you. Either way you're leaving the police have already been called. You're trespassing." She gasped the ghettoest gasp; she then used some rather colorful words as she cursed him out. Then she tossed the baby at him. Andrew caught him and the baby instantly laid his head on his daddy's shoulder. Nicole's friend Tanisha got angry and she ran up in Toya's face. The two of them started arguing. Toya accused Tanisha and Andrew of messing around. Andrew rolled his eyes and started walking away. Toya looked like she was going to jump on him and Tanisha tackled her and put her in a police hold where she couldn't move. Toya was crying and screaming as the police came along side the house. As the police hurried onto the scene Toya looked up and saw Andrew walking towards the house, but it was in my direction. As soon as she saw me she became enraged almost foaming at the mouth. The police officer handcuffed her and lifted her up from the ground. Tanisha and the other officer spoke calmly as if they spoke some kind of officer secret language. Nicole and Hubby spoke with the officers as I secretly watched from the doorway as Andrew focused on his son. The baby was the spitting image of Andrew. The baby looked to his father for comfort; right away you could tell he was very attached to his father. All signs of anger and tension were gone from Andrew's face. Andrew was focused on his son the way a father should be. The baby held onto his dad's shirt with his tiny little fist. Andrew kept rubbing his little head and speaking in a calm voice as he smiled at his son. I wondered how many scenes like this the baby had seen. The music started playing again outside and Tanisha and Nicole walked past me and into the house. They both walked over to Andrew, Tanisha gave him a strong pat on the back and Nicole gave him a hug. It looked as if he was telling them he was going to leave, but of course Nicole convinced him to stay. She even got the baby who would not leave his father to smile. He still held onto his father as if his life depended on it.

Sonya nudged me to go back into the room. Then she told me the whole story. Andrew broke up with Toya right after the wedding, but then a couple weeks later she found out she was pregnant. It appears that his disappearance during the reception planted the seed that evening. I thought about how insecure she was acting before their disappearance. And how unconcerned with me she became after they came back. I suspected something like that because he couldn't even look at me. I wonder if he broke up with her because of me. Or if he was just fed up period, cause he never called me.

He tried to make the best of the situation, but of course Toya was only concerned with how much money she was gonna get for child support. As soon as the baby was born she took him to court. At first things were fine, she was living off child support and she didn't care much about anything. Andrew had the baby whenever he could. Then she tried to take him to court for more money. When the judge denied her she went crazy. Whenever she can she acts crazy with him to drive him crazy.

"What's wrong with her?"

"She's just that type of female."

I felt really bad for the baby. I imagined him growing up to be just like Steve. Then all the sudden overwhelming thoughts of Steve kept hitting me like bricks. I hadn't thought about him in weeks. Eventually Nicole came in the room holding little man. He kept looking at Nicole with big brown eyes. When Sonya and I said hi to him he laid his head on Nicole in a shy manner. Sonya changed the subject back to wine tasting. Then she had the thought, "would it be ok with you guys if we paid for the trip and took some engagement photos?"

"So you mean bring the men?" I really wanted to say HECK NO! But all the sudden it became a free trip for me.

"Yea, I think it would be fun. We could have the person who did our makeup for the wedding come and do our makeup. Looking good, drinking wine, and having a good time. It should be just us."

"Who's us?" I asked

"Nicole and Hubby, me and my man, you."

And then Nicole said, "and Andrew of course" she was too eager to say it and Sonya shot her a look like be cool.

Both of them had looks of busted on their faces. We all started laughing. "Andrew is a good guy, but I think his plate is a little full." And then as if on cue. Little man shimmies off Nicole's lap. He wobbles over to me and puts his hands up. OH JUST MELT MY BLEEDING HEART! This was just like Joy's little man all over. I picked him up and he put his head on my chest. I almost cried, "This isn't fair you guys". He was so sweet, clearly he was all dad. "Fine! But I wanna invite my friends Joy and Anthony. They have a little boy as well."

"That's fine, let me run all this by Philip. I'm sure he'll say yes then we can set a date."

Then little man sat up and stared at my face. It was like he was making a mental impression of my face. Then he ever so gently started touching my face. Like he was studying the curves of it. I smiled at him, but he didn't smile back. He kept taking me in. Sonya and Nicole exchanged looks, but they didn't say anything about me and Lil man getting to know each other. A little while later there was a knock at the door. Oh yes! He's handsome, Sonya had a winner I could tell when he walked in the room. He said a respectful hello to everyone but his focus was his woman. They hugged and kissed, Lil man wasn't impressed. He remained stone-faced when Philip said hello. Sonya walked him out to the hallway to discuss the trip most likely.

Nicole looked at us and smiled. "This is the first time he's let me walk away with him. Normally he doesn't want to be out of eye shot of his dad."

"I thought you didn't know him."

"They came over a few times recently. Andrew really needed to talk to Hubby. He's been going through it. I'm surprised he came straight to you."

"Are you guys trying to get Andrew and I back together?"

Nicole said a very guilty, "no way Jose" we both laughed. Lil man watched my face while he had his head on my chest. "Look, it's not like I asked him if that's what he wanted or you for that matter. But I feel like its only right to put you two in the environment to see what could happen. If you guys get back together, that's on you. I know there's added levels, but what's life if it isn't complicated?"

I smiled as I looked down at Lil man. "What's his name?"

"Andre"

"Aw! I like that. Andre!" I said as I rubbed his head.

Then Sonya came back in the room dancing and singing. Her lipstick was pretty much gone. "He said yes, let's book it."

After looking at the calendar we came up with a date two weeks away. Then I called Joy. She confirmed that they could come. Then Nicole and Sonya agreed to come to my service on Sunday to meet Joy. Then Nicole disappeared for a minute. Andre watched her walk out the room. I thought he might cry but he held on to my shirt a little tighter as he rested his head on my chest. Nicole came in the room with a bigger smile telling us that everyone could make it. She and Sonya high fived as I shook my head at them. A few minutes later there was a knock on the door. Andrew popped his head in the door. His eyes got big when he saw Andre and I hugged up at the computer. As soon as little man heard his dads voice his head popped up. Andrew's eyes stayed stuck on us as he talked to Nicole and Sonya. Then Lil man wanted his dad so he reached for him. Then they both stared at me. It was weird seeing him hold a smaller version of himself. Same facial expressions and everything. I put my hand up to block their gaze. I smiled and then I walked out the room. The air in there suddenly became too stiff. So I went to the kitchen to get some water.

"I don't think we met, I'm Michael."

I didn't know if he had been there all night. That's it, if you wanna meet a handsome guy just hang around Nicole and Hubby. This Morris Chestnut lookalike was kind of hard to shrug off. Although he was a little more chocolate but very charming. Now I've never stepped back and checked a man out but with Michael you couldn't help it. I guess he was used to my reaction cause he smiled with a mouth full of pearly straight whites. "No, I don't think we have. Tracy" I said as I stuck my hand out to shake his.

"Where have you been hiding?" He said as he leaned against the counter and prepared himself for a conversation.

"I guess I could ask you the same. I've been here for hours." Did I just flirt with this man? Un huh this guy, no, no, no Tracy! Run! He wasn't slimy like Cameron, but I'd be lying if I didn't say there was something in the area that smelled like Steve to me. But he was so pretty and charming.

"Well had I known you were here I would've gotten here sooner." There was that smile again.

I couldn't argue with myself any longer I had to go back in the room with my girls. "Ok well, now that that's out of the way. I gotta...." I scratched my head trying to think of something. "I'm just gonna go."

He held his smile, "ok, we'll I'm sure I'll see you soon."

"Ok" I held in a giggle. When I turned on my heels I was so eager to get out of there that I almost walked into the wall! Ugh! I can't stand myself. Why couldn't I have a smooth sexy exit? No I gotta hit my knee on the wall cause heaven knows where and how I was going anywhere. We both laughed, but I hated myself for laughing. Just as I was leaving the kitchen I had a goofy smile on my face and Andrew stepped out of the room. He looked at my face and you could see the question mark on his face and then three steps behind me was Michael. He looked at Michael and then back at my goofy grin. He knew!

CHAPTER 16

"This is so beautiful!" Joy said as she excitedly ran from room to room. "There are so many possibilities."

"I know right. I think I want a white, grey, and cobalt blue living room. I want blue and silver through out the house."

"This is a really big house for just one person."

"You know, I thought about that. But how could I pass this deal up?"

"When will you move in?"

"As soon as I have my alarm system installed. Since I will be here alone this place will be locked up like Fort Knox."

We agreed to come to my house after having our makeup done. Sonya and Nicole went to get the men from Nicole's house. So Joy and I headed to the house and we called Anthony to meet us there. Joy was first to see the house out of all my friends. My family helped me move in the items that I planned to keep from my apartment. The rest of the stuff I donated or gave away.

I put my bedroom furniture in the room downstairs. As I want a new set for my new room. I figured my old comfy bed would be very welcoming to new guest. My old living room furniture went in the family room. I decided to make the really small room my home gym. A treadmill and a machine of some sort. I hadn't bought any of the equipment yet but I focused my mind in that direction for that room. I also decided that my office would be within my lounge area in my suite.

Nicole and Anthony both pulled up in their SUV's at the same time. You could see the looks on all of their faces as they got out of their cars. Andrew was the last to get out, but you could tell he was impressed.

"Girl, can I borrow five dollars? I didn't know you were baller status like this?" Hubby said as he gave me a hug hello.

"It's not like you think, but thank you." Andrew gave me a polite hug hello, but there was no passion or even real feeling in it. I tried not to let it bother me. "We got a few minutes before the limo comes, let me give you guys the Grande tour." I showed them around the house. Andrew hung to the back of the group. Joy kept the boys downstairs as they instantly got along and were in their own boy world together touring the downstairs and all the open space. Everyone oohed and awed, as I showed them around. Just as we finished the tour the limo arrived. Since the babies seem to hit it off we put their car seats next to each other and then everyone seemed to couple off. Andrew seemed uncomfortable and uneasy about sitting next to me. I didn't want the day to seem awkward so I kept talking to Andrew until he started to relax and act like his normal self. When we arrived at the first winery, we put the boys in their strollers and then we went straight to the tasting room. Our attendant was very lively and informative. The wine was good and hit the spot on our first stop to relaxing. When we got back in the limo Andrew was more relaxed as he actually allowed his body to barely bump mine along the way. At the third winery we had a picnic lunch, which was prearranged by the limo company. We all opted to sit in the grass and eat and drink while Sonya and Philip's photographer ran around grabbing candid moments. I noticed Andrew betraying himself by checking me out. Then he said, "You look really nice".

"Thank you, but you always look good." Did I really say that? Doggone Moscato!

He seemed pleased with my response but he didn't say anything else to me he smiled.

"I need you two", the photographer said Andrew and I followed him over to a picnic table. He instructed Andrew to sit on the table. Then he snapped a few shots. It had to be the wine messing with me as I watched him I was just in Aw. Andrew looked good the way his grey shirt hung off his broad shoulders. The softness of the grey color caressed his cocoa brown skin. I stood there asking myself how I never slept with him. I didn't realize I was staring until I realized he was staring back and the photographer was snapping away. He kept alternating between us. Then he said, "Ok now you go sit in front of him".

85

So I walked over and stood in front of the table between Andrew's legs. "Come on sit down I don't bite." I scooted back on the table and Andrew put his big arms around me. I melted in his arms. I leaned to the left so that his face would show in the pictures, exposing my neck. First I felt his breath then he gently kissed my neck, suddenly it seemed like we were alone. Completely forgetting we were being photographed I closed my eyes and let out a slow deep breath. Which made him kiss my neck more. Then he gently pulled my hair to move my face back so he could kiss me. It was the longest and slowest, gentlest kiss I've ever experienced. I couldn't tell you where I was but this kiss was the kiss of a lifetime. Then I heard someone clear their throat and they were standing in front of me. I opened my eyes and we both turned our heads.

"What are you guys doing?" Hubby said with the biggest grin on his face.
I looked at our picnic spot and everybody was looking some with their mouths open. "My bad!" I said totally embarrassed

"Dude! You are making the rest of us look so bad! Cut it out!" We all started laughing. Then Hubby pointed at the photographer. "Homeboy is over here sweating like he's in trouble." The poor Photographer, he had broken out into a sweat.

"Whoa!" Is all I could think.
I started to get up, and Andrew grabbed me a little tighter. "Don't move yet." He blushed and that's when I realized there was something poking me in my back.

"Ugh! Ok..."

Hubby shook his head, as he walked away laughing, "can't take them anywhere".

Then Andrew whispered in my ear, "we need to talk".
I shook my head in agreement. With the way I was feeling, I would've agreed to anything right there. It had to be the wine right? Joy had the craziest smile on her face. But when I looked at Sonya and Nicole they had the same looks. Andrew started to pull me back into him. But I hopped up, "I gotta pee" as I flashed him a

pleading look. He exhaled and I kissed his cheek and then I ran towards the bathroom. Without a word the girls came as well. When they came in the bathroom we all screamed and high fived.

"I was about to get the hose on you guys." Joy pretended to get burned when she touched my shoulder.

"So what does this mean?" Nicole said

"I don't know! I don't know! He said we need to talk." I said cheesing like a Chesser cat.

"Wait a minute! Hold the phone! What about Michael?" Sonya said

"Huh?" I said feeling confused.

"Somebody has to address the pink elephant in the room."

"I've barely spoken to him. He's not an issue. If Andrew wants me, why would I care about Michael?"

"I hear that, but Michael's not the kind to bow out gracefully."

"I know he's your brother, but do you know something you wanna share with the class?" Nicole asked

"I don't know what you do to these guys. But off that one encounter my brother is so gone. I've never seen him like that over a hello. And when he likes a female like he's liking you..." She shook her head, "I'm just saying he don't give up easily."

I sucked my teeth, "so.... I mean what am I supposed to do wait for him cause he flirted with me one night? Up until your brothers hello you were all for me and Andrew getting back together. Please don't do this to me, I really feel like Andrew could be the one."

Nicole squealed while Joy clapped her hands in excitement. "You really think so sweetheart even after everything that's happened? Children change relationships, that's a lot to consider." Nicole said

"Well we haven't even talked it out yet. We got a lot to talk about. But at least we both wanna talk. I really need you to still be happy for me. Please you've been my Jiminy Cricket in this whole thing, and I need that."

Sonya huffed loud, "fine! Fine! Fine! But if my brother starts acting up, I gotta bow out gracefully."

"Understood, I don't know why he would though. We only said hi."

Sonya hunched her shoulders. We group hugged and then we went back to the picnic site. The photographer was in a zone snapping pictures of the boys as they completely ignored him and played their game of what's in this grass. I stood next to Andrew and then our driver came over. He stated that we had two more wineries on the schedule.

"If you'll clean up we'll take the boys and strap them in." Anthony said to Andrew

"Sounds like a plan." They fist bumped to seal the deal. Then Andrew looked at me and bit his bottom lip as he smiled.

We hurried around collecting our things. Everyone gathered on the limo, I started towards the limo. Andrew grabbed my arm and I turned to face him he planted another slow, but DEEP kiss on me. I didn't think I could melt anymore than I already had. He pulled me so close it was like he was trying squish us into one person. I felt my leg move up and I knew I had to backup, but I couldn't move my body only my face. "We need to talk." He said as he rested his forehead on mine.

"I know."

"What are you doing later?"

"Nothing, after everyone leaves I'm going back to my parent's house."

"You wanna come by my place first?"

"Ok" we sealed it with a kiss and then we got on the bus. The rest of the day seemed to float by. The day was as it should've been we were all with the person we were supposed to be with. On the way home everyone was "Happy" from the wine. Everyone was pretty much in their own conversations. Andrew and I held hands as I laid my head on his shoulder and he rested his head on mine. When we got to my house we transferred Andre's car seat to my car. And we followed Nicole to her house so Andrew could get his car. As I followed Andrew to his place my heart started pounding. I hadn't been alone with him since that day on the beach. I parked my car in his guest spot, I grabbed Andre and he got the car seat. Andrew kept smiling, "I didn't think the evening would end this way." Once inside he took sleeping Andre from me and put him down in his bed. His place was nice. It wasn't put together like a female lived there but it was nice. Definitely lived in, but not overly done like he was a neat freak or something. I sat on the couch and waited for him. When he walked into the livingroom he hit the dimmer switch and then he turned on the radio to KBLX.

He sat on the love seat across from me. "So".

I shrugged and said, "so".

"What do you want or need to know?" He asked

"Is that how we're gonna do this? Put it all out there?" I asked

"Sounds like a good idea, yes, let's do that."

"Why aren't you and Toya married? After all it is cheaper to keep her."

He made a disgusted face. "Eeewwllll! That girl is crazy."

"But after all that stuff you told me I thought you'd be married before you had a child."

"Well it wasn't planned. At least not on my part. Toya and I were at the end of our rope when Dre happened. I knew it was a mistake the moment it happened. Guess it kind of was a good thing you turned me down on the beach that day. I kept asking myself how much different my life would've been if I would've stayed with you." He said

"I wondered what would've happened if I would've fought for you. It hurt when you broke up with me. And since we're being honest, I guess we both got caught up in cases of looking back."

"Oh right, what happened to old boy?"

"We broke up." I said matter of factly.

He gestured for me to continue. "Yea got that. But why?"
I swallowed hard. "We were at the end of our rope as well. Then I found out I was pregnant and he flipped out on me. He stressed me out until I miscarried."

"How did he handle the miscarriage?"

"He wasn't there. I changed my number moved out of my place."

"Does he know?"

"I sent a letter to his job."

"Whoa!"

"I know, but it was that bad. The way he treated me was horrible. I had nightmares for months afterwards. He acted like... It was my fault we were in that situation. I was gonna have the baby, and just when I warmed up to being a mother it was over."

"I thought about calling you, but I kept remembering how hard you were sticking to ole boy last time we spoke. I didn't want to put myself through that again."

"Yea you were right not to call. I thought about you all the time though." He smiled real big. "I thought you hated me, so I was scared to reach out." I said

"Why would I hate you?"

"You were really mad at me when we were on the beach. So I thought you were done with me."

"I thought you were done with me, and I figured once you found out about Dre you would be really done with me."

"I was trying to give my relationship the space it needed to grow if that's what it was going to do."

"Before I forget, I'm in the process of fighting for full custody of Dre. She doesn't want him, the only time she wants him is when she thinks I do. She didn't show up to the last mediation appointment so I think she's giving up."

"Has she called?"

"No, but she only called before to fight or complain about how she was sick of being in the house. Since I got him and have had him since she brought him to the party she's only called twice to curse me out."

"You left me for her? I'm not gonna lie Andrew that hurt. Yea, I might've been looking back. But I really liked you, and I was happy to be with you. I miss you, and I miss us. But I still feel very scared right now. Like is there anyone else who could come a long? I don't even understand your connection to and with Toya. It kind of makes me feel like I don't know you at all. Oh but while we're sharing. I started going to service with my parents. Going has helped deal with everything a lot better."

"That's how you reconnected with Joy right?"

"Right."

"Anthony was cool." He said

"Yea, he's perfect for her. But, I'm saying you know how we were heading towards that connection before. I don't know if I can put myself out there like that again."

Andrew sat there with his eyes fixed on the ceiling blowing air. I didn't know if that was a good thing or a bad thing. Then he fixed his eyes on me. "So let me get this right. We were together seven months and you wouldn't sleep with me. Had me second-guessing myself. We breakup, and you get back with your ex. Obviously he was good enough to sleep with because for a brief moment you carried his child. But now you're telling me that should we agree to get back together you're not going to sleep with me until we're married?"

Suddenly I felt like this could be the no go for him. I swallowed, "yes".

Then he got up and walked away. I was dumb founded; I sat there motionless. Then he came back in the living room, and sat directly next to me on the couch. "Tracy I love you. I want us to get as close as we can back to where we left off. I'm not gonna lie, I don't want to wait." He put his arm around me and as he laid down he pulled me on top of him. "But if I have to wait, I guess I gotta respect that. I'm just saying please be patient with me cause I've wanted to be with you all this time." Then he kissed me. I melted on top of him, this kiss became passionate rapidly. That fast I was forgetting myself and giving into the longing within. I was going to say "no stop don't" but he was sucking on my neck, which was rendering me in auditable. Then I heard Andre, he started crying and he was looking for his daddy. Andrew exhaled and rested his forehead on mine. "Don't move!" He said then he kissed me on the cheek and popped up. I listened to hear if he sounded irritated, but his tone was kind and concerned. He tried to get Andre to lay back down. But it sound like he had a bad dream and he wasn't going back to bed without sleeping in his dads room. When the sleepy Andre walked into the living room his face lit up when he saw me. He came directly to me with his arms extended. Andrew walked into the living room and as soon as he saw us cuddled up on the couch he sucked his teeth. "Are you gonna stay?" I shook my head no. He looked disappointed. Then Andrew sat next to us on the couch and he put his arm around me as he turned the television on. "This is my woman." He said to Andre, Andre looked at him and then at me. Then he put his head on my shoulder.

Then my cell phone rang. Andrew handed me my purse. I took my phone out, the caller Id said that it was Sean. I silenced the ring and then I put my phone back in my purse. Andrew didn't look happy.

"What?"

"Who's Sean?"

"Seriously?" Did I detect jealousy? This was new.

"Yea, who is he?"

"A friend I made at service."

"A quote unquote friend huh? You like him?"

"As a friend. We don't gel well enough to be anything more."

"Oh and while we're on the subject, what's up with you and Michael?"

"Nothing." Here we go.

"It didn't look like nothing." He said

"I thought I was supposed to be the jealous one." I said

"How you figure?"

"Hello you broke up with me to get with your now crazy baby momma. I know you haven't been single this whole time. Whether you were playing on Toya's emotions or there was someone else in the picture."

He sucked his teeth, "someone else."

"I'm just being realistic here. Do you have any loose ends you need to tie up?" I said

"Ok, so we're definitely going to be together?" I nodded yes, he smiled. "Being honest, there was someone but honestly I don't see it as being a problem. We weren't together together. What about you?"

"I wasn't with anybody."

"Ok so this Sean person isn't gonna be tripping cause you've got a man now?"

"I honestly don't think so, but I couldn't really tell you."

"What about Michael?" He stared at my face hard.

"What about him? We just met the other day at the party."

"Did you give him your number?"

"No"

"Did he give you his?"

I looked at Andrew with nothing but irritation in my face and voice. "Really?"

"I feel like I gotta ask these questions."

"Why because I cheated on you? Or because I left you?"

"I guess it's my guilty conscience." He said

"Why do you even want to be with me?" I asked

A huge smile came across his face. "I asked myself that last night. And I wrote out a list. You wanna see it?"

"Of course!" Andre's eye followed his father and when he hit the corner to go down the hall. Andre scooted off my lap and took off running after his father.

He was thinking about me last night. Wow! I felt so special, and then I remembered that he was always sweet to me like that. He called me just to tell me he was thinking about me all day or something. At first it took me by surprise, cause the only time Steve said anything remotely close to that was when he wanted some, so he'd try to barely butter me up. Oh crap! There I go, hadn't thought about Steve in weeks. I don't want to think about him now. Andrew returned with a huge blushing smile. His mini-me was fast on his heels. Andre climbed back on the couch and into my lap.

Andrew held a legal sized note pad in front of me. He cleared his throat," I didn't number them I just listed them. So here we go, I apologize now if it kind if sounds cheesy.

You're smart, but not arrogant about it

You've always been accepting of me from our first hellos

You always made me feel like a man

You're beautiful

You're very nurturing

I feel like I can talk to you about anything

His list went on and on, I felt special and appreciated.

"Ok but I'm coming off the top of my head so please bare with me. No matter what size I am, you make me feel beautiful and attractive. You're always a man, even when it's difficult. When I talk you listen, but not so you can hold it against me later, but so that you can know me. You never made me feel bad about being myself. Because when you hold me I melt. Because you always wear the same cologne and sometimes I wanna lick it off you. Because regardless of what's going on you don't let it affect how you treat your son. Because every Jill Scott song about love and loving a real man describes you. My list went on and on, until he couldn't take it anymore and he kissed me.

"Now about this whole celibacy thing?" He laughed, "you sure about that?"

"Sweetheart it's not about you. It's about me. I'm sure."

"Forgive me for going here, but I gotta ask. Why was your ex good enough to not only sleep with but carry his child, but for me you need to wait?"

"It's a long story, but I don't like talking about past relationships."

He grabbed my hand, "Tracy! I love you! And unless you've become a new person that I don't know, you're gonna be my wife. Please don't make me guess about this stuff, which will drive both of us, crazy. Anything you want to know about me just ask. I am a open book when it comes to you. Please be the same."

Melting again, I squeezed his hand. "Ok" I took a deep breath. I started sweating; I was about to hand over everything I kept locked inside. I opened my mouth, but there was a knock at the door. We both laughed, and then he looked at the clock.

He sucked his teeth; "there's only one person rude enough to come over this late at night without permission. She must've followed someone else in the gate. I don't feel like dealing with her." He picked up the phone. He dialed security guard service number. "Yes, this is Andrew Wallace in unit 303. There's an uninvited person at my door, please call the police. This will not end well."

Then she started banging on the door and ringing the doorbell like she lost her mind. Andre got nervous and tried to climb in his fathers lap. But Andrew gave him back to me. "Please keep him in here." Then Andrew got up. He started flexing and unflexing his hands. Andre started crying, Andrew rubbed his head and said a very calm, "I'll be right back".

My heart was pounding, as the beating on the door got louder. Andrew snatched the door open. "The police have been called you need to leave."
"Not without my son! I don't know who you think you are, but you can't just take my son!"
"Who is that?"
"I brought reinforcements! Give me my son and I will leave."
"Ma'am you have to leave you're trespassing!" Sounded like the security guard I guess.
"You ain't even the police! You can't make me do nothing!"
"Sir, please back up!"
I heard cursing and tussling. Then I heard glass break, and then I heard Toya scream. "You got me you #+%?|^!" I put my arms around Andre who was crying his eyes out. I wanted to know what was happening, but I knew better than to move. I knew Toya was gonna flip out when she finds out Andrew and I are back together.

Then I heard hurried footsteps. "THIS IS THE EL CERRITO POLICE! PUT THE BOTTLE DOWN NOW!"

There was commotion and of course the sound of Toya screaming. Andrew told the police he wanted to press charges. I never heard him raise his voice like that before. More officers came they took statements from all of us. They put Toya and her companion in patrol cars. Andre and I fell asleep on the couch holding each other. I woke up while the sun was coming up. Andrew was sitting on the couch brewing.

"You've been awake all night?"

"Tracy I don't think this is gonna work. Eventually she's gonna find out about us. She's gonna lose it once she finds out. I can't even think about what I'd do if something happened to you."

"Why does she get to win? Just because she's crazy, she gets to control our lives?"

"Well what am I supposed to do?"

"Monday, you file a restraining order. Contact the mediation court and push for full custody. Have them set up her visits as supervised. With all the stunts she's pulling I don't see why the courts wouldn't side with you. She doesn't win!"

"You think she will go away that easy?"

"Move! Pack up and move. Get a P.O. Box put that address on the paperwork. She doesn't have to know where you live." He was nodding his head, thinking about my words. "She doesn't win this time." I said

"Ok! Cool! Lets go find a place."

CHAPTER 17

The world smells great! I got a handsome man who loves me by my side. A little boy who adores me as if I were his actual mother. Good friends and association, life is good. Once I got my alarm system installed I had my new bedroom set delivered to my home. I've always wanted a HUGE four-post bed, and Yay! I finally have it. I'm not finished in my bedroom but as it stands my room is a complete haven. My state of the art alarm system helps me to feel more secure in that big ole house all by myself. The house is covered in video cameras; a bird can't land on a branch without my cameras capturing it. I've got sensors everywhere, and it's all set up with a backup generator that could run a week if need be. Even with all of that I want a dog or two. Even though this neighborhood is very nice, I watch the news I heard about the home invasion robberies. How long would it take the police to actually get to me? I'd feel a lot safer with my actual security patrol. Besides there's only a matter of time before Toya finds out about us and I wanna be ready. Although ever since the courts granted Andrew full custody and her only supervised visits, she's backed down. A lot of that could have to do with the fact that he moved to Emeryville, which is right by me, and he changed his number. Andrew said she didn't seem to pay him any attention the last few visits which was refreshing.

My custom made dinette set arrived this past Wednesday and this Saturday I'm having my family over to finally meet Andrew. My parents seemed concerned when I told them about Andrew. I didn't tell them about Toya and her drama, but they were concerned with me dating. I keep reassuring them that I'm not compromising my stand, but you know parents they worry. But I saw my mom sigh a little sigh of relief when I told her that I wanted them to meet. My brother and sister in-law were chill as usual, but happy to meet him all the same. And as if it were perfectly timed my sisters were coming into town to visit so they would be there. The twins both got accepted into New York State and after school they decided that they wanted to stay in the big apple. It's been awhile since I've seen them, so I'm so happy they'll b here and get to see my house. I invited Joy, Anthony, Nicole, and Hubby. I'm not gonna lie, I've been avoiding Sonya to an extent. When we went wine tasting her comments about her brother made me nervous. So in an effort to avoid the issue all together, I've been avoiding her. Although that time at the party was the first time I ever met him. I was afraid that anything could happen now that I was on his radar. Things were going so well with Andrew I didn't want anything to ruin it. Instead of slaving in the kitchen all day I decided to have our meal catered. My mom was disappointed when I told her I wasn't making the desserts personally, but she quickly got over it when I told her I ordered from Nelson's Bakery in Oakland. Friday night I set the table. I found a beautiful chocolate colored table cover. Well actually I had to buy two, but it worked perfectly because each one came with six napkins and I needed twelve. I put twelve silver chargers down. Then I put twelve cobalt blue water and wine glasses out. I put two cobalt and one silver vases along the center of the table. I bought a couple of bouquets of calla Lillie's of various colors. I cut them to stand out but not too tall. Then I placed simple white dinner and salad plates on the chargers. I folded the napkins like little teepees in the center of each one. I hired Charles a local chef to cater. He and his crew of two showed up on Saturday to set up and get to cooking. The house smelled wonderful. Andrew and Andre came shortly after. They were coming from visitation. I asked him how things went and he said fine. But I could tell he was thinking about something. Around two thirty Joy & Anthony arrived, as usual the boys were so happy to see each other. The men went in the backyard with the boys while Joy and I sat in the family room chatting.

"So, how are things?"

I couldn't take the smile off my face. "Things are good".

"Your mom is so excited about today. After service Wednesday it was all she could talk about."

My service attendance had started to slack off. I felt guilty about that but nothing could kill my happy vibe right now. "Yea, she's called me like three times already. She'll be here in a little bit."

"Your sisters aren't coming?"

"Yea they're coming, but they're gonna meet here. They went over a few friends' houses today. You know doing their rounds of hello." Then Joy grimaced and shifted in her chair. "Are you ok?"

She blew out irritated air. "That doggone Anthony! I think he got me pregnant!" She said rubbing her stomach.

"Congratulations! How exciting!"

"Thank you, I just didn't want it to happen so soon. I really didn't want to have any more."

"Well you know how that goes." I said

"Yea, what's done is done. Can't change that." She said in the same defeated voice I had when I was talking to nurse Sandra.

Even though I tried to fight it, there I was feeling horrible cause I actually thought about Steve. I doubt he even cared; he was probably relieved more than anything when he received my letter. By now he's probably found his way on top of twenty thousand females and couldn't even remember my name. The doorbell jarred me back to reality. Joy was looking at me like where did you go? I smiled and hurried to the door. It was my mom and dad. My mom was happy and I could tell my dad was prepared not to like him. This was going to be interesting. I showed them into the family room and Andrew and Anthony came inside. I introduced Andrew to my parents. My mom was impressed by the looks of him. But my dad was sizing him up. Always the man Andrew lovingly embraced my mother, gave my father a respectfully strong handshake. My dad liked that but wasn't giving up so easily.

"Let's step outside." My dad said

"Sure." Andrew replied

"Come on Anthony." My dad said. Anthony looked at us and mouthed something that looked like yikes and then he followed. They shut the sliding door behind them so all we could see we're their backs.

My mother gave me a huge hug! "Finally a man!" I smiled; I didn't know what she meant by that.

Thankfully the doorbell rang again and this time it was Nicole & Hubby and my brother & sister. Charles' assistant served us delicious lemonade as we waited for my sisters. Finally Tia & Tara arrived; they were full of bubbly energy. Dinner was ready so we moved into the dining room. The boys sat at the children's table on the side. It was so cute watching them mimic us. Charles and his assistants served us four courses. We started with salad and his special peppercorn dressing. Delicious! Then he served us potato soup. Delicious! Then he served us filet mignon with roasted potatoes. Delicious! Then he served both cakes, I ordered a strawberry and whipped cream cake, and a triple lemon cake. He also served his homemade custard ice cream. Each course was served with a wine that complimented it. The evening was wonderful. I could tell my family really liked Andrew, but I knew they would. He is a man. When I went in the kitchen to settle the bill with Charles he informed me that Andrew paid the bill, and he tipped them rather nicely. I had no idea he was going to do that. I couldn't stop smiling, my baby is the man! When he caught sight of my smile he winked at me. My sisters quizzed Andrew for thirty minutes. They tag teamed him, my baby rolled right with it. He seemed to be enjoying it. But it started to annoy me, so I made them stop. The girls loved the house, and asked if they could spend the night with me since I was gonna go to service in the morning. Of course I agreed, it promised to be fun. The girls grabbed their overnight bags out of their rental car. They explained that they kept overnight bags in the car just in case they decided to spend the night somewhere other than where they were staying. After everyone left I walked Andrew to the door, we talked for a minute. We kissed and then he left. I set the alarm downstairs and then I went up to my room, the girls had already showered and were in their pj's. I didn't realize I had taken so long. The girls made their selves comfortable while I showered and put on my pj's. They were both sitting on my bed. Tia was up against the headboard messing with her phone and Tara was surfing channels. When I walked in the room they both sat up straight and locked their eyes on me. "What's up guys?"

"So momma never told us why you were staying there. But she had that worried about you sound in her voice. Then she tells us about this house and she's happy. When we get here there's a new guy? What happened to Steve?" Tia said

"And there's more but let's get that part out of the way."

Tia blew out hot air and shot Tara a look. Tara shot one back. They were talking without speaking; they've always done that. "Obviously we broke up."

"Yea, but even when you guys weren't together you always guarded yourself like you guys were still together." Tia said

"Don't get us wrong, were happy you moved on. We're just asking what happened?" Tara said

"You guys didn't like Steve?"

"Never did!" They said in unison

"Ok well, I decided to do something about my weight. Shortly after making that decision I met Andrew. We dated for a few months and then we broke up. Then Steve and I got back together. A little over a year later he knocked me up." Tia laughed Tara gasped and covered her mouth. "He flipped out, I miscarried. I shut him out. A few months ago I reconnected with Andrew who now has a child. I'm happy!" They started looking at each other again. They were both trying to force each other to speak. "Guys?"

"Ok!" Tara said in a defeated tone. "We went over Carmella's house in Richmond. Her mom asked us to go to the grocery store to grab a few groceries for lunch. So I'm there minding my own business when this guy walks up to me." My heart sank! "I thought for sure he approached me because he remembered me. But as he kept flirting I realized that wasn't the case. So I stood there with a blank stare. Then he started trying to remember where he knew me from. Then Tara walked up, and he kept going back and forth between us. He looked confused but he said goodbye and walked away. As I'm telling Tara what happened, he came storming back!

Talking about WHERE's YOUR SISTER? WHERE'S YOUR SISTER???" I could now feel the sweat trickle down my back. "So Tara curses him out, and this fool was REALLY MAD! Carmella and her brother came over. Her brother got in his face and was like is there a problem? People were staring and scared, probably thought bullets were about to start flying. He wouldn't take his eyes off us. Then he walked away. When we left the store we didn't know if he was following us or not. So we drove the scenic route all through North Richmond. We hung around Carmella's longer than we wanted to, drove all around Oakland before going the back way to come here."

"Do you really think he was following you?"

"He looked so crazy there was no way to really know."

"Does he know you miscarried?" Tia asked

I felt embarrassed, "I sent him a letter".

They both blank stared at me. "You sent him a letter?" I nodded yes, "that is wrong on so many levels".

"Well calling would've meant talking to him, and I have no intention in speaking to him ever again. All the stuff he said was unacceptable. He was talking to me like I was some female he picked up at a club one night. I can't talk to him. And you guys look exactly like me. How could he not know who you were?"

"I don't know but it seems like you guys have some unfinished business."

"Not on my part. I'm done! I've moved on! I'm happy!"

"Ok!" They said in unison.

"So you're on top of your birth-control this time around?" Tia said

"Andrew and I have never had sex."

"WHAT????" They said in unison again

"Can you guys stop doing that? But, I told him I wanted to wait until I got married. When we were together the first time, I needed time and by the time I was almost ready we broke up."

"Does he know about the miscarriage?"

"Yes"

"He doesn't get jealous about that?"

"The one time we were gonna talk about it we got interrupted." Andrew did ask the question, so he's thought about it. The rest of the night the question bounced around my brain. In the morning I went for my run. I ran to Ashby Ave and then down past the hospital. I realized how distracted I was when I got to Adeline and I hadn't stopped longer than a wait for the traffic light to change. When I got home the girls were still sleep. After my shower I woke them, and we all got ready for service. I set the alarm and then I closed the front door. Andrew was in my driveway in a suit. My heart dropped. The girls said "Awwwww!" In unison.

"You guys need a ride?" He said holding the car door open. I thanked him with a HUGE kiss. I never expected him to come to service with me. But I never invited him either. When we arrived my parents were arriving at the same time. They didn't recognize Andrew's car, and my mom's face totally lit up when she saw us. When my dad saw us, a sense of peace came over his face. We sat towards the back; service was starting as we were walking in. Sean looked like a deer caught in headlights when he saw us. He was sitting on the opposite side of the auditorium from us and he kept staring, he thought he was being slick about it but I kept making eye contact with him. Then Andrew leaned over and said, "Sean?" I nodded yes. After service Sean came straight over to introduce himself to Andrew. I wanted to be involved in their conversation but Sister Harris came over with what she thought was veiled irritation. She said the fakest hello to Andrew; she didn't even give him the opportunity to respond. She had to know I wasn't interested in Cameron. But who knows what he told her. She busied herself with talking to the girls; she kept going on and on about how much they blossomed and how beautiful they were. Sean was inviting Andrew somewhere, I missed where. Then my dad came over and informed us that we were going to breakfast. I introduced Andrew to a few more families; they were all smiles and excitement. Andrew had the biggest smile on his face. Andre

who was slowly coming out of his shell, found his way to little
Anthony. It was cute to watch them mimic grown behavior. They
were talking, but since they were both barely two years old who
knows what they were saying to each other. I took a moment to
look at my man in my place of worship fitting right in and I
couldn't help but smile. Andrew wasn't really a religious person.
So the fact that he was here was all for me. I couldn't stop smiling
at him and at everyone. My dad had us follow him, and when we
got on the freeway headed towards Berkeley, I knew exactly where
we were going. We were going to Champagne Brunch at the
Double Oak Hotel. As if on cue the twins realized where we were
going at the same time as I did and we all started clapping at the
same time. This made Andre get really excited and he clapped
along with us. Andrew smiled flashing his dimples as he drove
along. My parents were very happy as we walked into the hotel.
My father instructed the waiter to bring sparkling cider for Andre
and to keep the champagne coming for the rest of us. I guided
Andre by the hand to the conference room next to the kitchen.
Wall to wall food. I told him that the dessert was last. And then I
showed him each table. The table full of salads green, pasta, fruit.
You name it and there was a representation of it on the table. There
was a omelets station, a carving station (that served roast beef,
turkey, and pork). A waffle station with fresh strawberries and
whipped cream, warm maple syrup Andres eyes got really big. I
showed him the fresh fruit, bacon, sausage, eggs Benedict, salmon,
crab legs, shrimp, and oysters. I know the choices should've
overwhelmed this two year old but he went right back to the
waffles. So we got him a freshly made Belgian Waffle with fresh
strawberries and whipped cream. Scrambled eggs and bacon. Now
I was not expecting him to finish this but he would be occupied for
a while trying. I took him back to the table, as I cut his waffle into
bite-sized pieces my father sat at the table. He didn't say anything
he watched as Andre and I interacted. Andre was telling me a story
he learned in preschool while I constructed his plate in a manner he
could manage. I asked my dad if I could leave Andre with him

while I went to get my plate. He looked at me with the biggest eyes and nodded yes. Almost dying of hunger I went straight to the omelet station. I asked for a kitchen sink omelet, basically everything they had to offer. While the chef manning the station prepared my omelet I grabbed some bacon and fresh fruits on a separate plate. As I waited for my omelet Andrew walked up behind me and kissed me on the back of my neck. I melted a little; the chef gave us a funny look. Andrew had two plates very neatly but separately organized. He waited for me and then we walked back to the table together. I put strawberries and pineapples in my champagne, and I put a couple in Andre's cider glass. His eyes lit up at the sight of it. His cheeks were full of waffles. The conversation at the table was lovely, who could've asked for a better brunch. My parents seemed really happy, my sisters were happy. My brother and sister in law couldn't make it. But we were happy all the same. On our final dessert trip Andrew grabs my hand and pulls me to the side. "It's time, are you ready?" I had a question mark on my face. "Are you ready to meet my momma?"

I got butterflies in my stomach. "Yes" and then I got on my tiptoes to kiss him on the cheek.

"How about after we leave here?"

"That's fine. Are you sure she's home? Do we need to call to tell her were coming?"

"Naw, she's expecting me this afternoon anyways. You will be an added surprise. She's been wanting to meet you for sometime now."

I smiled really big. I wasn't afraid of finally meeting his mother, but I was nervous. I was relieved when my sisters got in the car with us. They didn't know we were going on a trip real quick, we told them in the car. They were fine with it. We hopped on the 580 freeway and made our way to the Fruitvale area of Oakland. Quite a few turns and Tada we were pulling up to a Victorian styled house. It was styled like all the houses in Oakland. That old homie feeling. Andre got excited and took off running up the stairs to the front door. I took that as a sign that she was a good person. Andre seems to only like good people; at least it seems that way so far. Andrew held my hand as we walked to the door. My palms were a little sweaty, but he didn't seem to mind. Andrew knocked on the door while opening it with his key. "Momma? We got company." He called out. The twins were watching me like a hawk with big grins on their faces. I'll take that as another good sign. His mom was in the living room watching TV. She looked a lot younger than I expected her to be. She looked more like his older sister than mother. His mother was very fair skinned, which made me pay attention to the fact that he is a few shades lighter than me. Her hair was long and curly. She had on sweat pants and a t-shirt, with slippers. She smiled when she laid eyes on me.

"Come in, come in." She stood to hug Andrew, and then she said, "Who do we have here?" As she looked at my sisters.

"These are Tracy's sisters." The girls introduced their selves and she hugged them both. I guess he was saving me for last. "This is Tracy!" He said with the proudest grin on his face.

She smiled and hugged me. "It's nice to finally meet you Ms. Wallace". I said not knowing what to call her.

"Oh honey please! Please call me Amber."

"Ok"

"Are you guys hungry?"

"Naw we just came from Champagne brunch with Tracy's parents."

"That sounds nice, come in you guys have a seat." So we did, and then she pinched Andrew's jacket, "Andy, why are you dressed like you're going to work?"

We smiled at the nickname. "We went with them to service this morning. Then we went out to brunch."

"Wow! You're making a religious man out of him too. Impressive!" Amber said. A picture of a younger Andrew caught my eye. Amber followed my eyes to the pictures. "You guys wanna see pictures of Andy growing up?"

"Yes!" I said excitedly

Andrew shook his head, but he didn't protest. Andre grabbed her leg as she walked. "Aw! I'm sorry stank butt. Nana's not trying to ignore you." Then she picked him up, I could tell Andrew got his kindness from her. The decoration of the house was mostly antique, but it had a real sense of warmth.

She came back with three big photo albums, and Andre carried a small one behind her. She put the books on the coffee table and waved us down. We sat on the floor behind the coffee table and she sat in front. She made noise getting down, but she was smiling really big. Then she placed an album facing us and explained page by page who was in the picture. And when they were taken. The baby pictures of Andrew were so cute. Pictures of her with her pregnant belly. Pictures of his grandparents. Andrew was his grandfather's pride and joy. He is the oldest grandchild on account of his mother being so young when she had him. I never really assigned anything to Andrew's light skin or curly hair. His grandfather had blondish hair and hazel eyes, and his grandmother was almost dark brown skinned. His aunt was browner than his mother, and his uncles were both faired skinned just not as light as his mom. Not that it was something to point out, but revealed a lot. There were pictures of his parents, him and his dad. His dad was deep dark chocolate and very handsome. Andrew looked like him but more like his mother. You could tell his dad was too cool for school. Andrew didn't look at the pictures. He sat there watching us interact. There were pictures of his mom and stepfather in the album. His stepfather was chocolate as well, but his smile was a kinder smile, there was real warmth behind it. It wasn't until this moment that I realized he and his brothers had different fathers. He never mentioned it. But he didn't talk about his dad much at all. He said he left and he didn't go into much detail outside of that. Listening to Amber talk about Andrew was delightful. You could tell she really loved him and that he loved her. It was a refreshing change from Steve and his mother. She hated him, and he hated her for hating him. Steve's mom would take little snips at me, I guess because she didn't want him to have anything or anyone. I wouldn't say anything, which appeared to only make her more annoyed. There's no fun in insulting someone if you think they don't get it. Steve wouldn't say anything, I don't know if he cared. Amber was nice, and I liked her. She reminded me of Shirley in a lot of ways. In the teenage years, there were a lot of pictures of Andrew and Toya. If I didn't know who she was I would've thought about how gorgeous she was. But instead of seeing her beauty, I saw that little subtle look of evil in her eyes. Amber told the story of them very nicely as Andre sat in her lap following along with stories and pictures as she pointed them out.

"Where is everybody?" Andrew asked looking around.

"Who knows? They all running around trying to get their last thrills before the weekends over. Your brothers are gonna be mad they missed you guys. Ooh! Can I take a picture so they'll believe me?"

"Sure!" We said

"What do you mean believe you?" Andrew said.

"I wanna show then how pretty Tracy is. But they won't believe me when I tell them she has two sisters just as pretty."

We all blushed. We took quite a few poses for her. Then we had to leave to get the girls back to their car. They still had a few more people to visit before they left in the morning. Amber gave me a big hug goodbye, and she told me to come back. It was such a nice feeling to be liked by your boyfriend's mother. Andre asked to stay with his Nana, so Andrew agreed to come back and get him. We held hands in the car, life was good. Too good, I was so happy that Aunt Flow was visiting me. Otherwise I might've forgotten myself behind how wonderful the day had gone. The girls flew through the house grabbed their things. They gave us huge hugs goodbye, and that fast we were alone. When we finally agreed on a movie I remembered the thought that had been echoing in my mind all day. The conversation we never had. Right as I mustered the courage to open my mouth his cell rang. Not knowing I was going to say anything he answered. I could tell it was Hubby on the other end. His voice was so loud and animated. "That sounds good. Let me check with Tracy and I'll call you back. " Then he directed his voice to me. "So Nicole and Hubby are going to Tahoe, and they wanna know if we wanna go."

"How long, when, and is Sonya going?"

"Friday thru Sunday, two weeks from now, and yes. Do you wanna go?"

"I guess so. If you want to." I swallowed hard, "but before you call Hubby back can we talk?" I sat up on the couch to face him.

"Sure" I could tell he had no idea what I was gonna say so he braced himself.

"Well that night that Toya came we were gonna talk. But we never got a chance to have the talk. You asked me..." I tried to remember his wording.

"Why was your ex good enough to not only sleep with but carry his child, but for me you need to wait?" He said

I grabbed his hand. "Andrew I love you. You have always been special to me. Not sleeping with you is the hardest thing I've ever done. Steve came a long at a low point in my life. And instead of making me feel better sleeping with Steve only made me feel worse. Being with you made me strong. Being with you was confirmation that someone could be with me just for me and not because of anything I was giving them. I didn't jump right back where I left off with him. I did make him wait." Andrew exhaled, "I'm sure you don't wanna hear that. But what we have is beautiful. Please don't ever think that I don't want you. Sometimes I run to the shower and I make it as cold as possible."

"So... You want me?"

"Of course I do! You're an amazing man."

Then he kissed me deep and slow, his hands were roaming all over my body. "Then why do I have to wait? I love you! I'm gonna marry you. Why do we have to wait?"

"Do you want to have anymore babies?" I asked

"Of course!"

"How many?"

"It doesn't matter to me. However many you want to have."
He said

"What if when we do it, you think I'm horrible?" I asked
"What?"

"I know different people like different things. In the end, as long as I was there, I didn't have to be there. I hope we never end up like that." He just looked at me. I could tell he was filtering what I said. He didn't say anything he held my hand. "The night he got me, I was out drinking with my cousin. He picked us up cause neither of us could drive. I didn't even intend on seeing him that night, otherwise I would've at least had my diaphragm just in case. I barely remembered that night until I was trying to figure out how he got me. I always made him strap up. He said he was faithful but I couldn't tell. I didn't want to exert the energy to verify either." Andrew shifted but he didn't say anything. "Baby please say something."

"I hated seeing you with him. I HATED IT!" He opened and closed his fist. "But I also knew it was my fault you were with him. When I saw you at the restaurant that time. You were glowing; I knew I had lost you forever. I was trying to fight for you at the wedding, but you weren't having it. It hurt, but you were right it shouldn't have been that easy. Then a month later Toya's blowing me up. Talking about she was pregnant and we were gonna be a family. I have never felt so trapped in my life. I wanted my son just not with her."

"Can I ask you why she never even gave me the chance to be cordial?"

"I guess its cause of the way she got me. I was always her lovesick puppy. She'd break up with me and no matter what or who she could always pull me back. When I was with you, it wasn't that easy for her. She had to really dig deep just to converse with me. She came back for the money and the challenge. But I wasn't the same. I didn't take her crap like before, and I didn't bend easily either. She blamed you, when really she should've looked at herself. I should've never left you."

"We'll you're here now."

"But now you won't put out." I could hear the smile in his voice.

"Baby, I'm scared." I said

"I know, but are you hiding behind your religion? Or are you really into it?"

"Good question." I was silent for a long time.

CHAPTER 18

After a week into the idea we changed the itinerary and decided to go to Vegas. Amber agreed to keep Andre that weekend. So as a special thank you Andrew bought tickets for the carton ice show. He booked a whole touristy weekend for them through a travel agent right there in the bay. Andre was excited to spend the whole weekend with grandma. He hugged and kissed us goodbye and then proceeded to forget all about us. Andrew's brother Derrick was at the house when we got there. He was a little shorter than Andrew and a lot browner, but had those same dimples and curly hair. They favored but remembering the pictures I could see that he looked a lot like his dad. Andre did a nosedive on his uncle. Derrick pretended that Andre's strength was too much for him as he fell over. We chatted with Amber for a few minutes and then we were off. I was so excited about our trip. Steve never took me anywhere, but he never really had any money either. I normally footed the bill whenever we went somewhere more expensive than the Pancake House. The whole idea of going away with my man on a romantic weekend has always been a private wish. Andrew held my hand in the car while he sang along with the radio; that was pumping out hit after hit. Now my baby can't sing, but so what, neither can I. But let us tell it, we were Marvin & Tammie, "you're all I need! To get by!" To look at us in the parking lot we seemed like little love struck puppies. Just because the music was gone didn't mean our concert ended. The few people in the parking lot looked at us. Some smiled, others frowned, the rest acted as if we didn't exist. Not that we cared. We checked in the day before so we got in line to go through the FSA check. We were definitely giddy and full of smiles. The security check person who reviewed our ID against our boarding pass checked mine, but he kept looking at Andrew like he was trying to remember him. He gave Andrew back his stuff and we moved forward. After we passed security check Andrew needed to stop at the restroom so I held his bag while he went inside. I was texting Nicole to tell her we were at the airport. Then someone came out of the men's bathroom and stopped dead in their tracks.

"Tracy?"

I looked up and it was Cameron, "oh hey". I said unenthusiastically.

As he started to walk towards me I wanted to run in the other direction. The closer he came the more I leaned back. Then he opened his arms like he was expecting a hug. I tried to side step his hug, but I didn't clear my suitcase. And yea, I'm falling! Trying to fight this fall just made it worse and somehow I ended up tangled in our bags. Ugh! How embarrassing, and normally I would laugh, but today I got mad cause he made me fall.

"Dang girl! You ok?" He said as he put his hands out to help me up.

"Whoops!" I said irritated

I let him help me up but I didn't want him to touch me. And once I was standing he still went in for the hug. I stood there while he hugged me. AND OF COURSE Andrew walks out the bathroom while this guy has his arms around me. If looks could kill. Cameron was so busy focusing on me he didn't see Andrew.

"So how you been?"

"Fine!" I said focusing on Andrew.

"Hey how you doing? I'm Andrew." He held out his hand for a shake.

Cameron's eyes turned evil, "oh hey man, what's up?" He was trying his best to size Andrew up.

Andrew didn't pay him any attention, "you ready?" He said to me

"Yes!" I said handing him his bag and walking away.

"Aw! Like that?" Cameron said throwing his hands up.

I grabbed Andrew's hand and started walking.

"Aaaa! Tracy! How's Sean?" He yelled after me. I really didn't like him. I didn't react I kept walking. Then he mumbled something and Andrew stopped dead in his tracks. He dropped his bag and turned on his heels. I didn't know what he said but it wasn't gonna be worth any of this. Cameron's eyes looked scared, but satisfied that he provoked a reaction from Andrew. In that moment Andrew seemed taller, heavier, wider, kind of like a charging bull. Stupid Cameron looked like a cowering little child trying to seem grown. I ran around Andrew and I tried to stop him. His eyes were focused on Cameron and he didn't even see me. I put my hands on his shoulders and I pushed to stop him. He looked at me, "Andrew baby!" I said pleading, "he isn't worth a second look. Lets go to our gate." I pleaded. Andrew exhaled and that fast his eyes softened when he looked at me. Security started coming in our direction. I guess Oakland airport wasn't taking any chances.

"Is everything ok over here?"

"Yes, we're fine." I said

Cameron chuckled and kind of flexed especially after he knew he was safe. Andrew's eye turned evil again when he looked at Cameron. I rubbed his chin gently and I smiled. "Baby, lets go." As Andrew came with me I grabbed our bags. I kissed him once we got to the end of the hallway. He accepted my kiss but he wasn't happy about it. It felt like he was upset with me. He didn't say anything more than he had to me the rest of our time in the airport. I wondered if this was going to be our breaking point. I didn't understand why he was acting like he was upset with me. I didn't hug Cameron or encourage his behavior. On the plane ride I cataloged what happened and I didn't get it. I didn't get why he was shutting me out. When we got off the plane he kind of walked ahead with his hands in his pocket, not saying anything. Part of me wanted to scream at him right there in the middle of the airport. The other part was hurt that he would ever act like this with me and I didn't do anything wrong. I didn't say anything I just walked behind him. At about the two hundredth step, I got a little fed up. So I dropped inside the Smoothie Stand to order a smoothie. I ordered my Pineapple Peach. As I waited for my smoothie to blend I could smell his cologne behind me. He didn't say anything he just stood there. When I got my smoothie he turned around and kept walking. Ugh! That pissed me off. I texted Nicole to tell her we were on our way. She responded with a smiley face. I wish my smiley face was genuine. In the cab we said nothing, I kept my body as close to the door as possible, I turned my back to him and I looked out the window. I really wish I knew what the speed limit is on the strip. Every time I come out here, I swear people made it up as they drove. We flew down the street. The hotel couldn't even impress me when we pulled up, I just wanted out. Andrew got out the opposite door. He paid the driver and I walked into the lobby and sat in the lounge area. I didn't want to be with him acting like this. And it was clear he didn't want to be with me. Nicole found me in the chair.

I tried to put on a happy face but I knew I failed when Nicole's smile dropped and she immediately asked me what was wrong. She sat next to me, and I quickly told her the story. She couldn't tell me what I did wrong either. Hubby came down and he started to say hey to Andrew but they were quickly in a guy huddle. Nicole told Hubby that we were going up to their room.

"Girl, don't trip Hubby be acting that way sometimes too. I think it's in the guy handbook or something." That didn't make me feel any better. "Let's get ready to go out to dinner. If he don't get it together by then, you'll sleep here and Hubby can camp out in his room."

"Girl! Naw! Hubby's not about to be mad at me!"

"He's not gonna be mad at you. He's gonna be mad at Drew. He's probably telling him to fix this right now, cause he knows how I am. He will blame Drew for keeping him away from me." She hugged me, "go get cleaned up in the bathroom so that when he comes he won't walk in on you changing." I said a defeated ok. Right after I walked into the bathroom I heard Hubby come in. I heard Nicole talking, and then I heard Hubby blowing irritated air. I turned on the shower so they wouldn't feel like I was listening. I tried to hear what they were saying, but I knew Hubby wasn't happy. Then I heard the door close. Nicole came in the bathroom while I was in the shower. She told me Hubby was pissed but at Andrew just like she said he would be. She made him take his bag to our room. He was not happy. She kept reassuring me that it was ok, and not to worry. I let the water hit me in the face to cover my runaway tears. I told myself to suck it up, I wasn't gonna give him the satisfaction of seeing me upset. I packed more dresses than I needed; with this turn of events I was so happy to have options. I pulled out my purple short party dress. It wasn't fancy but perfect for tonight. It had a deep plunging V-neck, and it crisscrossed in the back and the back was open. This dress showed off everything, but it was in good taste. Legs? Check! Breast? Check! Badunkadonk? Check! Glowing skin? Check! Simple but gorgeous makeup? Check! Lip-gloss? Check! Check! Check!

"I got the perfect song to pump you up before we go out there." She put her iPod on the in room stereo. Yes! We sang along "sometimes you gotta go in the back of the closet pull out that freak em dress." She called Hubby and told him to go down and grab us a cab. When we emerged Andrew and Hubby were talking to the driver. Andrew's mouth dropped but he quickly closed it when he saw me. I didn't smile at him like I normally would. Nicole and Hubby kissed, Hubby was all in her ear, and she was giddy from the attention. I sat next to them in the back and Andrew sat in the front with the driver. He was extremely conversational with the driver. Nicole and Hubby left each other's attention when they realized he was talking to the driver. They exchanged looks and then Hubby reached forward and tried to smack Andrew in the head, Andrew moved just in time. When we got to the restaurant Andrew hopped out the car first, and then he opened the door on my side. He held my hand to help me out the car, and then he did the same for Nicole. When Hubby got out the car he looked mildly pissed off. Nicole and I walked inside, and the men walked in the other direction. Nicole gave the host her name and then we sat down. The host kept looking in our direction. He was looking so hard he didn't hear the server asking him a question. Nicole and I laughed a little.

"Girl, he is acting ugly. Why the attitude flip?"

"I don't know, and see with him it's always something like this that gets in the way." Nicole nodded her head in agreement, but I knew she didn't know what I meant. "He's been so patient with me. So kind and gentle. I was thinking this weekend could've been the weekend."

She looked at me, "the weekend?"

I swallowed, "we haven't slept together yet."

"WHAT????" She said so loud almost everyone stopped to look at us.

I put my hand on my face from pure embarrassment. "DUDE! I'm not long distance. Ssshhhh!"

"How in the world do you have that much control?"

"Well it hasn't been easy, but like I said he's been good to me. Until tonight.... I can't go out like this. You can't reward bad behavior."

"Nope you're right."

"If I gave in it would ruin everything."

The host was still staring, I wondered if he could read lips, because the way his eyes bounced back and forth between our lips you would swear he could. Then Hubby and Andrew walked in they were both smiling. Hubby sat next to Nicole, while Andrew stood staring at me. His eyes were soft again and he was almost smiling. I rolled my eyes and turned my body towards Nicole. The host's eyes bounced between all of us. Then he called us to take us to our table. Nicole and I walked a couple steps past him to give him space to lead the way. Then when the men approached he said, "I need to shake ya'll hands in hopes that some of what you guys got will rub off on me. You guys are my heroes!" He said as he shook their hands. They all laughed but I didn't, I was too disappointed. Andrew noticed that I didn't laugh and his smile faded. When we sat in our booth I scooted all the way to the wall. There was a library of space between us. Nicole and Hubby were all cuddly, Hubby shot Andrew a look.

Andrew turned his attention to me, "why are you sitting all the way over there?"

I looked around to see who he was talking to. "Are you talking to me?" He sucked his teeth. "It's warmer over here. You're freezing me out." I tried not to have too much of an attitude, I didn't want to spoil the night for Nicole and Hubby. He kept trying to talk to me but I would look at him and roll my eyes or just ignore him altogether. Hubby laughed, and Nicole rolled right with me. Then we went to a lounge for drinks and a nightcap. We all started drinking right away. The men went to the bathroom, but I'm sure Hubby was trying coach him on how to get out of the doghouse. We said they were forming a plan of attack. Nicole took my hand and we went out on the dance floor. We were in our own world having a good time when Hubby came out and started dancing with both of us. I knew he really wanted to dance with his wife so I bowed out gracefully. Andrew was at our table, but I didn't wanna sit with him so I went up to the bar to get another apple martini. Then this all WRONG brotha approached. Andrew was cracking up as he watched me wiggle out of dancing with this persistent guy. But then a smooth brunette version of Steve approached me. He started talking to me. If I was single he definitely would've got my number. We chatted for a little bit. We danced to an up tempo melody and he had a nice smooth rhythm. Andrew watched us like a hawk. He didn't look mad, but he was watching. His name was Kevin, he was from Florida. He was out here on business. I told him I was there with my boyfriend, and he was sweet enough to dance with me and chat it up real big. When Kevin walked away Andrew came over. He held out his hand and I took it. We danced the next couple of songs. I couldn't deny that he could dance. But, still I tried not to pay him attention. Then a slow song came on, he didn't wait for me to turn and walk away, he grabbed me and pulled me in close as if he could read my mind. I didn't fight him but my body was stiff and cold. I didn't melt like I normally would. Andrew stared into my eyes patiently waiting for me to return his gaze. I refused; I looked everywhere but at him. When the song was over he lifted my chin and when I looked at him he said, "I apologize". I released some of my tension but his apology wasn't good enough I needed to know why he did this. Why did he shut me out? What happened? In the bathroom I told Nicole that he apologized and that I would sleep in our room. She was happy; she said she and Hubby really needed to celebrate the night. Eeewwllll! Everyone was back to normal in the cab ride back to the hotel. Andrew followed us to Nicole's room so I could get my bag. Then Andrew, Hubby, and I went to our room so Hubby could get his bag. We were one floor higher, and on the opposite side of the hotel. The first thing I noticed was the huge King sized bed in the middle of the room. We had a view to the water show which was going when I looked out the window. Hubby was in and out before I realized he was gone. Andrew came behind me and put his arms around me. He gently kissed me on the back of my neck. I didn't reject his embrace but I didn't melt.

"What was this?"

Andrew huffed, "what?"

"This tonight? You shut me out, and I don't even know why."

"That dude pissed me off!"

"But why does that translate to treating me badly?"

"It didn't."

"Then why were you treating me like that? I expect more from you."

"What do you mean?"

"You communicate unlike any man I've ever known. I appreciate and value that from you. I expect you to talk to me no matter what."

He walked away from me. "I don't turn off and on like that, when I'm that pissed I gotta walk away."

"Even from me?"

"Yes, I needed a minute to calm down. You wanted to keep talking to me."

"Well how long should that minute last? I didn't say anything to you on the plane, and at the airport..." Tears started welling up in my eyes and I hated them for betraying me. I didn't mind showing anger but I didn't want him to know how much he hurt me. But it didn't matter cause here they were. "At the airport you acted like you were mad at me. You can't treat me like that."

"I was wrong. I didn't mean to spoil your night or the weekend." He came back and hugged me tighter.

All I could think was good thing I packed more than one nighty. I didn't feel beautiful anymore. I didn't feel sexy, maybe a little loved. But nothing like I thought I would. I was very disappointed and ready for the weekend to be over even though we just got there. I took another shower and I put on my nightgown. It had a picture of Betty Boop on the front and it said, I'm such a flirt. He was sitting on the bed watching TV when I came out. He looked at my nightgown, but he didn't say anything. I put my scarf on and climbed under the covers. I know I was still sulking but I couldn't help it. I got on the right side of the bed. I faced the TV and waited to fall asleep. When he came out the bathroom he stood in front of the mirror naked flexing. I could tell he put some lotion or oil on cause his skin was shining so beautifully. I pretended not to look although I couldn't help but look. His body was beautiful but not overly done like some bubbled up body builder. His entire body was beautifully toned. He knew how I loved his naked chest, but I wasn't falling for it... I think.

I brought my diaphragm and condoms but after the way the evening had gone I didn't even bother. I had never really seen his "package" before; when he turned around I tried not to act like I noticed his size. Goodness! Now I was scared. No wonder Toya didn't want anyone else to have him. Although he told me he was never faithful to her. They had been together since middle school off an on, even in College he said it was the most open relationship sometimes he wondered why he bothered to call it one. I laid there backing out of every idea I had. He wasn't elephant sized, but larger than anything I had experienced and I wasn't feeling too adventurous. He seemed to glide under the covers and immediately he was on my side of the bed with his arms around me. When I didn't protest his embrace he put his chest on my back. I was ok with that, then he kissed my neck and I jumped. "What?"

"Andrew I'm tired," I turned my face and kissed his cheek. "Goodnight sweetheart". My heart was pounding, I hoped that he would let it go but my fear was that he would be like every other guy I know, and not take no for an answer. He put his forehead on my cheek; his breath was heavy and disappointed. He relaxed and he was no longer poking me in the back. I was still nervous and sweating up a storm. I was surprisingly really scared. I could tell when he fell asleep his body completely relaxed and his breathing became heavy, he didn't snore, but I could tell he was sleep. My mind was racing a mile a minute. He was calmer now, but how would he be in the morning? After I completely freaked myself out I fell asleep lightly. Every time he moved I woke up almost in a panic. At four am I couldn't hold on any longer and I fell asleep deeply. When I realized the daylight was shining on me I opened my eyes and Andrew was laying facing me staring at me. I put the sheet over my mouth, "morning".

He smiled and mimicked me, "good morning" we both laughed. "Not that I wanna bring yesterday up, but can I ask you something?" He said

"Of course"

"What do you think he meant by mentioning Sean?"

"I guess maybe he thought I was talking to Sean at some point. But I told you all about that."

"I had a thought this morning." He smiled

"Un huh?"

"We're in Vegas, what if we got married today or tonight?" My heart stopped! "Are you serious?"

"Yes, I love you! I love you like I've never loved any other woman in my life. I want to be with you forever."

I started to cry but as my mouth opened to say yes, I thought of my family. How disappointed my father would be. My special day reduced to a few minutes in a random location. No matter how I tried to spin it in my mind I couldn't get around how disappointed not only my family would be, I would be. Besides, yesterday showed me that there was more I needed to know about him before

I dove right in. "Andrew, I love you. I want to be your wife, but not with a quickie marriage. My dad has always looked forward to walking me down the aisle; I can't rob him of that experience. Plus I've always dreamed of my wedding. I want that memory." I close mouth kissed him. "Oh and I want a real proposal, you know the ring, the emotions." I said

He looked like he knew all that already. "But, do you love me?"

"Are you kidding? I love you so much it hurts!"

"If you really loved me you'd kiss me even with morning breath." I gave him a peck on the cheek. He cracked up laughing, "what was that?"

"A kiss" I smiled.

Then he kissed me for real. CHEATER! He had already brushed his teeth. "You taste good in the morning." Then he kissed me again. "Can I taste all of you?"

"All of me?" I was nervous

"Yes, all of you." He said he kissed me deep and long. That kiss went on forever. Then he kissed my neck, he sucked my spot like there was a sign that said kiss her neck here and she will be weak. He moved to my chest and then to my peaks. His mouth felt wonderful. Then he moved down, I thought I was going to hit a operatic note. My eyes crossed, I saw spots before my eyes, color explosions. I even thought I was gonna pass out. When I was exhausted he came up for air. He laid on top of me. I could feel him on my thigh. I was done, and he hadn't even begun. "I brought condoms", I still didn't exactly want to go there but I didn't want to be selfish.

He looked surprised, he kissed me. "Naw I'm good." I was shocked and surprised I stared at him. "Listen I'm really sorry about yesterday." Then he thought about it, "you brought condoms?"

I laughed nervously. "Yes, things were going so well between us, I thought making love would've been a lovely highlight of the weekend. But then you go and act a fool. Made me rethink everything. And then..." I opened my eyes wide. "I really changed my mind when I saw you in the mirror. You're pretty hung sir, and I'm not gonna lie. That was scary."

He laughed so hard he relaxed a little from holding himself up, and now as his body moved from the laughter he was tickling me. "You scared now?"

"Your feet aren't even that big, how you gonna sneak that past the radar?"

His laughter was teasing me now. I acted like I was readjusting, but I opened my legs wider in the process. "My feet aren't little."

"No, but they definitely don't match the package. You should have boats."

He laughed again, and I thought I would die. "It's raining!"

I looked out the window and the sky was blue. I had a question mark on my face and then he slowly rolled his hips. Oooooohhhhhh! I see. I had completely giving in and I was ready, when he got up. I opened my eyes in disbelief. He stood up, he was at complete attention. My eyes got big and I couldn't help but stare at it. "Let's go have breakfast."

"RIGHT NOW?"

"You're gonna end up in trouble if you stay in that bed."

I debated whether to stay there and make him keep his word. Then I thought about how romantic it was that he got out of bed for me. His mind was telling him no, but his body was telling him yes. But alas I decided to be a good girl and I pulled the covers back over myself. He smiled and went into the bathroom. I heard him turn on the water. My body was still rocking from this morning's delight. I took off my gown and I looked at my body in the mirror. Now it seemed so long ago that I had all the love handles and rolls. I still had some stretch marks on my hips from my former self but fortunately they were pretty light after concentrating especially there with my cocoa butter mixture. Then I decided that I needed a shower too. I walked in the bathroom and snatch back the shower curtain. He jumped and then his eyes went all over my body as I stood there like a goddess. He had a question mark on his face as I stepped into the shower. He slowly shook his head no; he was paralyzed by my tractor beam of hauteness! He moved back to the back of the shower but he didn't say a word. His breathing was heavy now as I approached him and made him bend down to kiss me. Then I kissed his neck and he pounded on the wall as if to say he was now loosing his power. Still not ready to champion his gift, I decided to bless him with a gift like he gave me. At one point his knees buckled and he slid down the wall into the tub. I followed his and kept kissing without skipping a beat. I loved all the sounds coming from him, ones I'd never heard. Then that deep throat cry out, creamy lava on my neck and chin. The shower water was beating on my back and head. He grabbed me by the hair and kissed me so deep. Yep, now I felt good about myself. He laid on the bathtub floor. While I washed up. As I exited the shower I looked at him and he looked drunk still sitting there. I lotioned up and put on a sundress. Then I pulled my wet hair off my face, I towel dried it a little. Then Nicole called me. She said she and Hubby had a long night and a even longer morning, and now they were starving. She told me that Sonya and Philip arrived early this morning and that they would join us up at the brunch buffet. Then Andrew appeared in the bathroom doorway. He had a towel tied around his waist and he had a drunken smile on his face. I smiled at him but I kept talking to Nicole. He pretended to stumble around as if he was drunk. Nicole told me to hurry up as they were all waiting.

"Baby, you gotta hurry up they're all waiting for us." I said

"I think you sucked all of the life out me, pun intended."

I hit him with the pillow. It was nice to be back to normal. As he got dressed and sang some song I never heard of the thought crossed my mind. What if he turns out to be exactly like the guy I flew with and the rest of this is just a act? The thought of it scared me and sent a chill down my spine. Only time would tell.

CHAPTER 19

It was like old times with Sonya, she didn't mention her brother once. And as if Andrew couldn't seem more sprung, after that morning he was all over me and so in love. I thought that night he would press the issue or ask again. But he came to bed in his boxers and he was happy just to hold me, which is how we normally slept together. Sunday night my intentions were to go all the way. But trying to hang with the big guys I drank too much. I was drunk, but not so drunk that I wasn't aware of what was going on. During the limo ride everyone realized I was gone. Andrew kept laughing at me. I was so intrigued with the silliest things, eyelashes, nostrils, water, and the plastic in the signs. Apparently I was a hoot cause everyone was cracking up behind the things I said and did. When we got to our room, I confessed how much I loved Andrew, how scary that was to me. I asked him if he was gonna curse me out when I confirmed that he got me pregnant. He looked at me, with sadness in his face. I asked him if he was really done with Toya, cause I was afraid he might still go back to her. Then I asked him if he was going to cheat on me again. I told him I didn't want to count on him being in my life if he was just going to leave me. He tried to quiet me so I would sleep. But I popped up. I stripped down to nothing. I told him I want to give him some so he'd never leave me again. I was worried that he had better and wouldn't be impressed with me. Then I promised a million blowjobs as long as he never shut me out and treated me like he did Friday night. I started crying telling him how much that hurt me. He got my gown out and I told him to get a condom, and then I had the idea. I told him he could get me pregnant that night. I told him maybe having his baby would take the nightmares away. When he asked what nightmares. I started kissing on him. I kept trying to make him sleep with me. He kept trying to stop me. When he couldn't help but salute me I told him a snake hopped in his pants. I kept trying to undress him. We were tussling, and movement sent me to the bathroom hugging the commode. He kept cool towels on my head and the back of my neck. He kept giving me water. Which would make me feel better as I started to sober up I got quieter and quieter. He put me in the bed. My head was killing me. He kept rubbing my back, and telling me to rest. In the morning he had Aspirin and tons of water. He ordered room service, and then he called down to the front desk and told them we'd need the room an additional day. He called the airline and changed our flights for Tuesday. I laid there listening and slowly remembering everything I said the night before. He didn't look mad, and before I wouldn't have thought he would be, but now I was questioning everything I knew about him. Although the Aspirin heavily sedated me I laid down only getting up to pee. Andrew kept looking at me, but he wasn't saying anything. At about two o'clock we both were exhausted and passed out. I woke up about six pm. Andrew was sprawled out on the other side of the bed. I went to the bathroom. Then I sat on the bed watching him sleep. He was even handsome in his sleep with drool oozing out the side of his mouth. Suddenly his eyes popped open. That scared me and I jumped.

"How you feeling?"

"I'm good. Thank you for taking care of me."

He sucked his teeth then he sat up. He scooted next to me, I turned on the TV. He took the remote from me and turned it off. I didn't know what he was gonna say.

"What happened last night?"

"I had one too many drinks." I said with a big smile.

He smiled flashing his dimples. "Yea, but why?"

"I don't know." I said smiling and shrugging like a child.

"Baby please talk to me." The request made me feel so small. I thought I communicated so well. But right here in this moment when he asked me to have a real conversation, I realized I wasn't equipped. I grabbed his hand and I squeezed it. I started feeling like I couldn't breathe. "Why?" he asked.

I put my eyes on the bed. "I don't want you to break up with me again. I thought you invited me here for sex." I shifted a little.

"Why would you think I would leave after all of this?"

126

"Didn't we have all this before? I was blindsided before. I didn't get with Steve right away if that's what you think. I wallowed in my hurt feelings. I kind of hoped you would come right back. But you didn't. How do I know you won't do it again? I don't know if I could survive it."

"Ok, but why does sleeping with me drive you to drinking?"

"I'm not really ready for sex. I still have nightmares about Steve."

"Let me say for the record," his voice was deep and very serious. "Tracy I love you! I'm gonna marry you! I don't want anyone but you! I'm not going anywhere! One of us will have to die in order to get out of this."

"What happened Friday?" I asked

"I come out the bathroom, this fools got his arms around you. I was ready to lose it right then. When I come over I see he wasn't nobody. He was testing me. I... I had a hard time growing up. Fools thinking I was soft cause they called me light skin. I've done something's I'm not proud of. Just for future reference if I'm in that space let me have it. I'll calm down but don't try to calm me." Then he looked at me in the mirror. "Funny how we always want the fine ones, but we can't handle when someone notices our treasure."

"I'm no treasure, I'm just the girl you taught to run."

"You're my treasure. There's no way I can convince you of that either. You just have to trust me when I tell you."

"Andrew you know that sounds good, but I just don't know. We've both got a lot of baggage. Neither one of us even knows how to express what we feel while we're feeling it. You have been good to me, but I guess I'm scared because I don't know what I did to deserve what happened the first time. What signs I need to look for. I'm scared!"

"I apologize for hurting you." Then he pulled me on top of him so that I straddled him but we had eye contact. "I'm a sorry man for hurting you like that. I could feel that I was making a mistake. I knew it as soon as I was back with her. I messed up; I wish I could erase the past. But I mean it, as long as we're breathing you will be with me!"

"Ok, but what if I decide I don't want to be with you anymore?" I smiled

"What did I do last time you rejected me?"

"You knocked up Toya."

"Ooh! A little bitter? Well you rejected...." He paused for a minute as if he was checking himself before he said something he couldn't take back. "No I'm not gonna go there. Kiss me."

"No"

"Give me my tongue."

I was teasing him. "No it's my tongue."

He reached up and grabbed my hair. His breathing was heavy, and his face was serious. He pulled my face to him but I arched my back. He let go of my hair and then he grabbed my hips and pulled me forward. His eyes were full of desire. "Can I kiss you?" He sounded like he was about to explode.

As soon as he asked my body filled with desire remembering what happened last time. But I hadn't showered all day. "I'm not clean, let me go get in the shower." I tried to get up but he tightened his grip. I gave him a look like "get real". I loosened his hands and I stood up. I could see his inner struggle to remain seated. I grabbed my bottle of water and began to drink as I walked to the shower. In the shower the cool water felt good on my skin. My stomach did flips trying to absorb the liquid. As I stood there I started to think about it. I felt like I was in high school, how long would this new aspect run before it became really old and tiresome? It's not like he's a teenager. Not that I would marry him today, but I would accept his proposal. Suddenly my mouth started watering, and before I could react, I was up chucking all over the shower floor. My body was convulsing so hard that I dropped to my knees. The undigested eggs, bacon, and toast that I barely ate earlier were now on the floor of the shower, on my hands, knees, and legs. Andrew came running in, I was embarrassed and feeling weak. He helped me up, he washed me. He put a towel around me, and helped me to the bed. He went back to the bathroom to rinse out the shower, and soak up the water that was now on the floor from having the shower curtain open. He gave me some ginger ale, and then he got in the shower. I'm assuming it was a cold shower from the lack of steam coming from the bathroom. When I put the ginger ale on the nightstand I noticed that he had two condoms on the night stand. I was stunned; I don't know why I reacted that way. But I thought he said he was gonna wait for me. Disappointed and confused I laid back down. Hoping the ginger ale would stay down. He turned the TV back on and then he spooned me. He kissed my cheek and then he proceeded to watch TV. My mind was racing a mile a minute trying to understand what the purpose of the condoms were. I closed my eyes cause the effort to understand was hurting my head. Then he looked at my face, I guess he assumed I was sleep. Then he got up quickly and he put the condoms in his bag. That's when I realized that they weren't my condoms; they were a different brand than the ones I brought. My heart sank, as I laid there trying to understand. Did he mean anything he said, or was it all just game?

CHAPTER 20

Things have been strained between Andrew and I. Suddenly work has become really demanding on both our parts. In the past two weeks I've had to work from home in the evenings because my projects have been pretty demanding. Since Andrew has been working equally if not harder, I've picked Andre up from preschool and fed him dinner. I felt so grown up, but I couldn't help but think this is what my life would be like if I wouldn't have lost my baby. I found myself wondering if that baby was a boy or a girl. I gave Andrew a key to the house and a key fab for the alarm. I normally left his dinner in the microwave. By the time he normally came home, Andre was knocked out in my bed and I was working away in my office slash lounge area in my room. Since I was still working and Andrew would be ridiculously tired, he'd climb in the bed with Andre and I'd keep working. When we left Vegas I said I didn't feel well, but I didn't feel much like talking. I know I shouldn't have but I felt betrayed in a way. I had so many assumptions running through my mind. The sad part is that I didn't even want to discuss it with him. Suddenly I started to feel like the things he said were too perfect. I needed to watch him; my daddy said love is more than what you say its what you do. I didn't trust him. That condom thing was just a contradiction of everything he was telling me that weekend. Amongst the chaos a few times Andrew asked me if I was ok. I would nod and say yes. On the first weekend after Vegas, Andre had a visit with his mom. They came by afterwards, but I was so involved in "work" that I couldn't really pay them much attention. Around seven'ish Andrew had a weird look on his face. He asked me if everything was ok. I gave a very plastic smile and nodded yes. Of course he didn't buy it, but I didn't give him a chance to inquire more. Sunday night, we were watching TV. Andre and I were coloring in his coloring book. Then my cellphone rings, it was on the lamp stand closest to Andrew. He looked at it and then at me.

"Who is it?" I asked

"Sean" I couldn't read his face

"Answer it" I had no idea why he was calling me.

"Hello" his voice was deep and manly. "What's up man."? His tone was calm but inquisitive. "When is it?" He locked his eyes on me. "I'll have to make sure we don't have anything else planned but it sounds good to me." He laughed a little, "Alright, I'll let you know". When he hung up he sat forward on the couch. "So your boy wants us to come over next weekend." His eyes were real serious. "Do you want to go?"

"I don't know, do you?" I felt like he was looking for something. If I said no, it would look like I was hiding something. And if I said yes there was a possibility that we could have another incident like the airport. But Sean calling my phone didn't look good.

"It's up to you."

"Then lets go. " I said then I went back to coloring.

Andrew sat there looking at me for a few minutes then he leaned back on the couch. He called Sean back and told him we were in. Sean told him it was a cocktail party. I told Andrew I would be the designated driver. I had no desire to drink any time soon. This party was just another something to throw in the divide between us. Andrew kept looking at me. So fast-forward to today. I put my hair up in a up do, with long earrings. I put on the simplest makeup, eyeliner, mascara, and lip-gloss. I put on a black cocktail length dress. It was very cute; it had a empire waist and soft fabric. I put on a simple low black heel. I looked nice, but I was shooting for a look that wasn't over done. I had a feeling that Andrew would see it that way if I shot for really nice. When Andre and Andrew arrived they looked nice, they both had leather jackets on.

"You look nice" Andrew said taking everything in.

"Thank you," I said then I kissed him on the cheek.

In the car I reached down and grabbed his hand. "You look nice".

He smiled and flashed his dimples. He relaxed some as the navigation system in his car directed us to Sean's house. We pulled up at the same time as Joy and Anthony. Lil Anthony was so excited to see Andre. It had been a few weeks since he had seen them. I felt a little guilty about that but I shrugged it off. Joy looked fabulous, she was glowing.

"Anthony, your girl looks great." Andrew said

"Thanks man, pregnancy agrees with her."

Joy sucked her teeth and rolled her eyes at him. "Joy you do look really good."

"I didn't know you were preggers. Congratulations!" Andrew said

Anthony belly laughed. Joy rolled her eyes. "Thank you, you guys. I don't know why he's even talking to me."

"You're still not talking to me?"

Her neck started wiggling. "No I am not!"

Anthony smiled and made a kissy face. Joy rolled her eyes and walked ahead. Andrew grabbed my hand and we walked behind Joy and Anthony. Sean answered the door; he was even in his hellos with everyone. He didn't pay more attention to one person over another. There were a few other people there. "Come in the kitchen I'll make everyone drinks."

"Oh, none for me." I said

"Me either." Joy said

"What, I made sure I had everything for your apple martinis." Sean said

Andrew looked at me. I was shocked that he even remembered that I said I liked them. "I don't even remember telling you that."

"I'll take a Hennessey." Anthony said shooting Sean a look.

"Yea, me too." Andrew said still looking at me. I shrugged. At the back of the house there was a pool table. Joy and I walked to the back room while the men went in the kitchen. Karen was playing a game against a guy I didn't recognize. She was beating the pants off of him. I couldn't tell if she was enjoying winning or bending over in her dress, which was on the short side more. I guess since everyone there was our age she felt comfortable wearing her dress. Yes my dress was kind of short as well, but I guess since I didn't play "goodie two-shoes" in my mind it was ok for me.

"Hey" she said barely paying any of us attention.

"Hey" we said in unison.

After a few minutes the men joined us. Andrew put his free hand in the small of my back when he walked in the room. Karen didn't pay attention at first she was focusing on sinking the eight ball. In a perfect shot, the eight ball yielded to her command. She smiled a knowing smile. Then she stood up. "Who's next?"

"Let's get a double game going." Sean said. "Andrew, Anthony you play?"

"I'm no pool hall shark, but I can play." Anthony said

"I'll play." Andrew said

"Andrew?" Karen said, "I don't think we've met." Then she looked at me, "are you guys related?" She said pointing between Andrew and I.

Instantly that rubbed me the wrong way.

"Not yet, but we will be soon." Andrew said. Then he winked at me.

"You're not with Tracy?" She asked playing dumb

"Yes!" I said not feeling like playing this game.

Sean shot Karen a look, and she put her hands up in defeat. But now every time she moved there was a rotation in her hips, or extra enunciation on her now slow dialog. She wasn't only flirting with Andrew, but Anthony as well. Anthony looked uncomfortable, but Andrew seemed to not notice. Or at least he was playing dumb real good. But then I caught Andrew looking when she bent over for the millionth time. When he caught himself looking he looked at me and I shot him daggers. Finally the game was over and I stood up to go back in the living room.

"You wanna play another game?" Karen said.

"No!" Joy said looking completely pissed.

"You heard the boss." Anthony said walking away.

"How about you Andrew?" She said holding the pool stick straight up and sharpening the end.

My blood boiled, apparently I became invisible. Didn't we confirm that Andrew didn't come here alone! I looked at Andrew who looked like he was thinking about it. I put my hand on my right hip as I wondered what was there to think about. "Let me get a rain check."

"Sure" she said looking satisfied with herself.

"Rain check?" I said looking at Andrew. He shrugged and walked over towards me. I wanted to slap his face. Karen looked very pleased with herself. I walked away before Andrew could touch me. We sat on the couches in the living room. The boys were watching a kid movie on the television. They had a whole little setup milk in plastic bottles, grapes, graham crackers, and Jell-O squares. Joy inspected everything and then she gave me the nod to tell me it was ok. We sat in silence for a few minutes. I kept looking at Andrew who seemed pretty pleased with himself. Then Sean came back in the room.

"Oh yea before I forget. I gotta play a song for you." He walked over to his stereo and hit the play button. "Andrew, Anthony can I get you a refill?"

"Naw I'm good." Anthony said

"Yea, I'll take another." Andrew said

"All alone on a Sunday morning outside I see the rain falling!" Lisa crooned
Oh my goodness! I couldn't believe he remembered. I gasped. Everybody looked at me. Sean walked in smiling as he handed Andrew his drink. "I can't believe you remembered!" I said

Then Andrew downed his drink, he put his cup on the floor and he walked back towards the back of the house. Sean started talking about the song, but I wasn't listening. Joy and Anthony looked like they didn't know what to do. I waited for what seemed like forever for Andrew to come back. I don't even know what Sean was talking about; I stood up and walked to the back of the house. I entered the room just in time to see Karen with her finger on Andrew's chin as she shamelessly flirted with him. He had a confused look on his face, and then he saw me. His face dropped, I turned on my heels and stormed out the room. I walked into the living room.

In the calmest voice I could muster. "Andre come on its time to go."

"You can't leave this early." Sean said. I looked at him and I rolled my eyes. "What's wrong?"

"Aw! We were gonna watch Lady and the...!" Andre whined

"Baby come on, you have that movie at home. It's time to go."

"We're leaving too." Joy said to little Anthony

Both of the boys whined. "Mommy can Andre sleepover?" Andre's face lit up at the idea. He started clapping his hands.

"He has to ask his parents but that's fine with me." Joy said

"I need to go!" I yelled, Andre's eyes got big. He's never heard me yell. Then he took off running to his dad.

"Aw come on Tracy, the party's not over. It just..." I turned my attention to him, and he stopped mid-sentence. "If you don't move out of my way! I don't have time for you or your messy sister! If you don't want me to tear this house apart you betta move!"

I could tell he was shocked, "wait a minute! What did I, or my sister do for that matter other than be hospitable?" He said trying to sound innocent.

When I tried to walk out he jumped in front of me with open palms. Andrew walked around the corner Andre was in his arms. Karen was right behind him. When he stopped in the room, she stood next to him and put her hand on his shoulder. Andrew looked uncomfortable but he didn't move. In one quick motion I turned on my heels, kicked my shoes off, and I was in her face. Karen swallowed hard. "DONT YOU EVER IN YOUR LIFE PUT YOUR HAND ON MY MAN! I WILL MOP THE FLOOR WITH YOU!!!" Then I slapped her so hard my hand was stinging. Karen fell backwards. She couldn't believe I struck her. The slap was a warning; I squared off waiting for her to bounce back.

"Aw! Heck Naw! You can't be acting like this in my house Tracy!"

Andrew's voice was so deep it rumbled the whole room. "Acting like what? You been flirting with my woman since we walked in the door!"

Sean didn't have anything to say to that. He opened the door for us to leave. Both the babies were crying. Joy and Anthony were the first out the door. Andrew wouldn't move until I did. I grabbed my shoes and walked out the door. Once we were out the door I heard Karen screaming and carrying on while her brother held her back.

I didn't care about what she was saying because if she wanted to be outside she could be out here. Andrew and Andre kept looking at me. No one spoke in the car, I drove very determined all the way home. When I pulled in my driveway Joy called. She wanted to know if I was alright, and somewhat un-phased little Anthony still wanted to have a sleepover. I asked Andrew while my ear was still on the phone. Andre got really excited, Andrew agreed but I could tell he was still mad. As was I, I paced around my empty living room waiting for Joy. Joy and little Anthony came to the door. Big Anthony waited in the car. She asked me again if I was ok. Andre very happily greeted them; Andrew was pacing in the kitchen. Joy saw the look on my face and she told me to call her later. When they left I locked the door, and I went upstairs. I decided to run a bubble bath with my salts, etc. to calm my nerves. I was irritated with Andrew as well, but I knew I needed to calm down before I confronted him. I was completely emerged in the tub when he walked in the bathroom. I opened my eyes and I watched him but I didn't say anything. He sat on the edge of the tub, he put his finger in. Then he walked out. I couldn't tell what he was doing cause the lights were out in there. The only light was from my candles. When he walked back in the bathroom he only had boxers on. "Did you set the alarm?" He nodded yes; he completely stripped and climbed into my tub with me. He sat in front of me with his back to me, and then he leaned back and rested his head on my chest. I didn't say anything right away. I guess this evening was supposed to be a taste of my own medicine.

"I guess it's ok for you to be smacking folks." He chuckled

"What?"

"So some female pushes up on me, you can't even control yourself. You ready to fight. But I'm wrong if I wanna wring the neck of the dude who's disrespecting me and you."

"Who ever said you were wrong for that?"

"You did"

"No, I said you were wrong for shutting me out. Treating me like I did something wrong."

"So you don't think you were treating me like I did something wrong tonight?"

"How did I treat you like you did something wrong?"

I guess he was mimicking the way I sound when he said, "you weren't talking to me the whole way home. When Andre left you didn't even come and talk to me. You just shut me out to go clean yourself." Then he laughed, "How much is your water bill? You are the cleanliest person I know."

"Andrew you realize that doesn't speak well of your Ex's. I know I only want something clean coming at me. Bodily Odors can be a turn off and I don't care if its quote unquote natural. If nothing else, your body should be clean."

"Alright, I'll let you have that. But it's seems like the tables were turned tonight, and you couldn't handle it."

"Andrew I guess. I didn't encourage Cameron to hug me. I actually fell, busted my butt trying to get away from him. What you saw was right after I got up from that embarrassing display only for him to hug me anyways. My arms were at my sides. It was not a returned or shared embrace."

"You fell?" He chuckled

"Yea I fell! Got tangled in our bags and everything. But all you saw was his arms around me."

"You should've said something."

"When?"

He laughed "oh yea. But you still you didn't have to slap that girl like that. Poor Andre was scared."

Then I felt bad. I didn't feel anything about slapping that girl, but when he mentioned the baby I felt bad instantly. "I will apologize to him. That poor baby has been through enough." I exhaled

"I think Toya's pregnant." His body tightened

"Why do you think that?"

"A little after they gave me custody, she seemed to lose interest. Some dude has been dropping her off to the visits. She's been distant and it's almost like its..." he gathered his thoughts "She talks to Andre but she's not paying attention. Not that I want her sweating me. But her face is changing like it did when she was pregnant before. Her clothes have been baggy so I can't really tell. Instead of booking the next appointment she told the counselor she'd call. Sad part is I think Andre would be fine with not seeing her. I think he thinks you're his mother."

" I do love him as if he were mine, but I would never try to erase her from his life. She is his mother and that's that."

He relaxed and then he kissed my hand. "This bath is relaxing. I could get used to this." He wiggled a little. "So tell me something."

Oh man! Here we go! He's going ask me a bunch of questions about Sean as if I lied to him or something. "What's up?"

"Why have you been avoiding me?"

Not what I thought he was gonna ask, "huh?"

"Don't huh me. Why have you been avoiding me? Ever since we came back you've been," he put his fingers up to make quotes, "busy with work".

"Cause I have been. So have you."

"Yea, but you've been avoiding me. One-word answers, we've been busy before but we never stopped talking. If I wasn't with you all the time I'd think you were cheating on me." The way he let that hang on the air felt more like a question than a statement. "But then you start slapping folks so I think you still like me a little bit. Did I do something?"

I debated on whether or not to say anything. If I didn't say anything now it would just keep building. "Ok, um. That trip was a disaster. Would you agree?"

"To a point! There were definitely some high points." I could hear his smile.

"What did you think was gonna happen on the trip?"

"That we'd go out, have a ball. I don't know maybe somehow accidentally get married and come home." I could hear the smile in his voice.

"You know there's truth in a persons joke."

He started laughing, "yea I know".

"I think I've explained in detail sober and drunk what I thought the weekend was about. You talked me down, but why did you bring your own condoms if I was crazy for thinking that way?"

He wasn't laughing anymore. "I figured if we got married there would be no other birth control available last minute like that and I figured we should discuss it."
I thought about it for a minute. "You thought we'd get married randomly? Do you not know me at all?"

"I thought it was kind of romantic actually."

"Oh really? What part? Having some stranger give me away? The lack of a proposal? The only part you came prepared for was the sex. Yea I'll pass."

"Well you never made a big deal out of it until now. So how was I supposed to know?"

"You never ask. I don't want you to marry me just to sleep with me. I want you to want to share your life with me. If you don't put effort into our beginning what does that say about how you'll be during our marriage?" My heart was racing I was so mad.

"Why are you mad? We're just talking. I didn't know it meant that much to you."

"You never asked."

"Ok" he said in defeat

"But that still doesn't explain why you had two on the nightstand?"

He paused for a minute. "It sounds stupid when I say it."

"What?"

"I didn't want to pull away when it was time, so I took out a condom."

"Oh" I said deflating

"Do you swallow?"

"No!"

"Exactly!" It was quiet for a long time. "So I noticed you haven't started your period yet."

I gasped, "How have you noticed that?"

"I know your schedule. But that's not the point. I'm in a tub naked with my woman. What you wanna do?"

"I wanna get a slice of pizza from Bimbo's. Aren't you hungry?" I asked

He seemed disappointed, but he went with me on the idea. "What about Bart's on Solano? I don't exactly wanna see the kids."

"Students at Berkeley aren't kids. But Bart's does sound good." I said

"Let's go." He said

I was surprised he didn't try to keep us in the house let alone in the room. He watched me climb out the tub. He watched me dry off and get dressed. It took forever for him to get dressed by the time we finally got to Bart's it was not only closed, but it had been closed so long the lights inside were off and it was still inside no movement. We both still wanted burgers so we agreed to go to National Burgers. Something told me to say to go to the one off of University, but I figured a burger was a burger so the National Burgers in El Cerrito was fine. We sat down with our food in the dining room in the front of the restaurant. I was facing the door and Andrew was facing me. I looked whenever the door opened. Habit I guess. In the dark I saw a couple approach. They seemed really happy. He held the door open and she walked in. There were good vibes between them. I saw her small belly first and then her face.

My smile disappeared when I realized it was Toya. She had the nerve to be glowing and looking beautiful. Pregnancy definitely agreed with her. Then her man walked in, my heart dropped. It was Steve. He looked good, but how dare he look happy? Andrew saw my face and he turned to see who I was looking at. He had to do a double take. I didn't know what to do, but I definitely wanted to run. Toya

Locked eyes with me, she smiled then he pulled Steve's face to hers, they stood there kissing for what seemed forever. Andrew looked at me and I guess my face told it all. Andrew stood up and took me by the hand. Toya didn't notice that Andrew was with me, I don't know why. Instantly rage was on her face. She came storming in the dining room and in my face.

"I bet you feel real good about yourself right now!"

Steve came after her but he was only focused on her until he saw Andrew then he slowed up. And then he saw me; he had the same reaction as Toya. He started charging but this time Andrew jumped in his path. "Can I help you with something?"

He looked at me viciously angry! "Where's my child?"

Everybody looked at me, and when I say everybody. Everyone in the restaurant paused and looked at me.

"What are you talking about?" I felt like crawling under a rock.

"I have rights Tracy! I want to see my child!" Toya stood there with her arms crossed and a little smirk on her face. "Brotha my problem isn't with you, please move out my way." Steve said to Andrew who was standing like a brick wall.

"Right, its cool, you understand." Andrew said in a deep voice.

Toya sucked her teeth. "You're gonna stand here and defend this sorry excuse for a female? I didn't even keep you away from your child. Matter of fact I gave him to you. What kind of a woman are you?"

I guess she was supposed to be instigating a reaction from me. But I was scared still of what Steve would do to me if he could get around Andrew.

"Tracy! Just tell him so we can be done with this once and for all!" Andrew said not taking his eyes off Steve.

"Do you think this nigga is supposed to protect you from me!" Then he pointed to me and then to his head. "No matter what you do, where you go, who you're giving your sorry excuse for pussy to. I live in your brain! The rest of your life you will be thinking about me, where I could care less about you! I just want my child!"

"I.... Steve there is no child! I sent..."

He got mad and tried to rush past Andrew. Of course Andrew wasn't having that. He punched Andrew in the jaw, and you could hear the impact loud and clear. My heart sank! Andrew started throwing punches and each one connected practically breaking Steve! I rushed to Andrew and I was begging him to stop. I couldn't explain why it hurt to see Steve get beat down so badly.

"Really Drew? Over this trick!" Toya screamed as she kicked me in the back of my leg. She was ready to fight; she squared off to prepare for my reaction. All I could do is look at her stomach. I couldn't fight her! She followed my eyes, "don't worry my baby will be fine right after I beat you down!" She said as she jumped on me. She was pretty solid and we fell to the ground with her on top of me. She was screaming like a crazy person. I put my arms across my face cause I knew that's what she was going for. I moved my right leg up to kick her in the back. Then I remembered when my brother would try to pin me down. I arched my back and when she leaned back to balance herself I raised my right leg and I squeezed, she fell backwards and I rolled forward which put me on top of her. I immediately put my knees on her shoulders. She couldn't believe I pinned her and she couldn't move. She looked crazy. She was cursing and screaming, I heard footsteps, and I was lifted with the slightest ease. I was pinned to the table and my arms were pinned behind me. Something was put on my wrist to bind them together. Then I was slammed into a chair. One officer was with me while another picked up Toya off the floor and put her in a chair. There were more than two police cars outside the flashing lights made my mind swirl. Two officers drug Andrew off of Steve. Andrew put his hands up to show he wasn't resisting. One of the officers handcuffed him. Steve was hurt, he was barely moving. When they made him sit up he screamed in pain.

Toya yelled, "officer I'm pregnant and she attacked me!" It didn't surprise me that she lied, but who were they gonna believe I had her pinned when they came in. "I begged her to leave me alone, but she jumped on me. She knocked me down." Then she started crying, and the officer next to her started consoling her. I looked at Andrew and his eyes were locked on Steve. Steve was wounded, both lips busted, nose busted, all kinds of knuckle marks on his face. I could tell he was on his way to completely swelling up. Then he said, "officer she has kidnapped my child!"

"Ma'am, where's the child?" The officer standing next to me said.

"There is no child." I said as evenly as I could.

"SHE'S LYING!!!" He screamed, and I could tell he truly didn't believe me. "She's just mad because I don't want her, so she's keeping my child from me!"

"What's the child's name?" The officer said

"There is no child!" Andrew said his voice rumbling the restaurant.

"Sit tight!" One of the officers said. Then he turned on his heels. "Who called 911?"

The woman behind the counter raised her hand. He walked over to her. Then another officer asked the other couple, and the family of a mom a dad and a teenage son for details. Toya kept a sad weepy face while the officer near her was looking, and as soon as he turned his head she started mouthing all kinds of profanity and threats to me. The teenage boy noticing what Toya was doing told the officer to look in the window. When he saw her, he didn't turn around he just said, "ma'am please stop that, this is bad

enough!" Her dumb behind forgot about the window. She looked
surprised, and she started faking crying again. Then they took
everyone's names and ran them in the computer. Fortunately there
were witnesses who told the truth about everything they saw. Self
defense! I explained to the officer that I had a miscarriage, and that
I couldn't bare to face Steve so I sent him a letter. The officer
laughed, "That's cold blooded!" I started to defend myself, but I let
it go. The officer asked Andrew and I if we wanted to press
charges? "YES!" We both said at the same time. I also told them I
wanted a restraining order on the two of them. Steve laughed at it.
"Wait until they're not around! You think some piece of paper is
gonna stop me?" He said in front of two officers. They couldn't
believe he said it either. I got really scared. Plus his face was all
beat up so he really looked CRAZY! I looked at Andrew's
knuckles and they were slightly bruised. I asked the lady behind
the counter for some ice. She gave me two cups full. I got paper
towel from the bathroom. I put ice in them and I wrapped them
around his hands. He thanked me, and then we waited. Finally they
were taking Steve and Toya in. They caused the altercation, and
Toya had a warrant already. When we got to my house it was
dawn. I closed the curtains in my room to block the sunlight. I put
peroxide on Andrew's knuckles for the cuts then I bandaged them
up. I undressed him and put him in the bed. I undressed and I got
in the bed. My mind was racing with everything that happened. I
started to cry and at first it was only a few tears, but once my body
started moving I couldn't hide my cry anymore. Andrew put his
arms around me. I felt horrible like this whole thing was my fault. I
felt so stupid for getting back with Steve in the first place. I
should've never allowed him near me. While I couldn't do anything
about his busted knuckles, I knew I could take his mind off it even
if only for a while. He held me but I wiggled away. I reached into
my nightstand and I pulled out a condom. His head popped up
when he heard the paper sound as I tore open the package. It was
somewhat dark but I could see the question mark on his face. I was
still crying when I faced him and scooted towards him. He tried to

move his hips back, but he was at full salute so it wasn't hard to find him in the dark. I used one hand to slide the condom on him, but he was still weakly protesting. I wrapped my leg around him and I kept bringing my hips in. We were dancing all over the bed. Finally he got mad, he got up. I could see his silhouette and his salute that was diminishing. I stood on the bed and I leaped on him. Of course he caught me. I wrapped my legs around him best I could. He was trying to push me off. He slid on the floor. I tried to move quickly to mount him, but he rolled us over. He pinned my arms above my head! "NO TRACY! NOT LIKE THIS!" I was still crying, and then I realized he was crying too.

CHAPTER 21

When I woke up in the morning Andrew was gone. When I didn't hear him bumping around in the bathroom I figured maybe he was downstairs. I grabbed my robe and I made my way down the stairs. I got to the foot of the stairs and I saw the reflection of the alarm panel telling me the alarm was engaged. I didn't hear him leave at all, so I went back upstairs. After last night I was still a little shaky, I decided to workout inside. I put on my workout gear and hopped on the treadmill. I turned on a movie and started running. I kept turning up the speed like my life depended on it. In my mind I kept seeing that one good punch Steve got in, and then Andrew beating him down. I couldn't believe he actually thought he would win. Steve clearly is not a fighter; yea he loved to talk like he would hurt me. But clearly when up against a man he was pulverized. Andrew didn't seem all that phased by the fight. I thought his hands would be all busted up, but they were a little bruised, a few scratches here and there. But he was still whole. Hhmmmm what does that say about him? My baby is a beast! The way he moved Steve didn't stand a chance. Then I heard Steve's words... He always knows how to destroy my self-esteem. I know he's just trying to hurt me because he thinks I'm hurting him, but it still hurts like any part of it could be true. Doesn't sex vary from person to person? What one person may like another may not. At least that's what I thought, but maybe he's right. Maybe I'm no good; maybe that's why he always cheated on me. Just as my legs started to burn and my cellphone rang. It was Joy, I could barely breathe. "Hello?"

"Why are you breathing so hard?"

"Running... Treadmill!"

"Oh ok, well Andrew is here sounds like you had a pretty crazy night?"

I took my time, deep breaths just like Andrew taught me. "Yea, Monday morning I'm filing for my restraining orders against them. When did Andrew get there?"

"Um! He came pretty early. He needed to talk to Anthony. When you get a chance, you need to come over here as soon as possible."

In other words she was saying get over here now! I didn't sweat it though; I was still panicky about the night before so whatever could be going on at Joy's house couldn't be that bad right?

When I walked up to the house Andrew met me in the doorway. His eyes were red like he had been crying, which is something until this morning I hadn't ever seen him do. He hugged me really tight, he told me he loved me and led me by the hand inside. Suddenly the spot where Toya kicked me started to ache. Which was funny because it happened right now and not a moment sooner. Suddenly I knew I wasn't gonna feel too good after all this. The boys were playing in the backyard, while their lunch sat on the table. They'd come in take a few bites and then go right back out. Joy came out of her bedroom once she heard my voice. Something was wrong I could see it on her face. But of all the places why would they call me here to discuss it. Joy and Anthony sat on the love seat. Andrew sat on the couch so I sat next to him leaving the rest of the couch open. Everybody looked serious, my stomach was flipping if someone didn't open their mouth and speak soon it was gonna be problems. Andrew was leaning forward with his hands clasped together. He looked defeated and scared.

"OH MY GOD YOU GUYS!!!!! SERIOUSLY????? Somebody please just spit it out."

"Let's pray first." Anthony said standing up and closing his eyes. Joy and Andrew instantly bowed their heads, I slowly lowered mine. The whole time I'm eyeing Joy cause I know she can feel me looking at her. What part of the game is this? Somebody gotta speak up.

"Amen!" They both said. I was busy shooting Joy daggers with my eyes I missed what he said in the prayer.

"Tracy you know there's never anything too big to workout or work through. You and Andrew need to talk, but I beg of you to pray on it before you react one way or another." Anthony said, again I looked at Joy. Then they both stood up to leave the room.

"HOLD ON!" I stood up, "both of you know what's going on?" Joy nodded, "so why do you have to leave? Obviously I'm the only one in the dark here. And it's so bad that you couldn't discuss it with me first???" I said now looking at Andrew who had his head down. Suddenly I had a familiar feeling. He's breaking up with me! I could feel it! I looked at Joy and as if she could read my mind she looked away. They walked out the room in silence and I sat on the opposite side of the couch. Tears came rushing out of my eyes; I couldn't stop them even If I wanted to. I put my back in the corner of the couch and I brought my knees into my chest. I just sat there and waited, waited for whatever sorry excuse he was gonna give me. Yea all that bull that he fed me in Vegas now this. Now my family is gonna be asking what happened with this one??? They'll never like another guy I bring home. It felt like we were sitting there for years. I didn't say anything, and I tried to keep my sobbing sounds as low as possible.

"Baby, I love you!" He reached out to touch me, and I slapped his hand away.

"What is it Andrew quit playing with me! Tell me!"

He took a deep breath, "remember that night you came back to my house after we went wine tasting? The night we got back together." I nodded, but I waited for the boom. "You asked me if there was someone, and I was honest with you when I told you there was. But she didn't matter." He took a deep breath, "I know the assumption was that I just cut her loose, but I didn't." That was the first wound, but clearly he wasn't finished. " I hadn't seen her in a year. I didn't break it off I just stopped calling and wasn't taking her calls. She called me out the blue last week."
"This is why you had the nerve to ask me if I was cheating on YOU! The guilty always accuse the innocent of what they're doing. I don't want to hear the details. Did you sleep with her?" I looked him in his eyes.

"No"

"But you were going to?"

"Yes, I had a momentary slip. But baby I walked away."

"What's the difference if the intention was there? How could you? "I cried so hard it felt like my eyes were going to burst out of my head.

"But I have to tell you who." I could see tears fall from his eyes.

"Please don't tell me it was Toya. Is she carrying your baby?" He made a disgusted sound. "Then do I really need to know?"

"Yes you do."

"Fine Andrew! Fine!" I looked at him.

"Karen" BOOM! There was the upper cut she could've came back with last night.

"What?"

"I didn't know Sean was her brother. I never met any of her people. She wasn't there when I came to service with you. I had no idea that you knew her."

"You are killing me Andrew! Killing me! I gotta go!"

"Where are you going?" He said blocking my path

I stuck my finger in his chest. "Move outta my way!" He moved and I walked almost ran to the door. Joy called after me, but I couldn't hang around. Eeewwllll that HOE! Such a hoe that she knew how to play her hand acting like she didn't know Andrew, flirting with him all night in my face. I got in my car and drove; if I went home he'd know where to find me. I called Nicole, she was home relaxing. She told me to come over. She let me put my car in her garage. We sat at her kitchen table while I told her everything. She tried her best to sympathize with me, but I could tell in the end she was on Andrew's team. She was trying to talk me down. And she did make some valid points. No one doubts whether he loves me, I just don't want to spend the rest of my life dealing with other females. I wanted a tub of ice cream right in that moment. Then the doorbell rang. I told her to tell Andrew I wasn't there. But it wasn't Andrew.... Michael was coming to pick up some equipment that Hubby left out for him in the backyard.

Nicole was trying to quickly take him to the back without acknowledging that I was at the table. He stopped dead in his tracks.

"I was starting to think you were a figment of my imagination. How have you been?" Michael was all smiles.

And I was just too defeated to go through this again.

"Oh I've had better days, how are you?" I kept my puffy eyes to the floor.
"I'm good now that I see you."

I blew out air. I wasn't in the mood. "I'll leave you guys to whatever you were doing."

Then he went to the backyard with Nicole. He grabbed an arm full of things, and then he told her he'd be right back for the rest.

Nicole and I moved to the living room. She confided that Hubby has cheated on her before, and she him. They worked it out. "We promised each other and ourselves that we weren't gonna bring that stuff into our marriage. But that also explains why we dated so long."

"I just thought you finally decided to make it official."

"In a way, but it was more to it than that. Do you love him?"

"More than I ever thought I could."

"Do you still want to be with him?"

"Does it make me weak if I say yes?"

"Not at all, he has to understand that you won't continue to accept this behavior from him."

"I've never had someone in my life who's ever had my back like he did last night. I'm still amazed. But then.... How could he have known I knew Karen? Right? But what if I didn't would he have come forward? Before we went out he was trying to stay in. And if he wouldn't have held me down last night I'd be walking funny today."

Nicole scrunched her nose. "Walking funny?"

Now I love Nicole to death, but momma told me you don't talk your man up in that area with your girlfriends no matter who they are. "You know cause its been so long."

"Oh, well definitely let him sweat it out. Don't make any rushed decisions. Get your point across, but honestly you found this out from him. He could've not said anything and if that girl ever did say anything would you have believed her?"

"Heck Naw!"

"Exactly! Gold star for Andrew!"

Then the doorbell rang again. We gave each other a knowing look. Nicole opened the door and gasped in a "aw that's so sweet kind of way". Then I saw a huge bouquet of Lillie's come in the door. Michael handed me a card. It was one of those funny sayings cards. The pink and green characters sang a crazy song to cheer me up.

"Thank you Michael they're beautiful. But I can't accept this." I said handing him back his card.

He put the flowers down on the coffee table, and then he sat next to them on the table. "I know you're upset, I don't know what for, but I feel responsible to cheer you up."

"Thank you, but I'm not your responsibility." My tone was dry, and I didn't want to give him the impression that I was interested in any way.

"Michael the rest of the stuff is back here." Nicole said pointing towards the backyard.

I could tell he didn't want to go, but I wasn't giving any indication of a green light to keep going so he got up leaving the card and flowers. When I heard the sliding door shut. I leaned forward to look at this extremely expensive bouquet of flowers. Casablanca Lillie's are not cheap! And this arrangement was super duper nice! But still, I have a boyfriend so I can't keep playing these games. The door opened and I hurried up and sat back I plastered my unimpressed look on my face again.

"Stop acting, it's me!" Nicole said making a beeline to the flowers. "These flowers are beautiful!" I agreed. "You hungry?"

"I guess I could eat, I haven't eaten all day."

"Cool! What you got a taste for?"

"Ooh! You know what I haven't had in a long time?" Nicole raised and eyebrow. "E&J!!! Hhhhhmmmm I can taste it already! Can we go there please!"

"Barbecue? Really?"

My mouth started watering at the thought of it. "Ooh! Yes! I want greens! Yum! Links!!! Yum!!! Sweet tea!!! Oh how I've missed you!!! Sock it to me cake... No! Sweet potato pie done right! Ooh girl lets go!" My mouth was thanking me already.

"Ok let me go get my purse." Nicole walked down the hallway.

Michael came in the door. "Can you lock this, my hands are full?"

I got up and went to lock the door. "You know Tracy, I'm really a sweet guy."

"I don't doubt that, only a sweetheart would go through so much trouble to cheer me up." He smiled at my comment. "But I have a boyfriend. And I know he wouldn't appreciate any of this."

"But he should be up on his game making sure you're always smiling."

Ick! There's that slippery tongue stuff that reminds me of Steve. "Yea well in the real world no one smiles all the time." I started moving towards the living room. Nicole was busted standing in the hallway listening. We started laughing. Michael smiled. I didn't want to be completely rude, so I invited him out to lunch with us in Jack London Square. Nicole was shocked when I did it. But I figured it would be ok because there were three of us. Although I knew Toya and Steve were locked up at least for the weekend I still didn't feel comfortable sitting with my back to the door. So I sat on the side facing the door, Nicole sat facing me, and Michael sat on the side. I forgot they had a bar. I ordered a sweet tea and a Long Island. I downed the Long Island and I sipped on my sweet tea while I waited for my next one. I repeated this process one more time before Nicole told me three was my limit. Michael didn't say anything about my drinking. He kept talking as if he didn't notice. The food was every bit as delicious as I remembered, I loved when that happened. You know how you remember food tasting a certain way and then you actually get to eat it.... Um no! When I stood up to go to the bathroom I felt that third Long Island. I stumbled a little bit and Michael stood up to steady me. That's when Derrick saw me, and I saw him see me. He had a shocked look on his face. I walked to the bathroom as I almost peed on myself when I saw him. I sat on the toilet an extra minute telling myself to get it together. Nicole came in to check on me. I felt crazy, because my heavy heart only felt heavier now, and now I was uncomfortable from all the food I ate. When we emerged from the bathroom Derrick was watching me like a hawk. He took out his phone and started snapping. I knew he was sending them to Andrew so I tried to look as normal as possible. Michael asked for the check, and then here comes Derrick. I couldn't remember if Andrew said Derrick was the trigger happy one or Darryl.

"What's up Tracy?" Derrick said, in this moment he looked big. Definitely related to Andrew.

"Hey Derrick how you doing?" He pulled the empty chair out. "Nicole have you met Derrick before? This is Andrew's younger brother."

Nicole swallowed hard, "oh hey, I'm Hubby's wife."

"Oh hey! Hubby goes way back with the family." Then he turned his attention to Michael. "So you're Michael." He said

"Yea man, I'm Michael", he said as he stuck his hand out to shake it.

Derrick left him hanging; he turned his attention to me. "Why are you here?"

Nicole swallowed again and looked really nervous. "Can somebody bring us the check?" She said helplessly.

Michael sat back in his chair.

"I'm eating," I said trying to smile past my buzz.

"Seriously somebody can we get the check???"

"Why are you drinking?"

"You obviously talked to your brother, you know why."

"You know what I don't care. But I was told to bring you home. Now you can come willingly, but I'm not above dragging you out of here."

"Derrick please." I said dismissing him. He stared at me; he wasn't smiling or showing any indication of backing down from his promise. "I thought we were cool."

"I like you Tracy, you make my brother happy. My mom likes you. This isn't personal. Did you drive?"

His voice was direct, no friendliness to it at all. I guess if I was in my right mind I would've been nervous. But Nicole had that covered for the both of us.

"No we rode with Michael" Nicole said then she stood up and said in a loud voice, "Can we get the check please!"

"Don't worry about the check, he got this, you guys are riding with me." Then he stood up. Michael stayed seated and didn't say a word. Derrick looked at his table, "you guys cool or you wanna roll?" There were two other guys at the table. Big and scary looking. I looked at Michael and I mouthed I was sorry as I stood up. "He ain't stupid, he knows its best for him to sit there and shut up! Lets go!" Nicole and I followed like scared little puppies. When we walked out the restaurant he pulled his phone out his pocket, no guess who he was calling. Then he turned to me, "where's your car?"

"At her house." I said pointing at Nicole.

He returned to his conversation. Then he started walking again and we followed. He chirped a black SUV. "Get in" he opened his door, Nicole and I quietly climbed in the back. He drove straight to Nicole's house, not saying one word or asking for directions. We both looked at each other when he pulled in front of her house and unlocked the door. Nicole signaled for me to call her and then She hopped out the car. Once she closed her door he drove off. He picked up his phone again, "yea we almost there." Then he hung up, in complete silence we were heading to my house. He pulled in front of my house, Andrew opened the door. I didn't know this fool knew where I lived! He unlocked the door, and when I got out he said, "take care Tracy." Then he drove off.

CHAPTER 22

Still a bit wobbly from my Long Island adventure. I slowly made my way to the house. Andrew stood with his hands in his pockets. I couldn't read his look. I walked past him without looking in his direction. "Where's Andre?"

"Joy's house."

I walked in the kitchen; I filled my gallon bottle with water from my filter. Andrew stood at the island watching me. "Well I'm home, with no car. Happy now? Keep breaking my heart! And now you have your brother punk me into coming home. What's next you gonna hit me? Why don't you just get that out of the way too!" He stood there looking at me. "I hate you! You have made my life Hell! I hate you!" He didn't move or change his expression. "Funny how you will sleep with everybody else. But for me NO! The big dick is too strong! You don't care about blowing their backs out. But no, for Tracy you eat dessert, as the day is long. I might want some beef! Hell! I'm not a virgin, you know that right? You strut around here doing all these manly things! Saying all these manly things! Being the man, but when it comes down to it you can't follow through! What am I your kryptonite? You can't perform? Something's wrong with it huh?" His expression didn't change. "Let me look at it again." I walked over expecting him to stop me. But he didn't, he stood up straight so that I could open his pants. I drop his pants to the floor, and then I pulled his boxers down. I moved him around like I was looking for something. He stood there looking at me. He wasn't saluting me; he was as flaccid as his expression. When that made me mad I knew I was drunk. "I hate you! Andrew just get out!" I went back to my bottle. He pulled his draws and pants up, not taking his eyes off me. I took a swallow on my bottle. "Why are you here Andrew?"

"I want to work this out."

"So you have your brother punk me, and basically kidnap me? I'm not ready to deal with you. I didn't come home to you I was kidnapped. And wait a minute, how does your brother know where I live? He knew where Nicole lived? What is this? Why he gotta be so scary? Using his Darth Vader voice on us. Jedi mind tricks, Michael's gonna pay the bill. He wasn't ever like that before. What's wrong with your family?"

"Nothing"

"Oh so if I talk about your family then you talk?"

Then he came around the island, and he put his finger on my mouth and his other hand on the back of my head. He wasn't hurting me, but his hands were strong and deliberate. "After last night, I see why you freak out. But I'm warning you. Don't go there. Don't talk about my family." Then he let me go.

Um! I was quiet! I picked up my bottle. I took a long swig. Then I walked upstairs. He set the alarm and was right behind me. I closed the door when I went in my room. But he opened it and let himself in. "Hello! The door was closed!"

"Why were you with Michael?"

"Why were you with Karen? Why were you with Toya? Why were you with Tooty? Why were you with Judy?"

"You're not even making sense right now. Lets let you drink some more water."

I grabbed all the clarity I could muster. "Andrew you say you love me, but do you really?"

"Yes! You are my heart!"

"You protected me last night, does that mean you want to protect me always?"

"Forever!"

"Then why aren't you protecting me from this? Do you have any idea how this makes me feel? How much this hurts? I could totally jump off the Bay Bridge right now, and feel the impact of hitting that icy cold water and dying a slow agonizing death would feel a million times better than this. Do you understand I don't have to feel like this? So yea, I'm gonna over drink. I'm gonna over eat. Either way I'm gonna die cause I can't live like this. How am I supposed to trust you?"

He had a pained look on his face. "Tracy I'm here to fix this. I messed up. I have no excuse for what I did."

"You're messing with my head. You won't sleep with me, but you'll sleep with everybody else. How do you think that makes me feel?"

"You told me you wanted to wait. I was trying to honor your wishes. Besides I don't want you to have to be drunk in order to sleep with me."

"I wasn't drunk last night!" I screamed

"Yea, but I needed to talk to you."

"You weren't concerned with talking to me before we left. We could've talked about it as soon as we came home. "

"You were pissed when we came home. But you're right I could've talked to you then."

"Andrew I need some space. I need to think things through."

"That would be fine if that's what you were going to do. You can't handle what you feel, so you drink or eat. And I know how you are when you drink."

"What is that supposed to mean?"

"Hello? Vegas!"

"That was with you."

"So you're trying to tell me you wouldn't have kissed Michael in your current state?"

It was like he read my mind. "No!" I didn't say that too convincingly.

He smiled, I wanted to kiss him. But I was mad at him so I rolled my eyes. "So what am I supposed to do now?"

He grabbed me up and leaned in almost kissed me. I wanted the kiss so I melted. "Forgive me, I promise I'll be better."

I leaned in for the kiss and he pulled away making a wounded sound. "What?"

"If I kiss you now, later you will accuse me of not taking you seriously. If I apologize and just be here, at least you'll know I'm taking you seriously. Even if it kills me."

"What if I kiss you?" I said kissing his neck.

He pushed me away. "When you sober up you're gonna be mad again and regretting me again."

"Why won't you marry me?"

"I didn't think you would want to marry me after this."

"So I can't marry you, but you send the Mafia after me if I try to move on? Um, seems like everyone gets something out of this but me."

"No one sent the mafia. But that's a good point. But! You want to wait."

"Well it's not like I can go back there after last night."

"That's not true. Besides if she outed you, that would be outing herself. I don't know that she would be that bold. I highly doubt that."

"Ok! But!" I grabbed his shirt, "still doesn't change things."

He smiled, "I'm not doing this!"

I walked over to my bed and put my bottle on the floor. I took my shirt off, and then Andrew turned his head. I took my bra off. I took my jeans and underwear off. Andrew went and sat on my couch. I laid on my bed and spread my legs. "Andrew!" I sang

He said an irritated, "yes!"

"Please kiss me?"

He sucked his teeth then he made the mistake of looking at me. He stared for a little bit, then he waited a little bit then he looked again. I could hear him wrestling with himself. Then he walked over. I was smiling with a knowing smile.

"How sober are you?"

"I could drive if I had my car." Lied but so what.

He sighed a defeated sigh. He pulled off his shirt. I got excited. He stripped down naked and I pulled a condom out of my nightstand. He rolled his eyes at me. He kissed me very gently. He was at full salute. Then he kissed my neck, I got excited knowing what was about to happen to me. The relationship his mouth has with my body is out of this world! My eyes literally crossed multiple times. He out did himself this time. I know he was trying to erase the idea of anything else in my mind. When he laid down I grabbed the condom. He didn't protest when I put it on. I went down on him and as soon as I saw he was relaxed I climbed on top of him. He was shocked, and he tried to move me but I was already on his head. He shook his head no, as I slowly worked him in. HE IS HUGE! I almost rethought what I was doing as I had to tell myself to relax to take him in. I had to bob at each increase. I told myself to breathe, I could do this, just take my time. I was tighter than I remembered. Naw this guy was huge! When I finally had him in all the way I was afraid to move. But I was in peaceful bliss with him inside of me. Then Andrew rolled us over, my eyes got big cause if he lost control and started pounding me he was gonna break me in half. He moved slowly and gently my orgasm from earlier was back, and it kept rolling over me over and over. He remained slow but steady. Every part of my body sizzled; I couldn't believe I had him inside of me. Even inside of me he felt strong and powerful! He started groaning and his rhythm picked up, but it was still controlled strokes. I was in heaven my mouth and throat were completely dry. He bent down to kiss me. He cursed, he was coming BUT his face looked stressed!

"What?" I said as I surrendered to my fifth orgasm.

"The condom broke!"

CHAPTER 23

Now that sobered me up. I looked at Andrew's face and he looked horrified. It was my fault; I pushed him to this point. I kissed him and kept trying to tell him it was going to be ok. He told me that those little condoms didn't work for him, and how they always broke on him. With all the throbbing I was now feeling I believed him. I found myself comforting him. When I got up to go to the bathroom it was clear, he was the man. I was walking funny; it felt like I lost my virginity all over again. There was even blood, I didn't know if I was starting my period, or my body's reaction to his size. When I came out the bathroom he was laying on the bed with his arm over his eyes. I grabbed fresh underwear from my dresser in the closet. Andrew hadn't moved.

"Baby come shower with me."

He raised himself on his elbows, "you sure about that?"

I swallowed, "um, I just wanna shower. I'm good otherwise." He laughed deep and loud. In the shower he was back at full salute. Impressive! Outside of that night at the hotel, Steve was always a one shot kind of guy. Feeling kind of responsible, on my knees I went. He looked at me funny when he saw me put a pad on, but he didn't say anything.

"Ok, so seriously we need to talk." I said

"Right"

"Andrew I love you, but I cannot live the rest of my life worrying about you and any other female. I can't handle living that way."

"I understand. I wouldn't want you to."

"Can you promise to ONLY be about me from this point onward?"

"Yes, how about you?"

"Um, with that big beautiful gift where would I go?" I laughed, he smiled proudly.

"I've been blessed what could I say?" We laughed.

"There's another thing." I swallowed, his smile dropped. "Since you're here all the time. Why don't you and Andre move in?"

"Are you sure about that?"

"Yes! It'll actually help me out. I'll be able to finish furnishing the house. And it won't seem so empty here when you're not here."

"I don't have to move in here to buy you furniture. We can go shopping tomorrow."

I raised an eyebrow. "Just like that? You have it just like that?"

"There's nothing I couldn't buy you."

"Everybody has financial limits. I'm still paying on my student loans, etc. you know grown folks stuff."

"Whatever, what am I supposed to do with my loft? I just bought it."

"You can rent it out. Places in Emeryville go like hot cakes. That shouldn't be hard."

"Your parents aren't gonna be happy when they find out."

"I'm not a child Andrew. I'll handle my parents."

"Let me think about it. But if it's cool with you, while we buy furniture for the house we can set up Andre's room?"

"Yes! Of course!" I got excited.

My phone rang and it was Joy. She wanted to know how I was doing, and she was a little surprised to hear a smile in my voice. I told her I was fine, and then I invited them over for dinner. I gave Andrew a list of things I needed from the store, especially since I didn't have my car. I ran around sprucing things up. And prepping the things I did have in the refrigerator. Once all I had left to do was wait my mind started going over the weekend. It wasn't even Sunday yet and too much had happened. What did he mean by there wasn't anything he couldn't buy me? How much money does he have? He's never said no to me about anything I wanted to do, or ever seemed concerned about the cost. But let me be real, he graduated top of his class from college. He has a pretty high-powered job at his company, especially for someone so young. I know Toya felt like she should've been living larger than she was, but I really assumed that was based on her assumption of his job. But how in the world does Toya act like that if his brothers are who they are. Who are they? Ugh! Thinking about it made me scared and I didn't want to be.

I called Nicole who was still a little shook up. She called Hubby as soon as she got in the door, but she said he made her mad by not seeing what the big deal was. He told her Derrick did right, and really Michael shouldn't have been with us. She asked me if Andrew was mad, and I told her no. I told her we even made up. Then she called me a drama queen for the whole afternoon. I didn't think I was being a drama queen. I had every right to feel what I felt. Outside of inviting Michael to lunch, and throwing back too many Long Islands on a partially empty stomach. We asked each other what would've happened if Derrick would've only seen Michael and I as we were leaving? I shuddered to think if it. When we got off the phone I turned on the TV to block any unwanted thoughts out of my mind.

Fortunately Joy came with the kids. She said Andrew came and picked up Anthony a while ago. So I told her everything that happened. She got quiet when I told her about Derrick. "Who is he?"

"All I've ever known him to be is his brother, but today he was different. I'll tell you one thing they seem so much bigger in those spaces. I guess most men do, right?"

Joy started laughing, "did he really punk Michael like that? What if he couldn't afford it?"

"I know right. Those flowers weren't cheap in the least bit. I doubt he thought he was paying for lunch too. Oh well."

"Well you know he probably thought it was gonna go somewhere."

We both laughed, then I told her about shopping tomorrow and we both got excited. I took out a notepad and pen and I jotted down the good ideas we came up with. Since the walls were grey, the trim was white and the floors were dark cherry wood I went back over my white living room ideas. The furniture would have to either be espresso chocolate or stark white. We discussed frames even. Then we asked Andre which room he wanted of the twin rooms as we called them. He picked the one closest to my room. Both of the boys cheered when I told Andre it was going to be his room. Instantly they started talking about more sleepovers. I showed Joy my room, and she had some suggestions for a few things in there. Like a rug, candle holders, etc. but like I said my room was pretty much done. I still needed a family table for the kitchen. We had so much fun, by the time the men finally came with the groceries we kept talking about the ideas. The men made the salad, potatoes, and steaks. Joy and I made the cake. After dinner, I decorated the cake. Joy said I should've been a pastry chef. Everybody tore up that cake. First they raved about how beautiful it was, and then they devoured it. I loved watching them enjoy it. The boys had cake all over their faces, and they asked for more until there was no more. Andrew and Anthony did the dishes, while Joy and I put our feet up. The boys ended up conking out on our laps. Poor babies, they had played until they passed out. I laid them on the guest bed in the room downstairs. When the dishes were done the men came in the living room with us. We watched a movie together and it was a lovely cap to the night. Well not the cap I was hoping for, but my poor body screamed at me for even thinking of it. We walked our guest outside, then Andrew told me my car was in the garage. I didn't look for my keys; I didn't realize he had taken them. I didn't question it. When we walked back in the house we were awkward for a moment.

"Andre has to sleep with us until we get his room set up."

"That will be taken care of tomorrow. Did you start your period?"

"I think so, either that or you're too big." I smiled

"You're sore?"

"Yea, but it's ok. It's what I wanted."

He said ok, but his face didn't look so sure. He brought Andre upstairs and I set the alarm. He tucked Andre in and kissed his forehead.

"Let's watch TV for a little bit." He motioned for me to join him on the couch. I sat with my back to him between his legs. His arms were holding me. I could stay like this forever. "So lets discuss this." My heart sped up a bit, I don't know why; he was lovingly holding me. His statement scared me.

"Ok, shoot"

"Are we having sex now or was today a one time thing?"

"How could we go backwards, isn't that cruel? And I'm talking about me, I don't know about you. I have to master that beast you got. Whew!"

He laughed, "ok, so are we gonna get pregnant right away? Or do we wanna wait?"

"What do you want?" I asked

"I'm happy either way, I just want you to be cool with it."

"Provided that the seed wasn't planted today. I'd like to wait until we're married. I just don't want to be preggers in my wedding dress. It's not a good look in my mind."

"Ok so what type of birth control we gonna use?"

"I have a diaphragm and condoms should work just fine."
"What's that?"

"You don't know what a diaphragm is?"

"No"

"I'll have to show you, but it works by blocking the sperm from reaching your cervix. You also put spermicide on it each time you use it."

"Oh I think I know what you're talking about. I don't know if that's gonna work."

"Why not?"

"Um, the beast as you so lovingly named him will knock that thing into your ovaries."

We both laughed. "Ok but you'll wear a condom as well, so we should be ok."

165

"You can throw those little man things away. I'll buy my magnums." I laughed. "What's funny?"

"Please don't get mad, but it's about Steve." He looked at me. "I just remembered how he would buy those and more than once they slid right off. He wasn't packing at all."

Andrew didn't laugh, he kept quiet. I instantly felt bad about bringing it up. "I'm sorry".

"Any who, back to our conversation. Monday they're gonna want your address for the restraining order."

"I opened a PO Box while I stayed with my parents. I hadn't switched over all my addresses yet any ways. We could use that. Are you moving in tomorrow?"

"Hhhhhmmmm, I need to think about it."

"Seriously? What's to think about? You know where everything is in the cabinets."

"It's more to it than just that Tracy."

"Ok, oh but before I forget to ask, what's the budget for tomorrow?"

"You need a budget?"

"Yes! Joy and I came up with some beautiful ideas. We both have expensive taste, so I need to know when I should look for more cost effective options."

"Let's just see where we end up."

"You do realize you did this to yourself I'm trying to warn you."

He laughed, and I kissed his dimple.

The next day as promised we were up and out. I decided I wanted to paint Andre's room, we both agreed on a green color that I knew would make the items we picked out for his room pop. We decided on bunk beds, for him that could be taken down if we decided we needed a change. We got the matching dresser with a mirror and a adjustable desk that would grow with him, as he got older. He would need this for his homework, etc. we had such a nice time out as a family. We went to stores in Lafayette, Moraga, and Walnut Creek. When we came home that evening the boys kicked me out as they painted the room. I just knew they were gonna make a mess especially when I heard them in there laughing and playing around. By the end of the night it was finished and I couldn't have done a better job. Andre had paint all over his body, hair, and clothes. But they were both happy with their selves. I made dinner while they painted, and then they washed the dishes and kicked me upstairs. I could get used to that for sure. I took a long hot bubble bath while they were downstairs. At bedtime I bathed and tucked Andre into my bed and kissed him goodnight. Then wearing only my robe I went downstairs where Andrew was watching TV and talking on the phone. I sat on his lap as usual. I had no idea what he was talking about. He was pretty animated but not in a bad way, but I couldn't tell if it was good. He was giving orders, but I couldn't figure it out. After thirty minutes of feeling ignored I took his right hand and put it in my robe and I made him cuff my breast. He started rubbing my chest, but he kept talking. Then I started kissing his chin. He eyed me, and I smiled, then I showed him the magnum. He wrapped up his call; I think he might've hung up on the person even. We made love on the couch, no words just us. I was still a little tender, but it wasn't an issue. The pleasure was so worth the pain. Then he carried me in his arms. Initially I reverted back to my big girl thinking and he gave me a look. I shut up and he effortlessly carried me around to turn off the lights, turn on the alarm, and then to the bedroom. He tucked me in and kissed my forehead. Andre scooted close to me. Then Andrew got in the bed on his side. It was such a nice moment I didn't want it to end.

CHAPTER 24

In the morning, we called in to our jobs. We took Andre to school, and then we went straight to the courthouse to file for our restraining orders. I put everything in the report even the names and badge numbers of the officers that heard Steve threaten me. That afternoon the orders were ready and approved by the courts. We went to pick them up. He said he'd have his brother serve them. I didn't question it. I handed them over; I put the assigned court date in my phone so I wouldn't forget to ask for the day off.

We had lunch, and then my mom called. She said she was calling to hear my voice since she hadn't heard from me. Andrew and I decided to go over. She asked why I wasn't at work, but I talked around it. Andrew was really quiet on the ride over like he was thinking about something. I asked him if he was ok, and he said he was fine. When we got to the house, my mom showed Andrew where my dad's office was and then she came back in the living room.

"What's up with him?"

"Up?" I asked

"He seems a little different today. Maybe he's got a lot on his mind." When I didn't respond, she changed the subject. "Have you met his mother and father?"

"It's just his mom, and yes she seems really nice."

Mom started reminiscing over my grandmother; since my parent's families grew up around each other she already knew her mother-in-law and she loved her dearly. She asked what type of relationship I had with Amber. I assured her that things were fine, but we were still getting to know each other. We chatted for a while then Andrew and my father came in the living room. They had funny looks on their faces, it wasn't mad just weird. Then Andrew got a call that he had to take, he stepped out of the room. When he returned he begged my parents to forgive him but he had to swing by his office. We hopped in his car and headed to the small Hercules business park. In all our time together I had never been to his job or he mine. He introduced me to Jennifer the receptionist/administrative assistant at the front desk. She seemed to know who I was before he said. As we were saying hello, people in the nearby cubicles stood up to get a look at me. Andrew stood there proud as people came over to say hello. I wish I would've been more prepared to meet everyone, I looked fine. But I didn't feel beautiful. There were some older women and some younger. Older gentlemen and young guys. There was a good mix age ranges and backgrounds. Some of the hellos were genuine and others were sizing me up and so fake. Finally we made our way to Andrew's office in the far corner.

"So does the location of your office mean you're a big deal in this place?"
Andrew flashed his dimples, "I'm a pretty big deal. I don't make a big deal out of it but they do."

Then there was a knock at his door. He looked at the shoes through the frosted window. He sucked his teeth, "hold on!" He called out. Then he looked at me, "now look, this is my place of business so you can't be smacking folks here." Then he winked at me.

I knew I wasn't gonna like her by the disclosure. Then he called out, "come in" then she walked in. She was tall and heavyset; you could tell she tried to present herself as if she knew she was fine. Very narcissistic within moments of meeting me, she's sizing me up, and then acting like she's an authority on food and exercise, etc. She said, "girl I'm constantly trying to make sure he eats well. Sometimes it's like he doesn't come out of this office, so I try to bring him something."

"And what do I tell you?" Andrew said quickly

"Girl he's so modest he always tells me no, but sometimes I lure him into eating."

Andrew put his head down, while he peeked at me.

I started blinking my eyes, "lure?"

Realizing what she said she started trying to retract it, "oh girl, you know what I mean. My food always smells good." She said

I looked at Andrew, "you eat her food?"

Andrew smiled, and said, "No"

Then I looked at her, "what's your name?"

"Oh I'm Lisa."

"Lisa got it" I said then I focused my attention on Andrew. "Do I even have to say it?"

Slightly laughing Andrew said, "No you don't"

"Ok.... Well.... I'm gonna go."

I looked at her. She should've never come in here. Andrew kept his eyes down trying to keep his laughter in. She was exiting when I said; "I know you didn't bring me here for this."

He stuck his tongue at me. "No, I need to run in this office real quick. Promise you won't smack anybody?"

"At this point I can't promise you anything." I said rolling my eyes.

He stepped out of the office and disappeared into another. That heifer made me mad, how dare she try to come in here and act like she knows what's best for MY MAN! If she knew what he was working with she'd really be sprung, then I'd have to cut her. That's when I realized how possessive I'd become in this short space of time. I didn't want any female even attempting to look at him, the beast was mine! Maybe this is why Toya acts so crazy. For once I think I understand. It kind of made me laugh that I found myself relating to her. But I'd probably go crazy too if I was her. But what I didn't understand is how she could go backwards to someone like Steve. If you don't know any better Steve is great, but since I know she does I don't get it. I got up and walked around his office. It wasn't huge but he had a lot of windows behind him and a beautiful view. He had a picture of Andre when he was smaller, one of me and Andre, and one of the pictures he and I took on our Napa trip on his desk. No wonder everyone knew who I was. Then I had a seat in one of the chairs in front of Andrew's desk. Then Jennifer buzzed in on the speakerphone, "Andrew?"

"He just stepped out." I said

"Uh, ok. His father is on his way back there."

"K?" His who? His what? I didn't know he interacted with his father at all. I felt so out of the loop. Pretty soon a tall dark chocolate man walked in the office. He was about the same build as Andrew, and just as solid. He stopped when he saw Andrew wasn't in there, and then he quickly looked at me. His facial expression didn't change when he saw me, he sized me up too.

"Where's Drew?" His voice was deeper than Andrew's

"He stepped out for just a minute. He'll be right back."

I felt awkward; Andrew never talks about this man. For all I knew he could've been dead. He didn't try to make small talk with me or anything he just stood there. He didn't wear the same cologne as Andrew, but his had a distinct smell as well. He was dressed nicely in slacks, Stacy Adams, dress shirt, and Mister Rogers sweater. Then he walked over to Andrew's chair and sat at his desk. He picked up the phone dialed a number. "I'm gonna be a few minutes longer... No..... I said No. Alright!" Then he hung up and leaned back in the chair. He looked at the pictures on Andrew's desk then he looked at me. He didn't say anything he just rolled his eyes. Obviously he wasn't friendly so I sat back praying that Andrew would hurry up.

I could hear Andrew talking as he exited his coworker's office. He was talking about findings, and some business jargon I didn't understand. When he entered his office he stood in the doorway with his eyes locked on his father. He looked at me and then back at his father. He came in and shut his door behind him. "What do you want?" He didn't sound mad, a simple question.

"Darryl came by to see me." His father said

"And?"

"What's going on?" He said casually using his hands for emphasis.

"It's nothing right now."

"If I'm here, then it doesn't sound like nothing to me. Do we need a visit?"

Andrew blew air. "Not yet. Lets get the restraining orders in place, then I'll let you know."

"So he doesn't know?" His father said

Both of their tones were dry and both of them focused on each other; it was almost like I wasn't there. But the tension in the room was clear.

"You think if he did there'd be any of this? But it's good this way, right?"

"Yea I guess." Then he nodded towards me. "Nice!" That sounded more like a question.

"Yea" Andrew didn't look at me.

"Interesting." Then his father looked at me. "I'm Malcolm"

"Tracy this is my father." Andrew said as he sat in the chair next to me.

"Nice to meet you." I tried not to sound nervous. Malcolm reminded me of Derrick in a way. I guess it was that no nonsense approach, although until Saturday I never knew Derrick to be that way.

"You should bring her by." Andrew didn't say anything. "What are we gonna do with that other one?"

"Nothing, she's Andre's mother."
"Like that matters." He rolled his eyes. "You can't be soft with that one. I told you before."

Andrew's tone got a little deeper, "I'm not."

"So you went to Vegas."

"That was your boy, I know. Tell him to not be so obvious next time." Ok, that much I followed. I remembered how the security check guy looked like he was trying to place Andrew's face. But what did that mean? They were having some whole coded conversation. "We're heading out." Andrew said standing up, so I stood with him.

Malcolm stood up he walked around the desk. "Alright, I told Darryl to keep me posted."

"Alright."

Then Andrew looked at me, "you ready?"

"Yes" I didn't understand anything they were talking about. But Malcolm seemed focused and not into personal relationships. "It was nice meeting you Malcolm."

"Likewise." He said opening the door.

We walked out behind his father. Lisa kept eyeballing me as we walked. I felt a little bad for her, but lets face it, I was at capacity and she was getting on my nerves. When we walked out to the parking lot there was a fancy car. So fancy I don't even know what it was. My mouth literally dropped open. I looked at Andrew, and he nodded but didn't say anything. There was a female in the car, but I couldn't really see her cause the windows were tinted.

"Alright Drew! Later!" He said getting in the car.

"Later!"

When we got in the car I faced Andrew. He knew I had a ton of questions. I couldn't believe the way things were coming out. Andrew was always no less than a gentleman with me. He's always been a sweetheart, but for the longest Toya was the only link to this life of his. Andrew flashed his dimples as he focused on the road. "What? Alright let's hear it, what?"

"How come I assumed your father was dead?"

"I don't know why you assumed he was dead, cause I never said that."

"Right, you never said anything." I gestured with my hands for him to spill it.

"You think I look like him?"

"You do, but you look more like your mom."

"Yea, well he and moms were young. You know how tumultuous young love can be. It didn't last. They both moved on."

"What does he do?"

"He owns a couple barbershops, and a few recording studios, etc., etc. " he was being vague on purpose.

"Where does he live?"

"Oakland."

"Why doesn't he know about me?"

"He knows about you."

"It didn't seem like it."

"He's not that kind of father."

"What kind of father is he?"

"Everything is business to him. He cares but not like your dad. Your dad was the kind to put training wheels on your bike and still run along side you to make sure you didn't get hurt. My father was the kind to put you on a bike, tell you that you better not fall, and then push you down the hill. When you mastered the skill out of fear of him, he'd move on to the next thing. It took me a long time to understand him. He's just who he is."

"Who was in the car?"

"I don't know, don't care." I grabbed his hand. I could tell he didn't want to discuss it. I wanted to show I appreciated him opening up about it. "Oh and before I forget they've been served. Now what?"

"Now they'll probably counter with their own restraining orders. We go to court, and the judge decides how long if at all."

"Do we need lawyers?"

"No with your past with Toya, eye witness accounts, it should be a open shut case." Then my cellphone rang. The caller ID said it was Sonya. "Ooh!!"

"What?"

"Sonya, should I answer?"

"You got anything to hide?"

I reluctantly answered the phone. "Hello?"

"What happened?"

"It's a long story." I said

"How you gonna do my brother like that?"

"I didn't really have a choice in the matter. Please tell him how sorry I am."

"He did say you guys were kind of forced, but why did you invite him in the first place?"

"I felt sorry for him, he spent all that money on those flowers. I didn't want to be completely rude. How in the world was I supposed to know all that was gonna happen?"

"What flowers?"

"He bought me a huge bouquet of flowers. I told him he shouldn't have and that I had a boyfriend. I promise I wasn't flirting outside of inviting him to lunch. I was wrong for that. Please tell him I'm sorry."

"I guess I kind of understand. But you do understand that Michael's my brother."

"Yes" I said not understanding where she was going with this.

"I'm gonna have to un-invite you and Andrew to the wedding."

"That's fine, I understand." I did even though it hurt my feelings.

CHAPTER 25

I woke up in a sweat at three o'clock in the morning. I was going with Andrew to the courthouse, so why was I scared stiff about seeing Steve? The nightmares came back two weeks ago. Each one seemed worse than the one before. This morning we were back at National Burgers and instead of hitting Andrew he hit me. And then he kept hitting me, accusing me of being a liar. There was a baby carrier there and I kept trying to keep him away from it. Every time I tried to stop him he'd hit me some more. When I woke up Andrew was looking at me. He waited for me to wake up; last time he tried to wake me up I became all nails and scratched up his arm trying to get free. I sat straight up trying to get away. Andrew put his hand on my back and he started rubbing. "Are you ok?"

"Yea" I got up and went to the bathroom and splashed water on my face. When I got back in the bed Andrew looked at me.

"What can I do to help?" Andrew asked

"You're already doing it." I said, also trying to convince myself. I knew Steve was in my head, but I couldn't tell you why.

"It kills me every time you wake up like this." Andrew said still a little groggy

"I'm just sorry I keep waking you up like this." I threw my arm around him.

"Don't worry about it." He said as he dosed off.

I laid there listening to him breathe. After an hour I was restless and I knew I needed to sleep. I needed to burn some energy. I needed Andrew to wake up. I rubbed his back, kissed his ears, kissed his chest. He stirred a little but he wasn't fooling with me. Finally at a quarter to six I got on the treadmill. I put the speed as high as I could stand it, and then I ran my heart out. Tears and snot ran down my face. I ran as hard as I could for as long as I could. Andre came in my exercise room; I was running so hard I woke him up. I tried to get him to go back to sleep, but it was useless he was awake. So he sang a new song he learned in preschool for me, while I finished my run. My legs burned and they ached but I couldn't seem to run far enough. When Andrew got up Andre sang the song for him. It was a nice way to start the day. I held up black slacks and a black pencil skirt up, "which one should I wear?"

"Why are you dressing so professional?"

"Hello! We're going to court I want to be respectful of the space."

"The skirt is sexier."

I gasped, "we're going to court I don't want to be sexy!"

"Please wear the skirt for me." He was trying to make light of the situation.

"I'm just so nerved up!"

"With all the running you just did?"

"Yes! If my legs weren't sore I'd swear I needed to run again."

"I could've helped you burn some energy." He said raising his eyebrows

"Um! I tried to wake you first, but you were out."

He looked at the clock, "do we have time?"

"No, we gotta get going. We gotta drop Andre off, and we gotta go all the way to Martinez in commuter traffic."

He walked over behind me and put his arms around me and his breath was on my neck. I looked in the mirror; I love to watch our reflection. "Pppppllllleeeeeaasssseeee!" He begged kissing my neck.

I LOVED when he begged too. But my nervous energy wouldn't allow me to get into it. "Andrew we can't! You should've woke up. We don't have time."

Still kissing me he grabbed me tighter. "What about a quickie?"

I was taking everything in but my stomach was in knots, my body wasn't responding like it normally does. Normally I would be bent over by now. I turned around and kissed him long and deep. I didn't want him to feel unloved or neglected, but I couldn't do it. He hugged me in defeat. He was dealing with it, but I could tell he

177

wasn't happy. Great! One more thing to feel guilty about. Andrew remained quiet the whole car ride. Although he was driving he told me to stay in the car while he took Andre to sign him into his class. I didn't say anything, I kept telling myself to breathe. After that point we rode in silence, I couldn't tell you if the radio was playing or not. My mind was racing fifty miles a second, but I couldn't focus on anything. We had to park a couple of blocks away from the courthouse. We held hands on our way to the courthouse. As we approached there was a line that was growing as we approached. I didn't see Steve or Toya. They made an announcement but I was so nervous I didn't hear it. Andrew didn't appear to be phased at all. If anything my nerves seemed to be bothering him. So I tried my best to be quiet. We sat in the waiting area outside of our assigned courtroom. People were coming and going, the airport style security check before entering the building did make me feel a little better. We were there maybe ten minutes when Toya arrived. She had all her hair pulled back and small hoops. She didn't have any makeup on; I'd be lying if I said she looked bad. She actually looked really pretty. Her face didn't look all that different from the last time I saw her as far as fullness. Her belly was still there, but it was still small. I don't know what I expected in four weeks. She looked at us, but she didn't react. That was the first time EVER!

"Drew" she said acknowledging him.

"Toya" he said uninterested

Then she stared at me, so I stared back. Seriously??? When Andrew realized what was going on, he said "Hey!" Snapping his fingers "stop that!"

She huffed and then rolled her eyes. This was the most controlled I'd ever seen her.

Then Steve arrived. He sat next to Toya and started whispering in her ear. She laughed but didn't respond. My heart dropped when I saw him. He was still bruised slightly. I couldn't believe they were together. He couldn't even remember how he knew her or at least that's what he told me. Now there they sat together. Her pregnant and him seeming to be ok with it. Why was it ok for her to carry his child, but not for me? His eyes burned through me. I could visibly see him trying to restrain himself whenever he looked at me. It hurt that he hated me so badly, but I didn't know what I did to make him so angry with me. Well besides up and suddenly moving, sending him a letter to let him know the child he didn't want was dead, and/or when my current boyfriend beat the snot out of him. I diverted my eyes so I wouldn't look at him anymore. Andrew was not in the least bit concerned that Steve was there. They called everyone into our courtroom. The judge was a older black woman, and she was no nonsense. Straight to the point. There were couples fighting over custody, divorces, and rebellious teenagers. As people were heard and cleared out, the crowd in the waiting area got smaller and smaller. That's when I saw Derrick sitting quietly in the corner. Then I noticed Darryl sitting a few rows ahead of him but more towards the center. He was a couple rows behind Toya and Steve who had to be told more than once to quiet down. Steve kept staring at me; I could feel his eyes on me even though I wouldn't look at him. I was nervous and sweating like crazy, but seeing Andrew's brothers did make me feel better. A little more secure, but my stomach was still in knots. I think my palms got too sweaty for Andrew to continue holding my hand. He put his hand on my knee, every once in awhile he would start rubbing, but he didn't move his hand. Steve saw Andrew's hand he became visibly unglued but he didn't say anything. I wanted this to be over. Finally the judge called our names. Steve had an attitude walking towards the front he flinched at Andrew, and Andrew looked at him like he was an irritating pest. I don't know why Steve thought Andrew would be phased by his little threat. His face should be a reminder as to why Andrew could care less.

The judge went over the events of that night. The documented witness accounts, and the police officer testimonies of Steve's threat to my safety. I even provided my medical records to show that I did actually have a miscarriage. Just hearing the judge talk about it made tears stream down my face. The judge asked Steve if he understood that there was no child. He sat there shaking his head, he was pissed. Toya looked irritated at how upset he was.

"But your honor I saw her with a little boy about the age our child should be!" He exclaimed

Everyone looked at him. "And when was this?" The judge asked

"I don't remember exactly when. But it was a while ago. She left before I could catch up to her."

"Do you have any other children?" The judge asked me.

"No your Honor, my boyfriend has a little boy. I also have a friend who has a little boy. But I don't have a child."

That's when Toya lost it! "I know you don't let my son go anywhere with this trick!" She hopped out her chair like she was going to do something. As she stood up she glanced to the back of the courtroom and immediately she shut up! She sat down and folded her hands in front of her. Andrew didn't even react to her. "Your Honor I have full custody of my son." He handed a copy of the court order to the bailiff to hand to the judge. The judge had seen enough, she approved the restraining orders. Before Steve could get up Toya whispered something to Steve and they both remained seated facing forward. Andrew walked behind me; we walked single file out the door. Derrick and Darryl looked at me but neither acknowledged me. They looked then looked away. I didn't know what they were doing but by the way Toya was behaving herself I figured there was more to this story than I knew. So I kept walking. We got in the line to get our court-approved orders. Although there was a charge after the first copy I didn't care I wanted twelve of them. My plan was to put them everywhere. Andrew thought it was a bit excessive but he didn't understand how scared I was. I wasn't him, if Steve saw me somewhere he already threatened that he wouldn't respect the paper. But I felt better knowing that I had the paperwork.

As we walked to the car I calmed down a lot. "Why are you so afraid of him? Did he ever hit you?" Andrew asked looking straight ahead.

"No, but in the end he seemed like he wanted to, he would threaten it sometimes but I never gave him a reason to. I guess it's the way he always seems to think he's smarter than everybody else." I exhaled deeply. "I don't know why honestly. It's like something in the back of my mind says he wants to hurt me. He turned into a lunatic when I found out I was pregnant. I guess Toya's just crazier than him for him not to pull all that on her."

"I'm not even sure that's his kid. I could be wrong, but Toya got a lot going on right now. If she truly cared about that baby would she have been trying to provoke you to fight her?"

"I don't know. Do you know who the father is?" I said a little prayer that he wasn't trying to tell me it was his. Although I asked him before I still kept bracing myself for it.

"Some square from around the way. She got him so fooled. She knows how to play the roll. She had to do something when she got cutoff from me."

"So what is she doing with Steve?"

"He's probably just around for her DL thrills. That girl's a mess."

"How do you know all this?"

He opened my car door. "I got eyes and ears everywhere." Then he winked at me. As he walked around the car he looked at his phone. He smiled and then he answered, he stood by the door for a minute. Then he got in the car. "Yea lets meet there. Haven't been there in a minute... Ok, see you there." He hung up. "You hungry?"

I didn't really eat breakfast I was too nerved up. "Yea actually"

"Good!" He started the car and we drove. I was happy we didn't see Steve and Toya outside. I felt like I could leave this all at the courthouse. I felt free in a sense. Andrew was holding my hand singing along with the radio. I guess I was the only worried party here.

"Baby can I ask you something?"

"Shoot" he said lowering the volume on the radio.

"Did you feel like I was overreacting about all this?"

"Not overreacting but definitely needlessly worried. You think I would let that fool lay a hand on you?"

"No, but we're not together 24 hours a day. The Bay ain't that big, if he wanted to, he could find me."

"You don't need to worry about all that."

"I didn't know your brothers were coming."

He nodded his head, "they wanted to see what was up."

"Is Toya scared of them?"

"I don't know, maybe."

"Should I be?"

"Why would you ask me something like that?

"She don't care about nobody or anyone but herself. She was about to act ugly in that courtroom, but she looked in the back she shut up and sat down. She doesn't even act like that with you. I was just wondering."

"She knows I won't touch her. I don't like hitting women, so she tries to provoke me. But my brothers on the other hand. Well they'll do what they have to when they need to."

"How does she know that though? I never thought of either of them as threatening until Derrick made me leave E&J's and even then I didn't think he was gonna hit me. Pick me up maybe."

"Lets just say she has to learn everything the hard way."

"Dare I ask what that means?"

"She knows my family in a different way. Nothing to stress about. You know how she is, that's it. " Then he turned the music back up a tad bit. But that was really telling me to drop it.

We were at a mom at pop looking place in Walnut Creek "Sophia's" it was an Italian food place. I recognized Derrick's car in the parking lot. There were a few more cars in the lot. A white lady greeted us when we stepped in the door, she knew Andrew. She looked at me and smiled, "is this her Andy?"

He smiled real proud, "yes it is!"

"Oh Andy she's beautiful!" She says as she hugged me. So I hugged her back but I had no idea who this woman was.

"Tracy this is my cousin Sophia." Andrew said

I was a little shocked at first but why should I have been. I hugged her again, "hello, it's nice to meet you."

"The boys are at your table." Then she hurried off.

We walked towards the kitchen down a hallway then into a banquet room. The smells from the kitchen made my mouth water. There was a big table in the middle of the floor. Derrick and Darryl were there laughing about something. There were two other guys I didn't know at the table.

"Drew! It's about time I was starting to think you weren't coming."

"Aw no, we had to get some paperwork taken care of. This is Tracy. Tracy this is Joseph and Jeff. They're my cousins too."

I shook their hands and then I sat in the seat next to Derrick. Sophia brought in bread olive oil and wine.

He smiled at me. "Don't be acting like you scared of me." His voice was happy and light hearted.

"I'm not. Just couldn't believe you did me like that."

He laughed, Darryl looked at him waiting for an explanation. So he told the story from his point of view. The way he told the story made everyone laugh. If I wasn't there it wouldn't sound as serious as it felt at the moment. But his version of the story mixed with my glass of wine helped me relax. Everyone was laughing and telling childhood stories. Joseph and Jeff, Sophia's little brothers, had great stories about the trouble they would all get into growing up. They were family on Andrew's grandfather side, their stories about the shock on people's faces when they told them they were related. We laughed about how stupid people are and their ideas of what family should look like. Sophia brought in clams and pasta, spaghetti with meatballs, a small lasagna, manicotti, spinach and ricotta ravioli then she sat down at the table with us. She was very sweet, and she mothered them.

"So Andy, when you gonna pop the question?"

Andrew blushed, "we've been talking about it."

"Nigga you getting married???" Darryl said

"Nigga where you been? She's here ain't she!" Derrick said

They both laughed, but I didn't get the joke other than them being a little younger. "What does that mean?" I asked

"They don't bring just anybody around me. They know how I am." Sophia said with a smile but her voice was slightly deeper.

"Oh well then I'm honored." I said

Then they started talking about all the family I needed to meet. My wine started to get to me and I needed to go to the restroom.

"I'll show you sweetheart." Sophia said, we walked through the main banquet hall and then someone from the kitchen needed her. So she pointed me towards the bathroom and then she went in the kitchen. The bathroom was small but very clean. It had two stalls in it. The walls and floors were a soft pink and cream. The stall dividers were pink. Then there were brown accents. It was very nicely put together. I went in one stall and then someone came in the bathroom. They pushed on my door. "Occupied," I said.

They stopped and went in the other stall. As I was washing my hands Toya came out of her stall with the biggest smile on her face. I sucked my teeth and rolled my eyes "really?"

"Yea really! I've been looking for you."

"Why?"

"What do you mean why?"

"I never understood why you cared about me so much in the first place." The water was still running over my hands.

"Simple, Drew was mine and you stole him."

"But I didn't, you took him from me."

"What?" She grimaced at me.

"We were dating when you came back and took him from me. Then you got pregnant. I didn't see him or meet your son until he was about a year old."

"Yea but I saw you at Hubby's house."

"That's what I'm saying, that was my first time seeing him in what seemed like forever. And I didn't even get with him then."

Her eyes turned evil, "you're lying! Andrew's gonna come back to me. He always does. I was his first, the only one who knows how to get him like I got him, and I will be his last."

"Ok, so then why be mad at me?"

"Cause I can't stand your goodie two shoes ways. You think you're better than me. AND THAT PISSES ME OFF!!" Then the bathroom door opened slowly and of course it was Steve. I thought I was gonna pass out. I turned off the water and grabbed paper towels to dry my hands I scanned the bathroom for something to throw at him. But why this fool gonna come in the bathroom walking all slow and dramatic. I was already scared enough now he had to be creepy. His eyes were red, couldn't tell if he had been crying or what.

"So where's your piece of paper?" Then he laughed. "You are so stupid to think that I would waste my time caring about you. I had more important things to do with my day then waste it on you in court."

"So why are you here?"

"Cause I want you to stop lying to me and tell me where my child is." Then he grabbed me by the arm. Toya smiled really big when he grabbed me. His grip felt like a vice grip it hurt and he kept squeezing making it worse. "Woman if you don't stop playing these games with me!"

Tears streamed down my face. "I'm not playing games. I lost the baby Steve, there is no baby!"

He backhand slapped me with his free hand. My vision blurred and I thought I heard a ringing in my ear. The right side of my face felt like it was on fire. Now I always thought if it ever came down to it that I would fight a man. But complete and total fear had me immobilized. Toya laughed, he raised his hand to strike me again, and this time I screamed at impact.

Toya's eyes got big. "Steve you need to get her out of here. Somebody's gonna hear."

"I don't care!"

She scoffed, "you are stupid! They might kill you for this. I'm out call me later if you can." She said as she headed for the door. He let go of my arm and grabbed my neck. "I trusted you! How could you betray me like this!" He screamed at me.

When Toya opened the door, Darryl was walking past. He did a double take when he saw Toya. She tried to run then you heard bumping in the hallway. Steve looked that way for half a minute then he started squeezing my neck. "You think I'm gonna let some other man have you!" It felt like my eyes were gonna pop out of my head. I was trying to hit him, kick him, scratch him anything to get free. Then the door swung open. Darryl had Toya by the ponytail.

"Nigga if you don't put your hands down right now you're guaranteed to leave here in a body bag!"

Steve slowly released his grip. "I don't want no problems. This is between me and her."

As soon as air hit my lungs I hurried to the toilet and threw up. Everything in my body hurt!

"Darryl, I told him to stop. But he wouldn't listen to me!" Toya was pleading.

"But you brought him here! You know better!"

Then I heard footsteps. It sound like a sonic boom happened! Steve's body hit the tile.

"Wait a minute! Lets think about this!" I couldn't tell if that was Joseph or Jeff.

Then Joseph came in the stall. That big thing definitely ran in the family. He didn't seem like the guy we were just laughing with. "Stand up! Let me see you!" He said helping me up. His blue eyes were piercing as he looked at my neck. Then he tilted my head from left to right. He turned red, and he called out. She's got hand marks on her neck, her lip is busted, and both sides of her face are bruised. Then he turned around and booted Steve! "You coward!" Steve's eyes looked crazy. I didn't understand what happened to the guy I used to know. The guy I used to cuddle with, the guy I used to swear was my everything. This person was like a cracked out version of him. Nothing like the man I loved once upon a time.

"Send her out!" Andrew's voice came booming through the madness.

When Joseph motioned for me to come out, Steve punched me in the thigh.

"Are you kidding me right now?" Darryl said laughing, "you must want to die!" Joseph kicked him again. Darryl had Toya on the ground with his foot in the middle of her back. All I could think was what about the baby. But clearly she didn't care or else she wouldn't have come here. I did my best to walk out the bathroom. All the men were huge and their eyes were cold.

Andrew was standing in the doorway. "Go back to the room. When you have the restraining order in your hand call 911!" His voice was calm, and commanding, but he didn't look at me. His eyes were fixed on Steve.

"Andrew!" I didn't know what he was about to do, and I was scared.

He didn't raise his voice, "go!"

But I could tell he meant it. I felt horrible when I walked out to the main dining room no one was in there. All the customers were gone and the closed sign was in the window. Sophia came out the kitchen; she started crying when she saw me. Then I heard Steve screaming. She put her arms around me as we walked to the banquet room. I opened my purse pulled out the restraining order. Then I dialed 911.

"911 what's your emergency?"

"Please send someone quick! I've been attacked by my ex boyfriend who I have a restraining order on!"

"Where are you located?"

"I'm at Sophia's restaurant in Walnut Creek." The operator read off the address. "I guess I don't know the address."

The operator placed the call. "Ma'am where is the assailant now?"

"He's fighting..." Then I started crying and I couldn't stop. Sophia rubbed my back. I couldn't talk I was crying so hard. "He... He..." I'll tell you something the police in Walnut Creek respond a lot faster than they would've in Richmond. When we heard the cars pulling up, I told the operator they were there. Sophia told me to go open the door. Toya was sitting at a table with her hands on her face. The two officers at the door immediately put their hands at their waste.

"Back up! Where is he?"

"Officer he's back here!" Jeff said

Darryl walked past them and sat at the table with Toya. I couldn't hear what he was saying to her, but she was visibly shook up, she was crying real tears. Two more cars pulled up and shortly after an ambulance arrived. I went back in the banquet room. Sophia stayed with me rubbing my back. A female and male officer came to me. They took pictures of my face and neck, and then they told me to go to the hospital. But then they asked me to stay until they got statements from everyone. They took pictures of everything; they called up my restraining order information. One officer whistled when he saw that the order was signed hours ago. "This guy wastes no time!"

Andrew walked in the banquet hall with his hands in his pockets. He was talking to an officer. He hadn't looked at my face yet, and my heart dropped when I thought of how he'd react when he saw me. He stood next to me and then he put his hand on my arm, he didn't know this arm was sore from Steve grabbing me by my arm. I didn't realize it was sore until he touched it. I jumped which made both of them look at me. Andrew's eyes got big then angry when he looked at me. I looked at his hand; it was bruised worse than before. The other hand was in his pocket. The officer gave him his card and told us to let them know what the hospital found if anything. When we walked out the banquet room. Toya was in handcuffs, and she was complaining about pain. The female officer was telling her that she was going to escort her to the county hospital, after that she was going to be taken in for violating the restraining order. She looked really sorry and she shot pleading eyes at Andrew. He was so angry they bounced right off of him.

"What happened to the ambulance?" I asked

Opening the door Andrew looked me in the face, his eyes were cold. "They rushed him to the hospital."

Derrick's car wasn't in the parking lot anymore. I didn't know if he and Darryl rode together or not. But they were gone. We went straight to the hospital, which was up the street. In the ER it wasn't crowded as it was only midday, but the few people who were there looked at me with questioning looks. They took us to separate rooms and they asked me what happened. After they examined me they told me I was going to be fine and to keep cold compresses on my face and lip. They told Andrew just about the same thing. Andrew got print outs of everything and he said he' d fax them. We rode home in silence. Amber called to tell him that she was picking Andre up, and she'd keep him with her.

When we came inside the house Andrew set the alarm and then he followed me up the stairs. Toya's words kept playing over and over in my head.

"Andrew?"

"Yea." He sat on the couch he was about to turn on the TV.

"Were you with Toya when we met?"

He looked at me. "No"

"Did you sleep with her anytime after we got back together?"

"No" there was no expression in his face

"Do you still love her?"

"I love the person that I used to know. But her as a person no."

"If we broke up, would you get back with her?" He sucked his teeth. "I have to hear you say it."

189

"No! You see the stuff she does. We're getting too old for these games. She dang near got him killed...." Then he shook his head. "Seems like he's gonna be this way regardless though."

"I'm gonna be honest with you. I'm afraid of being in this house alone. He's not going to leave me alone. He doesn't care about my restraining order. He's gonna get out and he's gonna be looking for me." I started crying.

Andrew hopped off the couch and was holding me in less than what seemed like a second. "Tracy, you don't have to worry about him." He rubbed my back.

"Andrew! Please move in! Please!" I grabbed his shirt. "I was already scared before. Now!"

"It's gonna be ok. Tracy you're safe!"

"How do you know? Toya said she don't like me cause I act like a goodie two shoe! Do you think I act like that?"

Andrew smiled, "well you are compared to her. But I love you for it!"

I felt like a child. "So that's a good thing?"

"You grew up a different way, you had a different life. Don't ever sink to her level."

"K!" Then I felt sleepy but every time I thought about dosing off I'd see Steve's hand extending to slap me. I wondered if that's how Karen felt the night after I slapped her? I almost felt sorry for doing her like that, almost.

CHAPTER 26

Out of the blue Marie called me. We hadn't talked in what felt like forever! She didn't even know I bought a house, or that Andrew and I were back together. I told her everything from A to Z. She took a lot of pleasure in knowing that I slapped the mess out of Karen. Marie used to go to service with my parents she was very aware of Karen's double lifestyle. I invited her over for dinner on Saturday. Amber, Derrick, Darryl, my parents, my brother and sister in law were all coming over for dinner. Andrew said it was time for everyone to get to know each other. When I told Andrew that Marie was coming, I could see him shuffling through his mental Rolodex trying to place her. I tell him all the time that my family is huge, but I guess if he hasn't seen them how would he know.

Last week Andrew brought me two dogs. A two-year-old Rottweiler named Eve, and a Rottweiler puppy he named Cain. Eve was already trained and Cain is in school. I feel so much better being home alone on the nights Andrew doesn't come over. That doesn't happen too often, but sometimes he's had to fly a few places Andre is always with me, and he's a joy to have. I haven't seen or heard from his mother since that day at the restaurant.

After they released Steve from the hospital he went to the county jail. Something happened in there and he was sent back to the hospital. Andrew said he was gonna be released soon and yes, I royally freaked out. Andrew asked me if I wanted a gun, but the thought of that scared me as well. So that's when we talked about the dogs. They could go running with me, to the store, just about anywhere. Andre was so excited about the dogs when they came. We let Cain sleep with him while Eve sleeps on the floor next to my bed. Joy told me she wasn't coming over anymore, but I assured her that they were extremely good dogs and she wouldn't have to meet them unless she wanted to.

It was so much easier last time when I had the dinner catered, but to keep the evening intimate and real I decided I would cook what started out as a simple meal. I decided to make a chocolate toffee fudge cake that was inspired by Chef Emeril. I made a few changes to the cake to make it my own. As if the cake wasn't rich enough I added caramel between one of the three layers, and rum between another layer with the ganache. Then I made a couple red velvet cakes, one with pecans, and one without. I made the cakes on Thursday after work and the boys promised they wouldn't touch them. Friday I prepared everything almost to the finish. I made smothered cubed steaks, garlic loaded mashed potatoes, a pot of greens, Saturday morning I put a whole chicken in the oven as a beef alternative.

Marie arrived at the same time as Amber. I gave both of them a tour of the house. Having the house fully furnished did give me a sense of home. And I loved to look at the house all said and done. Andrew spent over a hundred thousand in the end. He didn't even flinch as I ran a muck picking things out etc. in the end I had this gorgeous house.

Amber really liked the house; she said it was exactly the way she imagined Andrew and I living. When we got to my bedroom Marie said, "this is where the magic happens!"

I got embarrassed and Amber belly laughed. Marie had forgotten that Amber was Andrew's mother not his sister and even then I still would've been embarrassed.

"It's ok honey, you guys are in love." She patted my shoulder, I shot Marie a look. She mouthed "sorry". My brother Terrence and sister in-law Amy arrived. Terrence entertained Amber with stories from our childhood. Amy and Marie helped me setup the table. Marie played bartender and made us all something to sip on.

My parents arrived a little later, my mom keeps asking why I haven't been to service in so long. I told her I don't want to discuss it right now. I know it hurts her feelings, but the thought of looking Karen in her face knowing what I know now.... It's hard to keep my composure. She knows my man in a way I'd rather forget. Toya was before me, but Karen was during me. Even after us being together that first year plus she was still a factor. My heart can't deal with that right now.

My mom and Amber hit it off which was a relief. I didn't see any reason why they wouldn't get along, but you know how sometimes some females don't mix well even though everything else says they should.

Andrew arrived with his brothers and Andre last. When they walked in the door they all had serious faces and they were talking about something tense. Andrew's face softened when he saw me. I love to recognize that change in his face. That equates to love to me. Andrew told me he was going to give them a quick tour of the house and then we'd be ready to eat. When I came back into the family room Andre was in his grandmother's arms while she and my mom chatted. When I walked over to Amy and Marie, Marie says, "who is the chocolate cutie?"
"You have to be more specific. They're both chocolate." And of course she couldn't be. They hadn't been introduced yet.

When Andrew came down with his brothers he introduced them to everyone. I noticed that neither one of them let the "N Bomb" slip once during dinner. Everyone was polite and courteous until the battle of the bay came up. My family are diehard 49er fans and of course Andrew's family support the Raiders. So there was a lot of back and forth banter but everyone kept it lighthearted and nice. Andrew helped me bring out the desserts. My mom smiled exceptionally big.
"You made and decorated these cakes yourself?" Amber asked with really big eyes.
"Yes, I hope you like them." I said feeling a little pressure, and saying a silent prayer as she put her first full fork of red velvet to her mouth. Her eyes rolled into her head. I smiled a smile of relief. Darryl told me I was in the family! He said he was going to need regular cake sessions to maintain my position in the family though.

Then Derrick stood up, but when he looked at Andrew, Andrew shook his head so Derrick sat down. Everybody kind of looked at each other. Andrew blew air and then he stood up.
"Thank you everyone for coming out tonight." Then he shot

Derrick a look, Derrick smiled. "Tracy and I know how busy you all are so we appreciate the fact that you're here that much more." My mom smiled at me, and then I realized Amber was smiling at me too. "Just so you know, I wanted to have this meal catered but you know Tracy. She was determined to have a personal hand preparing this meal." Then he turned to me. "Tracy I know our lives aren't perfect, and that things can get a little chaotic around us at times." Darryl busted up laughing; Derrick elbowed him to cut it out. Andrew shot Darryl a look and he straightened up like a child would for their father. "Ever since I saw you at that engagement party, you're all I think about. I can't imagine my life without you. " Then he got down on one knee, "I have a question for you that is long over due." Everyone was looking at me with big smiles on their faces. "Tracy, will you marry me?"

The words I was beginning to think were never gonna come from him, just came out of his mouth! "YES!"

Then he pulled out a blue tiffany box, he slowly opened exposing a ring that was so beautiful! It was a platinum setting a heart shaped center diamond, and blue sapphires on each side, and another diamond on each side of that. The jewels captured the light in the room beautifully and the stones looked like they were moving they sparkled so brightly. I hugged him and squeezed him so tight. Everybody cheered and congratulated us. Our families were instantly excited about the wedding. They started hitting us with all kinds of questions.

"You guys we haven't had an opportunity to go over the details yet. We will keep you in the loop as soon as we decide." Andrew said

Andrew and his mom were hugging and congratulating each other when Marie scooted in close to me. She put her hand out to hold my hand. Her eyes got big, "THIS IS BEAUTIFUL! How much do you think it cost?" She asked in a way that only someone close to me could ask.

I tried to keep my voice low, "girl I don't know"

"All I know is that ring shows how much you're loved!"

"Well if all he could afford was a string I'd be just as happy."

"Un huh says the lady with the FAT ring. " we both laughed. "It's Gorgeous! Congratulations sweetheart."

Andre came and sat on my lap he was smiling from ear to ear. Then he motioned for me to come closer so he could whisper in my ear. But you know how three years old can't whisper; he says "are you going to be my real mommy now?" Then he looked at me with the biggest grin.

"I'll be your stepmom is that ok?" He shook his head no. "Why not?"

"Charlie said step moms are mean. I told him my mom is mean but my mommy is nice."

How does this little boy know to say this to me? "How about this, tomorrow we will have a family meeting to decide. How does that sound?" Andre hugged me tight. I didn't realize almost everybody was watching us. I got embarrassed; Andrew and his mom had the same expression on their faces. They were smiling from ear to ear; Amber had a tear in her eye.

The night seemed to spiral after that everyone was having a good time enjoying each other's company. Every once in awhile Andrew and I would lock eyes. His eyes would become so soft and gentle whenever our eyes met.

"Excuse me gentlemen," Andrew announced in the Family room. "As a special thank you I ask each one of you to roll up your sleeves and help me bust some manly suds." Darryl blew air and shook his head. "Especially you two!" He pointed to his brothers.

"I'm coming daddy!" Andre said hopping out of my lap. Andrew hit a muscle pose and Andre did the same. My dad and Terrence followed them into the kitchen.

Derrick and Darryl murmured in the corner, and then Amber snapped her fingers and they both jumped into the kitchen. Everybody laughed, the boys were laughing as well. All you heard was Darryl comically complaining.

"Welcome to the family!" Amber said hugging me again

"Thank you! Thank you!"

"You know we should do something just us girls."

"We should, I like that idea." I said

"What's on the agenda for tomorrow?" Amber said

"I have service in the morning, but I'm free after that." My mom said

"Me too" Amy said

"If I can bunk here I can roll." Marie said

"That's fine with me." I said, "what does everyone want to do?"

Amber leaned in, "I say we have a pamper day".

"That sounds good to me!" My mom said

"Any opposed?" Of course there were no objections. "Cool! I'll set everything up for tomorrow. Lets meet here at 1:30." Everyone agreed.

Marie had a bag packed in her car just in case she decided to stay. That was the way we used to always operate. We'd prepare to spend the night at each other's house whenever we got together.

Soon everyone was gone. I told Marie to stay up so that I could introduce her to Eve and Cain. When I went outside the dogs were patrolling the yard. They didn't make a peep all night. They were quietly watching over everything and everyone. When I brought them into the guest room they stood besides me watching Marie. Then I told them it was ok to say hello. Cain approached her first, and instantly he was in love. Eve followed suit and Marie had two puppies loving her. I told her that Eve would stay downstairs with her. I asked if she preferred for Eve to sleep on the floor or outside the door. She chose the floor. So I told her what commands to say and how to say them. Then I left the happy couple downstairs. Since Marie was spending the night I told her not to open any outside doors or windows, I didn't set the motion detectors for the hallways downstairs or the kitchen. Andrew was tucking Andre in when Cain and I came into his bedroom. The two of them were always so cute and heart warming to watch. I always thought that fathers would be hard on their sons and less affectionate. But Andrew hugs his son, tucks him in at night, plays with his son, and he always tells him he loves him. All winners in my book. I gave Andre a kiss as well. He had a very big smile on his face as he said, "goodnight parents."

The thought of it touched my heart to think how devastating it was to find out about him, to now not even know how to picture life without him. We were barely out of André's room when Andrew turned me towards him and picks me up. So I wrapped my legs around him and put my arms around his neck. I was staring into his beautiful brown eyes. He carried me into the bedroom and shut the door behind him. "So Mrs. Wallace when would you like to set the date for?"

"I don't know, but I want to say thank you for loving me with all my faults and insecurities." Then I kissed him very passionately.

"Ooh! You can't be kissing me like that unless you're asking for it."

"Maybe I am!" I said and then I kissed him again. Up until tonight our lovemaking had always been gentle and kind. Tonight was full of passion, lust and pushing each other to the limit! He did things I didn't know he was capable of. I felt things I didn't know I could feel. My body orgasmed repeatedly, my toes curled so far up I thought they would cramp up, but they didn't. That did it! This man was more powerful than I could've imagine. He came twice before he needed a ten-minute break, then he was ready again. But even during that ten-minute break, he still had me going. I couldn't believe how freaky this man was, or how flexible he was. All I knew was at the moment when my mouth was completely dry, my body was completely drenched in sweat, and I couldn't feel my legs there was no way this man could ever leave me! I could see why Toya lost it. I couldn't understand how she could lower her standards to be with Steve. He may be handsome and have a few tricks up his sleeves, but that was all null and void the moment I got with Andrew. I know it's not fair to compare them, but I couldn't help it. Andrew held me tight, he told me he loved me again, and then we both passed out intertwined in each other's limbs. When I woke up a few hours later in the early morning Andrew was staring at me. He knew I'd try to run to brush my teeth so he pinned me to the bed and made me kiss him. That got us going again but this time we made gentle love. The Beast was making a slave out of me. I wanted to go running, but the Beast had me on my back obeying his every command. When I woke up, from round.... Six I think that was, Andrew was still knocked out. I sat there looking at him. I counted two passion marks on his neck. I wondered how he'd react when he saw them. I wondered if he'd freak out when he saw them or if he'd be okay with them. I wondered if he could still go again. This was a test; I needed to honestly know how much stamina I was dealing with here. So I kissed him, the thought of me coming on to him excited me. His red eye popped open. He looked at me in disbelief. Completely well almost completely spent he rolled over. The beast slowly rose his head to salute me. He wasn't at full salute but I could definitely work with him. Because the beast was so blessed I didn't need a full salute to feel full, but this time I took the drivers seat. Upon impact my body went right back to orgasm mode. When we were done I passed out on top of him, "woman! You're trying to kill me!" He jokingly whispered in my ear. I smiled as I fell asleep again.

When I woke up Andrew was opening his eyes at the same time. "I feel so drained," Andrew said with a smile on his face.

"Well you should. I love you!"

"I love you!" We kissed again, you never did answer my question." I looked at him with a question mark expression. "When do you want to get married?"

"Soon, BUT I want enough time to be able to order my dress."

"So I need a timetable."

"Lets say at least a year."

"Tracy! That's too long?"

"That gives enough time to plan and arrange things as needed."

"Baby that's too long. We're just about living as husband and wife now. I don't want to wait that long."

"But you don't live here. You're here all the time but you don't live here. Why won't you move in?"

"Cause, were not married yet. Once were married then we'll officially live as though we are."

I sucked my teeth and got off of him. I put my back to him. "Why is that an issue?" He said putting his arm around me spooning me.

"I don't understand where this is coming from?" I said angrily

"Where what is coming from?"

"You won't technically move in here. So why keep playing this game!" That fast I could feel anger turning in my stomach. "What difference does it make at this point when you move in? You're paying all the bills here, you only go there maybe once or twice in a whole month. It doesn't matter how many times I tell you I'm afraid to be here without you, you won't even do it for me! Andre can move in but you can't! You're too precious!"

"Tracy! You're being ridiculous! I never said any of that."

"You don't have to. It shows! Did you ask me to marry you to appease me?"

He looked at me; I could tell that question was too far. "I'm done with this. You're going with mom today right?"

"What do you mean you're done with this? I'm not done!" I said sitting up.

"You're being stupid right now, and instead of letting this irritation continue I'm changing the subject." He said as he got out the bed.

"I'm being stupid? I'm being stupid? I'm not being stupid, I just don't understand what the big deal is. Why can't we be here together all the time? I'm scared!"

"I told you, you have no reason to be scared. You need to stop being so paranoid."

"You would be scared too if you knew someone wanted you dead just because you don't love them anymore."

"I told you, you don't have to worry about them no more. Toya's not gonna mess with you anymore. She's not stupid."

"So she's not stupid, only me?" He blew air then he walked into the bathroom to pee. "Andrew are you sleeping with her?" He made a disgusted sound, but gave no answer. He looked in the mirror while he washed his hands. I watched him inspect himself. When he saw me looking he rolled his eyes. "You didn't answer me." I said

"That's a dumb question!"

"Maybe it is, but I'm waiting for your answer." Jealousy was raging in my stomach.

"How could you be so insecure especially after last night?"

"You're not answering the question!"

His voice lowered and was full of bass. "Thank you for ruining my morning." He snatched his clothes off the floor. When he reached for his pants I hopped up and grabbed them too. I could tell he was mad, but I didn't care, I wanted to hear his answer. "I will walk out of here with no pants on." I kept pulling on the pants. So he let them go and I fell completely helpless backwards on the bed. When I sat up he was trying not to laugh at me. This made me angry, so I took a running start and I jumped on him. I wrapped my legs around him. "Answer me!"

"Tracy stop!" He said now laughing.

I gently bit his ear, "no!" I said trying to stop him from putting his clothes on.

"Stop it!" He said trying to push me away. I then decided to mark up his entire neck or any part of his body I could get my mouth on. When I latched onto his neck it was as if he read my mind he just blew air. He just stood there while I climbed all over him sucking on him. "Um Tracy, you do know that in the world of females this just makes me more desirable. Keep going if that's what you desire."

I sucked my teeth and then I threw my body dramatically on the bed. This has to be PMS causing tears to seep out of my eyes even though my eyes were closed. What's happening to me? The Beast is just making me so insecure. I didn't even want to deal with myself. What am I gonna do? If this man cheats on me I'll be devastated, I can't keep going like last night and this morning. My family is so excited about our engagement. I don't know what to do, but I don't like this person that I'm becoming. I put my face in the pillow, and tried my best to muffle my cry. He walked out the door and I cried louder. I ran a bath, sitting in the warm water I stared at the ring. What did it mean about the rest of our lives? Why would he even love someone who's acting like I've been acting? My mind was racing a mile a minute. I had my eyes closed, I didn't hear anyone come in the room, but I could feel eyes on me. When I opened my eyes Andrew was standing in the doorway. I screamed! "Make some noise when you walk!"

"Didn't mean to scare you." Then he came and sat on the edge of the tub. "What's happening to us?"

"Baby, I'm sitting here wondering the same thing."

"I realize we have some unfinished business to discuss. But with your cousin downstairs, and you guys hanging out with mom's today I think now isn't the right time although it feels like this time has been chosen for us. What do we do?"

"Can we go over the basics right now?"

"Yes," he said kind of sounding defeated.

"Why would you propose to me?"

"Why would I..." He put his hands on his face. He took a deep breath. "Baby, I know that fool has gotten in your head. I know all this is outside of your level of dealing with. But you gotta let Steve go! I don't know what his deal is, and I don't care. But what he does to you pisses me off. He makes you second-guess who you are. He makes you second-guess everything you know to be true. Now you're doubting me."

It was silent for a few minutes. "Sweetheart, what you're saying is true. But there is another aspect to our relationship. Our lack of trust."

His eyes glazed over, "what do you mean?"

"I hate to keep beating a dead horse but, you left me for Toya. Call her what you want to today, but yesterday she was special enough to leave me for. You came back, but you brought Karen a long. In both cases you brought it to me. I have to respect you for that much. But at what point do you think I start to doubt the limits of your love for me? Sleeping with you doesn't automatically make you the faithful kind. Sleeping with you has only intensified my insecurities. I now understand why Toya acts so crazy about losing you. I don't understand why Karen hasn't yet."

"Ok so that's me, I didn't handle everything right. But you are the queen of running. Instead of fighting for your man. You let me go. When I came back to talk it out, who do I see walking in your apartment? Steve! Made me feel like you had been playing me the whole time. That's the reason you didn't care about me leaving. Despite that I still wanted you. Yea I came on a little strong but I wanted you. When we do get back together out of the blue might I add, I had something going on at the time. I didn't want to pass up the opportunity to be with you again. But did you think we'd be married just like that? What was I supposed to do? Just snap my fingers and be on board with being celibate for the next three years? Each time I came to you, you didn't find out from someone else that I was doing somebody else. So now you're questioning me like there's something to find out. I love you, but all these insecurities are driving me crazy."

"Oh so I'm the only one insecure? You can't even let me enjoy a lunch with somebody. Not screwing them, not even kissing them. Just eating, and you send your brother in scary mode to force me out. Matter of fact how did it just so happen that your brother ends up at the same restaurant at the exact right moment? Knowing where everybody lives? Do you have people following me?" His face changed to a surprised but busted expression. "You have people following me!!!!" I stood up in the bathtub. "You have people following me? So you don't trust me?"
I could tell he was trying to choose his words. Every time he thought he had a good answer he'd rethink the answer. "Yes and

no. Yes, I have people follow you. But it's not about trust anymore. It's about your safety."

"WHAT????"

"Ok I know it sounds bad, but let me explain!"

I stood there waiting, but he wasn't answering. "That's why you didn't remember Marie cause she fell through the cracks. You can be as secure as all get out. You know beyond a shadow of a doubt that I'm not cheating on you. But what about me? Who's been following me? How are you doing this?"

He put his hands on my shoulders, and slowly pushed me to sit back down. "Like I said I saw Steve going in your apartment minutes after we break up. I thought it could've been a coincidence, but he was ALWAYS around after that. I didn't know what to think about you two. You wanted to stay with him, fine. I left you alone, kind of. Every once in awhile I'd check up on you. So fast-forward, I'm seeing Karen and a few others. Nothing serious though, now you're open to the idea of us again. I didn't know the details of your falling out with him for a while; you can be tight lipped when you wanna be. I love you, I've loved you from the moment I laid eyes on you, but love doesn't automatically bring trust. I know some people would like to believe that, but it doesn't. So yes I've had people follow you since we've gotten back together. There's always somebody watching this house. They follow you to work, to lunch, to the grocery store. On your runs."

"When were you gonna tell me this? Maybe it might've made me feel a little better about being in this house alone. I don't know how to feel about the rest."

"We can talk about this some more later. But just know that I know you love me. I wouldn't intentionally do anything to hurt you. You don't have to guess about me. I tell you what you need to know."

"Well I need to know it all!" I said getting out of the tub. That was a lot to take in. As I walked past him. I paced in the room. I don't know why, but I did. He sat on the bed watching me. I was talking to myself, trying to sort out all of the details. "I DONT

KNOW WHAT TO DO!!!!!" He sat there watching me freak out.
"Stop messing with me! Is your family some kind of mob family?"

He laughed, "you're so dramatic!"

"Is that a yes or no?"

"No, but we're not like your family. Different backgrounds for sure."

"What does that mean?"

"I am a College educated man from Oakland, I know what's up, and sometimes what needs to be done is done. That simple."

"What does that mean? Are you a drug dealer?"

He blew air, "calm down this isn't some after school special."

"Andrew that isn't a yes or no."

"Tracy, you are acting crazy. No I'm not a drug dealer. I go to work everyday just like you. I make six figures a year, but that's just for now." He smiled

"I feel like I'm taking crazy pills!"

"Why?"

"I don't know what's real?"

Then he rushed me, I could tell his patience was wearing thin. He grabbed my arms. "TRACY!!!! Cut it out! I just told you I love you! I tell you I want to spend my life with you, and that a year is too long to wait. From that you're freaking out. Accusing me of cheating on you, accusing me of being a drug dealer. Are you looking for a reason? If you don't love me, tell me now. But stop this!"

My eyes got big because he's never grabbed me or rushed me. For a minute my brain tricked me and it wasn't even Andrew. My towel fell to the floor, and I was frozen. He didn't get it at first, but when he saw how stuck I was he had regret all over his face. He tried to hug me but I stood there, everything was silent. "Ok just breathe! Just breathe! You guys need to separate for the day. Tracy, keep it together!" I looked at the time it was 10:30. I went on autopilot; I went in the closet picked out an outfit. Andrew was talking to me but I don't even know what he said. Then he sat there looking at me. I hopped in the shower. Andrew kept following me and watching me. Once I was dressed, I walked out the bedroom door. Marie and Andre were watching a movie in the family room. Marie smiled at me, "good morning sleepy head".

"Good morning." I said, I sat next to Marie who then realized what time it was. She went back in her room to shower and ready herself.

Andrew sat at the table in the kitchen watching me. Andre climbed into my lap. "Remember you said we could have a family meeting."

"Yes I do."

"Daddy!" He called out. "Family meeting!" Andrew came in the family room and sat next to me. "I want Tracy to be my mommy."

"But she is, she's your step mom."

"But.... I want a real mommy."

"I know this is hard to understand, but Toya is your real mom." Andrew said

"But she's mean. I want Tracy to be my mommy."

"How about this, whatever you and Tracy decide is what it will be."

Andre smiled really big. "Please!!!!"

This little booger was persistent. "Fine Andre! How can I resist you?"

Andre ran to the kitchen to get a Capri Sun. His dad told him to drink it at the kitchen table.

"Are you ok?" His eyes were full of concern. I shook my head yes, although my mind was turning over. He watched my eyes he was reading me. "I'm sorry!" He said as he hugged me. I didn't say anything or react.

"Aw!" Marie said as she walked into the room.

Andrew kept looking at me, but he didn't say anything. The dogs were in the backyard. Suddenly they both ran to the side of the house, but they didn't bark. Then the doorbell rang. It was my mom and Amy. They were so excited and full of energy. Andrew was at the kitchen table with Andre. They were having thumb

wars, as Andrew privately watched me. Everyone was so excited
that no one noticed how I was just existing. When Amber arrived,
she came in the door full of energy and excitement. She told
everyone our limo was waiting outside, but she asked for lotion.
My mom and everyone went outside as we were going up the stairs
she said, "honey what's wrong?"

"What makes you think something's wrong?" I said trying to
plaster a smile on my face.

At the top of the stairs she put her hand on my shoulder.
"Honey I can read your face."

I took her by the hand, and brought her into my bedroom and
shut the door. "I was freaking out this morning. I was going from
A to Z; I know I was working his last nerve. In an attempt to make
his point he grabbed my arms. It has me a little shaken. He's never
done that before, and he became apologetic right away. It scared
the life out of me."

She hugged me, "he should know better! It's gonna be ok
sweetheart. Today were gonna go get massages, facials, Mani's,
and Pedi's. Oh we're gonna swing by and pick Sophia up too." I
smiled. "Tracy, I don't know all the dynamics of your relationship,
but I know you've been through a lot. Let some time pass get some
space today. Tonight it'll be better." She gave me a sympathetic
hug. And then we were off.

Our first stop was to pickup Sophia. Her house was
wonderful, and in a beautiful neighborhood in walnut creek. My
mom and Amy shot me funny looks when they saw Sophia. I loved
how Amber only said this is my cousin and there was nothing else
to explain. But I know my mom would be asking me later how this
white woman and Amber were related.

As if everyone wasn't already having a good time Sophia was
just what the doctor ordered for me. Pretty soon my nerves were
gone and we were all laughs and giggles. She made a HUGE fuss
over my ring. She and Everybody else had stars in their eyes about
the wedding.

"When do you think it will be?" Sophia asked

"Well, I told Andrew we needed a year to order my dress and plan." Everyone's smiles dropped. "But he says that's too long?" everyone started clapping like they were on a game show talking about "good answer." I laughed, "that's asking for a complete stress out! How in the world?"

"Oh my goodness child. Hire a wedding planner! Pay someone else to stress for you. And as far as your dress see if you can RUSH order it." Sophia said, "I would offer to cater for you, but I want enjoy the event I don't wanna be stuck in the kitchen."

"That's totally understandable and I wouldn't ask you to be." We ended up at a spa in Napa. It was completely plush! They rolled out the red carpet all the way. Champagne and fresh fruit. They had us strip down to our undies and walk around in plush robes and slippers. We had bottomless champagne service, top of the line everything. My facial was amazing; I fell asleep during the massage. My masseuse said I had knots and a lot of tension through out my body. When I woke up everything was relaxed, I felt great. I even fell asleep during my leg and foot massage.

Sophia jokingly said, "girl are you pregnant? All this falling asleep you're doing. I instantly looked at my mother's face and she had a horrified look.

"No!" I said, and then I started doing the count in my head. Maybe I was a little late, but I needed to look at the calendar. I thought Andrew and I were very careful to avoid exactly this. But nothing's a hundred percent right. Suddenly I felt a hot flash, Sophia and Amber cracked up. I shook my head at my mom to say no. But she kept looking at me out the corner of her eye.

"I'm not gonna stress about this." I kept telling myself.

Amber bought everyone gift baskets full of treats from the day. When we dropped Sophia off she told me to bring my family by the restaurant for dinner any day.

When everyone went their separate ways I went straight to my bedroom looking for the calendar. My calendar had nothing marked, but I knew I had a period the month before. I would have to wait until tomorrow.

CHAPTER 27

I sat on the bed in shock. What if I was pregnant? I don't want to be a pregnant bride. If Andrew thought a year was too far away he'd hate my answer if I was actually preggers. Eve looked at me while I sat there looking devastated. I heard Andrew come in the front door. Eve walked to the door sniffing, she watched me until I let her out. She and Cain went down to the boys. Andrew tucked Andre in then he and Eve returned to the room. When he walked in the room his eyes were on me the whole time. I looked at him with pleading eyes. "What's wrong?"

I braced myself for his reaction. "Do you know when my last period was?"

He stopped dead in his tracks. I could see his mind going a mile a minute. "Are you pregnant?"

"Sophia and your mom made the joke today because I kept falling asleep in all my massages. I can't remember when my last period was to start to count whether I'm a little or a lot late. I thought I was PMS'ing today, but could it be?"

"But we've been very careful." Andrew said

"I know, but nothing is a hundred percent." I started to feel nervous, was Andrew gonna flip out too? Once Steve had me trapped that's when he started acting like a crazy person.

Andrew sat on the bed next to me. He put his arms around me. "Are you scared?" I shook my head yes. "You shouldn't be. We'll figure it out no matter what the situation is."

I looked up at him; first thing I saw was all the passion marks on his neck. I felt bad about them, even though two of them were genuinely there. "Are you mad?"

"Why would I be?"

"Cause we said no babies until after the wedding." I still kept preparing myself for him to change up and go off at some point.

"Babies happen, that's a silly something to be mad about. Besides we don't know for sure, it's all speculation right now. Are you gonna be mad at me if you are?"

"Why would I be mad at you?"

"You seem to keep going back and forth in your mind. Like everything I do is compared to your past. Maybe you just wanna be mad at me. I don't know that's what it felt like earlier today. Like you were looking for something to be mad about. If you act like that again I'm just gonna walk away from you."

I laid my head on his shoulder. "I'm sorry. I was panicking."

"No kidding!" I kissed him. "You were drinking?"

"Yes, but we were drinking before the thought was planted. And if you would've saw the look my mother gave me. I told her I wasn't, but she was watching me so I had to keep drinking." Then I swallowed hard. "I told her I'd come to service with her on Sunday."

"You want me to go with you?" He said sounding defeated.

"Please!"

He blew air. "Fine!" Then I kissed him. I kept kissing him, and then I started on his neck. "Aren't you a little tired?"

"Yes", I said still kissing him.

"Can we just hold each other tonight? I'm still spent from earlier. I mean I could go, but I could use a breather."

"Fine." I said pretending to give up. I don't know why I felt like I needed to go one more time. But I did. "Shower with me." I said raising him to his feet. I undressed him, and then I undressed myself. When we got in the shower he turned to the water. "You know you're too tall you block all the water. " I said forcing my way in front of him. His eyes looked over my body. "They said I had a lot of tension and knots in my body. Can you massage my shoulders?" I said turning my back to him. His hands were strong but gentle. I moaned because it felt good but also to mess with him. He kissed my shoulders; I could feel the heat from the Beast behind me. I moaned again, when he kissed my neck he went straight for my spot. If he wasn't on board before he was now. He picked me up, and I put my foot on the ledge/seat I had installed in this shower for occasions just like this. When the Beast came inside this was the first time we were skin to skin. I didn't have my diaphragm in either, I guess we were gonna go for it. The Beast was smooth like velvet. Andrew held me in a bear hug while he worked me from behind. Something about the Beast would have me shivering no matter which angle he approached me from. The thought occurred, what if I'm not pregnant and this gets me pregnant? But as soon as that thought hit me, I decided to turn around. I loved the sounds of making love and the faces that would come from Andrew. As he erupted lava hit the shower floor. You could tell all of his power was drained with it. I watched him wash down the drain. I didn't want him to do that, but I couldn't complain about it either. Andrew sat on the seat in the shower, his legs were weak and he was red. I finished our showers then I dried him off. As I was drying off, he picked me up and laid me on the bed. He kissed me until any thoughts I had of jumping him later were gone. As we laid in the bed our fingers intertwined. I wondered what our child would look like. What it would feel like to carry the seed of the man who loves you. To be excited about my baby.

****

As I walked in the door this morning my phone was ringing. It was my boss telling me about my commute across the bay this week. "Tracy I know you try avoid the city office as much as you can, but Tuesday through Thursday we need you here. Tuesday afternoon through Thursday morning."

Instantly I started to breakout into a sweat. As far as I know Steve still works out there. But then I remembered Andrew. "I absolutely have to be there?" Nervousness in my voice.

"It's our annual Symposium. They decided to have it in the city this time. I need my entire team there. We've got a lot of networking to do. Come in by noon to have lunch with the team."

My boss was telling me more than she was asking me. I get it business is business. As soon as we hung up I took my cellphone in the stairway and called Andrew at work. "I'm freaking out!"

"What does the calendar say?"

"I didn't get a chance to look. My boss was calling as soon as I walked into my cubical. I have to go to the city for the next three days."

Andrew was quiet for a few minutes. "Let me make a call, don't worry. I love you!"

"Love you!"

We hung up. I pulled out my calendar in my drawer. The tenth was circled in red. Today was the 32nd day. Ok! Ok! Don't freak out, I could just be late. I recounted six times to make sure my count was right. I broke out in a full body sweat! I mean sweat was trickling down my forehead and back. I turned on the fan. I sat there staring at my computer. Although I just got there a few minutes ago working from the office wasn't gonna work. I emailed my boss and told her I wasn't feeling well and that I would continue working from home. As I was packing up my laptop Andrew called me back.

"Ok so, you're gonna be driven to and from the city. Someone will be with you all day there always is."

"Ok, but I'm going home."

"Why? What's going on?"

The thought of letting the words come out of my mouth made tears fly out of my eyes. "I can't talk about it right now."

"Whoa! Ok! Ok!" I could tell he was fidgeting at his desk. "Ok, call me when you get there."

I packed up my things in lightning speed. On the way home I noticed a green civic was following me. I didn't recognize the person in the driver's seat. Once I pulled into my driveway the car drove on. I hurried inside, I set the alarm and I took the dogs upstairs with me. I logged into my laptop and my fingers went crazy. I typed up proposals, reviewed project prospectuses, created files. I was sweating and focused on my task at hand. I was on a conference call when I heard Andrew come in the door. The dogs went down to greet him. When he came in the door he kissed my cheek. He threw his bag on the couch and went to the bathroom. I thought he had to use the bathroom. But he came back with a cool towel and he started wiping down my face, neck, back, and chest. He smiled a evil grin when he got to my chest. But the towel felt great, I don't know why I didn't think of it. He sat on the bed and stared at me. As soon as the call was over I looked at him, "what?"

"How far along are you?"

"We don't know that I am. I'm just a few days late. It could just be stress."

"Lets hope for the best and plan for the worst."

"And what's the best in this situation?"

"You having my baby of course."

"Why would me not being knocked up be the worst?"

"Because we'll have to wait that much longer to get started. Plus you'll be overly paranoid, which just means more of yesterday. We don't want that crazy lady back.... EVER!"

"I'm sorry!" I felt terrible for my behavior.

"Aah! I just hope you're so understanding when I start freaking out."

"Does Andrew ever freak out?"

"Heck yea! I freak out, but normally you're freaking out at the same time so you don't notice me."

"Oh really?" Thinking about it, I guess I am a bit of a drama queen.

"Ok so!" He said clapping his hands. "Tomorrow Yussef is going to be in the city with you."

My mouth dropped. "You mean my assistant?"

He smiled at me and raised his eyebrows. "Told you I got eyes everywhere. It's just nice to be able to talk to you about this stuff. Only thing is you don't have to stop singing my praises to him." Yussef was hired to assist me with my projects, etc. he was a little younger than me, an excellent assistant. I couldn't believe he knew Andrew and told him everything I said about him. "Darryl will be dropping you off and picking you up."

"Who drives a green civic?"

"Green civic?"

"There was a green civic that seemed like it was following me today."

He picked up his cell phone and walked out the room.

I couldn't directly hear his conversation, but he had a serious tone while he was talking to someone. I started working again; I needed to direct a call. So I jumped on the phone and I opened the conference call. When Andrew came back in the room he took Eve with him and they went outside. I wished I wasn't stuck on the call so I could see what they were doing. Cain was by my feet playing with his toy. A hour later my call was over and I went downstairs and looked out the front window. Andrew was talking to a driver in a grey colored sedan. I saw that car all the time; I assumed they lived in this neighborhood cause the car was always outside as far as I could tell. "Web of lies!" I shook my head and went into the kitchen. I threw together a quick stir-fry with chicken over quinoa. Andrew came inside just as lunch was ready. His face was very serious. I pointed to his lunch on the kitchen table. He came and sat at the table. I looked at him waiting for him to speak. "I was talking to Curtis, the grey car. He saw the car as well. We don't know who that was. I don't like that." He was staring off thinking.

"It could've been a fluke." I said

"Yea, it could've been." He was silent for a while then he put a fork full of food into his mouth. That broke his stare, "this is delicious!"

"Thank you!" I smiled brightly and watched him enjoy his lunch.

"So when can we find out for sure?"

"With this symposium happening, I figure if I haven't started by Monday I'll go take a test."

"Do you think you're pregnant?"

"I don't think so. I haven't gained any weight, just been moody. But I associate moody to PMS."

"Isn't PMS and pregnancy just about the same thing?"

"I wouldn't know." I shrugged. Then our conversation from the day before played in my head. "Can I ask you something about something you said yesterday?"

"Sure?"

"You thought about me after you broke up with me?"

"Yea, I thought you would've understood that at the wedding."

I exhaled. "I wondered why you never called me. I thought you were in relationship bliss, and you had forgotten about me. After the wedding I tried not to think about you. I thought you hated me by the way you walked away from me."
"No, I didn't hate you. I put myself out there and you rejected me. I was mad at the time. I got it later.," he said

"Why do you love me?" I asked

"You are a sweet and gentle person. You have a warm and loving heart; you bring out a gentler side of me. In a lot of ways you remind me of my mother. You acknowledge me, but you don't fall all over yourself for me. I mean I know I'm fine." He flashed his dimples. "You're smart, independent, and capable. You're gorgeous! I can take you anywhere. My son loves you! My mom loves you! You always want me around! And even though I know it's not fair that I know all this but you sing my praises to complete strangers, even when you're mad at me."

"Wow! That's quite a list!" I was blushing from the inside out. "You think I'm gorgeous? Wow!"

"Are you kidding? When I first saw you, I had to meet you. I was praying you were single, and that you'd go for me."

"That I'd go for you?"

"Yea, you could've had a specific type and that type could've been everything I'm not."

"Ok..."

"You saw me, but you weren't paying me any attention until I approached you." He said

"That was the beginning of my weight loss journey. I wasn't thinking anyone noticed me."

"Oh yea! Well chubby or not you're gorgeous to me. Doesn't change who you are." Then he kissed me, I melted.

I kept looking at him with big eyes.

As we walked back upstairs to get back to work my cellphone rang it was Nicole. She was calling to tell me that at the last minute Phillip called off the wedding. Sonya's wedding was supposed to be last weekend. Nicole didn't know the details yet, but she was pissed because she had paid for everything for the wedding and then he called it off. And because he waited until the last minute they still had to pay the vendors all full price. I asked how Sonya was holding up. She said everything was chaotic at the moment. She said she thinks Sonya's embarrassed so she hasn't been answering her phone or responding to anyone. I felt bad for Sonya, they had a long engagement and then to get so close. I debated whether or not to share my news, so I waited until the subject changed. Nicole screamed into the phone, "you should've answered the phone screaming it!" Then she got on my case for not calling her right away. She said I should've called her immediately afterwards. That reminded me that I needed to call Joy. Andrew was working hard on his laptop. He looked at me from time to time and smiled, but his face was so serious as he looked at his paperwork and clicked away on his computer. Nicole like everyone else wanted to know when our wedding would take place. I told her I didn't know yet. I told her that Andrew and I hadn't agreed on time frames yet. She had to get back to work so we got off the phone. I did a little more work then I called Joy. She screamed at me as well. She couldn't understand why she wasn't there. She promised to be my right hand in the whole process. Then I walked out the room and I went into the closet in the empty twin room and shut the door. I sat in Indian style in the furthest corner. "There's one problem, I'm late!" I whispered.
"Whoa girl!"

"I know! And I'm sorry I don't want to be a swollen pregnant bride. I would rather wait until the baby was born, but I know

Andrew's not gonna like that. I don't even know how to approach that with him."

"Well you don't know for sure yet. Find out for sure before you get paranoid."

"That's what were gonna have to do. This has the potential to be horrible." I said not wanting to think it through.
Then we went back to daydream land. "What do you think your wedding budget will be?"

I hadn't thought about that. "I have no idea. Since he's been paying for everything, I have a nice little savings nest. But the cost will mostly depend on how many guest." I said still whispering.

Joy was so excited, she was in her last trimester so she was happy that the baby would be here and she wouldn't be pregnant during the wedding.
When I came back in the room Andrew laughed at me, but he didn't say a word.
We both worked some more, around 4pm I couldn't take it anymore. I shut down my computer.

"Lets talk wedding." I said with a nervous smile. He smiled and placed his laptop on the couch. "How many people will you need to invite?"

"My family is huge, so I'd guess at about three hundred just on my side." He said

"Three hundred! Good grief my family is equally as big. What do we do? It's gonna be too big!"

"How about we stick to two-fifty each?" He said
"Andrew that's still five hundred people. Do you have any idea how much that's gonna cost? Even if we had a basic setup with nothing special, five hundred people is expensive."

"Your point?" He asked

"That's a lot of money. What's our wedding budget?"
"Good question, I want a nice wedding. And if there's something we want I think we should have it."

"Even with five hundred people?"
"Yes, even with." He said

"How much money do you have?"

"However much you need, I got it."

"What does that mean?"

"I get paid very nicely to do what I do. I also get nice bonuses. I'm part owner of my father's shops, and studios, etc. I have quite a few investments that I get nice returns on." He said matter of factly

"Really? So then if I wanted to be a Bridezilla you'd let me?"

He laughed, "I think I know you better than that. But whatever you want we can have."

I swallowed hard, "I don't want to be pregnant and fat in my dress."

"I know that."

"So then what if it turns out that I am preggers?"

"I would rather have the wedding sooner than later, but I'm guessing you'd want to wait?"

"I don't know, I think my parents would have a cow. I guess we'll cross that bridge when we come to it." Suddenly I started sweating again. "Oh lord Andrew what if I am pregnant. The thought of it SCARES ME!" Tears came rushing out of my eyes.

He walked over to the bed. Took off his shoes, and then he sat behind me. He pulled me into him and he held me. I feel so safe in his arms. "I don't even know what to think. I thought we were so careful. But if it turns out that you are pregnant please know in your heart that I am excited, and completely on board. I don't know about you," he said sarcastically. "But I've already had the horrible why is this happening to me experience. I'm actually toning down my excitement out of respect for your anxiety. The thought of a little girl who looks just like you calling me daddy." He squeezed me a little tighter. "I can't wait!" That made me cry more. He softly kissed my neck. "What?"

"You are so good to me. I know it's stupid to keep looking back, but a lot of the time I wonder where we would be right now if we never broke up. I honestly didn't know I had the option of fighting for you. I thought your mind was made up, so I didn't fight you. I was sad when you broke up with me. Steve was hanging around waiting for me to get over you. Like a vulture waits. I missed you so much. I thought about you all the time. When I found out about Andre I was devastated I thought that meant you were married. I wondered how you handled the situation. What did you say when she told you?"

"It wasn't a surprise I knew I messed up when it happened. But I didn't think she'd keep him."

"She had been pregnant before?"

"When we were in high school, taught me a lesson. When we were in College, but I honestly don't think that baby was mine. And then Andre."

"Can I ask you, what happened with you two?"

"I told you, when I was with you that was the first time I've ever rejected her. She didn't know how to handle it. No matter who I was with before, she came first."

"Why?"

"Because we went so far back."

"Because she was your first?" I said

"When did she tell you that?"

"At the restaurant, she said you will always come back to her cause nobody can work you like she can." The thought made me sweat more.

"So she thinks."

"What made her special?"

"Back in the day I thought she was pretty."

"She still is."

"Not with that ugly heart. Her true colors came out when she was pregnant. I wouldn't get back with her even though she was pregnant. She.... She showed me who I had really been dealing with. She used Andre as a tool to hurt me. She only wanted him when she thought I did. I'm trying not to...." He squeezed me tighter. "When I saw you at Hubby's... You didn't even see me. I was happy and sad at the same time. I didn't know if you were still with ole boy, if you were feeling me if you weren't. Then Toya showed up, I thought for sure you weren't gonna look at me. I wasn't sure about the invite to Napa especially when I saw you and ole boy in the kitchen. There was something about that moment when I held you for the first time in years. I knew I didn't want to let you go." He inhaled and hugged me again. "That was one of those moments that stay with you forever! I didn't care what it took I wasn't letting you go again." He exhaled! "You are precious to me. My most precious jewel. I know you're freaking out, but I would be so happy if you were pregnant, no regrets. No regrets you hear me! I love you so much it hurts! He was a fool to let you go. I won't be that fool again!"

"Well alright Daddy!" I said patting his arm.

He softly growled in my ear, "call me daddy one more time and see what happens!"

I smiled and innocently said, "daddy"

Well you can only guess what happened next. He looked a little disappointed when I went to get my diaphragm, but I didn't want to push the issue.

"Can I ask you something?"

He looked at me, "shoot!"

"Am I horrible in bed?"

He started laughing until he realized I was seriously asking. "No, you're not."

"Am I ok?" I felt so stupid asking but I really needed to know. "I know it sounds stupid, I'm sorry for asking but I need to know."

"You're great! No you're amazing! Phenomenal!"

"Stop clowning!" I swallowed. "You sure you want to spend the rest of your life with just me? Won't you get bored?"

"Well let me say, The Beast loves you!"

"But couldn't that be just because I made you wait so long?"

"No, you take the whole Beast, not everybody can do that. We are getting to know each other just fine. We are good. I have no complaints or anything like that."

"He said I was bad at it."

"He was messing with your head. If you were even a quarter of the things he tells you, why does he even bother? Shouldn't he be running from you? He better be happy I'm a changed man!"

I didn't want to push the issue by asking him what that meant. I kissed him and rolled over to sleep. He woke me a few minutes later to go get Andre and then go out to dinner. We decided to invite his mom. But she had already cooked and so she convinced us to come over. When we got there Darryl was working on a economics paper. His information was compiled but it didn't flow. He asked what I thought, and before I knew it two hours passed as we discussed his ideas and I showed him how to make his thoughts flow on paper. His face was very serious and concentrated as he listened to me. He was smart like his big brother, but his thoughts made him move too fast at times. Derrick came over while Darryl and I were working. He sat close by and listened. A few times I caught him nodding his head to what I was saying to Darryl. When we were done Darryl gave me a hug (the first time he's ever touched me on purpose) and thanked me for helping him. When we came home I put Andre in the bath while Andrew finished up some work. I felt really nervous about the next day, but singing songs with Andre helped to calm me down a lot. To my surprise when my head hit the pillow I was knocked out.

****

Darryl was at my house at a quarter to eleven. He came right after his morning class. During the ride over the Bay Bridge we talked about his classes, and what he liked most about them. Darryl had never been this talkative with me before. I felt like he was opening up to me, which made me feel more comfortable. Like clock work as we pulled up to the building I spotted Yussef walking down the street. When I got out the car, he greeted me like he normally did. I didn't know whether to speak on it or not, so I didn't say anything. He gave me the normal updates on the task he was working on for me. Everything felt completely normal. Yussef was dark brown sugar colored and medium build. He had long dreads that were very neat and kept up. He was well spoken, and educated. I didn't know how he fit in with Andrew but I really didn't want to know. Like what was it about this man that made Andrew ok with trusting my life to him. The question in its self scared me. Walking into my old office sent all kinds of feelings through me. I avoided coming out here as much as possible. I walked over to Shirley's cubicle and pretended to yawn. She immediately noticed the ring. She pretended to be blinded by it. I missed working with her; she and I were really close. She told me I looked great, and then she brought me up to speed on her life and the things that were going on. At lunch we sat at the same table as Yussef, I introduced them. Yussef was very charming and Shirley said they needed more young men like him at the company. During our afternoon meeting I looked at Yussef a few times and he was really paying attention. If Andrew hadn't told me anything, I would've never connected him to Andrew. Then Shirley leaned over, "your ex watches our building all the time. He always speaks, and says hello. But you can tell he misses you."

She made my stomach flip. I grabbed my purse and squeezed as if that would make my restraining order activate and turn into a force field. At the end of the day I called Darryl to see how close he was. He told me he was circling the block, and that he would call me back as soon as he was out front.

"Have you spoken to Steve since the incident?" She was speaking of the miscarriage.

"Um, kind of. He's very angry with me so I try to steer clear of him at all cost."

"Really cause he always seems like a love struck puppy when I see him."

"Really?"

"Yea, he tells me how much he misses you. How he wishes he could talk to you. He really wants you back."

"Steve?"

"Yes, Steve." Shirley said smiling an innocent smile.

"Have you told him anything about me?"

"No, not really. He knows you don't work out here anymore. But I didn't tell him that. I hadn't seen him for a while and then he told me about your new boyfriend. He said your boyfriend over reacted when he simply wanted to talk to you. He thinks your new man is insecure about him."

I couldn't believe this. Over reacted? That fool is trying to kill me! "What did you tell him?"

"Well I tried to comfort him and let him know that real love will wait a lifetime. I told him he needs to be patient."

"Oh Shirley! Please don't tell him anything about me. He hates me, and every time he sees me he becomes violent. Please stay away from him, he's trying to find out information about me." I pleaded.

"Steve become violent? I don't believe that."

My phone rang; it was Darryl telling me he was outside. "Shirley please! I have no reason to lie to you. Please! I have to go my ride is here. But please!" I grabbed my purse my nerves were on edge.

"You're not gonna ride Bart with me?"

"Oh no, I got a ride. I gotta go I'll see you tomorrow." I walked out the door. Yussef was in the lobby walking almost ahead of me but along side me from across the lobby. When I exited the building he was within arm's reach of me. All the people outside made me nervous. I hurried to the car. Yussef strolled onward towards the Bart station.

"You ok?" Darryl asked he could clearly see I was unglued.

I told him what Shirley said, and he cracked up laughing like I was a comedian telling a joke. "He should be ashamed of himself for working that old lady like that. But let me ask you something. Why are you still working?"

"I don't understand the question." I didn't.

"My brother got you, why are you working?"

The thought of not working was foreign to me. "He's not my husband yet, and even then why would I stop working?"

"I guess. My girl won't work. I don't know about marriage though."

"What's wrong with marriage?"

"Look at what it did to my parents. I don't want no part of that."

I didn't exactly know what happened with his parents. Other than one day he left. "If you love someone regardless if you're married or not it will devastate you if they leave you."

"That's true, but there's no paperwork saying they're entitled to anything when they do leave you. They can kick rocks!"

"Do you still see your father?" He looked at me in the rear view mirror. He started laughing, but he didn't answer me.

The rest of the ride was silent. On the way home we stopped and picked up Andre from school. He was so excited from the day that he filled the car with chatter. When we pulled up to the house there was that grey car on the corner. As Andre and I got out the car, the green civic came down the street, but it went by so fast I couldn't see who was driving. The grey car took off after the green car. Andrew came rushing out the house. "Go inside!" He said as he hopped in the car with Darryl. Cain and Eve sat in the doorway. To the best of my ability I tried to remain calm as I took Andre in the house. Andrew had dinner ready. I checked the oven and I caught the garlic bread just in time before it burned. The spaghetti was ready. He had components out for salad so I finished the salad. We sat at the table waiting for Andrew. He had a big smile on his face.

"Everything ok?"

"Yea, so the green civic lives a block away. Some older hippie looking guy. He was cool." He said with a big smile.

"Wash your hands we're ready to eat."

He washed his hands, he kept his smile. "So I hear someone is heartbroken." He laughed. "Is she really falling for that?"

"I guess so. She's old school for real."

"Hhmmmm" he started thinking. "Be careful with her. She sounds very idealistic, and she might have good intentions but end up putting you in a bad position. You understand what I mean?"

"I do. I'm even more afraid to go tomorrow."

"Why are you scared?" Andre asked

"There are mean people at this new place."

"Oh I don't like mean people."

"Me neither." I said

"Do you want me to beat the mean people up?"

"I think daddy has that covered." I smiled

He had a evil grin on his face, "call me daddy again".

I smiled at him.

CHAPTER 28

Yesterday was long! Darryl picked me up early, as we had to get through rush hour traffic. When we pulled up Yussef and Shirley were walking to the building but behind me when I got out the car. All I know is this guy was GOOD. We sat together for breakfast and lunch. Shirley didn't mention Steve at all yesterday. She was her normal sweet self. The day kind of dragged but also flew by. We had a little time to network in between workshops. I made quite a few connections. People that I've worked with on projects but never met face to face. Even this one guy, Edward. Edward works in our Charlotte office. He was so impressed with me when he worked with me that he raved to my boss about me. When my boss Becca introduced us his eyes got big. He pretended to bow to me. He was a lot more animated in person than I thought he would be. He turned out to be very charming, I think I even caught him checking me out which was weird cause I didn't think of him as someone who would be attracted to someone like me. But oh well stranger things have happened I suppose.

This morning I asked Andrew about the afternoon. I told him the symposium would be over at noon, but I didn't know if our team was going out to lunch afterwards or what. He told me to call him as soon as I knew. We kissed and went our separate ways. When we pulled up this morning Yussef was standing outside putting his ear buds and things in his backpack. We had breakfast together and Shirley came in just before our first workshop. She was a little out of breath. She said she over slept and just couldn't get it together this morning. She grabbed coffee and a pastry, and then she was right on my heels.

"To be young again!" Shirley whispered

"What do you mean?"

"Don't you even sit there and try and tell me you haven't noticed the men who've been noticing you these past few days."

"Like I care," I held up my hand. "I got a man!"

"You're better than me. All these different flavors would make me hungry." She said looking around.

Then Becca came over and whispered, "we're gonna have lunch at the Cheesecake House with Edward's team. Make sure you tell Yussef." Then she walked away.

Shirley hurried over to Yussef to tell him. So I excused myself and went into the lobby. I called Andrew. "We're going to the Cheesecake House afterwards. I don't know how long we'll be there but I'm guessing a hour and a half to two at least." I said

"Ok, shoot! Darryl has afternoon classes." My heart sped up. "Yussef will be right there. Call me when you leave the restaurant, I will pick you up at Ashby Bart."

I was silent for a minute. I was scared but what are the chances right? "Ok, I love you!"

"I love you! Have a good day."

As I walked back into the conference Yussef was walking out with his phone in his hand. As I sat down Edward looked at me and smiled, I barely smiled back my nerves were starting to kick in. With emotions like this no wonder I'm late. My poor period may never come.

"What do you think of Edward?" Shirley whispered

"He's a nice guy."

"But do you think he's handsome?"

"I guess"

"You guess? Child if that man was looking at me like he's been looking at you... Shoot!" She wiggled her neck and shifted in her seat.

"You'd jeopardize your job like that?"

"As long as we remained professional, I don't see the harm."

"Shirley! What has gotten in to you?"

She tisked at me, "nothing. You're young I don't want you to look back with a life full of regrets."

"I'm not. I've got a FINE man at home! Nothing about no one else is appealing to me."

"If he's so fine why is he so insecure?"

"Really?" I was starting to get irritated. Who was this woman? What happened to my friend? "Who said he was insecure? A better question is why would that person divulge all this information to you suddenly when they don't even know you? He's lying to you please don't believe him."

She looked at me, but she didn't say anything. It may have been my paranoid state but it did feel like eyes were all over me. I went to the back of the room and stood by the wall for a bit. When the workshop was over I was looking at my watch.

"You actually still wear a watch. Wow!"

I didn't know who he was. "Yes, I like to keep my time on my wrist."

Then he reached out his hand to shake mine. "I'm Matthew, I report up to Edward."

"Tracy, nice to meet you."

Then he whistled as he looked at my ring. "That's a nice couple of rocks."

"Thank you!"

"Are you married or engaged?"

"Engaged." I blushed

"Aw! Isn't that nice. Your fiancée is a lucky man."

"Thank you."

"When is the date?"

"We haven't set one yet. The engagement is pretty new. But if he chooses it would probably be this weekend." I said

"Aw! He's eager to get this show on the road. Can't blame him for that."

"Thanks" I didn't know what to say to that.

"So I see you've met Matt. Are you ready to head out?" Edward asked

Becca walked over with Shirley and Clara. "Let me rally the rest of my team one moment." Becca said rushing over to Bill and Enton. Yussef stood next to me but he didn't say anything. "Ok, we're all here. I guess we can do the whole introduction thing at the restaurant. Lets go."

Shirley fell back; she was talking to Clara and Bill. Enton, Yussef, and I were talking about working in the city. It was a beautiful day out, and although the city is always chilly, the weather was really nice. Once the hostess brought us to our reserved table I attempted to sit next to Yussef, but Edward insisted that I sit between him and Becca. Yussef didn't have a reaction to that at all, but why would he? And really I was now sitting across and over one seat from him.

"So Matt tells me you're engaged?" Edward said

"You're engaged? How come you didn't say anything?" Becca said

"I didn't really get a chance to tell you. It just happened."

Then she looked down at my hand. "Oh my word! That's beautiful. Congratulations Tracy." Becca said

Everyone gave their congratulations.

Then we went around the table introducing ourselves one by one. Then conversations broke off from there.

"Yussef is the newest member on my team. He works directly with Tracy. Yussef how do you like working with Tracy?"

Everyone seemed to stop talking to hear his answer. "She's pretty great to work with as you all know. Her ability to boss people around, and do it in a way that you don't always realize at first is pretty amazing." Everybody laughed.

"Is she approachable?" Shirley asked

"Oh yea, she's always available to discuss anything. But if you really wanna get her to talk your ear off, ask her something about her boyfriend. She's definitely in love."

Ok that was embarrassing. Yussef smiled at me. "I hope my girlfriend talks about me like that when I'm not around."

Shirley looked at me, "I guess we haven't talked in a while."

Irritated I said, "what do you mean by that?"

Catching her tone, she sweetened her tone. "Oh nothing honey. I just meant it sounds like you have a new best friend at work. So I wasn't privileged to hear all the details of your new fella." She smiled.

"Communication goes both ways Shirley. Do we need to go to the bathroom?"

Did that heifer roll her eyes at me? I looked at Becca.

"Shirley can I talk to you?" Becca said getting up from the table. Shirley sucked her teeth and walked with Becca.

"Wow!" Edward said, "sounds like everybody wants to be your friend."

"I guess!" I felt bad, and I didn't exactly understand what was going on. I got really quiet after that and watched people. Edward kept shooting me looks but I acted like I didn't see them.

"So where does your fiancée work?" Edward asked

"Cooper Financials"

"I know the company. What does he do there?"

"He's the Senior EVP of Community Banking"

"That explains the ring." Edward said jokingly. I smiled. "Out here in California, do you guys sign pre-nups like they show on the news?"

"That really depends on your situation. They're not necessary for everyone." Matt said

Becca and Shirley returned to the table, Shirley still seemed huffy.

"Do you plan to have children?" Edward asked

"Yes" I said as Shirley rolled her eyes. I could feel my blood starting to boil so I excused myself to the restroom. It was really hurting my feelings that Shirley was acting like this. I thought we were friends. When I came out the stall Shirley was waiting. I rolled my eyes at her.

"I guess I deserve that." She said

"What's wrong with you? I thought we were friends?"

"We are friends. I don't want to see you make a mistake. Steve really loves you!"

Fire started burning in my stomach. "No he doesn't! He's lying to you!"

"Honey, he loves you! At least talk to him, before its too late."

"Shirley! Listen to me! Steve is trying to kill me. I have a restraining order against him. Last time I saw him he choked me and he hit me. Only reason I'm here now is because someone stopped him. Shirley he's messing with your head trying to get to me."

"I remember how much you love this man. Funny how now that you got a new man Steve is all these horrible things. I remember how you two were."

"So then you remember how depressed I was. You remember how stressed I was. You remember how heartbroken I was when I lost my baby! You remember how crazy he was which is why I switched offices in the first place!"

"I know he didn't handle the news right, but you're throwing away years! It was always about Steve."

"You don't get it! Steve is NO GOOD! I have a restraining order against him for a reason. You're supposed to be MY friend! Why are you defending him?"

"Because honey I'm looking at the big picture. You're so sprung off this new guy that you can't see the truth."

"I'm done! I can't do this! I'm standing here crying, screaming at the top of my lungs and you choose to believe him over me? I guess there is a fool born everyday. You are the FIRST person not to hear me on this."

"That's because I love" I put my finger up shushing her.

"Shirley I was raised to respect my elders. But you're gonna make me lose all that respect. You can go back to the table." Then I turned my back to her. She hugged me then she walked out. I called Andrew from the bathroom I needed to hear his voice. But he didn't answer his cell or his desk phone. I wet a paper towel and dabbed my face.

Becca came in the bathroom "are you ok?"

"Yea, I'm fine. I don't know what's up with Shirley. We used to be friends."

As my boss I knew Becca couldn't really say anything. So she smiled an empathetic smile.

When I came back to the table some were leaving and others were staying for dessert. Yussef was looking at the menu, so I opted to stay. At three I was ready to go. Everyone was finishing up, so we all walked out the restaurant together.

"Yussef can I walk with you to the Bart?" I asked

"Sure" he nonchalantly said.

Shirley left thirty minutes before we did. I was glad cause I didn't want to sit next to her on the train if she realized I was taking Bart.

"You and Shirley were going at it!" He smiled

"I don't know what her problem is. I thought we were friends."

"Friends come and go."

"Ain't that the truth." Then I looked at him. "Do I really talk about Andrew that much?"

"It's not like you overly do it. But you light up when you talk about him. It's sweet."

"Thanks. You never told me you have a girlfriend."

"I was just saying that for when I do."

"Oh" I said.

Then Yussef took out his phone "we're on our way". Then he hung up.

As we walked down the stairs I caught a glimpse of Shirley. My stomach flipped and I knew it was all-bad. Instead of standing on the escalator I walked down on the left with the rest of the hurried people. Yussef looked at my face and then he started looking around. He kind of glided while I moved hurried and clumsy, bumping into people and apologizing. When we got down to the platform Yussef stood in line and he told me to come stand with him. When Shirley rounded the corner I held my breath, and yep sure enough there was Steve walking with her. He looked like he put a little weight back on but he was still too skinny. He didn't look crazy, he actually looked normal. They walked right up to me.

"I thought you were getting a ride today too?" Shirley said. I shook my head no, but I wouldn't take my eyes off of Steve. He was staring at me but his face had no expression. "Neither one of you has anything to say?" I guess she was proud of herself.

A tear ran down my face. "How you doing I'm Yussef." He said as he moved me to the other side of him and reached out to shake Steve's hand.

Steve frowned and pointed at Yussef while looking at Shirley with a "WHY?" Expression on his face.

"That's just Yussef, he works with us."

"How you doing Tracy?" Steve said ignoring Yussef. I wanted to say something but I was paralyzed in fear. With all these people here he wouldn't try anything would he?

"Tracy talk to the man. He ain't gonna bite you!"

"Steve I have a restraining order. Please go to the next station and leave me alone." A couple of the people in line ahead of us heard me. They looked at Steve then at Yussef and some moved.

"Baby I don't know why you're acting like this I want to talk to you. You owe me at least that."

"I'm not your baby and I don't owe you anything." I grabbed Yussef's arm. "Can you walk with me over there?"

"Ok, ok. I just wanted to apologize for the way I acted when I found out about the baby. It wasn't fair for me to treat you like that. But you never gave me the chance to make it right."

Still holding Yussef's arm I took a deep breath. "Can we go? He's gonna go from zero to sixty in no time flat."

"Did you hear me?"

"I heard you when you were trying to kill me! I have NOTHING to say to you!"

Shirley got a funny look on her face. She looked at Steve. He shrugged, "I don't know what she's talking about."

"Aw man! She's asking you to leave her alone. Go on get!" Yussef said shooing him like a little pest.

Steve looked Yussef up and down. "I suggest you mind your own business! This is between me and her!"

Shirley looked horrified, "Steve, come on."

"Naw! Every time I just wanna talk to her she got some fool in my face. She do you too? You risking a beat down for some weak pussy! She ain't worth all that!"

"Steve! Stop talking about her like that!" Shirley said

"Shirley you don't know this tramp like I do! Now she wanna hide over there like she's scared. I ain't gonna do nothing to her!"

"Boy come here!" Shirley said putting authority in her voice. And to my surprise he did it. "This is nothing like all the stuff you were saying to me! How dare you talk to her like that!"

"You don't know her like I know her! She always trying to play Ms. Innocent when other people around! But at home.... Ooh!"

"You told me you loved her, and that you wanted her back."

"I do!"

"Do you really think this is how you get anyone back?"

"She's over there acting like she's scared of me. That makes me mad!"

"That doesn't justify you acting like this. This may be your only opportunity to talk to her. And you over here acting a fool! You better talk to her. Tell her the stuff you told me. Man up!"

He exhaled and then he kissed Shirley on the cheek. "I'm sorry Tracy!" He said walking towards us. "I miss you, and I wish you would talk to me." I kept my head down and I clung to Yussef's arm. "Can I call you?" I shook my head no. "Can I email you?" I shook my head no. "Why are you acting like you're scared of me?"

"Cause you tried to kill me!"

"No I didn't stop saying that. I was trying to bring you with me so we could talk."

"Richmond bound train in one minute!" The automated system called out.

I shook my head no. "Ok, that's enough she don't want to talk to you. Now I think I'm asking nicely, leave her alone." Yussef said.

"Whatever punk! Ain't nobody concerned with you." Yussef was no longer relaxed. He put his hands in his pocket and start jingling change.

"Come on Steve. Leave her alone." Shirley said she ushered him to get in line a couple of cars ahead of ours. As soon as we got on the train Yussef told me to move two more cars back. We were in the last car. Yussef didn't say anything his jaw just kept flexing and unflexing. My heart was beating out of my chest. I didn't like Yussef being so calm, but I understood that his hands were tied as there were so many people around and all Steve really was doing was talking. Shirley was gonna get off at one of the transfer stations she needed to get on a Fremont train, but I know she got on this train for Steve. I didn't know what he would do once she got off. She obviously had a calming affect on him.

There was standing room only in the last car. We pushed through towards the end of the car by the last door. I stayed behind Yussef not knowing what to expect once Shirley got off. Each stop my heart sped up and then slowed down. When we got to MacArthur station a lot of people got off. Yussef asked me if I wanted to sit. But I told him I was getting off at the next stop. I couldn't make Shirley out as the train pulled off. But all I could think was "I'm almost home!" Then I saw Steve coming through the door I almost lost my wind. Yussef was shaking his head and laughing.

"Yo boy is stupid!"

"Something funny?" Steve said, that crazy look was settling over his eyes I wanted to scream.

"You are the stupidest fool I know! You just don't know how to leave well enough alone." Then Yussef grabbed my hand as my stop was coming. "Come on! He ain't gonna do nothing." I followed and Yussef put me in front of him. "If you smart, you'll stay on this train!"

Steve sat still and looked at me. When I got off the train Yussef walked behind me and at the last minute Steve was up and sliding through the doors as they closed. He was running straight at

234

us, Yussef turned around and stuck out his hand. You heard a zap noise and Steve was falling twitching and jerking. Yussef smiled and then he turned to me "keep walking". I did as I was told when we exited the Bart station Andrew was parked on the street waiting for us. He was smiling until he saw my face. Instantly his face went serious and he looked at Yussef. Andrew opened the car door and I got in. Yussef was telling him what happened and both of them started laughing. Another car pulled up and Yussef got in it. As we pulled away paramedics were arriving. Tears streamed down my face. "I thought she was my friend." Andrew didn't say anything he kissed me and held my hand.

The next morning I couldn't bare to get up. I powered up my laptop and I sent my boss an email letting her know I wasn't feeling well. Then I laid back down. I kept seeing Steve's body jerking, and I would start to feel bad until I remembered how he was talking about me. I remember when he used to be sweet. I remembered Nicole's wedding, he wasn't even concerned with Andrew. He knew he had me and that Andrew was my ex. He didn't even question me, now this cracked out looking fool uses every opportunity to abuse me. He's calling me a hoe when he always cheated on me. I was the stupid faithful one.

Andrew walked back in the room. Normally I'm up and almost ready but this time. I was in the bed with the pillow over my head. "You not going to work today?" He said tapping my foot. I shook my head no. "Are you sick?" I shrugged my shoulders. He walked over to my side of the bed. He took the pillow off my head. He sat next to me and started stroking my curls. "Are you playing hooky today?" I shook my head. "You want me to stay with you?" I rolled over and looked at him so surprised. "Wait I gotta reply to a couple emails, and then we could have the day. How does that sound?" I sat up and kissed him on the cheek. He flashed his dimples. "I'll take Andre to school be ready by the time I come back." I ran to the shower. The hardest part was deciding what to wear. I decided on my dark blue jeans, a white button up so that I could flash my cleavage at him all day. A taupe jacket, black shoes, and a red purse. When I looked in the mirror I gave myself the nod. Eve even looked like she approved. Andrew called when he was outside. I made sure there was enough food and water out for my babies. I set the alarm and I headed out the door. "I love those jeans!" He said when I got in the car. I kissed him. When we pulled up to his office I wanted to wait in the car. But he wasn't having it. When we walked in the door, everyone was dressed more casual I guess because it was Friday. Everyone seemed surprised to see us walk in the door together. When we walked into his office he shut the door. Then there was a knock, he looked at the shoes then he said, "enter".

Jennifer walked in; she smiled at me "are you taking off early today? You know I was sent to ask."

He smiled, "tell them they can leave at 12 today."

"Yes!" Jennifer pumped her fist. Then she looked at my hand. "Oh my goodness! He finally did it! Congratulations!"

"Finally?" I thought to myself, but I smiled and said thank you.

Lisa was walking by right at that moment. "Congratulations?" She popped her head into the office. She spotted my ring and said the fakest "congratulations". Andrew looked at her and shook his head. "Andrew don't look at me like that."
Then I looked at him. And he looked at her, "don't you have some work to do?" She sucked her teeth threw her head back and walked out.

Jennifer tried to cover her laugh, but it was no use. We all kind of chuckled. "Congratulations for real!" Jennifer said as she backed out of the office.

"Thank you Jennifer" I waited for her to close the door, "Good grief! That girl be on you."

He smiled, "kind of why I like having you pop up from time to time." Then he winked at me.

I played solitaire on my phone, while Andrew focused on his emails. Then my mom called to confirm that I was coming to service on Sunday. Right after I hung up with her Nicole called.

For her fourth wedding anniversary they wanted to have a skate party. She said they rented out the skating rink in San Ramon next Saturday night. I got so excited, I hadn't skated in years. Andrew laughed at how fast I was talking. In the car I gave him all the details. He laughed at my rambling. He drove for a while I talked about everything but nothing. After awhile I finally realized we had been driving for well over an hour.

Eventually we arrived in Monterey.

"What are we doing here?"

"I thought it would be totally romantic to randomly drive out here."

I got so excited I started clapping my hands. I gave him a hug and a kiss. We followed the signs to the aquarium. It was so nice; there were a few field trips. The kids were so cute. While we were in the jellyfish exhibit he pinned me in the corner. "I can't wait until you're carrying our child."

I put my arms around his neck. "We can start trying on our honeymoon night."

"You started?"

"No, I'm trying to be positive."

He sucked his teeth, "well you think your way and I'll think mine." Then he kissed me. After we kissed in almost every corner of the aquarium we left to find a place to eat. "Do you wanna stay over night?"

"What about Andre?"

"He'll be happy to spend the night with Nana." He called his mom who was happy to have Andre spend the night.

Then we checked into a REALLY nice hotel. We ordered a couple's massage in our room, and we sent our clothes off to be laundered. We ordered room service. There was a Jacuzzi tub right next to our window so that it was like you were looking at the ocean. As crazy as it sounds in this romantic setting, we kissed, we touched, but we didn't make love. It was quite nice actually. In the morning we did everything but make love. We drove home along the coast talking and taking each other in. Andrew said we needed this impromptu trip cause things were about to get crazy with our wedding coming up.

CHAPTER 29

I woke up in a panic, I slightly overslept. I ran around like a crazy person waking the men. Fortunately I knew what I wanted to wear. I put on a black dress, and it has this electric blue swirl in it. This dress lovingly caressed my curves, but it wasn't tight or clinging. I twisted my hair up in the back while the front was curly and nicely framing my face. I put on a little makeup, but not a lot. I stood in the mirror taking my look in. I thought I looked nice; the test would be the reaction from the men. Andrew was helping Andre with his tie when I walked out the bathroom. Both of them looked at me smiled and then stared.

"You look pretty!" Andre said

"Thank you sweetheart", I gave him a kiss on his cheek. "You look very handsome as well."

Andrew kept looking at me. His eyes were running all over my body. His face said he approved, but he didn't say anything. When he finished André's tie. He told him to go wait by the door. Then not even waiting for Andre to exit the room he pulled me close and put both of his hands on my butt. "You sure you wanna go? Cause I can think of something else we can do." He smiled

"My mind's telling me no! But my body's telling me yes!" I sang, we both laughed.

He patted my butt, "lets go".

When we got to service the parking lot was full. So we parked on the street. My parents saved us seats next to them. As soon as we sat down Andre whispered, "I gotta pee".

I told Andrew I'd take him, and we went to the bathroom. I held the stall door closed while Andre was inside handling his business. Karen comes out of the stall next to us. She was startled when she saw me.

"Well, well, well if it isn't little miss insecure." Karen said as she walked to the sink to wash her hands. In the mirror she was sizing me up from head to toe. She was moving real slow. Andre came out the stall full of energy. He stood on the stool at the sink next to hers to wash his hands. "Hello" she said to him.

Andre looked at her. Looked her up and down and then he looked at me in the mirror. I smiled at him, and then he said an uninterested, "hi".

Andre dried his hands and then he handed me the paper towel. She was still watching me in the mirror. Then I saw her see my ring. Her eyes got big, and then she looked pissed. I smiled at her and walked away. When we sat down Karen took her seat next to her brother. I could feel the heat from their laser beams as they stared at the back of our heads. Andrew put his arm around my chair and I smiled at him. After service my parents were bubbling forward about our engagement. A sea of people surrounded us. Karen stayed on the other side of the auditorium. She kept staring and she was clearly upset. When Andrew saw her, he looked like he felt bad. He nodded at her, and she rolled her eyes. Then she left, she looked like she was about to explode. Andrew didn't look happy, but he tried his best to fix his face when he realized I was watching him. I didn't like that display of empathy one bit. Anthony distracted him by saying congratulations. They started talking and I walked over to Joy, she was due any day now. "Girl, it was just too many people over there. I need to sit down. Let me see the ring." I showed her my hand. We had a whole giggle fest about the ring. "How we doing on the other situation?"

"Still nothing, but I'm not gonna worry about it. Whatever happens, happens."

"You still gonna wait until after if you are?"

"I don't know, I think I'd be the only person ok with that. We'll see. You guys gonna come to brunch with us? Our treat!"

"That sounds a lot better than going home. And making a mess to clean. Sure! We'll go."

My mom, Amy, Joy, and I rode in Joy's car while the men drove their cars. Anthony and little Anthony rode with Andrew and Andre.

"Do you at least know what your colors will be?" Amy asked

"Yes, my colors royal blue, silver, and white. I need another week then I can start focusing on the wedding."

"Why do you need another week?" My mother asked suspiciously

"I got stuff going on mom. I don't want to be distracted. Plus as it stands the guess list is too big. We need to figure out a budget and how many people."

"Un-huh" my mom said looking out the window

I looked at Joy, "I gave her a see what I'm saying" look.

Brunch was lovely, everyone was happy and conversation flowed. I could tell Andrew was a little sad though, and I prayed that it didn't have to do with Karen although I knew it did. When it was time to go Andre asked if Anthony could come over. I agreed as I could tell that Joy needed to rest, and Anthony needed the space to wow her with his supportive husbandly technique.

"Penny for your thoughts." I said as Andrew drove us home.

"Hhmmmm, nothing I can express. Just thoughtful today."

I tried to stop my lips from curling up. "Did Karen speak to you? Congratulate you or anything?"

"Naw, I saw her from across the room. But I think she might've feared another smack down cause she didn't come over." He smiled

"I guess she can be smart when she needs to be."

When we walked in the door Andrew introduced Anthony to Cain and Eve. Then the boys took off upstairs with the dogs in tow. I sat on the couch in the family room. Andrew paced around the kitchen for a minute. Then he announced he was gonna go take a shower. I looked at him to read his face. He never announces like that. He smiled, kissed my cheek then hurried upstairs. What if he calls Karen while he's up there? I waited until I heard the water running then I went upstairs. The boys were playing with trucks; Cain seemed very amused by their game. Eve as the true female was in the corner laying down and unimpressed.

When I opened the door I could hear the shower running. His wallet, cellphone, keys, and change were on the nightstand. I sat on the bed and picked up his phone. He had two missed calls. My heart dropped, I looked at his call log. His mom and Derrick had called. I went down the whole list and no calls from Karen. Then I looked in his contacts, she was still there. I guess I couldn't exactly be mad at that, I hadn't gone through my contacts and deleted anyone. Feeling a lot better I put his phone down. I put on sweats and a t-shirt. Then as the water turned off his phone rang. Expecting it to be his mother I looked at the Caller ID. Of course it said Karen. "Babe!"

"Yea?" He answered

"Karen's calling you!"

He blew out air in a defeated way. "Answer it!"

I picked up the phone quickly, "hello" I said with a smile in my voice.

She hesitated, "Can I speak to Drew!" She sounded like she had been crying.
"Who's this?"

She blew air, "Karen"

I hit the speaker button then I handed Andrew the phone. He looked sad, "hello"

"Drew what is going on?" Tears returning to her voice.

He kept his eyes to the floor. "What do you mean?"

"You're gonna marry her?"

"Yes"

"Why?"

"Because I love her, and I want to spend the rest of my life with her."

"What about us?"

"Karen I told you. I love her and I couldn't see you anymore."

"I didn't think you were serious."

"Why?"

"What do you mean why? You've said that before, but it's not like you held true to that. Drew I love you!"

He shook his head. "How could you? I've never taken you out. I haven't done anything for you." He swallowed hard, "all we ever were was sex."

"How can you say that? I know you care about me."

He blew air, "look I know it's hard enough to deal with the fact that I'm getting married. And I don't want to say anything else to really hurt you. But think about it, we only ever had sex. I told you before that I'm in love."

You could hear her crying, "but you always come back."

"Not this time."

"What am I supposed to do now?"

"I can't answer that for you. I don't wish anything bad on you. I just won't be a part of your life anymore."

"Drew please don't do this! Please!"

He exhaled, still keeping his eyes to the floor. "I gotta go."

"You love her that much? Why?"

"I'm not gonna do this with you." His voice got deeper, "Karen!"

"Yes?" She said through her tears

"Stop it! Just stop! If you want to continue this dramatic scene, find somebody else. I already told you I wasn't fooling with you no more. So I don't know why you have to have this whole dramatic scene. You are making a fool of yourself!"

"How dare you talk to me like this! I could call her right now and tell her everything! Mess up your whole situation, and you gonna sit over there like I can't mess you up!"

"Tell me now!" I said

"You got me on speaker! I can't believe this!" She blew air and did her best to try to take the tears out of her voice.

"Tell me!" I said

"That the whole time you've been seeing him he's been with me."

"What do you mean by whole time?" I said

"Before you were pregnant." She said

I shot Andrew a question mark look. "How long before?"

"About six months."

I did the math in my head, I was with Steve and he was with Toya then. Why would she think Toya and I were the same person? She came over my parent's house before Andrew and I got back together Andre was born then. All she has to do is think about it. "And when was the last time you were together?"

"Right before the party at my brother's house."

I looked at Andrew who hadn't taken his eyes off the floor. "Excuse me?"

"I didn't stutter! To think all these years if only I knew it was you! I can't stand you!"

"Yea! Yea! Yea! Back to this last time."

"Oh what you want pointers?"

"Get real! You're telling me you slept with my man right before the party?"

"Yes!" You could hear the smile in her voice.

"No! Tracy, I told you I did not sleep with her."

"So I guess cumming in my mouth don't count then?"

"Eeewwllll!!!! You're nasty!" I looked at him. "Oh so oral sex isn't sex to you?"

"It's not the same." He said

Karen laughed, "I bet you think putting a dick in your mouth is beyond you. You little prissy snot!"

"Oh no, you've already let your hair down. Don't try to act like a lady now. Are you really sitting over there priding yourself on being somebody's secret? Someone they'd never be seen in public with. A man can get sex from anywhere and if that's all you're offering him, he will move on. You have the nerve to ask him not to marry me, but you're fine with being on the DL if we're just dating? You need to learn to respect yourself!"

"Oh so I guess you learned all this from messing with Steve! I know how he did you, I had him too." My stomach turned. What she do follow me around? "And Cameron told me how you just lay there like you're too pretty to do anything!"
Andrew flashed me a look!

"Who?"

"Don't act like you don't know who Cameron is. Sister Harris' son. He told me how boring it was to sleep with you. How you just laid there with your legs open like a stiff board. I had to show him how a real woman puts in work."

"You should really stop talking."

"Why? Drew should know, which is why he always came back to me. It made all the sense in the world once I found out you were the girlfriend. Poor baby was bored."

I calmed my voice, "first of all! That's news to me that you were with Steve, but I can't even care about that now. I NEVER touched Cameron, sounds like he used that lie to sleep with you. I was NEVER interested in Cameron! He called me a few times but yea those were just courtesy conversations. His momma wanted that not me. I don't know why he felt like he had to trick you, sounds like you would've gave it up either way. Now regarding MY MAN!!! All I have to say is call this number again and see what happens to you!" Then I hung up the phone. I was so angry I tried to throw the phone at Andrew, but it hit the wall and shattered. He was mad, but he didn't say anything. "You lied to me!"

"No I didn't!"

"Yes you did! You told me you didn't sleep with her!"

"And I didn't!"

"Andrew oral sex is still sex!"

Then Andre knocked on the door. "Are you guys ok? I thought I heard something."

"We're fine baby, go back to playing." I said in the nicest voice I could muster.

"Can we go in the backyard?"

"Yes take Cain and Eve with you." Andrew said, and then he went to the key panel and unlocked the alarm on the back door and windows. He opened the patio doors in the bedroom so we could hear the boys. "I know oral sex is sex, but...." He was shaking his head.

"Were you sleeping with her when we were together the first time?"

"No! I didn't even know her back then. But you were sleeping with her when you were begging me to get back with you!"

"Yea, but..."

"Eeewwllll Andrew! What if I would've said yes?"

"But you didn't! So it doesn't matter."

"Why does she think Toya and I are the same person?"

"I didn't want to date her, so it was easier to let her believe Toya and I were still together. This is not an issue."

"Why all your Ex's gotta be so crazy?"

"WHO ARE YOU TO TALK ABOUT CRAZY EX's? Got me running around here like the secret service."

"Why they have to always go behind me?"

"That's your interpretation, they could say you went behind them."

I got mad cause he was taking me off the point. "Doesn't matter, you lied to me! As if it wasn't bad enough to tell me about this whole thing why would you then only tell me part of the truth?"

"I told you the truth!"

"You're making it very hard to trust you!"

"I told you the truth!"

"So what if I said I didn't sleep with Sean, but I let him eat me out? Would that matter to you?"

His knee jerk reaction was angry. Then he sat on the bed, he was quiet. His hands kept flexing and unflexing. He was quiet for a long time. Then he looked at me, his face was hard! "He would die!" He said real even.

"Die?"

"You heard me." Then he got up like he was going in the bathroom. Right when he was in front of me, he put his arms around me and he grabbed me. The angle he was holding me in I couldn't tell if he was angry or what. He threw me on the bed, and then he laid besides me holding me down with his leg and his arm. He put his face next to mine. "Tracy, I'm sorry! I love you! But let me make something clear. We have to finish the way we start. If we didn't start off in a open relationship, we will not end up in one either." His voice was a low rumble, I'd never heard or seen him like this. I was scared! "No man will ever touch you again. Or else someone will die! You will not leave me! You're stuck with me until the day YOU die! So for both of our sanities don't ever paint a picture for me like that AGAIN! You understand me?"

Ummmmm, was this fool crazy? Yes he's crazy cause now he's just laying there staring at me. His arm and leg were strong but not heavy. Did he just manhandle me? Aren't I supposed to be his delicate flower? Suddenly I had to pee, but I was scared to say anything. So I just laid there. Then I remembered who this is and who I am to him. "Move!" I said pushing his arm. He fought me at first but he let me go. I went into the bathroom. As soon as he heard me peeing he started laughing. "I hate you!" I said while he kept laughing. "You play too much!"

"But I'm not playing with you. I'm serious!"

"Whatever Andrew! Keep testing me and we'll see who's playing."

He smiled at me, and then I shut the bathroom door. YES! My period came.

CHAPTER 30

I bought Andre a pair of skates. Everyday we went in the backyard and practiced. He's such a quick learner that he picked it up in two days by Friday he looked like he was born with skates as feet. His little self was going and going on those skates. Andrew wasn't my favorite person all week. He kept eyeballing me ever since he did the scare the pee out of me routine. I would roll my eyes at him, or blank stare at him.

By day four my period was gone. And normally as soon as I was off I was ready to go. But since I was mad at him I had to put those feelings to rest. At night we would do the whole stare down thing. He said before he could tell when I was on my period by the things I wore especially to bed. Thursday night I saw him do a double take when I wore my long black nightgown to bed. His attitude softened a little. Then he took a shower, oiled up, and came to bed in silk pj pants. I am a sucker for the feeling of soft silk on skin. But I laid on my side and wouldn't look in his direction no matter how inviting he tried to make his chest look. In the morning he was on the floor doing push ups. I pretended not to notice his beautiful back stretching and flexing as he went up and down. I pretended not to notice him watching me get dressed in the morning. After work I met up with Nicole at Chase's to celebrate the week being over. I told her about Karen and she shook her head. Then I told her about our whole show down. She laughed at Andrew and I, she said we were silly. I looked around the bar, no one there looked familiar; I figured maybe he called off the followers. I exhaled took my shot of Patron, and then started on my Grande margarita. Nicole smiled really big, "I guess you're right! We can't go anywhere!"

I looked up and Hubby and Andrew were walking towards us. I rolled my eyes cause he looked good too! I kept telling myself to be cool. Had I known he was coming I wouldn't have drunken anything.

"Hello my name is Hubby, can I ask yours?"

"Nicole" she said with a huge grin

"Nicole, I was coming to have a drink with my friend. But I saw you, you are breath takingly beautiful!"

"Thank you!"

"I had to come over and introduce myself."

"Well I'm glad you did." She said

"Really?"

"Yea, me and my girl was hoping this place turned up something nice."

"Well I see you have drinks, can we get the next round?" He said

"You're welcome to join us."

I looked at her while finishing my drink. "Speak for yourself!" I said

"Why you so angry? Where's your man?" Andrew said

"I fired him!" I said matter of factly

Hubby started laughing. Andrew smiled real big, "why did you do that?"

"Cause he play too much! I don't have time for that." I said

Andrew sat down and leaned in, his cologne invaded my nose. I tried to pretend I didn't notice, and that I didn't love his smell. "You don't like games?"

I sighed and put down my drink. "What's your name?"

"Mauricio, and you're?"

He gave his middle name, fine. "Laureen"

"That's very pretty."

"Thank you, anyways, Mauricio? You are a good-looking kid; you're wasting your time over here. I'm not interested." I rolled my eyes and went back to drinking.

All three of them laughed. "Please excuse my friend. She's leery of new people." Nicole said

I rolled my eyes. "That's ok, she's feisty. I like feisty women." Andrew said

"Really you like living dangerously!"

He leaned in. "I'm a very dangerous man!"

I rolled my eyes, "I trust that!"

"You too pretty to be so mean."

"Didn't anybody tell you that the pretty ones have the worst attitudes."? I said

"Ouch! Why don't you retreat to your corner, refresh your game for a minute." Hubby said

Then Andrew waved down our server. Can you bring the ladies another of whatever they had and four fingers Glenlivet neat. Hubby?"

"Jack and Coke" Hubby ordered

"Can I get you anything to eat?" Our server asked

Everybody looked at each other. "How about nachos and the fresh made Guacamole?" Andrew asked, no one objected. "Good we'll have that."

"So pretty Nicole, what you got going on for the night?"

"After this nothing, I was meeting my friend for drinks and then I'm open. Do you have something in mind?"

Hubby sat there eyeballing her then he turned to Andrew. "I wanna go dancing, you down?" Andrew and Hubby fist bumped. "So you down to go dancing?"

"Yes!" She said too excited

"No!" I said

"Aw! Come on girl! They look like fun guys. What you gonna do tonight anyways? Sit at home with your son and watch wheel of fortune?" Nicole said

"Sounds better than this." I said rolling my eyes. "We're not even dressed to go dancing."

"You have a son?" Andrew said

"Yes"

"How old is he?"

"Almost Four"

"That's a fun age."

"It is," I said. Our drinks arrived. I took the shot, and then sipped my margarita.

"Listen, I would be really happy if you would come with us. I don't wanna be the third wheel to these two." Andrew said

I rolled my eyes, "still doesn't change the fact we're not dressed to go out."

"I know you've gotta have something at home. " Andrew said

"Maybe I do. I still don't see why I should waste any of it on you!"

"Come on girl do it for me. We don't know these guys they could be dangerous. You would never forgive yourself for leaving me alone with them." Nicole said

"I'll think about it." I said. I peaked at Andrew out the corner of my eye. He looked GOOD! Why do they always do that when they know you're mad at them? Funny how only when he's mad do I recognize how big and solid he is. But I'm mad at him for trying to put back on me what he did wrong. He didn't tell me the whole truth, and then as I'm trying to help him understand my point he loses it. Oprah says when a person shows you who they are pay attention. But what did he show me? That he can't handle the idea of another man touching me in anyway. He lost it! I guess that's not the worst. To know that you're the weakness of the guy who's your weakness. But he has to pay for scaring the pee out of me.

Nicole and Hubby were falling all over each other. Andrew kept watching me and I kept rolling my eyes at him. He kept winking at me, flashing his dimples, trying to wear me down. If I was gonna remain strong I was gonna have to stop drinking. So I turned down round four, as I was already tipsy.

"So, what's the verdict? Are you ladies rolling with us?" Hubby asked

"It depends on my friend." Nicole said

Everyone looked at me. "Whatever, we can go." I rolled my eyes.

I could tell Andrew was a little tipsy as well.

"Cool! We'll come pick you guys up from your friends house." Hubby said

Nicole was so excited, she rambled the whole way home. After I introduced her to Eve and Cain we ran upstairs to raid my closet. I found the perfect strapless little black dress. I gave Nicole a purple one-shoulder number that looked great on her. I hopped in the shower while she washed up in Andre's bathroom. I wore my curls down, I put on a simple necklace, fabulous heels, and I grabbed a clutch that would stay on my wrist all night. Fortunately Nicole's shoes went nicely with her dress, as we didn't wear the same size shoes.

I'm not gonna lie, this role-playing was kind of fun. I just wish we were in a happy place when we decided to do this. I looked out the window as a NICE car pulled up. "They're here!" I yelled as I ran back upstairs. I gave Nicole a bag to put her things in. She went down to put her stuff in her car. I ran in the bathroom, I put my diaphragm in just in case. I grabbed a few condoms out of the nightstand, and a lightweight sweater. As I walked down the stairs Andrew was standing in the doorway. He smiled really big at me showing his approval, and I rolled my eyes. That made him laugh.

"This is a nice house you have." He said looking around

"Thank you. I'm gonna need you to step out so I can set the alarm. "

Andrew chuckled as he stepped out. I petted the puppies goodnight, gave them a treat and closed the doors before the alarm set.

"Ok so, I'm gonna take my car home so we can all ride together in that snazzy car." I started walking towards her. "Where are you going?"

"Um! I'm riding with you." I got in Nicole's car.

"Girl how much longer you gonna give Andrew the cold shoulder?"

"I don't know, until he apologizes I guess."

"What kind of car is that?" She said looking through her rear view mirror.

"I don't know but it's beautiful! They got a driver and everything."

Nicole was so excited about the night. All four of us squeezed in the back of the car. I didn't pay attention to which way we went, but we pulled in front of Elegant Affairs a club in Oakland. The line was down the block to get in. Everybody was looking at us when we got out of the car. There was no waiting for us, "Drew! Hubby! Haven't seen you guys in quite a minute. Come on in!" One of the bouncers said.

This club was amazing inside. I wondered why, if the bouncers knew him, why was this my first time here? This place was beautiful! There was a lounge area where the music wasn't as loud. A table area where you could sit and enjoy the music and watch people dance. There was a bar with a ton of bartenders. They were all moving at all times but gliding harmoniously together. I thought we were going to sit at one of the tables, but Andrew guided us to the roped off VIP section. It was over to the side but in plain view of everything. I immediately recognized his father who was sitting with some OG looking fellas and they all had their eyes on the dance floor. We sat in a booth two booths over from theirs. As soon as we sat down a waitress came with single malt for Andrew. She asked what we would like to drink. I couldn't decide. Our waitress was really nice. I told her I had been drinking margaritas already. So she told me she'd bring me something along those lines. Nicole asked for the same thing. Hubby gave her a hard time for forgetting his usual Jack and Coke. She was back lickety split with our drinks. Hubby told our waitress that he had a request for the DJ. Then he whispered it in her ear. She smiled real big then she disappeared. The next thing I knew the music changed. Everyone who was sitting grabbed their partner's hands and made their way to the dance floor. "You're all I need to get by!" Hubby looked at Nicole, they were on their feet making their way to the dance floor. Method man explained his situation. The music was so clear, the bass felt like it was pumping through you.

Andrew slid right next to me. "Tracy, I'm sorry for how I acted. I was wrong not thinking of how you'd see the situation. I just couldn't handle the picture you painted for me. It was too real. But I shouldn't have reacted that way. I'm sorry." He said

I wanted to still be mean, but one look into his eyes during his short little speech and all my meanness floated away. "You wanna dance?" I asked

He smiled and I took him by the hand. We floated past Nicole and Hubby into the center of the floor. Our groove started slowly, when the song changed to the next one the pace was a lot faster. We worked up quite a sweat dancing song after song. My baby always moved effortlessly. As we danced I wondered if there was anything he couldn't do? We danced, we did a little bump and grind, even two stepped. It was like we were in our own little world. I didn't pay attention to whoever was around us. Andrew was my focus. Then the DJ announced that they were going to have and impromptu performance by one of the regulars. With all the liquor in my system I now needed to pee. When I looked in Nicole's direction she was signaling to go to the bathroom. Before I walked away from Andrew he picked me up and we kissed long and passionately. Since the dance floor was clearing everyone saw us. Some people clapped while others cheered us on. I smiled because I was embarrassed. Andrew and Hubby headed back towards the VIP. I followed Nicole since she seemed to have been here before and knew where the bathroom was. Even though there were six stalls there was a small line.

"Girl you guys were breaking it down. I guess you guys made up."

"He apologized, so I guess so."

"Are you still roll playing?"

"I don't know, if we are he broke character to apologize. Are you guys?"

"Oh girl yes! It is so exciting. I love when we do stuff like this."

I smiled, and then we went into our separate stalls. I came out before Nicole, so I washed my hands. There wasn't much room so I told Nicole I would wait outside the bathroom for her. As I stood against the wall, I was looking down at my feet that were surprisingly comfortable in these high heel shoes.

"Tracy?" A unidentifiable voice said,

I looked up and the guy's face looked familiar, but I couldn't place him right away.

He was average height, so with my heels we were about the same height. He had beautiful cocoa brown skin. His hair was nicely lined and his hair was curly. Not as curly as Andrew's, but soft looking. Even though I couldn't place his name I knew I knew him from somewhere. "Hey! How are you?" I said as he came in for a hug. "How have you been?"

"I'm doing well, how about you?" He said

Then Nicole came out the bathroom. I motioned to her to come to me. "This is my friend Nicole."

"Hello Nicole, I'm Jesse nice to meet you."

She smiled real big. "Nice to meet you."

I grabbed her hand as a way to tell her not to leave. Last thing I needed was for Andrew to walk around the corner and get the wrong idea. I remembered Jesse. We went to middle school together. He was always nice to me, but we never dated or anything. Not that I didn't think he was cute back then, but his attention never swung my way. So I never thought of him. "So are you here alone?" I asked

"Not really, but I'm working tonight. They're setting up the stage for me right now."

"Oh yea. I forgot you sang."

"Jesse come on!" Someone called from the end of the hallway.

"Ok, I got to go. But don't leave before I get a chance to catch up with you."

"Ok" I said as he hurried away.

"Girl, I don't know if that's a good idea."

"What do you mean? We weren't flirting, he's just a friend from way back in the day." I said defensively

"You don't realize where we are?"

"No! What club is this anyways?"

"This is one of Andrew's spots. If you felt like you were under surveillance before. Just assume almost everybody in here is affiliated with Andrew in some way."

"But there's nothing between me and Jesse. We were always cool back in the day."

"Ok but don't say I didn't warn you."

"What do you mean Andrew's spot?"

"He either owns or is part owner. I get it confused."

"How do you know?"

"Hubby and I used to come here from time to time."

"Hhmmmm" seemed like he's still a regular, but I didn't say anything.

Nicole told me to come on. The dance floor was empty the tables, bar, and lounge area were full. Malcolm was sitting with Andrew and Hubby. He was telling them something, but with his gestures it looked serious. Andrew and Hubby were both tipsy but focusing on him while they continued to drink.
Jesse was on the stage preparing for his first song. He was kind of watching while he prepared to sing.

Not knowing what to do, whether I should wait for them to finish or go sit down, I opted to go sit. I sat on Andrew's left side since his father was on the right. There was a fresh drink waiting for us and a large pitcher of water with four glasses next to it. I poured a glass of water. I debated whether I wanted the new drink. But the last one was so good, I could barely taste the tequila in it, but I could feel the affects on the dance floor. Malcolm's face was always serious; when I sat down he looked at me like I was intruding. "Nice to see you again Malcolm."

"Likewise" then he looked at Andrew. "So when is the big day?"

"We haven't set a date yet. But it will be soon."

"I don't know why young folks wanna get married. I guess you guys like the show."

"We wanna put it on paper." I said

Malcolm looked at me with cold piercing eyes. He made me nervous, and I don't think he likes me. "Paper can be destroyed."

I put my arm around Andrew's. "True, but we've vowed to each other so paper or not this is it." I said trying to stand my ground although I really wanted to run away.

Malcolm looked at me for what seemed like forever. It was that same evil look Andrew had when he scared the pee out of me. Why do the men in this family have to be so scary?

"Alright then!" Andrew said breaking the silence. He put his hand between my knees, and rubbed my thigh. "You run your life your way, and I'll run mine my way. Comprende?"

Malcolm look at his hand then he looked at me. "Toya's here!" He said as he stood up.

"I already know. And trust she knows better. Plus she's here with her L7, no worries."

Malcolm walked away. Hubby and Nicole were busy making out; they didn't hear a word of what we were saying. "She's here?" Andrew nodded.

"Where?" Andrew pointed to a table not too far from us. She was staring at us when I finally understood where he was pointing. Her hair was done up, and she was beautiful. The guy she was with looked as clueless as me. When he looked at her she smiled as if she had been looking at him the whole time. He was talking about something and she nodded and smiled. Whenever she could she'd cut her eyes back our way. "How long have you known she was here?"

"Since I sat down. She's not gonna do nothing. She's playing good girl tonight." Andrew said

"And how do you know that?" I asked staring at her.

"Her hair, and the way she's acting. If she was gonna do something she would've been over here especially while you were in the bathroom or talking to Jesse."

"How do you know about that?" The hallway to the bathroom was on the opposite side from the VIP section.

"I told you I got eyes and ears everywhere." He leaned back with a huge grin. "By the way, we got our own bathrooms up here. You don't gotta go down there."

"Nobody told me."

"So..." He smiled. "How do you know Jesse?"

"We went to middle school together."

"Aw! That's cute!" He said smiling at me. "He has a booth up here maybe we can all chat, when he's done."

"Ok" I said looking back at Toya.

Then Jesse performed a few songs for the crowd. He was an excellent performer. He had the whole house rocking. We all went down and danced while he sang to us. A couple of idiot young girls were dancing at Malcolm's table, the smile on his face said he was enjoying the show they put on for him. On the slow song Andrew pulled me in so close I didn't know where he stopped and I began. His lead was strong, I never guessed about which way he was leading me. We moved so in sync together it was almost like we were making love right there on the dance floor. All I knew is I was ready, Andrew looked at my face and he flashed his dimples. I kissed him, I would love to blame it on the alcohol but I knew it was all me. My baby was Fine! And always the man! No matter what was happening. How could you not love someone like him? When we went back to our booth, Andrew looked at the tramps performing for his father. He looked at them then his dad. He shook his head. His dad smiled and shook his head yes.

We sat down, and Darryl appeared, "Nigga! I see you finally brought her out to come kick it with the fam!" Then he gave Andrew a fist bump.

"When did you get here?" I said rising to give Darryl a hug.

"I been here for a minute. I was hollering at this hoe in the lounge when I looked up and see ya'll making babies on the dance floor." He said cracking up.

"We were not." I said embarrassed

"It's cool sis. Nice to know you know how to let your hair down." Then he did a quick study of my face. "And you twisted too. Oh this is about to be fun!" He chuckled.

"You gonna bring your friend up here?" Andrew asked Darryl blew air, "please! You the only one who be weak over females. I don't know that hoe to be bringing her up here. Only the worthy can come up here. I'll send her a drink though." He said looking around. "A! You know Toya's here?"

"Yes I saw her!" Andrew said

"Is that her baby daddy?"

"I think so, I think they're married too." Andrew said

"WHAT????" Darryl sang cracking up. "I gotta go mess with her!" He got up with a huge grin on his face. Toya started shaking her head no. Darryl shook his head yes, as he walked over. Toya shifted in her chair. She shot Andrew a pleading look, and he smiled at her with a evil look.

"How do you know she's married?"

"I told you I got eyes everywhere." He said appearing to be amused by Darryl's actions.

"How long she been married?"

"Not exactly sure, but I believe it happened after she got out from her little stunt at the restaurant." He said not taking his eyes off of them.

Darryl was talking to them and he kept bumping Toya for confirmation to what he was saying. You could tell she was uncomfortable but she was trying to be cool. There was a girl in the lounge area staring at them. I could tell she didn't like Darryl's interaction with Toya even though her man was sitting right there. She walked over to them with a ton of attitude. Her neck was wiggling and her finger was in Toya's face. Toya's man stood up. Darryl laughed and put his hand on his shoulder. Toya looked scared, as she tried to calm her man. Her man wasn't happy, he was talking mostly to the girl, and Darryl dismissed the girl still laughing. She went back to her corner still brewing and talking to her friends. They all started looking at the table. I guess he said the wrong thing; cause although Darryl was still smiling he slightly opened his jacket. Then he patted her man's shoulder who now did as he was told and sat down. Toya put her hand on her face as she shook her head. Then Darryl went over to the bar. He pointed at their table and then he came back to our booth. He was cracking up. The bartender brought a bottle over to their table. Darryl was cracking up as he slapped Andrew's hand.

"What just happened?" I asked

"I went over to say hey and introduce myself. Her man got a little heart, but he's still a loser. That hoe came over talking about she don't like Toya, and Toya playing little miss innocent acting like she don't know her or why. He got mad about the accusations. I had to let him know he doesn't know where he is and he needed to calm down. I sent them some Cris to celebrate their nuptials."

"Aren't you sweet!" Andrew said making fun of him.

"You know I do what I can."

"Darryl!" Malcolm's voice came booming out of nowhere.

Darryl was up and over there in no time flat. "Excuse me, I'll be right back." Andrew said as he made his way towards his dad.

Hubby and Nicole came back to the booth. I couldn't hear what was being said, but the vibe over there was serious. Toya was trying to look without looking. But then she kept looking behind herself as well. Nicole saw me looking and she followed my eyes until she spotted Toya. "What is she doing here?"

"I don't know, but Andrew said she's with her husband."

"Her what?"

"Yep, somebody married her."

Nicole scooted closer to me, "what does he look like?"

"I can't tell. I've only seen the back of his head."

Jesse finished his final song, everyone was going crazy. Especially the ladies. He was smiling from ear to ear as he entered the VIP and sat down in the booth next to ours on the left. He stood on the seat and leaned over towards our booth. "What's up Tracy!"

Nicole and I stood up on our seats to look at him. He was still sweating. "Hey Jesse you were great!"

"Thank you! Thank you! So you're with Drew? Wow!"

"Why is that a Wow?"

"I just didn't know you had it in you."

"What does that mean?"

"Drew handles his business. He's the man! Just didn't take you for such a high profile guy."

"What does that mean?"

"I thought I was the biggest news to come from Portola Junior high."

"I'm not big news, he is. I happen to be the woman he loves." I said with a big smile.

"They're engaged!" Nicole chimed in.

Jessie's eyes got big. "Whoa congratulations! When's the wedding?"

"Soon, how about you? What's new with you?"

"I'm married. I got two girls."

"Is your wife here tonight?" I said looking into his booth.

"No she's not here tonight. Our youngest is sick. But she's normally here."

"Aw! I hope I meet her soon."

"Meet who?" Derrick said as he walked over to our booth.

"Hey D-Rick!" Jesse said as he walked around.

"Aw! What's up man!" Derrick said giving Jesse a pound.

"I was just telling them how my wifey is normally here, but our youngest is sick. "

"What up Jesse!" Darryl said, "good set tonight!"

"Drew!" Jesse said as Andrew approached.

"Hey man!" Andrew said then he looked at Nicole and I who were still standing on the seat in our heels. We quickly got down. "No wifey tonight?"

"Nope, one of the girls is sick."

"Sit down, relax, you just finished a set." Jesse sat down while the rest of his entourage filled in at his booth. Andrew sat down, "so how do you know Tracy?"

Derrick and Darryl sat down; Hubby leaned in to hear his answer.

"We went to Middle school together."

"Is that right?" Andrew said taking another drink of his drink. "What was she like in middle school?"

"We were always cool, I guess she was your average 12-14 year old."

"Did you guys date?" He asked bluntly.

"No" he thought about it. "Tracy why didn't we date?"

"Um, I don't know. Neither of us ever showed an interest in each other. We were always just friends."

Suddenly the music stopped and the lights on the floor came up. Two girls were fighting. I instantly looked at Toya's table, but she was still seated. Two bouncers came out of nowhere. They each grabbed a girl and promptly picked them up and escorted them out. Andrew didn't flinch he as watched. His eyes bounced around the room. Then I noticed the eyes that floated our way looking for Andrew's approval.

"Derrick when did you get here?" I asked

"I was here before you guys."

"Oh I didn't see you."

"I'm learning to be stealthy like Drew." He said

I looked at Andrew who was finishing his drink. As soon as his glass touched the table his waitress was at our table collecting. She came back with another fresh glass, and a appetizer sampler platter. The platter was loaded with fried mozzarella sticks, chicken fingers, potato skins, jalapeño poppers, fried zucchini, and chicken wings. We all went in on the platter; I needed something to soak up the alcohol. But I also drank the next two drinks brought to me. At one point Andrew needed to talk to Malcolm again, so he asked Jesse to dance with me. As we danced to a couple of fast songs Toya brought her man on the floor to dance. I tapped Nicole to look at them. Her man was nice looking, and he appeared to be completely in to her. I couldn't understand why she would bring him here. Andrew came on the dance floor. He walked right between Toya and her man. Her man looked like he had, had enough. Andrew was now completely toasted. "You ready?"

"Yes" I said, "let me grab my sweater." Jesse walked with me after giving Andrew a pound. "Thanks for the dance Jesse. It was good seeing you again."

"You too, Andrew is good people. Just be careful."

"What does that mean?" I asked

"I know you're a good girl, and this whole lifestyle is beyond you." Then he put his hand on my shoulder, "take care".

I grabbed my sweater, when I turned around Andrew was staring at me. I joined him on the dance floor. He put his hand in the small of my back to guide me out. Nicole and Hubby were already waiting at the curb. Both of them were gone, they were so drunk and giggly. Our car pulled up and we piled in. When we drove off Toya was looking at us as she walked with her man in the cold to their car. She did not look happy. Nicole and Hubby were all over each other. Andrew's mouth tasted sweeter with the taste of alcohol on it. We dropped Nicole and Hubby off first since they lived in Oakland. Andrew didn't move from his corner of the back seat. I laid across the backseat with my head in his lap looking up. He smiled down at me and stroked my head. "How do you like the Rolls Royce?"

"Is that what this is? We were trying to figure out what kind of car this was."

"Yep, how many guys can say they've rode in a Rolls?"

"How many guys have gotten laid in a Rolls?"

"What about the driver?" He asked as I sat up

"Duh! That's what the curtain is for!" I said pulling close the curtain. I pulled a condom out of my clutch. He smiled a relaxed smile. I pulled his pants down, and my dress up enough to mount him.

"You are so beautiful Tracy! I love you so much!"

"I love you!" The excitement from driving on the freeway, being just about drunk, that was definitely "a ride to remember". Our driver was completely red in the face when we got to our house. I couldn't look him in the face. When Andrew came inside after settling the bill. He threw me over his shoulder, set the alarm, and then he playfully spanked me all the way into our room.

"When did you put your diaphragm in?" He asked as he put me down.

"Before we left." As I started to walk away he grabbed my arm while undoing his pants with the other. He dropped his pants and drawers to the floor. Then he grabbed me by the waist as he squatted. He picked me up and made me straddle him. Skin to skin again I surrendered to the feeling. I thought alcohol was supposed to make you sloppy and hinder your ability to perform. This man continues to blow my mind.

As we sat on the floor, he looked at me completely drunk. "What do you think of Toya's man?"

"I didn't"

"Do you think he's better than me?"

"Absolutely not! But why do you care?"

"I don't! But I didn't like seeing her tonight! Sometimes I forget how pretty she can be."

I knew he was drunk cause he'd never admit to me that she was pretty. "She was pretty."

"But she's evil! Evil! She always wanted me to fight somebody, to show I cared about her. She cheated for attention. I like how you don't do that. You just want me to show you love and that's enough to make you happy." He scratched his head. "And you know what?" I looked at him. "She couldn't handle the Beast. One time she cried and said I was trying to kill her. But she got mad when I was with someone else. Honestly I think she didn't mind. As long as she was number one." He looked around the floor. "You know that time when we made Andre?" I nodded yes. "She was on my nerves, acting so insecure. She was convinced you had put something on me, cause things weren't the same. But that time I made her take the whole Beast! I didn't care if it hurt her or not. I was so mad! I thought I lost you forever!"

"Look at what being mad got you." I said

"I love my son! I'm just happy she's not connected to him anymore."

"Does it bother you that she's married?"

"A little bit. When I proposed to her in college she told me she needed to think about it. Took her dear sweet time, then she told me No. I vowed I'd never ask her again. But she only got pregnant cause she thought I would marry her. She thought she was gonna get all this money from me for having my baby. She was mad that I controlled everything. She didn't love me, I was sorry that it took her being pregnant for me to understand that."

Then he pulled me by my arm into his lap. "You love me don't you?" I shook my head yes. "I know, cause you bent your vow with God for me. You show my son so much love. You listen to me when I'm talking. You let me protect you. You let me be the man. And the most important part to me is that you didn't run from me. When Toya pulled that stunt at my old place, I knew you were gonna run. I didn't even wanna deal with it. I was gonna be through with you. But you stayed, you fought for me." He smiled, with tears in his eyes. "My life is crazy, as I'm slowly letting you see. You give me so much peace and calmness."

"Can I ask you something?"

"Shoot!"

"Why haven't you officially moved in?"

"Your dad asked me not to. Ssshhhh! Don't tell him though."

"When was this?"

"Remember that time we went over there? We went to get restraining orders and then we went over?"

"Yes!"

"I told him I loved you more than anything in the world. I asked him for your hand. He asked me if I was living with you. I told him no, he made me promise not to live here until we were married. It's been hard! I get tired of going back and forth for clothes. But when a man gives his word he has to stand by it. Besides I know how much you love your dad."

"Why didn't you tell me?"

"It's a conversation between me and him. You don't need to know."

"But you just told me." I said smiling

He had a confused look on his face. "Woman you pumping me for info?"

"Yes! I am." Then I swallowed hard. "Was Karen the only one you cheated on me with?"

His eyes glazed over. "I don't wanna talk about this."

"Why? It would really make me feel better." I said

"In the beginning no. But in the end yes."

"What was it about Karen?"

"She seemed nice enough. But I always held back with her. She never met my son. I just needed sex and she liked it. I didn't know she was religious. I came over did my business, went home."

"Then why were you sad when she found out about our engagement?"

"I don't like hurting females, even when they are asking for it. I saw my mom cry too many times not to be affected by it."

"What happened to your step father?"

He got real quiet, tears started rolling down his face. But he didn't say anything. I put my arms around his neck and kissed his tears. He didn't talk after that. He cried himself to sleep.

CHAPTER 31

In the morning I made Andrew drink a ton of water. I took Cain to the store with me. I put the guide dog in training handle and jacket on him so that the stores didn't give me static about bringing him in. Most people would look at his size and still move out of my way completely. I got some Gatorade, watermelon, and anything else I could find to hydrate him. I made Andrew some eggs, bacon, and toast when I got home. I brought it all to him on a tray. He was appreciative; he didn't appear to be hung over like I thought he would be. But I knew he was definitely drunk last night. He was quiet most of the morning, I didn't know if he didn't feel well or if my questions bothered him. I chugged on water and everything else as well. I wasn't nearly as gone as he was, but I was definitely on the dehydration bus. Amber brought Andre home at about noon.

"Next time you guys go to EA I wanna go."

"You go to clubs?" I asked surprised

"Child please! How old do you think I am? Of course I do."

"What about skating?"

"Oh yea! I skate my behind off." She said snapping her fingers looking less and less like an older woman. I forget she isn't much older than Andrew.

"We're going to Hubby & Nicole's anniversary party tonight. It's gonna be at a skating rink if you wanna come?"

"I wouldn't be intruding?"

"Not at all. Nicole would love it."

"Excellent!" She smiled really big. "What time should I be ready?"

"We'll pick you up at about four thirty to five."

"I'll be ready." She smiled as she started to turn towards the door.

"Can I ask your advice about something?"

"Sure Hun, what's up?"

"Is your ex husband a taboo topic?"

"What do you mean?"

"I asked Darryl about him the other day and he stopped talking altogether. I asked Andrew about him last night and he got really upset. But he won't talk to me. I don't like seeing him like this."

She touched my shoulder. "It's a sensitive subject with all my boys. When he's ready Andrew will tell you about it. Just leave it alone until he's ready though. If there was ever a topic that you shouldn't push, that's it." We were quiet for a minute. Then she said, "did anything exciting happen last night?"

"Not really. Oh but Toya was there with her husband."

Amber's eyebrows went up, "HER WHAT????" She sat on the couch waiting for me to tell it all.

"I didn't know she was there until Malcolm pointed her out."

"Malcolm was there?"

"Yes."

"Was he with a girl?"

"Not exactly." I said not knowing how to explain what I saw.

"I guess it figures that he would be there." She had that same look on her face that Andrew would have as he connected dots unsaid. "What did her husband look like?"

"He was nice looking. I guess he was alright."

"Why would she bring him there?"

"I don't know. I was wondering the same thing. She didn't look happy about it. You know how she gloats all the time. She looked like she was trying to be low profile. Andrew said she was gonna be a good girl, he could tell by her hair."

"How was her hair?"

"It was in a up do." I said

"Oh yea. Most of the time she pulls her hair back in a ponytail she's plotting. When it's down she's happy and most vulnerable. Which is why she doesn't wear it down often at all."

I wondered if I assigned any emotion to my hairstyles. How closely did they pay attention to people to pick up on little things like that? Fortunately Amber changed the subject and we started talking about the wedding. "When are you going dress shopping?"

"I haven't decided. Andrew and I can't agree on the size of the wedding. Last we talked we were talking five hundred people. That's too many people."

"Oh honey if you got five hundred people willing to travel, etc. just to see you say I do I say go for it."

"But that's gonna cost a lot of money. I haven't discussed budget with my parents. Andrew thinks we, and when I say we I mean he, should pay for it. And with that he's not worried about cost."

"Are your parents expecting to pay for the wedding?"

"I don't know, but they're completely excited."

"Stop worrying about the small stuff lets get this wedding on the road."

Andre was sitting at the table eating a peanut butter and jelly sandwich. "Hi dad!" Andre said

Andrew came around the corner with a smile on his face. "I thought that was your voice. Good afternoon." He said reaching for his mom to hug her.

"Good afternoon baby. I heard you guys had fun last night."

He kissed me on the forehead. "Yea we did." He said as walked over to hug his son.

"Oh babe I invited your mom to go skating with us."

"Perfect!"

"So Malcolm was at the club?"

"Un huh!" Then he cut his eyes at me. "Yea, Toya was there too. She was with her husband." He said nonchalantly

"What did she have?" She asked

"A boy." He said sounding uninterested.

"She looks good for having just had a baby." I said

"I guess," he said shrugging his shoulders

"Is the baby cute?" His mom asked

"Momma I don't know!" He sounded irritated, "and I don't care!"

"I just wondered if the baby looked like the guy or not."

"It's Toya! That could be anybody's baby." Then he turn his body away from me.

I looked at Andre, and he was wonderfully unaware that they were talking about his mother.

Amber dropped the topic, and then she left to buy skates and get dressed.

Andre was so excited about going skating; we picked up Anthony who was also excited. Then we picked up Amber, she rambled just like Andrew and Andre when they were excited about something. Andrew on the other hand was very quiet all day. He didn't have an attitude; he was kind of deflated if that makes sense. Amber and I exchanged looks the whole car ride. When we got to the skating rink, Amber took each of the boys by the hand and she walked ahead. I got over to Andrew's door before he stood up, that's how slow he was moving. "Baby you ok?" I said putting my hand on his chin and stroking him gently. He shook his head yes as he closed his eyes enjoying my touch. He stood up, kissed me quickly and then started walking towards the rink.

Inside there were all kinds of people. I spotted Sonya, Philip, and Michael sitting at a table as they all laced up. We got rental skates and a training bar for Anthony. As soon as their skates were laced up they hit the floor. Everybody went crazy when they saw little Andre out there on that floor. It looked like he was only going to do one lap, but since everyone loved his skills he did a second lap. Then he was by his buddy's side helping him get the hang of his skates and helping him up when he fell. Andrew was talking to Hubby, it didn't look serious. I sat next to Amber as we laced up our skates. Sonya came over to us. "Hey Tracy!" Sonya said with what sounded like fake energy.

I stood up with one skate on. "Hey Sonya how are you?" I said giving her a hug.

"Oh I'm just falling apart over here, and I didn't hear from you."

I didn't know what to say to that. "Amber this is Sonya, Sonya Amber."

"Hello" Sonya didn't look at Amber.

Amber didn't say anything; she was definitely Andrew's mother with the look on her face. I reached down and touched her shoulder.

"After you uninvited me to your wedding, I figured the topic was off limits. How are you doing?"

She started crying on the spot. "Everything got so crazy! I was Bridezilla times ten thousand! Philip and I started to have real problems. He decided that he didn't want to get married especially seeing what it was doing to our relationship. So we decided to live together for now, and later if we do get married it will be really small and quick."

"Are you ok?" I asked cause she was still crying.

She hugged me. "I missed you girl! Don't ever leave me like that again."

Amber looked at me like I was crazy for hugging her. "Ok, then don't un-invite me to your wedding."

"Oh girl. I was acting on behalf of my brother. He was really embarrassed when Andrew's brother came at him like that.

Amber's neck snapped. "Did you tell your brother I'm engaged?"

"NO! Cause I didn't know! When did this happen?" She said looking at my ring, a hint of jealousy was in her face.

"A couple weeks ago."

"Michael's gonna be crushed, but oh well." I smiled, "let me get back over the to Philip and my brother. I'll see you on the skating floor. Then she went back to her man and brother.

"So spill it! What happened?" Amber said

So I told her the story about E & J's. I just told her that Andrew and I had a fight, I didn't tell her what it was about. She laughed so hard; I didn't think I told the story in a funny way. But she was quite amused by the story.

After Sonya told Michael I'm assuming about my engagement he was clearly upset. I could feel his eyes on me. I did everything in my power to ignore him. Amber noticed him staring;

she said he was giving me puppy dog looks. I refused to look at him. Last thing I needed was for Andrew to think I was encouraging him. I stayed close to Amber since she was actually skating. The boys went back and forth between playing video games, and skating. Andrew stayed on the edge of the party. It was Nicole and Hubby's party so they played host all evening, stealing a few skates for their selves.

As I skated by I saw Tanisha walking over to Andrew, they were hugging hello as I skated by.

I hadn't really put my finger on what Andrew's type was. Toya was a beautiful ebony brown, Smooth skin, long permed hair, average bosom, big butt and legs, thickness at its finest. Karen was light skin, short haircut, small bosom, no butt, and kind of tall, and thin, and very tomboyish, although she has her girl like moments. Like at her brother's party. Then there's me, although I like to tell my sisters I'm dark chocolate, I'm just brown. I wear my hair naturally curly. It has gotten some length on it now but when we met it wasn't long, not an Afro but not long. I have the larger bosom out of the three of us, but since I've lost weight my chest did go down tremendously. Toya's butt is bigger than mine, but I definitely have one. I'm average shortness. I'm not tall at all, but most people don't pay too much attention to how short I am. So now there's Tanisha, I never asked why she got in Toya's face that day at the anniversary party. She had his back, but she didn't seem to come up again or come to mind for that matter. Tanisha was a little shorter than Andrew. Honey kissed complexion. She kept her hair braided, at least whenever I saw her. She was always very nice, but don't make her mad. She was also very tomboyish. And I never saw her in a dress or looking very girlie. But that doesn't mean she's not his type. Mister eclectic, with his variety. But that's only the three I know of. I decided not to worry about it. Amber noticed Andrew and Tanisha as well. At one point he was smiling a real smile, that didn't make me feel good. I couldn't keep circling the floor anymore I was tired, sweating, and thirsty. I was happy Amber was with me, cause she gave me someone to talk to.

Something about Sonya felt off, and although her relationship isn't going the way she would've hoped she can't say congratulations? I was trying not to think about that, and just have a good time. We skated to the concession stand and got water bottles and sprites. Then we sat at a table close to the floor so we could watch as we cooled down.

"Woo girl! This is good exercise!"

"Tell me about it. I'm gonna feel this in the morning." I said with my eyes glued to Andre and Anthony who were having a blast with each other.

"So I hear congratulations are in order." Michael said pulling up a chair

"Yes" I said looking at Amber. She was smiling at Michael, no doubt admiring his handsomeness. "Amber this is Michael" she smiled harder and reached out to shake his hand. "Sonya's brother".

"Oh" her smile faded a bit.

"Uh oh what did I do?"

"Nothing. I told her the story about the last time I saw you."

"That was crazy huh!" He said

"To say the least. I thought you might've hated me for it."

"Hate you? Naw! You told me you had a boyfriend. We were having a friendly lunch. He over reacted. But oh well, what you gonna do."

Amber's smile went away completely. "What do you mean by over reacted?"

"We weren't doing anything inappropriate or disrespectful. We were eating ribs, and talking." Amber sat back in her chair sucking her teeth. "You see it differently of course?" He asked

Amber sat up straight, her gestures became very strong but her tone didn't rise. "From my understanding of the situation my son acted accordingly. You..."

"Wait a minute! Did you say, your son?" Michael's eyes got big.

She smiled shyly. "Yes my son!"

"Whoa! Whoa!" He shook his head. "This is your mother-in-law?"

"Yes." I said, although his reaction was funny to me. If I didn't know Andrew and his brothers and I saw the four of them together I would've thought she was their sister, but never their mother. So I understood his reaction. I hoped he'd tone it down some though.

"Ok, whoa ok. I'm sorry for interrupting you. I just wasn't expecting you to say that. Please go on." He said

"What was I saying?" She was blushing, "oh yea! My son acted accordingly. Body language says a lot. If you were sitting in E&J'S with the body language you got right now, I'd have snatched them out of there too."

"What's my body language saying?"

"Honey please! You are on the prowl. You are looking for a way in. I wouldn't trust you alone with my daughter." She looked him up and down. "Not one bit. And you better hope my son doesn't see you over here."

"That's not fair I came over to congratulate Tracy on her engagement."

"Sell stupid to someone else cause I ain't buying!"

"Why wouldn't you be cautious about me coming to meet you?"
She blew air, "boy please!"

"Um! What's happening here?" I said completely confused.

"I just came to say hello. Find out what's new." He said smiling

I looked at Andrew; he was completely into his conversation with Tanisha. He didn't even see Michael at our table. Hubby was talking to someone; Nicole quickly skated to him and pointed at our table. Hubby looked disappointed. He came over quickly. "Get up!"

Michael was mid-sentence he look confused. "What?"

"Man! Get up! I don't want this at my party." Hubby said "Want what?"

274

"Man! This! Do you know wifey was so shaken up I was on lock down for three days because of you! I won't have this again! Get up!"

"But I'm not doing nothing" Michael said raising his empty palms

"Don't make me get loud! Get up! You can talk to anyone except them. Go run be free! Just get up!"

"Alright! Alright!" Michael said in defeat, "I'll catch you ladies a little later."

"Not tonight you won't. I'm getting laid tonight!" Then he put his hand over his mouth. "Sorry Ms. Amber!"

Amber was cracking up. "Boy you are a mess!"

Hubby walked away with Michael, he was still giving him a hard time. I glanced towards Andrew and he hadn't even noticed. What could they be talking about that was so interesting? Amber was watching me. "Girl! He's fine! I know exactly why Derrick did what he did."

"What do you mean?"

"Don't play dumb, you and Andrew were fighting. You're drinking and there's a man there waiting for the liquor to do its job. Lower your inhibitions enough to give in. He's still looking for an opportunity. He's bold to come over though."

"Yea, but somehow that turned into him flirting with you."

"Only to get a reaction from you. Check the game!"

"I don't know or recognize games until its too late."

"That's ok, some games aren't meant to be played."

"Ok so what game is Andrew playing right now?"

She turned and looked at him talking to Tanisha. "I don't think he is. They're just talking. Besides they go way back. I was good friends with her momma all through school."

It was starting to annoy me that they were still talking. "You ready to go back?"

"Whew! Honey not yet. You go ahead and I'll catch up."

I went back on the skating floor. When Andre saw me he caught up to me. He was telling me about all the fun he was having. Anthony was playing a game in the arcade. Then the DJ announced that he was going to play the next few songs for the couples. "I'll skate with you" Andre said.

I looked up and yep they were still talking. And now Amber and Michael were talking again. Andre and I held hands. Then a couple skated past, the guy was gliding backwards while holding hands with his partner. "Cool! How do you go backwards?" He asked

"I have no idea, I only know how to go forward."

Andre was studying their posture, feet movement, everything. I knew it was only a matter of time before he had that down too. Ok so enough was enough we're half way into the second song and they're still talking.

"Andre I think we should invite dad and Amber to skate with us."

"Ok"

"I'll invite dad, you go invite nana."

Andre took off, he moved so fast and naturally. I skated over to Andrew and Tanisha. "Hey Tanisha how you doing?" I said once I was close.

"Hey girl, how you doing?" She said standing to hug me.

"I'm good." Then I looked at Andrew who was now all smiles. "Sorry to interrupt your convo, but it's couples skate."

"Oh ok, I'll catch up with you guys later." She said walking away.

Andrew laced up his skates and we were off. Is there anything this man can't do? He could skate so good I just kept looking at him. He smiled at me as he had one arm around me and the other I held onto as a guide for which way he maneuvered us to go. We glided in and out of the others. Andre got so excited when we passed him and Amber on the floor. I bet he knows he has the coolest dad ever. Hubby got excited when he saw Andrew and I. "Finally!!!! Ooh! It's about to be on!" He announced to the floor. Andrew smiled but didn't say anything. Michael sat on the side watching us like a hawk. Andrew didn't seem to notice, but that doesn't mean he didn't notice.

"Feeling better?" I asked

He kissed me on the cheek, "I'm cool".

We skated to the last couple's song then the DJ invited everyone back on the floor.

"Flashlight" was playing by Parliament by request from Hubby. "Lets do it! Uh! Uh! Lets do it!" He said as he skated past Andrew and I. Andrew let go of my waist and they were off. "Quincy! Lamel! Ya'll get out here! We about to go!" Hubby shouted. A lot of people exited the floor myself included. I wanted to see the show, Andre stayed on the floor. I could tell he was taking notes. They danced around that skating floor like it was what they were born to do. They had a little routine, they were really good. Nicole came by Amber and I. We were dancing in place on our skates, and cheering them on. I could feel Michael's eyes on me, and when I looked at Amber I could see him standing on the other side of the hallway behind us. His stare was determined and deliberate. I looked at him and desire was all over his face. I shook my head no at him, and he smiled kind of like my resistance fueled him on. I turned back around and focused on my man on the floor. Andre was trying to get the hang of skating backwards and doing the fancy turns all at the same time. Andrew slowed down. He was showing Andre how to move his feet when skating backwards. Andre kept falling and getting right back up, and right back at it. He got it fast; once he had that then Andrew showed him a turn. Andre had the mechanics down but his execution was lacking. Andrew smiled so proudly while his son kept falling and getting right back up. Andre needed to practice; Andrew left him to it while he rejoined his friends in their four-man skate show. Anthony was on the sideline cheering them on. After the song was over the stars glided off the floor while everyone applauded them. As Andrew approached Michael was still standing there. "This fool is bold and stupid" is all I could think.

"Thirsty!" Andrew said all smiles.

"What do you want to drink I'll go get it." I said

"Water or sprite" he said

"Why not both?" I said

"That's up to you." He said

I skated away; Andrew started talking to his mom. Michael waited a couple minutes then he approached the concession stand. The line was kind of long from when everyone left the floor originally. I was hoping some one got in line between us but of course not.

"That was some fancy skating."

"Yea, he's pretty awesome." I Said smiling proudly.

"You were good too."

"Thanks" I said dryly.

"Can I ask you something?"

"You just did." I grinned the line moved two steps, so did I. Michael took three.

"What happened with us?"

"Us?"

"Yea, when we met I thought we had a connection. But then you disappeared."

"Nothing happened. Andrew and I got back together."

"Were you guys talking that night?"

"No, but the stage had been set for us to get back together."

"So I had a chance until he came back?" I looked at him. "I just need to know for my own peace of mind."

"There's nothing to know, I'm engaged."

"So should I take that as a yes? It sounds like it to me."

"You like living dangerously."

Then Sonya walked over. She eyeballed her brother. "What ya'll talking about?"

"I was just about to tell Tracy how fine she is, and how I'll wait twenty five years for her to get a divorce so I can have the best of her."

Sonya smacked the back of his head, "Please excuse him, he was dropped on his head as a child."

"I'm just saying one day she won't be protected by the secret service, and when she's free I got next." He laughed. Sonya and I looked at him with blank stares.

"Why are you in this line?" She said

"I'm thirsty." He said annoyed with her interference

"Un huh. Go on and learn the hard way. I already told you."

"You know me sis," he said with his hands spread out.

"Look Michael, I can't handle this right now. This is not the time or the place to do this. Please respect my relationship and stop." I said

"Ok, I'll drop it. But first admit for the record that you were feeling me when we met."

"Yes, I was single then." I said

He smiled real big. "You like playing with your life!" Sonya said totally pissed off.

"You know something I don't?" Michael asked

"A heck of a lot! Don't let the skates and the good times fool you. Her fiancée ain't one to be messed with or messed over. He's a good guy, but you are so fortunate his brother didn't throw your body in the bay. That family don't play! I could tell you stories."

My face said "Yea" but my insides wanted to ask her what she knew.

Finally it was my turn. I asked for two water bottles and a sprite. I didn't turn to look at them I skated off.

CHAPTER 32

I tucked the boys into theirs beds. Andrew was finishing up in the shower when I came in the room. He was still pretty quiet on the car ride home. So Amber and I talked to each other while the boys talked and played thumb wars. I sat on the bed, he came out in a towel. I noticed that he left his clothes where they fell on the bathroom floor. He kissed me, removed his towel, and then he got in the bed. He turned his back to me.

I couldn't put my finger on why but I felt bad. "So, what were you and Tanisha talking about?"

"Nothing special, just catching up. Did you have fun tonight?" He asked with his back still to me.

"Hhhhmmm, I guess."

"Why do you only guess, you and mom's seemed like best friends tonight."

"Amber was great! Sonya was weird, and well it was Nicole's party so you know."

"Sonya was weird huh."

"Why do you have your back to me?"

"I'm just tired." He said

"So you want me to leave you alone?"

"No this is fine, go head." He said still keeping his back to me

I blew air and went in the bathroom. I turned on the faucet to run my bath. He put his damp towel on the floor. I snatched it up and put it in the hamper. I really wanted him to talk to me like he talked to Tanisha. They'd probably still be talking if I hadn't interrupted. But for me he has no words, and he doesn't even wanna look at me. I was so jealous I couldn't even see straight. I felt bad for feeling this way, but it is how I'm feeling. As I sat in the tub I stared at the ring, true it's only been two weeks, but it seems like one drama after another ever since. All week Shirley was sending me apologies, and I let them sit in my inbox, or I didn't respond to her instant messages. I was done! She put my safety in jeopardy because she believed him over me. We were friends, not she and he. I don't know how he had her ear so well that she believed him over me. Then I thought about Karen! Eeewwllll! She was a nasty hoe. She had Steve too? And she said that like it was something to be proud of. I can't believe, no wait yes I can believe that Cameron would lie on me like that. He's a coward and ridiculous. Talking about I just laid there! Please! I didn't even have to check with Andrew to make sure he was ok. He knew that mess was a lie. But is she in some kind of competition with me? Why she gotta have someone just because I did. When did she have Steve? Was it before, after, or during me? Knowing about Steve was kind of like whatever, who hadn't had him? But thinking about her having Andrew even if it was only physical, hurt. How was he with her? The tricks he keeps pulling out his hat, did he learn them with her?

Aw! This is why it's not good to think about the past. Even if she crossed over into my present. Who is Tanisha???? I gotta know! I wish I could have someone follow him like he does me. Is there anybody else I should be worried about? What if he is still cheating on me, and I'm blissfully unaware? He's definitely got the stamina. I huffed! Why would he come home and go to bed? When does he ever do that? Even if we weren't gonna make love, normally we cuddle, make out or something! Could he be saving himself for her? Maybe they made a plan to hook up later. Maybe he's gonna dip out for a minute, dip in her, and then come home. All my insecurities were running wild in my head. My brain kept turning over and turning over. Finally I got sick of listening to myself. I soaked a good while, took my time about lotioning my body, I put on a nice short black nightgown then I walked over to my side of the bed. Andrew was knocked out! I thought about it, making love wouldn't make me feel better so I needed to let that idea go. No need for the diaphragm tonight. I laid down and just as I was about to disappear into la la land the house phone rings. I popped up; I looked at the clock it was after two. Andrew didn't move.

"Hello?"

"Tracy my water just broke. Anthony is taking me to the hospital now. Can you bring Lil Anthony in the morning?"

"Of course! Do you need anything now?"

" Yes, an epidural on the rocks."

"You still have a sense of humor. Nice!"

"Yea until the next... CAN YOU TRY NOT TO KILL ME ON THE WAY TO THE HOSPITAL PLEASE!! He's swerving in and out of traffic as if the baby is flying out of me right now!"

I laughed a little at the thought of mister cool losing his cool. "Girl I might as well come down there. There isn't much use for me here. Andrew can bring the boys in the morning."

"Only if that's ok with him. Let me go, I'll talk to you when I see you."

"Ok, love you!"

"Love you!" Joy said

I hung up the phone Andrew was still on his side with his back to me. "Why are you going now? She still got a long road ahead of her."

I wanted to say, "BECAUSE AT LEAST I KNOW I'LL BE WANTED THERE!" But instead I said, "I wanna be there for her. I missed Lil Anthony's birth at least I can be there for this one."

"If you say so". I could hear the sleep coming back into his voice.

"So you can bring the boys in the morning?"

"Yea sure whatever." He said falling back asleep.

I threw on a sweat suit and a T-shirt. I pulled my hair back into a ponytail. Eve walked me to the door. As I stepped outside the air was crisp and fresh. I saw the grey car on the corner. I wondered if they would follow me this early in the morning. I got in my car and as I drove past the car there was no sign of life in the car. I drove down Ashby looking in my rear view mirror for lights to suddenly appear. Nothing! I was free for the first time in years. I drove to the hospital with a huge smile on my face. When I got to the labor and delivery in the Oakland Hospital, Joy was already laboring. It was too late for a epidural so Joy's body was responding naturally. Four pushes and Veronica was born. She was beautiful! She was very alert, responding to her parent's voices.

Seven pounds and two ounce of adorableness! By four they were transferring Joy to the Postpartum section. I knew I should've been tired but after witnessing that I was wired. Well the birth and the feeling of my freedom. Remembering that Andrew left his clothes in the bathroom on the floor his cellphone wasn't next to his ear. I sent him a text message:

Veronica is here! I got some running to do. I'll be home LATER!

I kissed Joy goodbye, then I ran to my car giddy like a kid ditching class. When I pulled out of the garage I started laughing out loud when I was the only car on the street. Where am I gonna go? If I went East, that could be predictable. So no Sacramento. Up north? Naw, I had no idea of what to do out there. I called Marie. She answered the phone "this better be good"

"I need you to play hooky. Please tell me you don't have any clients today?"

"I don't I was gonna stay in today and relax."

"Please get up, brush your teeth. I'm in Oakland I will be there in a minute."

"Is everything ok?"

"I'll explain once you're in the car. Just come on do me this solid." I pleaded.

I flew down the freeway to Marie's place in Walnut Creek. She was ready and hurried into the car. I got back on the freeway and I headed south on the 680 freeway. I was driving as fast as I could without being too daring.

"What's going on." Marie said looking very concerned by my crazy behavior.

I explained the last two weeks to her. I told her this was the first time in forever that I felt free. Andrew would have to wonder where I was, who I was with, what I was doing. I didn't understand what he was going through yesterday, but it wasn't fair to just shut me out. She nodded, she understood my craziness. I thanked her ten million times over for coming with me. She was the only safe person I could think of. I didn't know if he had people watching everybody else's houses or only knew where everybody was in case. I appreciated the protection when I had to be in the bay; who knows where Steve was gonna pop up. But today I wanted to be free. Around seven am we were winding and twisting through trees headed for the boardwalk.

"I haven't been out here in years!" Marie said

"Me neither! You think we can make a day of it out here?" I asked

"Of course!"

"You wanna eat?"

"Sure! You're not tired? You didn't sleep last night."

"Nope! I'm on an adrenaline high." I was too happy.

We stopped at a place called Walnut Street it was just after eight and people were starting to come in as we sat at our table. Looking at the menu while sipping my coffee, even coffee tasted better out here. The choices looked amazing! I decided on Chilaquiles and I had them add chorizo to it. Marie couldn't decide, so finally she decided to have the same thing as me.

As Marie was telling me a story about one of her friends Andrew texts me:

What running do you have to do at four in the morning?

Me:

I just needed to get away for a while

Him:

Where are you?

Me:

I'm with Marie

Him:

That's not what I asked you

Me:

We're near San Jose, but we're wandering

He didn't respond. I couldn't tell if he was mad or didn't care. I told myself to worry about it later. Marie and I had an amazing time. We went shopping in a bunch of mom and pop places. We walked on the boardwalk, rode a few coasters. We ate a bunch of fried food. We stayed in Santa Cruz until about six. I dropped Marie off around eight. I thanked her so much for running away with me for the day. She talked to me the whole way home. She was nervous about me passing out on the way home. Our call disconnected in the Caldecott tunnel. I called her back as soon as I came out. She was almost hysterical, I reminded her of the tunnel, and then she calmed down. I was home in less than ten minutes from there. The grey car was gone. A tan car was parked there now. It was completely dark in the house. Eve and Cain greeted me at the door. I set the alarm; I threw my bags in the closet. I stripped down to my underwear crawled in the bed and I was out before my head hit the pillow. I had a dream that Michael kept trying to get with me in front of Andrew. Then Andrew proceeded to beat the stuffing out of him. Even in my dreams Andrew was a beast. The next thing I knew my alarm was going off. I wasn't ready to get up, but I had snoozed until the absolute last minute. Andrew didn't come home last night. It was weird to not even have Andre to care for in the morning. My body was begging for more rest, but I had to get up. I let the shower beat me until I felt a little awakened. Knowing that I would pay for the caffeine withdrawals later I made a pot of coffee anyways. My coffee attempt was ok. But after three sips I poured the cup out, rinsed it and put it in the dishwasher. I looked at my watch I had enough time to stop by Starbucks on the way to the office if I hurried. I made sure there was plenty of water and food out for the puppies. I set the alarm, and I hurried out the door. The tan car was gone. I looked around as I walked to my car. Nothing looked out of place, but it's not like it ever did. I drove to work like I normally did. When I exited the garage I went into the Starbucks in the middle of the Civic Center. When I walked out of the store like clockwork there was Yussef. I wondered how he timed our meet ups to make them look natural.

"How was your weekend?" I asked

"Same ole same ole. How about you?"

"It was interesting." Then I stopped, "why do you do this?"

He smiled and looked down at the ground. "Do what?"

"This! I see you everyday. You're always nice and respectable. But don't you get tired of babysitting a grown woman?"

"What happened over your weekend?" He asked smiling

"Oh come on! Tell me."

"I don't know what you're talking about." He said, as he looked me dead in my eyes

"Fine!" I said, and then I walked a little ahead of him. He didn't seem to care; he strolled along behind me. It was hard to focus all day. My mind kept wondering. A couple times I woke up not realizing I had fallen asleep. I couldn't wait for four o'clock to come. I made a beeline out of the office to my car. I went straight home. I took another quick shower then I got in the bed. I was almost asleep when Cain started growling. Eve and Cain were at my door and they wanted out. I sat up and I looked at them. Even these dogs were about business. I opened my bedroom door and Cain ran downstairs. Eve was at attention but she stayed next to me. Then the doorbell rang. Cain stood by the door, he didn't bark but he wasn't happy. Eve waited for me to throw on pants and a T-shirt. Every step I took she was next to me. I put my house keys in my pocket as I disarmed the front door so that I could open it. Cain and Eve sat side by side in front of the left front door, and I cracked open the right door.

"Yes?"

"Good evening, were offering free carpet cleaning to you and all your neighbors." The guy said

"We don't really have carpet here."

"We also offer floor polishing." He said trying to peak through the door.

I opened the door enough so that I could see who I was dealing with. The dogs stood up. Their bottoms weren't wagging, they were at attention. "Aren't you pretty! Would you prefer that I speak with your husband?"

"What does that mean?"

His partner was standing at the bottom of the porch and his eyes kept darting around; like he was definitely surveying the house. "I know that a lot of the housewives up here prefer that we speak with their husbands."

"No thank you!"

"Wait a minute, the demonstration is completely free to you." He was looking around me. "You have beautiful floors, we can help you maintain them."

"That's ok the system we have now works perfectly fine."

"If you let me show you our system I guarantee you will be begging me to give you what you need." His smile gave me the creeps

"Thanks but no thanks."

"I noticed there's only one car in the driveway. Is your husband home, or maybe we can come back when he's here."

"My car?"

"There's normally two cars, but today I only see one. Will he be home soon?" He said as he moved closer to the door. Then he put his foot in the doorway. His partner was looking around at the street. I jumped when he put his foot there. Cain lost it! His bark was loud and deliberate. Eve was growling.

Both of them jumped! But he didn't move his foot! A guy I didn't recognize at all was at the front gate standing in the walkway, I didn't know where he came from, nor did I see him coming, he suddenly appeared. "Can I help you guys with something?" Cain was still barking like crazy and Eve was growling.

I opened my door completely and Cain jumped in front of Eve and I. Both of the guys jumped back. "I'm not interested please leave!"

"Are you the husband?" The second guy asked

The guy in the walkway tilted his head to the side, as he looked at the guy crazy. "Are we gonna have a problem?" He said opening his jacket. There was something shiny, but I didn't see what it was.

287

Both of the guys straightened up, and backed away slowly. They didn't know whether to be afraid of the guy or Cain. When they started hurrying down the street. The guy said something in a different language and both of the dogs instantly shut up. The guy waved his hand and a white car cruised by in the direction that the salesmen went in. The guy backed away slowly, but he didn't say anything to me. I wanted to see where he went but he stood in the middle of the street staring at me.

"Thank you!" I said and I waved at him. He nodded his head, but he wouldn't walk any further until I shut the door. When I shut the door my puppies were back to normal. I tried to see where the guy went, but he was gone and I didn't see a trace of him or that white car. I set the alarm and then I went back up stairs. The puppies went back to laying on the floor in my room. It was only 6:30, but I hadn't heard from Andrew all day. I guess he's mad about yesterday. I called him, but he didn't answer. Now that I was up, I couldn't sleep. I decided to go by Andrew's place to see if he was home. I put both of the dogs into the car, and we headed down Ashby to San Pablo. I parked in front of his building. The lights were on inside, but when I called him again he didn't answer. I cracked the windows and then I went up to the gate. I buzzed his unit. He didn't answer right away. So I buzzed again. "WHAT?" He barked

"Open up!" I said, why didn't I have a key to his place? I couldn't believe I just thought of this. He buzzed me in and then I ran to his door. My stomach was in knots. Was someone with him?

Andre opened the door, "mommy!" He said so excited to see me. He literally jumped on me.

"Hi baby, Cain and Eve are in the car. Will you help me?"
"Yes!"

I peaked my head inside. It was quiet. Andre and I walked hand in hand back to the gate. "What were you doing?"

"Watching TV. Daddy doesn't feel good."
"Did you eat dinner already?"
"Yea, we had pizza."

"Ok, you hold the gate open. I'll bring them over."

The puppies were so happy to see Andre. Eve actually beat Cain to Andre. They were going crazy licking him, Andre laughed. I loved the sound of his laugh it was so cute. Andrew was standing in the doorway without a shirt. He didn't look happy to see me. When we walked in the door the puppies attempted to show him the same love they gave Andre, but he very firmly told them to "SIT!" and they did immediately. Then he told them to stay and they both laid down. "Andre, go back in the living room."

"Can Cain and Eve come too?"

He looked at the dogs, "GO!" And they immediately followed Andre. His face was mad, he looked at me then he turned and walked down the hallway to his bedroom, I followed him. It was dark in his room. He turned on the lamp on his nightstand. Then he sat on the bed and stared at me. "What do you want?"

"What do you mean?"

"Like I just said, what do you want?"

"Andre said you aren't feeling well. What's going on?" I walked towards him. "Do you have a fever?" I touched his forehead and he wasn't warm.

"I'm fine!" He barked.

I jumped because I didn't expect that reaction from him. "What's wrong then? Why aren't you answering my calls?"

"I'm giving you your space."

"What do you mean?"

"You didn't have to run away."

"I didn't run away."

"Yes you did!"

"The first opportunity you found to run you ran!"

"I didn't run. I wanted a day to myself, I...."

"And you were with Marie!"

"Yes! I told you that."

"RIGHT!!!"

"I was with Marie, you can ask her."

"I don't have time for these childish games. I'm just glad this happened before we got married." His eyes were cold, and so was his body language.

"What? What are you saying?"

"I don't want you sneaking around at all hours of the night. If you wanna be out there, then be out there!"

"What are you thinking I did?"

He stared at me, "you know what you did!" His whole demeanor was scary to me. I wanted to run out of there. Which is probably why I stayed by the door.

"Oh I see! So if your goons aren't following me around all day you don't trust me? Your trust only goes as far as you can see?" He kept staring at me. "Well how is that fair to me. You are the loose cannon in this relationship. You're the cheater not me. But somehow I gotta have faith in you to do right by me. But you can have people following me all day every day. Even having conversations with me, pumping me for information about you! But I don't have that, so I gotta trust you, but you don't have to trust me? If that's the way you feel then you're right I'm happy this happened before we got married. I don't wanna live like this." He rolled his eyes. "The ONE DAY I get to be out, and you flip! Who do you think I was with since you don't believe that I was with Marie?" He stared at me. The more he thought about it the bigger he got. I wanted to back out and say I didn't want to know. But at the same time he wasn't gonna punk me like he did the dogs. He stood up, I put my hands out. "Please stay over there! You're too mad right now!" He stood there thinking about it for a minute then he sat down.

"Who were you with?" He asked calmly

"Call Marie!" I reached in my pocket and tossed my cellphone at him.

He got mad again, "you said she lives alone!"

"She does!"

"Then why were people in and out of her place all day!"

"What?"

There were people in and out of her place all day." He repeated himself

"Call her!" I said, my heart was pounding

He called her and put her on speaker. "Tray-Tray!" She said all happy

"Hey Marie, it's me and Andrew." I called out from by the door.

"Hey guys what's going on?"

"Nothing much. Hey I got a question."

"Un huh, what's up?" She said all happy

"Did you get a roommate?"

"No! What I look like having a roommate in a one bedroom?" She laughed

"I know right." I was trying to think of a way to ask her without letting her know what was going on with us. "We're going over the guest list. I wanna send you an invitation, can you confirm your address for me?"

"Sure it's."

"Hold on," I grabbed a pen and paper from his desk. "Ok go ahead."

"121 Robles Rd #1201, Walnut Creek, CA of course"

"Thanks girl, listen I'm gonna call you back in a little bit."

"Ok, bye Andrew" she said in a silly voice

"Bye Marie." His voice sounded friendly but his face wasn't.

"Now call whoever and find out which apartment they were watching. I guarantee they had the wrong apartment."

He picked up his phone. He put the call on speaker. "Yo!" The person said

"Sunday!" Just like that, no greeting or anything? Wow! "What apartment were you watching?"

"A! What apartment was that?" He asked someone in the background. I heard papers. "1203!"

"Are you sure?" He said sternly

"Yes." The voice said

"You have the wrong apartment!" There was silence, except the noise in the background. "I will deal with you later." Then he hung up.

Well, well, well! Guess I'm not the only one with insecurities. His demeanor didn't soften, so the butterflies didn't leave my stomach. "Who did you think I was with?"

"I don't know Tracy!" He barked again

"Yes you do! Who?"

He stood up again. I put my hands out, but he walked towards me anyways. He walked straight into my hands and put me in a bear hug. "I was about to call this whole thing off!" Then he kissed my forehead.

"Why? Who did you think I was with?"

"Baby I'm so sorry." Finally he softened but his bear hug got tighter. I don't think he realized he was about to pop me.

"Can't breathe!" I said pushing on him. He was rock solid. Not my normal cuddly tear bear.

He loosened his grip just a little. I gasped for air as dramatically as I could.

"I'm sorry!"

"Andrew! What exactly are you apologizing for?" I was trying get to out of his grip but he wouldn't let go. "You don't trust me, but you want me to trust you?"

"I know! I know! I'm sorry!" He said still holding on to me.

"If you can't trust me, I would be a fool to trust you!" I said still trying to get away. It seemed he knew every move before I did it. If I tried to drop to the floor he held me. If I tried to put my arms inside his hug to push he wouldn't budge. I started sweating trying to get out of his hug. His eyes were soft and full of pleadings. "Let me go!"

"I can't! You might not come back!" He said kind of laughing.

That made me laugh a little. "I'm not gonna run from you, we both know you're faster than me. Just let me go!"

"No!" Then he kissed me but I didn't kiss him back. He stopped and looked at me. He let me go, and he took a step back. He put his hands in his pockets.

I looked at my reflection in the mirror above his dresser. My hair was all wild, my T-shirt was completely wrinkled, and sweaty. "Who! Did you think I was with?"

"I don't know, you could've been with anybody."

"We're you with somebody?" I asked with my finger out
He blew air, "No!"

"Then what, did you call somebody? We're you about to call somebody? What?"

"No, and no." He sat on the bed.

"Then what???"

"I was about to assign you all kinds of mean and hurtful things in my heart. I called you out your name so many times yesterday and today. I was angry!"

"Clearly! All because you didn't know where I was one day?"

"It's the way you did it."

"How did I do it?"

"You slid out in the middle of the night, and then away like a thief. You were very vague."

"You're always vague!" I said

"Am I?"

"'What do you or, what does that mean? Have become regular parts of my vocabulary now. I always have to ask."

"Didn't realize I did that. I'll work on it." He said

"Ok so what were you talking to Tanisha about?"

He blew air. "Seriously we're back to this?"

"Um yea! You're mopey all day, but you perk up for her. Then you go back to moping when we come home. How do you think that made me feel?"

"Oh ok, so you're the only one who can have melt downs? I can't need a minute to take in everything that's going on? How my life is changing? Who I'm becoming? Who I'm gonna be?"

"Why would your life with me make you depressed? If that's the case why even get married?"

"You're the one who needs the paper. I don't need the paper to say I'm gonna be right here, that I'm not going nowhere!"

"So I'm forcing you to get married?"

"You can't force me to do anything!"

"So then what are you saying? It sounds like the thought of marrying me depresses you. Sounds like you're gonna fall apart at the idea of spending the rest if your life with me!"

"No! No! I'm not saying this right."

"Sounds like you're telling me how you truly feel. Why don't I make it easier for you." My insides were screaming as I took off my ring. "Keep this until you know what it is you're trying to say to me. This way I won't have to deal with you taking it back, or ignoring me until I go away."

"Baby, you're not understanding."

"So make me understand then!" I crossed my arms. " I'm listening!"

He opened his mouth and closed it but nothing was coming out. I put the ring in his hand. "I hope you figure it out soon." Then I walked out the room. Andre was sitting on the couch watching cartoons. The puppies were at his feet. They sat up when I walked in the room.

"Are you leaving?" Andre asked his eyes were so big and brown. It was like they were pleading with me.

"Yea, baby I'm gonna go home. I'm gonna see you later ok." I gave him a kiss on his cheek.

"Why are you leaving?"

"I'm really sleepy I need to get some rest."

"Go sleep with daddy, I will turn the TV down." He said grabbing the remote.

"But I want to sleep in my own bed."

"Can I go home too? I wanna sleep in my own bed too."

"No baby I think you should stay here."

"But I miss you! I wanna go with you!"

Andrew stepped into the hallway just as the tears started rolling down Andre's cheeks. "Can't I go with you?"

"No! You're gonna stay here." Andrew's voice boomed down the hallway and into the living room.

Now Andre was not a crier. He was actually really good about sucking it up and toughing it out. So the fact that he was crying only let me know he felt the vibe between Andrew and I. I looked at Andrew and I gestured to say it was ok. Andrew blew more air and he went back in his room and slammed the door. Andre was heartfelt sobbing. "Come on baby!" He ran to me and put his arms around my waist. "Where's your jacket?" I said he grabbed it off the chair. Andre and I held hands as Cain and Eve followed us out the door.

CHAPTER 33

When we came home that night Andre followed me around the house. He even sat at the table telling me about his day at school and even the night before. I listened while I ate a bowl of cereal. I lacked the energy or desire to think of anything more nutritious to eat. Then we sat on the couch eating ice cream and cookies. I didn't say too much. I just let Andre talk and change the channels to whatever he wanted. Inside I was hurting, and it was a familiar ache. One I know all too well. I didn't want to get off the couch. I didn't want to do anything. The man I love is depressed at the thought of choosing me. When I thought about it, he had been drinking more lately than I remembered him drinking before. Although Friday was the first time I ever saw him drunk. He would say to me when we're married, and that we would never be apart. Now that he decided to put up or shut up, he put up and shut down. I don't want to be his demise, and I don't wanna feel like this. I smiled at Andre. I had no idea what this little boy was talking about.

"Alright sweetheart. It's time for you to take your shower and get in the bed."

"Will you sing me a song when I get in the bed?"

"But you know I can't sing."

"I don't care, I just want to hear you sing."

"Ok baby, but you gotta do your part first."

He took off running up the stairs. Cain followed him, Eve stayed by my side. The way she kept looking at me it was like she could read my mind. I rinsed the dishes and put them in the dishwasher. My heart was hoping that Andrew would call and tell me I was overreacting. Tell me how much he loved me, and how much he wanted to be with me. As I thought about it maybe I've been pushing his buttons too much lately. Making him reassure me more than he wanted to about his love for me. No man has ever told me as much or told me as often as he has how much he loves me. Maybe I'm too needy for him. Yea, maybe he loves me, wants to be with me until I start acting all insecure and needy. Maybe this is all my fault and I lost the best thing to ever happen to me? Tears poured out my eyes. I took a deep breath, set the alarm, and then I went up to Andre's bathroom. He was patiently sitting on the edge of the tub with his towel wrapped around his waist. I turned on the shower for him, made sure the temp wasn't too hot, and he waited for me to exit the bathroom before he took his towel off to get in. He said he's a man now, and unless I'm his wife I can't see him naked. I laughed when he told me that. I don't know where he picked it up from, but I respect it.

"I'm ready!" He sang from his bed.

When I walked in the room he got really excited, he started kicking his feet in anticipation of my horrible singing. I looked at him grinning from ear to ear and wondering how his mother could walk away from him. How she could just, wash her hands of this beautiful child. Andre has been like one of my pride and joy's the last few years. I don't feel so empty when he's around. I don't know how this is supposed to work now the boy is already calling me mommy. I'm over here caring for him as if he's my own. I guess we'll figure it out when we have to. "What do you want me to sing?"

He giggled, "I don't know. Anything!" He laid there flashing his daddy's dimples. Staring at me with his daddy's eyes.

When all else fails, sing the song your mom used to sing to you. "I love you! And I love you! And I love you! And I love you! And I love you! Please love me, like I love you! Cause I love you and I love you! And I love you!" The song goes on but you see where I'm going. He inhaled deeply and exhaled slowly. He had the biggest smile on his face as he laid there falling asleep. I rubbed his curly locs, and I kissed his forehead when I was done.

"Good night mommy!"

"Good night sweetheart, sweet dreams!" I petted Cain on the head as he scooted closer to Andre. Then I went in my room. There was no point in closing my door so I left it open. When I looked at my phone I was praying I had a missed call or something. Nothing! I put the phone on the pillow on Andrew's side of the bed. I leaned over and his smell was still in the pillow. I picked it up and squeezed it like my life depended on it. I cried into the pillow as hard as I could. I turned off my light and I laid down to go to sleep. I don't know how long I was sleep, but suddenly I heard Andrew's ringtone. I tried to find the phone, but my eyes wouldn't focus. By the time I found the phone he was gone. Still trying to focus my eyes the house phone rang. "Hello?"

"Did we break up?"

"I don't know. Kind of feels like it though."

"I don't want to breakup."

"What is it that you want?"

"I want us to be together... I can't explain it right..." There was silence. "Can I come over?"

"Of course! You didn't have to ask."

"I'm outside. I didn't want to come in unless it was ok with you."

"Its ok, come in." I sat up and tried to finger fluff my hair. I ran to the bathroom to brush my teeth. When he came in the room he didn't turn on the light. He still had his sweats on, no shirt, and a leather jacket. He looked how I felt. I said a silent prayer that he could have whatever he wanted as long as he didn't leave me. I begged.

I turned off the bathroom light and he snatched me up in a huge hug. I hugged him back and we both cried.

"I need to tell you something, but I don't know how." He said between his tears

"You can tell me anything!" I said squeezing harder.

"No, I mean there's something, but I don't know what it is. And it's bugging me. I do want to marry you! It's all we've ever talked about. It's just that there's something in my heart that I need to say, but I can't wrap my mind around it to tell you."

"It's ok! Whatever it is, it's ok."

"I flip out too you know. I have the same insecurities that you have if not more. We didn't grow up the same way."

"Ok" I said

"You gotta be the calm head for me when I'm flipping out, just like I am for you."

"But you're so much better at it than I am." I said

We both laughed. "Andre is really attached to you."

"I see that, but I feel the same way about him." I said

"I was like that about my stepdad." Then he started crying. "He was a great dad! He wasn't perfect, but he was a good dad." His tears became so heavy. I sat him down on the bed while I got him some tissue. He couldn't even talk he was crying so hard. So I told him not to talk. I kissed his cheek and put my arms around him. I took his jacket off, and I took off his shoes. I pulled him to the top of the bed, and I tucked him in. I was so happy that he was here, he could've told me he was having twins with Toya and Karen and it wouldn't mattered to me at this point. I just wanted him with me I wanted our family. I kissed his forehead and rubbed his back.

I woke to my alarm. Andrew was looking at me. Didn't look like he slept all night. I kissed him, "are you going to work today?" He shook his head no. "Did you go yesterday?" He shook his head no. I felt bad. "You want me to stay with you today? Like you did for me."

"No, you don't have the pull I have. I'll go get my laptop from my house in a little bit."

"Ok, I'll make you breakfast before I leave."

"You don't have to do that."

I kissed him, brushed my teeth, hopped in the shower. As I was in the closet attempting to get dressed. I kept getting frustrated. Nothing was fitting the way it should. My clothes were getting on my nerves. In defeat I picked a pair of slacks and shirt that I knew would fit.

"You ok?" Andrew called out

"Yea, I've been slacking on my workouts. It's showing in my clothes. It's just annoying the past two weeks have been too busy."

"It happens, don't worry about it."

I woke Andre; I put his clothes at the foot of his bed. Then I ran to the kitchen. Since I didn't really eat dinner last night I was starving. But I didn't want anything in my kitchen. So I made whole-wheat toast, turkey bacon, and egg whites for my boys. Andrew came down stairs with Andre. Andre was moving at the speed of molasses so Andrew told me he'd take Andre to school. I kissed them both and I ran out the door. When I got to the cafe in the civic center, I wanted something GOOD so I had a bacon avocado omelet with home fries. The lemon pastry was calling my name so I got that for a mid morning snack. I told myself I would stick to fruits and steamed veggies for dinner.

As I hurried towards the office, "ooh! What did you get?" Yussef asked

"An omelet"

"Sounds good," then he looked at my face. "What's wrong?"

"Nothing" I said hoping it really didn't show on my face. "How are you?"

"I'm cool," he said studying my face.

"That's good, lets hope it last all day." I said hoping to make it through the day.

Yussef just kept watching my face all day. He kept coming to my cubical to ask me work related questions, but he could've sent an email or an instant message. He didn't have to keep coming to read my face. At three o'clock he came in my cubical and sat in the guest chair. I spun around, "what's up?"

"What's wrong Tracy?"

"What do you mean?"

"You've been on the verge of tears all day. You're acting weird." He said

"I don't know what you mean." I said as a rebel tear ran down my face as if it was timed. I grabbed a Kleenex. "It must be my allergies." I said dabbing my eyes.

"Come on!" He said as he raised me by my arm from my chair. He took me out the office down to the courtyard. We sat by the fountain, "spill it!"

"Spill what?"

"What's going on with you?"

I smiled at him the same way he smiled at me the other day. "I don't know what you're talking about."

Understanding what I meant he laughed and bumped me as to say, "come on". I shook my head no, "nope, not doing it. I know nothing about you. You already know everything about me."

"That's fair, what do you want to know?"

"Hhhhmmmm" I tap my finger to my chin showing that I was thinking about it. He noticed I wasn't wearing my ring. "Answer my question, why do you babysit a grown woman?"

"Cause I'm paid to."

"Wow! Cause you're paid to?"

"Yea that's why I came here. To check you out, report back. Fortunate for you, you're pretty cool people."

"I'm cool people?"

"Yea, you alright. You remind me of my sister. She's always about her business, and she's always real with people."
"That's a nice compliment, thank you. You have any other siblings?"

"Not that I know of."

"Know of?"

"Father died when I was young. My mother knew about my sister, but she couldn't tell me if there were more."

"Wow!"

"So now you spill."

"Only if you promise that you will keep sharing."

"Deal!"

"Cause I don't think caring about my emotional makeup is part of either of your job descriptions."

"Nope, you're definitely off today. So spill it!"

"It's just so weird. I've never loved anyone harder than I love Andrew. I'm so afraid to lose him. But we never really resolve anything. It's affecting our relationship."

"In what way?"

"Like I get why the protection is necessary. I've seen how it benefits me. It's just unfair."

"How you figure?"

"He should know by now who I am, how much I love him, how much he's the only man I want in my life. But the one time I'm off his radar he flips. And I have to take his word for everything. I don't have proof like he does."

"What other kind of proof do you need? He takes you everywhere with him, the only time you're not with him is when he's handling business. He's paying a ton of people VERY WELL just to make sure you're safe. He comes home to you, and he tells you everything."

"You're taking his side."

"How is that taking his side? I'm telling you what I know. I know he loves you!"

"Doesn't take away from him cheating on me."

"Did you guys talk about it?"

"Kind of."

"Kind of?"

"I was almost to the point where I was gonna reach out to him. But instead I was forced to come home and deal with him when I should've waited for a clearer head."

"We're you gonna breakup with him?"

"No, but..."

"But what? I don't understand females in situations like this."

I tried to think of an example. "Have you ever had shark before?"

"Yes! I love it."

"Eeewwllll! You have?"

"Yes, I try different stuff on the regular."

"Ok, what about Orca?"

"No, I've never had whale." He said sarcastically

"Ok well say you're starving. I tell you I'm gonna feed you. You know me so you think you're gonna have steak or something like that. But instead I slap a piece of whale tongue down in front of you. Nothing about it looks appetizing, but you're starving no other option so you're warming up to the idea. I get impatient and I put a gun to your head and tell you to eat it. How does it taste now that I've taken your choice away?"

He thought about it for a minute. "I see your point. But you still had a choice. You could've said no."

"I didn't wanna say no. It would've been nice if it was my choice."

"You had a choice, and you chose. So the question is now are you gonna hold on to the past cause you can't move forward."

"We had a big fight, I decided that nothing matters. I gotta let it all go. None of that matters now. As long as we're together I'm happy."

"But you're not happy."

"I am happy." I said unconvincingly

"You're so happy that you're sitting over there stuffing your face all day?"

"You're faulting me for being hungry?"

"Hungry is one thing. You're using food as a crutch right now. I saw you, you were satisfied but you kept going. Like you're trying to punish yourself for something."

"Seriously, so you're judging me when I eat now?"

"I'm telling you what I see. There's no judgment I'm just asking you why."

"I don't know"

"You do"

"All this time and I still don't know him."

"What do you mean?"

"I keep finding out new things about him, it's starting to feel like every week there's something new."

"Bad things?"

"Not necessarily bad. But like, why am I just finding out about this?"

"So when you met Andrew, who did you think he was?"

303

"When I met Andrew I was sixty pounds heavier, and he was just a very sweet guy. I had no idea he was this big."

"Now put yourself in his shoes. There's always some female scheming, plotting, and trying to play innocent to get on his team. He finally had a chance with someone who doesn't know all the hype and who looked at him like he was just a guy." He looked at me, "I know it's a lot to take in. But your man is a big guy. He always has been a big deal. Look at it like an adventure. He's offering you everything he has. Don't let it scare you, embrace it."

Yussef was making me feel so much better; I could feel my soul getting lighter. "Ok, I hear you. But the dangerous parts. That's the scariest. I don't know if Sonya was kidding or not when she said something about her brother could've ended up in the Bay. That made me nervous! I'm afraid to ask if he's capable of something like that."

Yussef was quiet for a long time. He was trying to respond with the right answer. "Put it this way, is that Steve guy still alive?"

"As far as I know."

"Do I need to say more?"

He had a point. "You have a good point." I exhaled. "Ok so I'm a drama queen. Insecure, the whole bit. He probably doesn't even wanna marry me anymore. I gave him his ring back last night. He didn't give it back this morning."

"Just give him the space to see you. Stop stuffing your face with that crap. You guys need to talk, but stop with the drama."

"Wow tell me how you really feel." I smiled, "are you gonna tell Andrew about this?"

"What do you mean?"

"I know you report back to him, you gonna tell him about today?"

"Come on Tracy you know I have to."

I huffed, "ok but thank you for talking to me. I really needed this."

I drove home feeling a little better but worried about what shape I'd find Andrew in. I asked if I was picking up Andre. Andrew said no, and that he needed me to come home. I started to get a lump in my throat. His tone didn't sound happy to hear from me. Tears started rolling down my cheeks when I turned on my street and I saw the limo in front of the house. I felt like tons were lifted from my shoulders. I pulled my car into the garage. Andre was standing next to the open limo door dressed in his suit. He had the biggest smile on his face. "Hi baby!" I said giving him a hug.

"Hi mommy! We're going out to dinner! Get in." He said excitedly.

When I got in the limo there was a garment bag hanging, and a bag on the seat next to it.

"Where's your daddy?" I asked Andre

"He told me it was a secret. And secrets are commitments! So I made a commitment not to tell." Andre said with a big smile.

"Ok baby." I smiled to match his. "How was your day today?"

"Great! I stayed with daddy!" Then he put his hands over his mouth. I guess that was part of the secret too.

"That was my fault baby. Lets sing songs." I smiled

So we sang songs on the way to our destination. I had no idea where we were going once we hit the Caldecott tunnel I stopped paying attention. We sang quite a few songs, before stopping at the Lafayette hotel. We were escorted from the limo to a huge suite! Both bags were laid on the bed in the bedroom. Andre turned on the TV in the living room. I closed the door and looked at the bag in fear. Reliving my fight with my clothes this morning, I wondered what he picked. The bag contained beautiful cream-colored shoes. The lines and curves were so smooth. There was a matching purse with silver hardware. The leather was so soft. There was a black strapless body suit inside. Then there was a gift box. I hopped in the shower and then I put on the bodysuit. It sucked everything in without making me feel like I couldn't breathe or feel uncomfortable. I admired myself in the mirror. I opened the box, to find a pair of beautiful diamond earrings with a matching necklace and tennis bracelet. I couldn't even begin to imagine how expensive this gift was. I laid them out on the bed. I couldn't procrastinate any longer. I slowly unzipped the garment bag. The hanger was from Bloomies. I never shop there! The most expensive I ever went in that shopping center was Norm's, and even then only for sale items, etc. I walked around Bloomies once and I knew it was too rich for my blood. When I saw the dress the beautiful blue of the dress caught my eye first. The dress it's self was soft and billowy. It was a strapless, sweetheart neckline, trumpet styled dress. The bodice had a asymmetrical design with a few lines of silver beading. The bottom was pretty and full. I searched inside the dress for a size. There was no tag. Little beads of sweat popped up on my forehead. "What if this dress doesn't fit?" Is all that ran through my mind. When I picked up the dress I noticed the cream colored pashmina behind it on another hanger. It was beautiful and so soft. I wondered if everything feeling so soft to the touch was a sign of quality or a underlining message. I looked in the mirror. I tried to fluff my hair, as I didn't have my products or utensils to do something else to my hair. I stepped into this gorgeous gown holding my breath. I pulled it up; I zipped it as far as I could reach. I looked in the mirror and the dress fit perfectly as if it wouldn't fit at all tomorrow. As I started putting on the earrings there was a knock at the door. I opened the bedroom door and Amber was standing there. She was dressed up as well. She had the biggest smile on her face.

"How's it going?" She said

I was relieved to see her. "I need help!" I said with a smile.

"Oh honey you look beautiful!" She said holding my arms up to get a full look at the gown.

"Thank you." I appreciated the compliment. But I felt weird about myself in this gown. "Can you zip me?" She tried to zip but it wasn't budging. I sighed in disappointment.

"I know what it is. Push your breast in as flat as you can. Ready, set, push!"

It worked! The dress zipped up nicely. Then she helped me put on my necklace and my bracelet. "I always wanted a daughter. This is like a dream come true."

"That's so sweet! I'm so happy that we get along." We hugged.

"You ready?"

"Yes, where are we going?"

She smiled a evil grin. "Can't tell you, but I think you'll like it. Are you ready?"

We collected Andre and then we got back in the limo. Since I'm not all that familiar with that area, I had no idea where we were. Then we pulled in front of a beautiful building. There were twinkle lights everywhere. The driver opened the car door. Amber told me that she and Andre were going in first, and that the driver would tell me when to enter. I watched as Amber and Andre disappeared inside.

"Mam, you're up." The driver said.

I walked down the red carpet not really knowing what to expect on the other end. When I entered the building there was a high ceiling with a beautiful crystal and bronze chandelier. The hallway was long and there was a door at the end of the hallway. I assumed it was the door to the banquet hall. I took a deep breath, although Amber said I looked good. Andrew's reaction to me would make or break how I felt. I caught a glimpse of myself in the floor to ceiling length mirror, not bad. "Oh my goodness!" I thought as I caught the reflection of my butt. Very slick Mr. Wallace I thought to myself. This dress hugged my butt if nothing else. When I crossed the threshold the lights in the room were romantic and low. Everyone was standing and yelling "SURPRISE!!!!" Andrew was steps away from the door. He had a mile wide smile as he admired me in my dress. I hurried over to him, and hugged him. "What is this?" I whispered in his ear.

"Our engagement party." He whispered back

"You did this for me?" I asked with the biggest smile

He flashed his dimples, "of course! What wouldn't I do for you?"

Everyone came up to me to offer their congratulations. Then Andrew led me to our Sweetheart table. Andre was already sitting at the table with the biggest smile on his face. I sat in the middle of Andre and Andrew, and they put their arms around my chair.

"When did you do all this?"

"I've had the idea for sometime. Tanisha was helping me map out the last minute details at the skating rink."

I felt horrible. "I'm sorry!"

"We both showed our butts it's ok." He kissed me.

"Hey girl!" Tanisha said as she approached the table. She had on slacks and a button down shirt.

"Hey" I said as I stood up to give her a hug. "I hear I owe you a huge thank you."

"No thanks necessary, just glad I could help. Please let me know if you need my help with the wedding."

"I don't know why I thought you were in law enforcement of some kind?"

"I am, but..." She turned around and looked for someone in the crowd. Then she waved them over. A very pretty young lady appeared. She seemed somewhat shy and totally sweet.

"Hey Andrew." She said shyly.

"Hey Carina!" He said as he stood to hug her and kiss her on the cheek.

"This is the woman of the hour! This is Tracy, Tracy this is Carina."

"Hello" I said extending my arms to hug her not exactly knowing why.

"Carina is the event planner, I fill in where ever she needs me to. So she's really responsible for tonight. I only helped."

"Nice to meet you, this place is beautiful!" I said

"I'm so glad you like it! I was so worried about your opinion of this space."

"Have you had a chance to take it in?" Tanisha asked

"Not yet." I said looking at the crowds of people.

"As soon as we eat, I'll show her around." Andrew said

Then my brother stood by our table with a microphone. "Everyone, our lovely couple would like everyone to take their seats. The servers will serve the Wallace's first and then they will serve the tables. Then my brother winked at me, and Andrew nodded at him. A server brought us salads. I noticed that as soon as we started on our salads, servers seemed like they were pouring out of the kitchen. In a matter of minutes everyone was served salad. I noticed that Andre had a very simple salad with romaine lettuce. My salad was chicken and spinach. Andrew's salad had chicken, spinach, and strawberries. Andrew noticed me noticing the salads. He smiled at me very sweetly. As soon as we were done with our salads one server cleared our plates while another was placing our entrees in front of us. Andre had spaghetti with two meatballs, and garlic bread. His little face lit up so big when he saw his food. I had chicken Lombardy it's basically chicken breast, mushrooms, artichoke hearts, and these round shaped pastas in a white sauce. As I picked up my garlic bread I looked at Andrew with love in my eyes. We went to Chord's Italian food restaurant in El Cerrito once. I ordered this dish, and he assured me that I would love his cousin's version. I couldn't believe he remembered. Andrew had linguine with clams. Again moving in perfect harmony the guest tables were cleared, and plated. I was in Aw of the execution.

"How many people are here?"

"A little over a hundred."

"I don't know how you're doing this but it's amazing!"

"Do you like it?"

"I love it!" I put a fork full of my food to my mouth and I was in heaven. The sauce was creamy and flavorful. Everything was perfect. "This is so good!"

"Sophia made our dishes personally. She let her catering staff handle everyone else's food." he said

"Are their meals personalized too?"

"They had options to choose from. What do you think of the execution?" He asked

"I love it! No one's waiting for food and looking impatient. This is executed so well baby, you are the man!"

Andrew blushed. "Lets go look at the cake." When I grabbed his hand it was a little sweaty like he might've been nervous about tonight. "Now I doubt that the cake will be as good as anything you could whip up, I figured we needed a cake for the night so I went for it."

In the corner there was the cake table, and a dessert table a couple steps away next to it. The dessert table was long with apothecary jars full of different cookie assortments, brownies and blondie's, candy, dessert condiments like sprinkles, whipped cream, hot fudge, caramel sauce, strawberry and blueberry sauces, marshmallow topping, and last but not least an assortment of ice cream tubs. There were two servers stationed at this table awaiting their turn to provide service. The cake table had a silver satin tablecloth, with a blue over lay. There were twinkle lights all around the table. The cake it's self was a full sheet, but it was decorated to look like a quilt. The patches were all kinds of pictures of Andrew and I. There were even some from when we first met and initially dated. Pictures from Nicole & Hubby's wedding, that day in Napa, and more recent photos. The picture that caught my eye most was one from the very beginning. My face was so full, and so was my body. Andrew had that same proud look on his face that he always has had with me. Right in that moment I felt horrible for panicking about my weight or my appearance period. This man has always been attracted to me, why do I give myself such a hard time. Tears streamed down my face as I took in the whole cake. Andrew put his arms around me, "I bet you thought I forgot your makeup. But I knew I'd get a few good tears out of you so I didn't want you worrying about your makeup. You are beautiful naturally anyways!" Then he kissed my cheek. I threw both of my arms around his neck as I cried like I just got beat. Andrew rubbed my back. With those tears I released all the angst and panic I had been experiencing over the past two weeks. I was now ready to plan our wedding. "Oh yea, before I forget." He reached into his pocket. "If you take this ring off one more time there will be consequences." He said smiling. He slid my engagement ring back on my finger. I now felt complete. Then he took me to the photo booth. We took tons of pictures. Guest came over as they finished eating and we took pictures with all of them.

Terrence came over to get us. We sat down at our sweetheart table. There was a spotlight placed on us as the lights were lowered even further. Then on the projector screen was Joy. She was waiting for her queue. "Ok Joy you're on!" Terrence told her.

"Oh my goodness look at you guys! I was supposed to go with Andrew to pick out your dress today. Even though he called me numerous times to go over your ensemble, he and Andre did a very good job I see. Just know that I will be up to help you in four weeks. Carina everything looks great! Have a wonderful time tonight, and I look forward to being present for everything."

"Thank you girl! I'm gonna hold you to that."

Then the screen went black. Then there was a spotlight on Sophia. "Hello everyone my name is Sophia for those of you who don't know me, I am the soon to be Groom's cousin. I wanted to wish them well tonight, and to tell Tracy for the hundredth time how excited I am to welcome her into our family. As many of you may know, I don't like everyone." The audience laughed, "but I've always liked Tracy from the first time I met her. She's a lovely addition to our family." Everyone clapped in agreement.

Then the screen lit up again, this time it was Tia and Tara. "Oh my goodness Tracy! That dress is beautiful!" Tia said

"Yes, the whole place looks nice. We're so sorry we couldn't make it for the engagement party, but we promise to be there for everything else." Tara said

"Yes and we'd also like to welcome Andrew into our family. When we met Andrew, it was obvious to the world how much he loves our sister. We're so happy for you Tracy. You've got a real man who loves you to death. We wanna say welcome, and we too will be there every step of the way." Tia said while Tara nodded in agreement.

"We can't wait for the wedding." Tara said

Everyone wished us well on our nuptials, and then we cut the cake. The cake was pretty good. It was chocolate chiffon cake with a caramel custard filling. Of course I had to have a scoop of coffee ice cream to go with it. The night was perfect, when the party was over the limo driver took Amber, Andre, Andrew, and I back to the hotel. Amber had her own room, she took Andre with her.

When we entered our room Andrew kissed me long and passionately. He didn't pack a overnight bag for us; I kind of figured that was by design as well. As we kissed some more both of us took turns yawning. We laughed at how old we felt in that moment. So we kissed one final goodnight kiss, and then we both passed out.

CHAPTER 34

"Baby we really need to figure out a budget."

"I know! I don't know why I am fighting the idea. I want you to have everything that you want."

"I really appreciate that, but I gotta know when too much is too much."

He raised an eyebrow, "too much?"

"Ok let's dream here. If I came at you with a million dollar wedding budget that would be ridiculous."

He looked at me, "is that what you want?" There was no expression on his face.

"No! I was saying hypothetically." I remembered Yussef's comment about Andrew being a big man. "Baby can I ask you something?" I started to feel nervous at the thought of asking. He looked at me. "How much money do you have?"

He laughed, "what do you mean?"

I swallowed, "you said there was nothing you couldn't buy me. Then you drop a hundred grand without flinching to furnish the house. You paid off my student loans, my car, and all my debt. You pay my mortgage, and yours, you pay for everything. My paychecks have actually started earning me interest. And you still continue to buy things and pay for things without really giving it a second thought. I'm starting to get curious."

He laughed, "I do come off as straight balling huh." He laughed again. "You mean liquid cash?"
"Whatever, all of it." I didn't want to sound money hungry so I asked, " Do you want a pre-nup?"
He was quiet for a minute. "Before we discuss the money, is divorce an option for you?"

"I really don't want it to be. But you know how people change. What if one day you lose your mind and go upside my head? Or if you cheated on me? In those case scenarios I would say yes it's an option. I would do my best to work with you through anything else."

313

"Yea I want that same clause too. You can't be going upside my head and think I'm gonna roll with you forever." He laughed, "here's the thing. If our wedding budget was a million, I could manage it. But I don't know why it would need to cost so much. Especially since it's only for one day. But it's important to me that entire families are there, children should be included. But let me get back on the point. Money!" He exhaled, "I'm not gonna lie to you. I have a lot. Some of it is from my job, but I think I told you. I have a lot of investments that perform very well."

"Ok so that's still vague. But there's no pressure. Just give me an idea, NBA or NFL status or lower?"

He smiled really big. "Bigger!"

My eyes bulged. "Really? Wow! So it's not pushing to think of a hundred grand as our wedding budget?"

"That's fine, but lets set the ceiling at 5! Nothing higher than five."

"It must be nice!" Then I started thinking about it. "Andrew, with all that said I would feel better if we had a pre-nup."

"Why?"

"I never want it to be confused why we we're together. I love you, and I'm only marrying you because I love you."

"That is sweet, but I don't think it's necessary. Let me think about it. Right now I'm looking at things through rosé colored glasses. But you're right the world we live in is not like we imagine. Just know that I love you, and if I think about it and ask you to sign please understand it doesn't mean I love you any less."

"I understand. But at least we have a wedding budget. Look at that we're making progress. Now all we need is a date." I smiled

"I guess so." Then he looked at his watch. "You ready to make our way back?"

"Yes" since it had been ages since we worked out together. Andrew suggested that we take the puppies up to Wildcat Canyon in Tilden park and walk the trail. The walk within its self was pretty nice and it kind of gave you a feel for hiking in the woods. And then there's a huge hill that you have to walk up. I was out of breath when we got to the top. Once you reach the top there was Lake Anza. It had a small beach. We were sitting on a big rock by the water. We had been here for over an hour sitting on the rock talking about anything and everything. It was nice to have this time alone with him. We started walking on the trail back towards the hill. "Hey in all honesty, I need to ask you something." I said holding on to Cain who was very excited to be walking again.

"What's up?" He said watching Eve's footing.

"Do you think its weird that we haven't had sex in a month?"

He stopped in his tracks, it was clear that he hadn't realized it. "Has it been that long?" I could see him trying to retrace our steps. "Whoa!"

"I'm not complaining..." Then I looked at him. "YET!" He smiled. "But when I looked at our condom stash, I realized that it hadn't moved since the last time I checked it."

"I don't know how that happened. I must redeem myself."

"No worries, I just realized it myself."

As we walked back he kept looking around. When I realized what he was doing I smiled at him. "We can wait, home is right around the corner." But that didn't stop him from becoming all hands and chasing me back to the car. We were so out of breath when we got back to the car we couldn't even kiss. We were laughing and carrying on. Our car was the only car parked by the trail. The sun was starting to set so no one would be our way any time soon. Andrew picked me up and set me on the hood of his car. As he was kissing me I caught glimpse of a light.
"What was that?" I said pushing Andrew back by the shoulders.

He looked over his shoulder and he didn't see anything. "Inspiration" he said laughing

Then I saw it, a spotlight shining ahead on the grass. A car was coming and it was moving really slow. "Andrew somebody's coming!" I said pushing his shoulders.

He grunted, and then he looked over his shoulder. I guess he didn't believe me until he saw the light coming around the corner. It was a police car; I guess they were making sure there wasn't anyone in the park before they locked the gate to this area. Andrew stood up really quick, and I sat up. We looked so guilty.

"The park is closed!" The officer said

"Ok, we are on our way out right now." Andrew said helping me off the car. The officer ran Andrew's license plate number. Andrew blew air, "here we go!" He put the dogs in the car. I got in the front seat, and he started the car. The officer followed us out of the park, and all the way to Shattuck Ave. he finally turned right on University. Andrew was livid! He memorized the car number, and he went on and on about how he should've got his badge number. When we walked in the door instead of picking up where we left off. He went straight for the home computer. He was on there for hours. At one point I heard him on the phone. I don't know who he was calling, but he had that business tone which also meant leave him alone. In defeat I went down stairs, warmed up leftovers from the night before. I ate in front of the TV. Then I set the alarm, and went upstairs. He was still on the computer, he was typing at an extremely fast pace, which led me to believe he hadn't let the incident go yet. I showered, and I put on my feet pajamas. If nothing else sent a leave me alone vibe, feet pajamas were my voice. I got warm and cozy, and fortunately fell asleep fast. After a while he came to bed. As if he didn't get the hint from the pj's he tried to kiss me awake. He was trying to see if I was up to the task. I shooed him away like an annoying pest as I did my best to stay sleep. Eventually he stopped trying. He turned his back to me and went to sleep. In the morning, I ran in the closet. Grabbed my clothes took them in the bathroom and I hurried. I got too comfortable hitting the snooze button and it was now later than I needed it to be. Andrew was up before me running on the treadmill. He was drenched in sweat when he came in the bedroom. I kissed him on the cheek and I flew out the door. He looked disappointed, but I didn't want a quickie, and as that's all we had time for, I'd rather not. "Call from Andrew!" The car called out.

"Answer" I told the car. "Yes sweetheart?"

"Um! Yea, what was that?" He said sounding annoyed

"Baby, we didn't have time."

"There's always time!" He huffed

"Dude, you were on your own tangent last night. We had the whole house and the whole night, but you stayed on that computer."

"So is this supposed to be payback?"

"No, I didn't want a quickie this morning."

"Eeewwllll Tracy! You are such a tease!"

I laughed! "Am not!"

"Are too!" He laughed, "I'm not done with you yet."

"You promise?" I tried to say as cute as I could.

"Alright, talk to you later."

"Talk to you later."

As usual Yussef was walking across the street at the same time I was. "Good morning"

"Good morning. Well isn't someone bright and happy this morning. Your diet must not be on your nerves this morning."

"Why you gotta remind me? I got ten more to go and then I should be good."

"Whatever you say!"

"What you trying to say I need to lose more?"

"Not at all. I personally think you're fine where you are. You could stand to gain a pound or two."

"I like the way my body feels ten pounds lighter."

"If you say so, it's your body." He said

Yussef has become one of my best friends. It helps that we see each other every day Monday through Friday. But he gives me a male point of view when I need one. Although I know he's probably telling Andrew everything we talk about its still nice to have him around. When we walked into the office as we rounded the corner Shirley was walking away from my cubical. I instantly felt a heat wave flash. She saw us, just as we saw her. She eyed Yussef who stayed planted at my side.

"Good morning Yussef." She said in a way that made you wonder what she meant by that.

"Good morning Shirley." He said not moving

"Good morning Tracy." She said with soft pleading eyes

"Morning." I barely said

"Can I talk to you?" She pleaded

"I don't have time right now. I have to jump on a call." I said brushing past her to my desk. I put my purse away, and I hung up my jacket. She stood there with pleading eyes. "I don't have time for this." I said booting up my computer. I put my headset on and I dialed in to the conference line.

Shirley walked away deflated. Yussef made a face as he passed my cubical. My call only lasted five minutes, which was great! Then Danielle tiptoed in my cubical. "There's someone in the lobby to see you. He said he didn't have a meeting but it was urgent that he met with you." She whispered. "And since I know how you are about unexpected visitors I figured I should walk back instead of calling you."

My heart dropped! Ain't this some junk! Did Shirley REALLY bring Steve to my job???? My stomach started doing flips. "Thank you Danielle I'll be right out."

When she walked away I ran into Yussef's cubical. He gave me the "woman you must be crazy look". I whispered in his ear, "Danielle said someone's in the lobby for me!"

His face turned serious. He stood up and as he walked out of his cubical Shirley was coming as if she was coming to see if I was off the phone yet. She rolled her eyes as she saw me step out behind Yussef. I walked three steps behind him. My heart sped up, as we got closer to the door. Yussef looked out the glass door, and then he went through. I came through the door as his hand was in the air. He was giving Andrew a hello handshake. Instantly I was excited and I couldn't believe it. He's never come to my office before. I started jumping up and down; I forgot I was at work for a minute. Andrew was definitely on his way to work. He had on one of my favorite blue suits, with a cream shirt, tie, and handkerchief.

He looked good enough to eat. Danielle was sitting at her desk smiling. "Danielle this is my fiancée Andrew!"
Her smile changed, "oh man! I was hoping he was a vendor, I was gonna ask for details. Nice to meet you." Danielle said

Yussef's smile was kind of weird, but he was smiling all the same. "I'll let you guys talk." He said as he walked away.

"What are you doing here?" I had the biggest smile.

"I wanted to come see you, you know surprise you." Andrew said flashing his dimples and biting his bottom lip.

"You wanna see my workspace?" I said, I was so happy he was here.

"Sure." He said

I badged back through the glass door. We walked past Yussef's cubical but he wasn't there, and then we went into mine. "Here's my tiny little piece of real estate."

He smiled as he looked at my pictures and my knick-knacks. "Cool space!"

I smiled, and then as if on queue Shirley was walking past she slowed down when she saw Andrew. "Hello I'm Shirley." She said sticking her hand out to shake his.

She always did that when we worked in the city together. A vendor or anyone would be in my cubical and she would ALWAYS butt in and introduce herself like the person needed to explain to her why they were there. When we were friends it didn't bother me, but now it pissed me off. "Oh you're Shirley!" Andrew said turning to get a good look at her.

I guess because he was smiling and looking her up and down she thought that meant something positive.

She smiled really big, "yes I am. What company are you with?"

"Cooper financial" he said casually

She was trying to place the company in her head. "I'm trying to remember if I worked on anything with you."

Annoyed I stood up. "Lets go in a conference room where we won't be disturbed." I said grabbing Andrew by the hand.

I signed out the Bullwhip conference room for the next hour and a half. It was the only conference room with no windows and it was used last because of this. I locked the door, Andrew sat at the head of the table and I leaned against the table next to him. "What a lovely surprise! To what do I owe the honor?"

He flashed his dimples along with a wicked smile. "I wanted to see where you work, etc."

"Un huh, what's the etc.?"

"Yussef's reports have been less detailed lately so I wanted to 'pop my head in' (pun intended) and see how things are going."

I blushed, "we can't do that here. Someone will know." I whispered but I was thoroughly excited by the idea.

"How will they know there's no windows?"

"It'll smell like sex in here."

"We gotta go somewhere, I think I'm about to explode!" He said caressing my thighs.

I couldn't think, especially when he started kissing my stomach. "The Marriott is a block away. I could take my lunch hour."

He moaned in agony! "Seriously??? We're already here." I pushed his shoulders back as he went for my neck. It took everything in me to keep my composure. "Andrew please!!!" I begged

He smiled, "I like the sound of you begging!"

"Baby you have no idea!" I grabbed his jacket. "And you wore this suit! You knew what you were doing to me when you got dressed!" He kissed me! Long! Deep! And hard! I almost forgot what I was saying by the way he kissed me! "You gotta go!"

"Lets walk over together."

We kissed one more time to seal the deal. Then I hurried to my desk. I blocked my calendar for the rest of the morning. I sent my boss an email letting her know I was leaving for and appointment. Yussef looked around the wall at us. Then he went back to work. I hurried out the door before Shirley could come and disturb the feeling I was having. We hurried down the street like we were on our way to meet up with our pusher. Although check-in was rather quick it seemed like it took forever. In the elevator I was all over him. He kept hugging me although he was getting weak in the legs. Once we were in that room we were both in marathon mode. My extreme workout for the day! We had a lot of frustration to burn off. As we took a moment to catch our breath, we talked about the wedding and how this should be our last hooray before the wedding. So as a last memorable touch we made slow passionate LOVE. It was so beautiful and powerful. I've never connected with someone like I connect with Andrew. We were really quiet for a long time after that. We felt it, it was like our souls became one. I laid there staring at him as he stared at me. Yep! I'm sprung! Our bodies were still rocking, Andrew moved his leg and it was still shaking. I had been waiting for this feeling my entire life! I looked at the clock on the nightstand and that fast two hours had flown by. I sat up.

"I don't know how I'm supposed to focus after this!" Andrew said

"Me neither!"

We showered together, and we headed back to my office. Although I told him I could go back up on my own, he insisted on walking me to my desk again. When we entered the office Shirley was in Yussef's cubical. She was talking to him about something work related, but he got distracted when we walked past. Andrew sat in my guest chair, as I logged into my computer.

Shirley cleared her throat. She was standing at my cubical now. "I'm sorry suga, I didn't know you are the fiancée."

"Andrew" he said as he stuck his hand out.

"Nice to meet you." Shirley said

"So Shirley what do you have against me? I'm a good guy."

She shifted from side to side. "I only know what I've heard."

"Now I know, you know, you can't believe everything you hear."

"Yea, but she's been so tight lipped about you."

"I guess it depends on who she's talking to." Andrew said in a way that knocked whatever she was gonna say out of her mouth. "Now tell me Shirley, are you gonna bring Steve here too?" He gave her direct eye contact on that one.

She turned her eyes and looked around the cubical. "I wasn't trying to cause problems in your relationship. You don't know her like I do. She was so in love with that man, and it doesn't add up for her to suddenly turn her back on him."

"So you feel she should be with Steve?"

"I think she owes it to herself to at least talk to the man. Get some closure before she tries to pretend like she can move on."

My head snapped so fast! What does she mean by pretend?? Andrew put his hand up to say he got this. "What are they supposed to talk about?"

She put her hands out "stuff".

"Can you be a little more direct?" He said

"Stuff, like they never discussed the miscarriage. Or even agreed that their relationship was over. He still loves you!" She said looking at me.

"Do you think I love her?" He asked

"I guess, but I don't really know you." She said

"Well see that's kind of the point. You don't know me, you don't know the whole situation, but yet you're trying to make your opinion stand out as the only opinion that matters. Shirley you really need to mind your own business. Does it even matter to you that you lost a friend behind this? And as soon as he realizes he can't pump you for information, or use you in whatever ways he already has he's gonna drop you like a hot potato." She stood there with her face all twisted. "Tell me something, what do you get out of all this? Why are you pushing this?" She blew air, and then she walked away. I knew Yussef was listening, how could he not be. Then Andrew kissed me goodbye.

After ten minutes Yussef came over. "Good lunch?"

I smiled really big, "UN HUH!"

Yussef didn't look amused. He started talking about work stuff then he went back to his cubical. The rest of the day he stuck to business, no small talk or chit chatting like we had been doing. At four I came to his cubical to wait for him to shut down. "How come you're so quiet? It's Friday, you got any plans?"

"No" he said uninterested in talking to me.

"Yussef what's wrong?"

"Nothing." He said

"Is it a girl?" I asked

"Why you ask me that?" He stood still to hear my answer.

"Cause you're over here all withdrawn like a little love sick puppy." I said teasing him

"But what if it was a guy?"

My eyes got big "really?"

"No! But I'm saying you don't know what you're talking about."

"Well something's wrong with you."

"It's been a LONG day!" He rolled his eyes at me. "I'm tired!"

"Ok, good grief! I was just asking."

Yussef was very huffy walking me to my car. He didn't say much; he wasn't in the mood for me. I wrote it off as a long day.

As I walked in the door my cellphone rang it was Amber.

"Hello"

"Hello honey, you guys got plans tonight?"

"Not really, what's up?"

"Sophia and I wanna go to EA, can you guys go?"

"I'll have to check with Andrew but it should be fine. But wait a minute, if you go out, who's gonna have Andre?"

"Sophia's daughter Sabrina is gonna babysit."

"Ok, let me check with Andrew." I said

Amber's voice got really excited. "Ok, talk to you in a minute."

I called Andrew at work. He said he'd leave after another hour, but he was fine with it. When I called Amber back she was so excited. She wanted a driver so we could all drink without worry. So of course that meant hiring a limo. Now the ugly part. I went to my closet to find something to wear. Rebounding from my twenty-pound fluctuation has been a little harder. I'm a big girl at heart. And eating is something I do especially when my emotions get the best of me. Andrew doesn't seem to notice, or seem to care. When I start complaining or having meltdowns in my closet, then Andrew suggests things we could do as a family. Like our little hike in Tilden park yesterday. I tried on dress after dress. I was getting so frustrated. Of course in the back of the closet I found a very forgiving black blouse, which I paired with a short red skirt. I hopped in the shower again. I wondered why Yussef started acting funny. But who knows what Shirley said to him when I was gone. I will make him tell me on Monday. Then I thought about Shirley. Even after looking at Andrew and hearing him speak how could she think I'd want anything to do with Steve? I can't believe she's still swinging from his nuts like that either. Yes, so back in the day I loved him. That's when I didn't know any better. She saw the way he talked to me how in the world could she think he had anything pleasant to say to me. I don't even understand how she could still think there's anything between us. When Andrew came home he gave me the biggest hug.

"I couldn't stop thinking about you all day!"

"Same here, I love you so much!"

"You sure you wanna go out tonight? Honestly I could chill here with you."

"Me too, but your mom was really excited. She's getting a limo and Sophia's coming. Maybe we could go for a little bit and then take a cab home."

"That sounds like a plan." He hopped in the shower.

I called out while he was in the shower. "Is it ok to use your phone to call Tanisha? I wanna connect with Carina."

"Yea, sure."

I put the phone on speaker, "hey Drew how's it going?"

"Hey Tanisha, it's Tracy actually."

"Oh hey girl, what can I do for you?"

I grabbed a pen and paper off the nightstand. "I was wondering if I could get contact information for Carina. I meant to get it that night, but it got away from me."

Tanisha laughed, "we were beginning to think you might've went with someone else. Carina's right here, hold on." I could hear her saying something, but I couldn't make out her words.

"Hello!" Carina said very excitedly

"Hello, how are you?" I said with a smile in my voice.

"I'm great! Especially since you're on the phone." She said happily

"Aren't you sweet!"

"So what can I do for you?"

"I need your contact info. I need to know what services you offer, etc. Andrew and I finally came up with a budget."

She got really excited. "I can email you my information. There will be a PDF attachment, you can take a look at my brochure."

"Sounds good." I gave her my email address, and then we got off the phone. She sounds so happy, I would like to believe that excitement was for me but I knew she was excited about her commission.

Then Nicole called me, I told her we were going to Elegant Affairs, and I asked her if she and Hubby would like to come. She said they would meet us there. While Andrew got dressed, I looked at Carina's brochure. And then I went to her website. I could tell she was just getting started but I was still impressed with what I saw. She did a wonderful job with our engagement party. Then a sinking feeling thought hit me.

"Andrew"

"Yes" he called out from the closet.

"Did you ever date Tanisha or Carina?"

He started laughing. "Why are you asking me that?"

"You asked Jesse directly. I know your list runs long so I'm asking."

325

"I only know Carina through Tanisha. No I've never dated her."

"Ok so what about Tanisha?" He popped his head out the closet and he had a crazy look on his face. "Is that look supposed to tell me something?"

He started laughing. "Ok, I'm gonna tell you the story. We were in elementary school so I don't think that really counts. You know the whole I go with you stuff. I don't remember why we broke up cause it was that stupid. Junior high school we're at a party, were talking about stuff. You know how the teenage years go. She asked me to help her out. So of course I was down. She was my buddy. She was my first." I gasped. "He put his hands up, but you gotta understand it wasn't like that. She was trying to come to terms with who she was. You are the only person I've ever told this. I guess that's why Toya thinks she was my first. But anyways, we gave it a few more tries. But she wasn't into it. She don't like men. We've been cool ever since, and she said she's thankful to me for helping her. I didn't do it for her. Carina is her girlfriend. I thought you would've picked up on that." He smiled

"How would I have picked up on that?"

"I don't know. But trust she don't want me."

"Why did I have to ask you this? Why didn't you tell me?"

"I didn't think it was a big deal. But if that's what you want I can give you back ground stories on everybody."

That was a lot to take in, in thirty seconds. I sat on the bed wrapping my mind around it all. "Why didn't you tell Toya?"

He shrugged, "it wasn't none of her business. Plus she liked the idea of being my first. I got in her pants that much faster."

"Faster?"

"Yea, you think them little girls wasn't on me? I came at her like, I don't wanna be a virgin no more, if you wont do it somebody else will. Not my proudest moment. At the time though, I thought I was the stinking man!"

"I see... You just nasty!"

He smiled real big, "YES! YES I AM!"

"But Tanisha was your first! Mind blowing!"

He stopped, "you get hung up like that? Such and such was my first, I'm stuck to them, or some stupid junk like that?"

"Not exactly, but everyone's not like that. Some people don't get over their first."

"What about yours?" He sat down at the foot of the bed.

"Ick!" I mimicked a bad taste in my mouth.

"Come on, spill it."

"Mine doesn't have a happy ending."

"Yes it does, your story ends here." He said

"He was my first heartbreak, my first serious relationship, my first everything. And he was horrible! He wasn't gentle or kind. The whole ordeal was just painful. He made me feel broken, like there was something wrong with me. He actually made me hate sex." Andrew frowned. "When we broke up, I didn't get what everyone was going crazy about. What was the big deal about sex? But I wanted to know, and I really wanted to know if it was me or just my reaction to him. There was one guy after the mistake. He was alright, but he didn't exactly know what he was doing. I cared about him though, but that was over shortly after it started. Is it ok to tell you all this? You NEVER asked."

"Yea, go ahead." He was listening, but his face was sad.

"Ok... Then there was Steve, the most experienced of the three of them. But for all intents and purposes he was like my first. I was able to give him what I couldn't give the mistake. Steve would always act jealous of the mistake even though they never met or crossed paths as far as I know. Steve always felt like my first and it's not until recently that I've been able to truly let that go. I don't understand why he hates me so much."

He exhaled, "he hates you because you left him. He's the kind of person who holds onto people in his life. You got in there pretty deep and then you left. He feels like you abandoned him. It's not right, but that's how he feels. So instead of putting himself out there for fear of rejection he lashes out at you. He doesn't want you to move on. But he didn't do what he needed to, to keep you either." He said matter of factly

"Ok..." I said. I don't know why that made me feel weird. But it did. "Since we're sharing..."

He looked at me like oh no here it comes. "What?" He said

"Have you ever had a STD?"

"Yes" he clapped his hands. "I had the clap, talk about eyes crossing!" He shook his head. "It could've been worse. But I stayed suited up after that and with my own stash. Like I said those little things ALWAYS break on me. You?"

"No, Steve only got me that one time. Thank goodness I didn't catch anything." The thought of it made me shudder. "Have you heard of any of your partners catching something and it freak you out?"

"Not besides babies."

"Are you sure Andre's your only son?"

"Yes, I told you I wasn't slipping up. Aren't I even careful with you?"

"I guess, but you've been raw dog with me too."

"Twice!"

I laughed, "didn't realize you were counting as well."

He made his voice sound like he was crying; "you have no idea how hard that is. Every time I wanna say forget it, and go for it. Then I think about how dramatic you are." He shook his head, "cause you know you'd be pregnant. My soldiers know how to march! Ten hut!" He saluted me, "your mom and dad would be mad talking about how I violated their little angel. Yea Id rather not."

"You don't think I'd stop you?"

He started laughing. "Yea right! Both times you acted like I was reading your mind. You never object to anything the beast does. Well almost anything." He laughed

I rolled my eyes. "Whatever! I'm not into back door exploring. And even if I was the beast is too tall to ride this ride."

It was the nonchalant conversations like this that made my heart sing. I like how he didn't flip out when I told him stuff, and how later on I wouldn't hear about it when he was mad at me. The mistake taught me early on that you don't talk about your past, men can't handle it. Steve would ask questions here and there and then fill in the blanks with assumptions and then I'd hear about it whenever he was mad. Now it was my turn to try and for once not hold something he's told me in confidence against him.

When Amber and Sophia arrived they were happy and loud. They kept saying they were letting their hair down as they flipped their long tresses backwards. They looked good.

"Oh no! I already know I'm gonna regret this. You guys look like trouble!" Andrew said grinning from ear to ear.

"Amber, I think that's your son's way of telling us we look good!" Sophia said flipping her hair.

"You could be right! Thought I taught him better than that, but oh well." Amber said fanning her hands at him.

When we got to EA the line was down the street again. I know that could only be good for business. The bouncers high fived Andrew as we walked in. We went straight to the VIP, the waitress brought out Andrew's drink immediately and then she asked us what we would like. So I ordered a Tokyo Ice Tea. After explaining it to Amber and Sophia they asked for the same. "AND KEEP 'EM COMIN!" Amber hollered after the waitress

"Momma there's no need for that. Unless you say otherwise they will continue to bring you the same drink all night." Andrew said sounding embarrassed already.

"Ok well, I didn't know. I wanted to make sure they knew." She said taking off her jacket and looking around the club, she had a huge smile on her face.

It wasn't until that moment that I thought about the mother son dynamic of the night. Fact is Amber doesn't look old enough to be his mother. She looks every bit as young as me, maybe even younger depending on who's looking. And she wasn't carrying herself as if she has three grown children. Andrew sat back and watched the crowd of people on the dance floor.

Then he bumped me, "look it's your boy." He said pointing out Cameron on the dance floor.

"Uh oh what if Karen's with him?" I asked

"Then they better act right, or they gonna have to go." He said nonchalantly.

As Darryl approached our booth he stopped in his tracks when he realized his mom was with us. "OH SNAP! YOU HANGING WITH US TONIGHT???" He said heck of excited

"Go on boy! You too silly!" Amber said all smiles

"Wait until I tell D-Rick!" He said opening his phone and walking away.

Our drinks arrived and they both gave me thumbs up. We finished our drinks like we were in a race. When we set our empty glasses down at the same time then we started laughing. "Lets go dance!" Sophia commanded.

"You ready?" I said to Andrew

"You guys go ahead, I'll come out when I'm ready."

"Lets go!" Amber said grabbing my hand

When we got on the dance floor I felt like I was with girlfriends. We grooved to two songs before Nicole found us on the dance floor. She said Hubby didn't wanna be the only guy out here with us. It was only a matter of time before Cameron spotted us. He came trying to dance up behind me. I rolled my eyes and walked away. I headed for the VIP and everyone was in tow. Our fresh drinks were waiting for us. Andrew was smiling with his eyes locked on someone; Cameron was standing there looking stupid. I guess he felt like I dissed him, but whatever. Then Amber gasped and she and Sophia started fidgeting, I was wondering what was wrong with them until I saw Derrick walking alongside Malcolm. Malcolm had his eyes locked on Amber. I wondered how these two were ever together, Malcolm is just mean from what I can tell and Amber's a sweetheart. I thought Malcolm was gonna sit in his own booth like he did before. But he planted himself right in our booth.

No Mister Rogers sweater for him tonight. He had on a leather jacket, turtle neck sweater, slacks, Stacy Adams. "Amber" he nodded at her.

She smiled, "Malcolm".

"Sophia" he nodded at her

"What's up Malcolm! We haven't seen you in a minute. What you been up to?" Sophia said obviously not intimated by him.

"Oh you know, a little of this and a little of that." Then he looked Amber over, "you look good".

She smiled, "thank you".

I looked at Andrew and he wasn't even paying them any attention. So I tried to do the same, but I really wanted to see them interact. Nicole and Hubby went back on the dance floor. Malcolm scooted next to Amber. Wow! To see them next to each other. Suddenly Malcolm didn't seem so old. Suddenly he looked a lot younger. Suddenly I realized he was just a guy with a sweet tooth for Amber. He said something to her and she blushed.

Derrick sat next to me, and Sophia asked Andrew to dance with her. He agreed and they were off. I wanted to see how things unfolded up here anyways. Did I really just see Malcolm blush? Wow! Derrick wasn't interested in the Amber & Malcolm show either. He was watching the dance floor. Then he tapped me. "Who's that?" He gestured with his head towards Cameron. Cameron was shooting daggers at Andrew with his eyes. Even from the VIP you could see his panties were all in a bunch. "His name is Cameron Harris. He's a pest that won't go away."

Derrick was unimpressed, "he need to watch himself. Guess he don't know who's house this is." Derrick said in the tone he had with me at E & J's. I said a little prayer that Cameron acted right. There's no way it wouldn't get back to my mom if something happened. Then I noticed Darryl on the dance floor with some girl. Derrick was sitting and surveying the land. Amber convinced Malcolm to dance with her. It was amazing to me to see Malcolm act normal, even if he didn't say hi to me when he sat down. Amber led Malcolm by the hand to the dance floor. He was reluctant at first to dance he stood there with his arms folded, but grinning. Amber danced around him; she dropped it, and everything. I was in aw behind the scene. Derrick got tired of me gawking at his mom. "Lets dance!" He commanded, and of course I went, finishing up my drink. The waitress was on her way to our booth with a drink. I'm assuming it was Malcolm's she took my empty glass as she smiled at me. Derrick became nice Derrick again as we danced. The music changed and everyone got excited and started stepping. "You know how?" He asked

"Not really."

First he showed me the foot movement, once I got that. He held me, "follow my lead". His lead was strong, and although I've always not fully understood the male lead in a dance, I didn't have to guess with him. He turned me this way and that way. It was pretty cool.

I looked over and the dance floor wasn't as crowded as everyone couldn't do this dance. Sophia and Andrew were all over the floor. Amber and Malcolm were "dirty stepping". He had his leg between hers. They were twirling and stepping like professionals. Then suddenly Derrick twirled me and I landed in Andrew's arms. I could hear Sophia speaking my thoughts about how smoothly they pulled that off. Andrew flashed his dimples at me. His lead was stronger, and way sexier. Maybe because I realized I've felt this lead by him before. When the next song came on we stayed on the dance floor. The crowd came back. I couldn't see Amber & Malcolm all that well any more. Nicole and Hubby were at the booth and they were coming back to the floor. Andrew and I were in our own world when someone bumped into us so hard I almost fell. Andrew's face was pissed before I even saw who it was.

"Oops my bad!" Karen said with her hands out.

"You better be cool or else I will have you thrown out of here!" Andrew said completely annoyed. Derrick and Darryl were both looking.

"It's ok, I'm ok." I said trying to pull Andrew's attention back to me. He was annoyed, but I didn't get the impression that he was going to have much patience.

Karen mouthed something that I assume was directed at me, but I didn't care to find out what she said. We kept dancing and here came Cameron and Karen. Now she should know I didn't care about her dancing with Cameron but I guess I was supposed to be upset by all the extra they were doing on the dance floor. Amber even stopped her groove to give them funny looks, cause they were pissing a bunch of people off. Cameron high fived about four or five guys on the dance floor. I guess he was trying to show he had backup. Derrick bumped into Cameron so hard he fell into Andrew. "MAN WHAT IS YOUR PROBLEM!" Andrew barked

"My man over here having a hard time keeping rhythm." Cameron said pointing at Derrick who wasn't paying attention to him as he kept dancing with Sophia.

"Lets go sit down." I said to Andrew

"Naw!" Andrew said resuming his dancing. Then he bumped into Cameron really hard and this time he fell into Derrick.

"I GUESS WE GONNA HAVE A PROBLEM TONIGHT!" Derrick said

Cameron seemed rightfully nervous. "Naw! Naw! My bad!" His dumb behind kept dancing, even though Karen was saying lets go sit.

He moved away from us and Derrick. But!!!! Darryl bumped him and he fell into Malcolm. The music stopped! Lights came up, and it seemed like the room spun. Malcolm didn't say anything he looked at Cameron like he was a bug about to be squashed. I started praying again. "Who are you?" Malcolm said putting his hands in his pockets.

Cameron's dumb behind starts yelling talking about people bumping into him. Malcolm walks up to him, "if you wanna live to see tomorrow!" Then he looks around the room. "This little boy is bothering me. Put him out!"

"WHAT! WHAT! I DIDN'T DO ANYTHING! THESE FOOLS DONT KNOW HOW TO DANCE!" He yelled

"Man! Shut up!" Malcolm said signaling for the bouncer to come.

"You gotta go!" One bouncer said as he put hands on Cameron to remove him. Cameron started to fight back, the bouncer put him in that hold where your arms are up in the air kind of behind your head, and his hands were on Cameron's head. His "boys" started to move like they were gonna do something. Suddenly the crowd shuffled and all you saw were men who had looks on their faces like "I wish you would!" The people sitting around started laughing. "They punked you and your friends!" Someone yelled. Everybody started laughing. Karen looked completely embarrassed. She looked at me, she was so mad! She looked like she wanted to do something but she looked at the crowd, and she decided against it. The bouncer drug Cameron out of the club. They started preparing for Jesse's set. As we went back to the VIP, I saw Toya standing by the lounge area. I pointed her out to Nicole. She had on black pants and kind of a long jacket. Her hair was up in a ponytail, and she looked mad. As Nicole was telling Hubby she walked out towards the door. The vibe in the club kind of stood on its head. I felt self conscious, about all the eyes on us in the VIP.

I leaned in to whisper in Andrew's ear, "why do they even let her in here?"

"Karen?"

"Yea, well her too. But I'm talking about Toya."

"She's here?"

"She was, Nicole saw her too."

He thought about it for a minute, and then he said something to Darryl. Darryl was gone. I didn't want to drink any more. Andrew didn't touch his drink anymore either. All I could think was we had to go out there to go home. We should've stayed home. Jesse was into his set and doing a good job, but all I wanted was to go home. Andrew grabbed my hand; it was like he could read my mind. I looked at Amber and she was chatting Malcolm's ear off, she looked so happy. Funny thing is he looked happy too.

"Are you ready?" Andrew asked it was like he was reading my mind.

"Yes, but I don't know..."

"It'll be fine." Then he turned to Hubby, "how long you guys staying?"

"Nicole was just saying she was tired. We about to bounce."

"I'm getting tired too." Sophia said obviously ear hustling

"Tired? Who's tired?" Amber asked. Our group raised their hands. "Wimps!" She said disappointed "I guess I gotta go."

"What?" Malcolm said sounding disappointed.

"We came together, we gotta leave together." She shrugged.

"But I can take you home." He said holding her hand

"Some other time." She said completely teasing him. She grabbed her jacket then walked in front of him on purpose. No doubt teasing him some more.

Andrew blew air; he stood up and reached for my hand.

"We might as well go too." Malcolm said to Derrick

We all walked out the door together. The air was crisp and cool. I looked at the line that still wrapped around the corner of people waiting to get in. We were waiting for the limo. I spotted Toya across the street looking at us. That's when I heard the footsteps hurrying towards us. Everybody's sense of alarm went up. Andrew grabbed me as I turned around in time to see Karen running up. Derrick pulled his gun out and pointed it in her face, "female you must feel like dying today!" She stopped dead in her tracks.

"Seriously Karen? You wanna fight outside a club? How old are you?" I was mad but I also had a few Tokyo teas in me.

Sophia laughed, "she's a stupid somebody!"

Derrick put his gun down. "This is what you're gonna do! Take you're little busted self and go tend to your man! Next time you think about running up on somebody, just say no. If I ever hear about my sister having problems with you, well. I'll just have to pay you a little visit at 2121 Arlington Ave!" She gasped! I kind of did too. How could he call to mind a random chick's address like that? Whoa! Karen didn't move right away she was stuck out of fear. "If you stay, well that's gonna irritate me. You won't like me when I'm angry but the choice is yours." She started backing away slowly. "I thought so!" Then he looked across the street at Toya. "If you don't stop instigating!" He put a fist up, "you know what's up!" She walked away annoyed.

Malcolm looked at Andrew, "I keep telling you about that one." He said in an authoritative tone.

"Malcolm not right now!" Andrew barked

"Mark my words! You gonna have to do something about that one." Malcolm said matter of factly.

Andrew was completely pissed off, but I didn't understand why. I knew they were talking about more than they were saying.

"She needs a visit." Derrick said matter of factly.

"She needs more than a visit." Malcolm said

"Come on you guys," Amber, said trying to calm everyone down. "Lets not talk about this tonight. Lets go get something to eat. I need something to soak up this liquor."

"We could go back to my restaurant. It's almost closing so we can have the place to ourselves." Sophia suggested.

Everyone liked the idea, so Hubby told Nicole to ride with us, and Andrew went with him. He was so angry I wondered what "a visit" meant. Obviously Derrick knew who Karen was to rattle off her address like that. I knew Derrick carried a gun, but I never thought I would see it.

"You ok?" Nicole asked

"Yea" I said, but I wasn't.

When we got to the restaurant Sophia called all her staff out. She asked who would be willing to stay for double and a half overtime pay. Only one lady couldn't stay. She had to get home to her kids. I heard Sophia tell her she'd get paid anyways. The lady gave her a heartfelt hug. You could tell she was a good boss and her staff loved her. They made a long table for us in the middle of the main floor. We had wine and delicious food. Sophia told her staff to bring out all the specials and to keep the wine coming. I needed to pee, but I really didn't want to go in that bathroom again. When I couldn't take it any more I asked Nicole to go with me. Walking down that hallway was a trip. And walking into that bathroom even more! I saw Steve's angry face as he choked me. I went in the stall, tears streamed down my face. Being in this space was too much.

"Are you ok?" Nicole asked through the stall door. I came out and washed my hands. She was completely alarmed once she saw my face. "What's wrong?"
"Oh I'm tripping out a little bit. Tonight's been a little crazy huh." I said

"Just a little but how often does it happen?"

"I knew I should've listened to Andrew and stayed home with him."

"Yea, but then you wouldn't have seen Derrick put Karen in her place. She almost peed on herself." Nicole said with a smile.

"Yea but what does paying Toya a visit mean?"

"Ugh! Trust! You don't wanna know."

I looked at Nicole, "you know?"

"I mean well the context clues aren't that hard to figure out. But how you gonna be in here all worried about her, when she's trying to get people to fight you?" I hadn't thought of it that way. "If somebody doesn't do something soon, you're gonna end up hurt." She had a point.

"This bathroom is where she brought Steve and he attacked me." I said looking at the floor like he was still there.

"What??? When was this?"

"A long time ago. I had handprints on my neck for days."
Her eyes got big, "where was I?"

"It was a long time ago Andrew gets mad every time he thinks about it."
Then we heard yelling coming from the dining room. We hurried out the bathroom.

"Son get mad at me if you want to. I'm telling you what needs to be done!" Malcolm's voice was booming as he talked to Andrew.

Andrew was livid pacing back and forth on the opposite side of the table. "You're always so quick to make those calls! These are people's lives!"

"You think she cares about your life? Does she care how she affects you or your son? The way I see it, it's either you or her. I can't let it be you!"

"Like you care!"

"Andy!" Amber said

"Oh I don't care? Who paid the way so that you could have something different?"

"You paid the bill, but I got myself there despite you!" I had never seen Andrew so unglued.

"Son we can go round and round, but I am your father!" Malcolm's voice boomed

Andrew yelled, "I KNOW! I KNOW!" I didn't understand what they were arguing about. But I couldn't move, Nicole stayed back with me.

Darryl looked sad, but Derrick kept a matter of fact look on his face. The difference in their expressions were like night and day. Darryl seemed like he wanted to rescue his brother, while Derrick seemed unattached.

Amber looked at Nicole and I. "Come sit down ladies." She said

I didn't want to but I didn't know what else to do. "NO! WE'RE LEAVING!"

"Andy come on, lets not let this ruin the evening." His mom said

"YOU DON'T EVEN CARE!" He screamed

Amber's eyes filled up with tears. "Of course I care, but people have to make their own beds."

"That's how you felt about dad? He made his bed, so he had to lye in it?"

"Andy that's not fair!" She started crying. Sophia came over to hug her

"I'm just saying..." He said

"You always move slow when a female's involved. All this could be resolved!" Malcolm said

Andrew looked at me, "lets go!" His fist were flexing. Hubby stood up, and took Nicole by the hand.

"Andy! Don't leave!" Amber pleaded

Andrew looked at her sitting next to his father. He rolled his eyes and his face was like stone. He gently grabbed my hand, and he led me out the door. Nicole and Hubby followed.

CHAPTER 35

We rode that whole car ride in silence. Hubby and Nicole dropped us off. Andrew said he would be back and he left. He came back with a sleeping Andre in his arms. He tucked him in, and then he stayed by the bed watching him sleep. Cain kind of looked at him like he felt his pain. He laid at the foot of the bed watching them. He told me to let him go through it when he was in these spaces, so I went in the room and shut the door. Eve looked at me like she wondered why he was staying out there and not coming in the room. Eventually I went to sleep, but barely. I wanted to know what was going on, and obviously Andrew didn't want to discuss it.

In the morning I was awakened to a beaming Andre. "Good morning mommy!" He said giving me a kiss on my cheek.

"Good morning baby. I missed you!" I said giving him a hug.

"I missed you too. Daddy said we're going to have a family day!"

"He did?" Andre shook his head yes. "Did he say what we were going to do?" Andrew was standing in the doorway watching us.

"Nope, but he told me to softly wake you up so that we could get going. Did I softly wake you up?"

"Yes baby, you did. Did you take a bath or shower last night?" I asked

"Yep!" Then he started jumping on the bed. "And then Sabrina read me a story. She said she's my big cousin. But I told her she wasn't because she's white. Then she told me that I was too. Am I white daddy?"

"You're brown Andre." Andrew said laughing

"Then how is she my cousin?"

"Our family has many different shades within it. Just because you're the same shade as someone doesn't make you family. And just because someone is a different shade doesn't mean they're not related. Ask Nana to show you pictures of my grandfather. As long as the person is a good person it doesn't matter what shade they are. Was Sabrina nice to you?"

"Yes, and she was funny!" Andre said still jumping

"Then that's all that matters. Now lets go get you ready, mommy needs to get ready too."

"Ok!" Andre kissed me one more time then he ran out the door. Andrew followed him to his room.

I did as I was told, and I got in the shower. Part of me wanted to stay at home. But Andrew was acting weird, so I'm going so that I don't rock the boat.

Andre wanted to go to Pancake House, so we went to the one in Emeryville. Our waiter was nice enough, but André's reaction to his funny face pancake is priceless. He laughs so hard when he sees it, and then he talks to the face. He explains to the face that he's his breakfast and he has to be eaten. Then the face tries to cry out for help. He acts like a monster and eats it all up. It is the cutest thing to watch. Then Andrew explained to Andre that he wanted his most prized possessions with him today. I didn't want to split hairs over a word so I let it go. But I'm not a possession. My phone rang and it was Amber. I attempted to answer, but Andrew took the phone from me. He hung up the phone and put it in his pocket. He shook his head no.

We drove over to Golden Gate park. First we went to Stow Lake. A little man made lake in the park. Andrew and Andre paddled while I sat on the back like a queen being taken around the lake. Andre had and absolute blast. Then as we walked around the lake, Andrew mentioned the zoo that was nearby. So we went to the San Francisco zoo. Andre loved seeing all the animals. He especially loved the petting zoo. I decided his name for the day was nature boy. He liked that. Those animals got a little pushy in the petting zoo, so I decided to watch the boys from outside the area. We spent hours in the zoo. I couldn't tell if Andre or Andrew was having more fun. Since we were right next to the beach of course we had to stop over. I planted my feet in the cold sand while Andrew and Andre ran around like crazy people. They were having such a good time together. It did make me feel good to see them enjoying each other so much. But I also knew Andrew was avoiding me. I didn't have it in me to pull it out of him right now. He was very guarded when it came to certain topics. I know he knows I want to know what happened last night, but I could wait until he was ready to tell me. Andre started playing with some little boys not too far from me. Andrew came and sat next to me on the sand.

"Don't you look pretty, shades on, wind blowing your curls back, sun set beginning in your face." He said leaning in to kiss me. I smiled, and I returned the kiss, but even his kiss was lacking something. He started staring at the water. "Yesterday morning was pretty amazing huh." He said fidgeting in the sand. I smiled at him. "I couldn't have planned that any better than it happened if I tried." He threw a rock. I looked at him with nothing but love on my face. He looked at me. "We should've stayed home. Something told me last night wasn't a good idea. But you know hind sight is always twenty-twenty." He exhaled. "I know you wanna know, but I'm not ready. I'll tell you, I promise." I nodded. "My dad was a good man. He loved me like I was his son."

"So he's dead?" I asked

He shook his head keeping his eyes to the sand. His eyes turned red, and tears started welling up. I leaned over and kissed him. He accepted my kiss, but his heart was hurting. He kept drawing stuff in the sand. Then he'd start over. I didn't ask him anything else, I put my arm around him as the sun set. I stared at the water and imagined us fifty years later still together. Our kids would be grown, and life would be good.

It started to get really cold so we loaded up back in the car. We stopped at Mellow's Diner for dinner. Andrew's phone had been going off all day. He'd look each time to see who it was, but he kept sending them to voicemail. I wished he would answer or allow me to answer mine. But his face told me not to even mention it. I didn't exactly understand what was going on at this point, I figured this was one of those times when I had to support him even though I didn't understand it. I could see pain in his face, and it seemed like it was more painful for him to keep it locked up inside.

When we got in the car I could hear my mother's ringtone coming from the glove compartment. I looked at Andrew and he looked away. I opened the glove compartment and I answered my phone.

"Tracy!" My mothers voice was troubled.

"What's wrong?"

"Sister Harris' son was in a car accident!"

"What? When?"

"Early this morning."

"Is he ok? What happened?"

"It looks really bad right now. He was out with Karen and some friends. They probably were coming from a late prayer meeting or something."

"Is Karen ok?" Andrew looked at me

"She's pretty banged up, but she's gonna be ok." Mother said

"What happened?" I asked, there was a knot in my stomach.

"They lost control of their car, they were on San Pablo Dam Rd between Orinda and El Sobrante. We don't know yet, maybe they tried to avoid a deer or something."

"Where's Karen now?"

"I'm not sure if she's still at the hospital or if she went home. But I think everyone is at the hospital with Cameron."

"I'm sorry to hear this momma. How's Sister Harris?"

"She's a mess, this is a mothers worst nightmare. He was a good kid, he didn't deserve this."

Clearly my mother didn't know how much of a jerk he was. But even with that he doesn't deserve to die. "I'm sorry to hear this mom. Please give Sister Harris my best."

"You're not going to go to the hospital?"

"No" I blew air, I didn't wanna seem like a jerk. However there was no way I was going to that hospital. "Last time I saw him it didn't go well. It would be in everyone's best interest if I sent best wishes through you. But please keep me posted on his progress."

My mother huffed. "Well keep your phone on. I've been trying to call you all day."

"Sorry about that, I will. I love you."

"I love you sweetheart, talk to you later."

I hung up the phone, Andrew looked at me with a curious look. "So Cameron and Karen were in a car accident last night. Karen's pretty banged up, but they don't know if Cameron's gonna make it."

"Do they know what happened?" He asked like he was trying to piece the pieces together.

"They're not sure, but they were on San Pablo Dam and they lost control of the car somehow."

"That's messed up. Hope he makes it."

"Me too. He's annoying but not deserving of this."

He reached over and grabbed my hand. With my free hand, I scrolled through my phone. My mom had been blowing up my phone. Carina called, and Amber blew up my phone too. My mom left a message telling me to call her back and that it was urgent. Carina very excitedly asked if I had any questions. Amber mournfully asked me to have Andrew call her. Then she said in the next message to please tell Andy that she loved him whenever he gave me my phone back. I laughed. I played her message out loud, and he smiled as well. "When are you going to call her back?"

"Not today! Today is André's day!" He said authoritatively I looked in the back, and Andre was knocked out. "Um, Mr. Wallace your son is sleep. Next excuse?"

He sucked his teeth, and then he peaked at Andre. He shook his head like he was busted. "I don't wanna call her back today! She's just gonna make me more sad!" He whined.

We both laughed. "Call your mother back."

He huffed, "I don't want to!" He pouted.

I smiled at him, "but you will!"

He sucked his teeth but I knew he was going to do it. When we got home, he put Andre in the bed. When he stepped into the hallway I saw the idea to sneak downstairs flash across his face. He looked to see where I was. He jumped when he realized I was standing in the doorway of our bedroom in the dark. We both laughed, he pulled out his phone. I could hear Amber's voice, so I closed the door. I bathed, and then I watched a movie. I could hear Andrew's voice; I could tell they were having an emotional conversation. Part of me wanted to listen to their conversation, but I wanted to give him the space to talk to his mom privately. I dozed off; I was awaken to Andrew spooning me. "Everything ok?" He squeezed me but he didn't say anything.

Early in the morning Amber texted me to tell me she was outside. So I went down and let her in. She thanked me several times for letting her in. She sat next to him on the edge of the bed. His back was to her. She started singing a song as she stroked his back. I went in the closet to get my workout clothes. When I walked out the closet he was sitting up. Amber was cradling him and rocking him. Just a big ole momma's boy. I smiled at Amber and then I went out the door. I changed in the exercise room, I warmed up. Then I put Boomerang on. This movie is my absolute favorite! The Halle Berry character always resonates with me. I told myself I would walk until the thanksgiving scene, and I had to run the rest of the movie. As soon as I started running Andre came in the room barely awake. I stopped the movie; the language was not ok for him. We went downstairs, as I looked in the fridge to see what I had to make breakfast. We didn't have much, but we had a gallon of milk and lots of cereal boxes. So Andre and I had cereal at the kitchen table. Andre gave me a play by play of everything we did the day before as if I wasn't there. But the way he told the story was very colorful. He made me laugh, Andre was such a joy. Amber came downstairs, "Nana!" Andre screamed as he ran to meet her.

"Hey honey!" She picked him up. "Your daddy's gonna go get donuts. But he doesn't know what kind I like."

"I know!" Andre yelled, "I can go with him, I can tell him."

"Would you do that for me?"

"Yes!" He gave her a big hug and a kiss on the cheek. Then she put him down. He ran up the stairs to his dad.

Then she came and sat at the table. "And how are you this morning?"

"Ok I guess." Then I relaxed some. "My mom called yesterday, she said that Cameron and Karen were in a car accident."

She nodded her head. "Yea I heard about that. Are you ok?"

"I'm fine. I'm kind of curious to know what happened to them. Cameron is fighting for his life right now. I feel bad for their families is all."

"How do you know them?"

"His parents and Karen and her brother go to service with my parents."

"Why was Karen running up on you?"

"I don't know exactly. But she used to see Andrew, she didn't take the news of our engagement too well." And then I remembered the party. "Oh and I slapped the mess out of her at her brother's party."

"Why did you hit her?" Amber smiled

"I didn't know about her and Andrew at the time. But she was disrespecting me. I got mad and I hit her before I could even think about it. No one was expecting me to do that. She was so shocked that she fell."

Amber started laughing. "Yea when I dated Malcolm seems like there was always some female coming out of somewhere laying claim to a piece of him. Andrew is like him in so many ways."

"What's the deal with them." I asked

"Malcolm was never the warmest father. He didn't want children, he considers them liabilities. But we were young and I was idealistic. At fifteen you think having a guy's baby will get you somewhere. And that's fifteen when he was born. Malcolm was always a hustler, but he wasn't a family man. He always had a taste for new female. He'd make sure we had what we needed, but he wasn't into being tied down. He didn't have natural father instincts. Where his stepfather was very hands on. Andrew loved his stepfather like he was his own father. David was a good man." She said then she closed her eyes and took a deep breath. It seemed like she was gonna tell me everything, but then it became too painful for her to talk about it as well. "He misses him a lot. I think being engaged, and having a family is a little hard on him at times."

It felt like she was trying to tell me I was a burden. "Why?"

"He doesn't want to end up like Malcolm. They have a relationship now, but it's strained. He misses David, and for the most part wants to be like him."

"How long were you married?"

She looked at me funny. "David and I never married. We were engaged though."

"Oh, I'm sorry I thought you were married."

"No need to apologize. My dad was against it. He didn't like David, he tolerated me and Malcolm."

"Why?"

"Malcolm was a thug, shoot he still is. And David..." She closed her eyes. That same pained look was on her face. "Well, David had his ways about himself."

I wanted to ask more questions. I wanted to know more, but I could tell Amber was doing her best to keep it together. So I put on a pot of water to make us some tea.

"You know I've never seen Malcolm smile until the other night. He seemed so human I couldn't believe it."

"Really?" She smiled

"Yes, I know I'm not on his favorite people list. "

"What makes you think that?"

"For one he didn't acknowledge me. He never really does. And he never acknowledges me any more than he has to. But honestly I thought he was dead. Andrew didn't talk about him much."

She smiled, "he likes you."

I was floored, "how do you know that?"

"Malcolm does his own background check." She laughed, "but he says it all the time. He's just different."

I couldn't believe it. "If you say so", that did make me feel a little better. "I don't understand how you ended up with him?"

"Can't you tell Sophia and I thought we were the stuff! Although I wanted a daughter, I was kind of happy I didn't have one. I was afraid of what I would get. I know how I was, caused my parents a lot of unnecessary pain." She closed her eyes. "I realized it too late to make it up to my Momma. But my Daddy and I talked."

"Andrew doesn't talk about her much. What was she like?"

"STRICT!!!" She laughed hard suddenly. I jumped, which only made her laugh more. "She was more upset about my pregnancy than my father was. She tried to beat it out of me." She said laughing.

Then Andrew walked in the kitchen. He had a small smile on his face, and Andre was right on his heels. He looked at his mom and then he gave me a quick kiss. "So this weekend we're killing your diet. We're going to get donuts. Any specific request?"

"Why are you on a diet?" Amber asked Andrew with a lot of attitude.

"It's not me momma. I told her she's fine. But she insist." He said putting his hands out.

"Now you sound like Yussef." Andrew's neck whipped at me. I instantly knew I shouldn't have said that. "I mean everybody keeps saying that. But I feel more comfortable in my skin ten pounds lighter."

"When did Yussef say that?" His tone was serious and he wasn't letting it go.

"It wasn't like that Andrew. Please forget I said it."

He eyed me for a minute. Andre was watching his dads face, and then he started Mimicking the look. Amber started laughing. "Like father like son."

Andrew smiled looking at André's face. "Is that what I look like!" He asked Andre.

Andre smiled real big, "yea".

"Come on boy, you are too much." Andrew said.

When I heard the front door close I exhaled a temporary sigh of relief. Amber was grinning. "So, who's Yussef?"

"He's just my friend at work." I explained

She eyed me just like her son did. "Un huh!"

I started to explain, and then the bell saved me. "Hello?" I didn't wait for caller ID to announce.

"Tray-Tray!"

"Hey!" I said, I knew it was one of my sisters but I couldn't tell which one yet.

"Ok so, Tia and I want to know when you're going to pick out dresses so we can make sure we're there." I didn't say anything, "that is assuming that we're in the wedding?"

"Of course you're in the wedding! I hadn't gotten that far yet."

"Oh ok, cause your silence was sounding..."

"I know, you caught me off guard. I guess I could schedule the bridesmaid part on the weekend. That should work better for everyone anyways."

"Ok let us know when, and then we'll book our flights."

"Ok will do."

"So how you been?" She said

"Ok, how about you guys?" I said

"We're good, nothing new for me."

"That's good, how about Tia?"

"She's good, we just wanted to touch base with you since we hadn't heard from you." She said

"I know, it's been crazy around here. We just agreed on a budget the other day. I'm assuming that depending on the venue we should have a date soon."

"Ok well keep us in the loop. We'll try to save our time off for two weeks before the wedding so that we can help with whatever or just be there."

"That sounds good."

We talked for a few more minutes. When I got off the phone Amber had moved to the couch. She was watching TV. I went and sat next to her as I prayed she didn't pick up where we left off. I hadn't thought of how to explain my friendship with Yussef without offending anyone. But when you spend everyday with someone who's cool like Yussef you can't help but be friends with them. Nothing more, nothing less, just friends. I wish he could be here to show them. We talk about Andrew all the time, and I know he reports back everything we talk about. So really I don't know what the big deal is. But I also dare not bring it up again. Amber and I talked about the wedding. Then we called Carina together. I asked her to come by the office tomorrow to go over her proposal for the wedding. She was very excited by the time we got off the phone. Andrew and Andre were back with sugary goodness. They made the trip all the way to Richmond to go to Andy's donuts. I took him there a couple of times when we first met. I didn't realize he was going into Steve territory for donuts. Although he was smiling there was sadness behind his eyes. I figured the sadness is what kept Amber around all day. Mid-afternoon Andrew got on the treadmill. From the sound of it he was on a level seven, pounding it out. We all went up to see what was going on. He had earplugs in, we stood in the doorway watching and talking. He knew we were there, but he ignored us. He ran hard for a long time. After awhile I was amazed to see how long he was going. I tried to pretend I knew he could last that long running like that but I was amazed. I ordered some pizzas, and then the doorbell rang ten minutes later. Andrew was finishing his run. Andre, Cain, and I went to the door. I almost passed out when I saw it was Malcolm.

"Tracy."

"Malcolm?" I said so surprised

His face held no expression. He looked down at Andre.

"Is this a bad time?" He asked not taking his eyes off Andre.

I didn't know what to do, so I invited him in. I had him sit in the living room. "How you doing little man?" Malcolm said cracking the second smile I've ever seen on his face. His voiced echoed off the walls.

"Hi" Andre said holding on to my leg.

Andrew was standing at the top of the stairs. I could see him battling with himself with each step he took down the stairs. I could tell by the shock on Amber's face she wasn't expecting Malcolm either.

"How you doing?" Malcolm said to Andre

"I'm good, how are you?" Andre said, Malcolm belly laughed which made Andre happy. I thought he would be scared of Malcolm, but he wasn't.

Andrew's face was serious. "What do you want Malcolm?" He said walking into the living room.

"Lets go up to my room and wait for the pizza man." I said to Andre.

Andre looked at Malcolm and then his father. I could tell he wanted to stay, but Andrew shot him a look and he came a long with me.

"What do you want Malcolm?" Andrew said as we were walking away.

"We need to clear the air about some things."

"Like what?"

"Do you really blame me for what happened?" Malcolm asked

"Is that why you came?" There was calm anger in Andrew's voice.

When I reached the top of the stairs, I could see the debate within Amber whether to continue to eavesdrop or go with us. Eve stayed downstairs with the men, but Cain came up with us. We went in my room and I turned on music so that we wouldn't hear them unless they shouted.

When the doorbell rang Amber and I ran over each other to get to the door first.

"They have my card on file, so I have to sign. I'll bring plates and soda." I said and then I stuck my tongue at her as I slipped through the door. I hurried down the stairs and to the door. Andrew and Malcolm were in their own world. They weren't paying me any attention. I signed for the pizza and I gave the driver a nice tip. He smiled really big. I hurried into the kitchen, I set the pizzas on the table then I walked back into the living room. "Excuse me gentlemen." They both looked at me with pain on their faces. "The pizza is here. Would you like me to leave you some, bring you some? Anything at all?"

Andrew inhaled, "would you like to eat with my family?" He said

"Yes, I'd like that." Malcolm said

"Excellent! I'll be right back." I said I ran up the stairs in double time. When I came in the room Amber's eyes were on me. I turned off the TV. We're gonna eat downstairs with them."

Her hazel eyes doubled in size. "Andy said its ok for him to eat with us?" I shook my head yes. She ran to the mirror to check herself. "Does he know I'm here?"

"Only if Andrew told him."

Then we walked down the stairs single file, with Cain leading the way, Andre, myself, and Amber bringing up the rear. The look on Malcolm's face when he saw Amber let me know he still cares about her. I don't know the story as to why they aren't together. Amber and Malcolm hugged, Andre smiled. "Nana you know him?"

"Yes baby I do."

"Who are you?" Andre asked Malcolm

"I'm Malcolm." He said not knowing what else to say to him.

"Lets go eat." Andrew said I gave him a hug and he squeezed me tightly. We sat at the kitchen table. Amber kept talking until everyone became conversational.

"This is a nice home you guys have. And you got dogs coming from everywhere." Malcolm said jokingly

"Thank you" Andrew said.

"You wanna see my room?" Andre offered

"Sure," Malcolm said.

"Me and my dad painted it ourselves. It was fun."

Malcolm looked at Andre and then up at Andrew. "It's like looking at you all over again."

"I say the same thing all the time." Amber said

Andrew grabbed my leg under the table. He held onto my thigh like his life depended on it. As they stood Andre invited Amber to come with them. Then Andre mimicked the way Andrew and I show the house. He started pointing out each room with brief introductions. When they started up the stairs, I put my hand on top of Andrew's, "are you ok?"

His face changed to stone. "I'm fine."

I rubbed his hand, and his face kept going back and forth from stone to sad. I took him by the hand and had him sit on the couch. Then I sat on his lap. I kissed him gently, and he softened. I love the feeling of comforting him. I didn't know exactly what the drama was, but I was here for him. I kept kissing him, until we heard them coming. I put my forehead on his. "I love you!" He said

"I love you!" I said. Then they entered the room. Andre sat next to us on the couch. It wasn't unusual to him to see us like this. "Do we need to leave?" I said attempting to get up so they could continue their talk.

Andrew held on to me. "No, we're good for now. Have a seat you guys."

Amber sat next to Andre. And Malcolm sat on the other side of the other couch. There was nervous energy in the room. We all kind of stayed around until Andre announced he was getting in the bathtub. Andrew looked at me, "this is your influence". I smiled, and then Amber volunteered to help him get his bath ready.

"Do you guys have any bones?" Malcolm asked

Andrew blew air, "Yea right! You don't want none old man!"

"Wash 'em!" Malcolm commanded. I went to the hallway closet and I pulled out the dominos. Both of their faces lit up. They played a couple games, and they were so loud you would've thought they were arguing. But by the smiles, they were finally enjoying each other. At first Cain sat there with his head cocked to the side like he was trying to understand what was going on. After awhile he became immune to it. Eve paid the whole scene no never mind she stayed by my feet. Andre came down and said good night to everyone and then Amber put him to bed. When Amber came down she suggested we play teams. I didn't want to play, but I faked the enthusiasm for the sake of the evening. Even though Malcolm was being "different" I knew not to think he'd be like this the next time I saw him. I actually had fun playing dominos with them. Amber and Malcolm beat the pants off of us, but it was never by much. They played so fast. It was like they knew their next three moves before I found my one.

At ten o'clock Amber yawned, "I've officially been here fifteen hours. I think it's time to go home." She said standing.

"I'll walk out with you." Malcolm said

Andrew stood up, "I'll walk you out.... Mom!" He said looking at his father.

Malcolm laughed, "cock block all you want to your mom knows what's up."

"Gentlemen please, we've had such a lovely evening. Lets end on a high note." Amber said

Malcolm put his hands up in defeat.

"Good night you guys." I said turning on the dishwasher.

The three of them walked out the door. Eve went with Andrew. I went upstairs and took a quick shower. Andrew and Eve were walking in as I turned off my light to fall asleep. Andrew hopped in the shower and then he got in bed. He spooned me and kissed my neck, I looked at him in the dark, as he knows better than to start with me. He laughed, "I wanted to make sure you were awake. I need to ask you something". He had a smile on his face so I figured it was safe.

"What's up?"

"What did you mean by I sounded like Yussef?"
I cringed as soon as he asked me. You mean to tell me after all this man has gone through today, he still remembers this ten-second piece of the day???? "Baby! I'm tired!" I whined.

"So answer the question, then you can sleep." There was no kidding in his tone.

"I knew as soon as it slipped out of my mouth you were going to overreact!" I huffed sitting up.

"Overreact? How am I overreacting? I just wanna know where the comment came from." He was now irritated with me.

"It's not a big deal. We were talking about my diet, and he asked why I was still dieting, and he said I didn't need to lose any more weight. That's all."

"Then why are you acting all guilty?"

"I'm not, it was the way you responded to it. I regretted saying it."

"What else You guys talk about?"

"You should know better than I do."

He shook his head, "nope I've been getting no events, no events. Why you think I came down on Friday?"

"To see me!"

"Yes, but to also pop my head in to see for myself." He was quiet for a minute. "Maybe it's time to switch him with someone else."

"NO!" I took a moment to calm myself. Even in the dark I could see him reading my face. "Baby please don't do that. I'm comfortable with Yussef, I don't want to have to break a new person in."

"For all you know I could have someone new on you already."

"Why would you do that?"

"Think about it. You're spending everyday with this fool. I've seen the bodyguard, I know what happens."

We both laughed. "The difference is that she wasn't engaged to you. The whole world knows how much I love you. And especially after Friday why would you care?"

"That was pretty amazing wasn't it." He said grinning from ear to ear.

"Yes my lord! You are the man!" I said shivering from a flashback.

"What if we can't make it? We don't even have a date yet. Are you gonna go into dramatics and act like you're disappointed in me?"

"You know I'm a drama queen so I can't make you any guarantees. Lets do our best. How about that?"

"What about tonight? I really need you!"

"See! That's how it will start and then it'll be like we never had an agreement."

"I know! I know! I didn't anticipate this weekend being so hard. I am an emotional wreck over here. If we don't, tonight imagine how pent up I will be tomorrow. Think of my office mates, think of their children. If not for me, do it for them."

We both laughed, "how about we cuddle." I knew good and well that wasn't gonna satisfy him. But I also didn't wanna give in without making him work for it.
"Cuddle? What am I ten?" I looked at him with a take it or leave it expression. "FINE!" We both laid down and I put my arms around him. "I don't know what I was thinking anyways. My legs are killing me! Every time I stood up my legs were on fire. But I wasn't giving him the satisfaction of seeing my pain."

I touched his legs, "where do they hurt?"

He started cracking up. I LOVE the sound of his uncontrolled laugh. "Don't tickle me." He pleaded.

The night ended with me straddling him.

****

When I walked out of the parking garage as usual Yussef was by me. I was still smiling from the night with Andrew. "Good morning Yussef, how was your weekend?"

"Same ole same ole. How about you?" He asked

"It's was ok, hung out with the in laws mostly."

"Did Shirley call you?" He asked

"No, she called you?"

"Not exactly. Your boy called me from her phone." He said

"What do you mean? How would he call you from her phone?"

"I put the emergency contact roster in my work phone. Just in case I lost the list the phone numbers would already be saved. Her number kept calling my phone, but it was him. Is he a user?"

"I don't know what he is now."

"Well he was acting a little crackish."

"What did he say?"

"First he acted like it would be hard for me to figure out who he was. But what guy is gonna call me from her phone? Then he wanted to know why I tazed him. I told him that he threatened my precious cargo. Then he started going on and on about how disgusting you are. All the mistakes you've made, etc. he kept going on and on. So I had to level with him. If you were all these things why does he keep going out of his way to cause you pain. Then I told him that he needed to leave you alone. I told him that he was playing with his life and he was too stupid to see it. Then I told him that he can't hide behind a cell phone and that I knew exactly where he was. When he didn't believe me, I gave him the address, the room, the chair, what he was wearing, and the fact that he just scratched his head." He started laughing. "He was so spooked!" I wasn't laughing, I was dumb founded when he called me precious cargo, and then how did he know all that. He looked at my face, "what?"

"How did you know that?"

"I followed him to her house." He said waiting for my smile to return.

"He goes to her house?" I asked curiously.

"Yes" he said not wanting to talk about it anymore.
"He visits for a little bit then he leaves?" Yussef looked at me. No expression on his face. Which meant he didn't want to talk about it but I had to know. "He spends the night like, he sleeps on the couch?" Yussef hurried into the elevator. It was kind of packed so I squished in close to him. He inhaled and closed his eyes. I didn't take my eyes off him. He knew I wasn't gonna let it go. When we got off the elevator he was trying to walk fast. When we badged into the office I followed him to his cubical. "Don't make me pull your dreads. I'm not scare of you. I will do it." He stood there looking at me with no expression. "Yussef!" I said stomping my foot. His expression didn't change as he stood there. I huffed to my desk and I logged in. Yussef came to my cubical and I ignored him. After ten minutes he walked away laughing. Then he came back. "Ok, ok. He sat in my chair and scooted in close to me. You cannot tell your boyfriend cause you're not supposed to know about this unless she tells you." I nodded yes in obedience. "Your girl and ole boy are shacking up." I grabbed my chest, Yussef looked at my hand as if my reaction was odd.

"Seriously?" I was in shock. "How long?"

"Not too long after the whole Bart Station incident. I don't get it they argue a lot. But I think it had been awhile since she had anybody tap that cause she acts like he's moving heaven and earth."

I put my hand over my mouth, I felt like I was going to be sick. I wasn't going for dramatic effect either, my mouth started watering. I jumped over Yussef and ran to the bathroom in time. My protein shake was staring back at me. I splashed cold water on my face. This had to be a nightmare, a imaginary story of some sort. When I finally got it together, and went back on the floor Yussef was standing outside my cube smiling as he talked to someone. When I heard the excited pitch I knew it was Carina.

"You ok?" Yussef asked with a concerned look.

"Yea, I'm ok." I couldn't describe how I felt anyways so that was gonna have to be my final answer. "Good morning Carina." I said mustering up the best smile I could.

"Good morning!" She said all bright and chipper. Yussef was smiling like oh yea. Until he saw the way she looked me up and down. He turned on his heels and walked away. "I love those shoes." She said staring at them.

"Thank you. Come with me, I have a conference room checked out for us."

Carey Anderson

CHAPTER 36

"Talk to me!"

"Ok so I have good and bad news." Carina said

"Give me the bad!" I said

"The St. Regis isn't available for eighteen months."

"18!" I was disappointed I really liked that hotel. It was really nice and it wouldn't sound like we were doing too much on the invitations. I sighed, "what's the good news?"

"A date just opened up at the Ritz-Carlton in seven months. I told them that we tentatively want the date pending your approval."

Ok, it is what it is. We're gonna look like snobs. Oh well! But! Putting The Ritz-Carlton on the invitation might also drive home the formality of the event. Anyone dressed casually would not be admitted. "Ok, I'm warming up to the idea."

"You saw the hotel wasn't it beautiful? Imagine the suite."

"Fine! Send me the numbers."

She said an excited, "OK! You'll have them in an hour. See you Saturday."

I hung up with her and I called Joy. "So the St. Regis is out, unless I can convince Andrew to wait eighteen months."

"What? No way! So what's plan B?"

"The Ritz-Carlton, it's in the city as well. Not too far from where we were shooting for any how."

"Oh yea their Ballroom was lovely. I can see that working for you."

"You don't think that will sound too pretentious on the invitations?"

"No, you're having a formal wedding, the setting should fit the dress code. The more I think about it the more I like the sound of it." She said

"Yea that's the way it hit me as well. The idea is definitely growing on me."

"Ok so tell me the plan for Saturday again."

"I'm asking everyone to be here by 9am with fun attitudes cause we have a long day ahead of us. Everyone should wear something comfortable to get in and out of. The limo will have a car seat for Veronica so you don't have to worry about bringing yours. We should get to the store by 10am; our appointment is at 10:30am. I really hope to find a dress and bridesmaids dresses all in the same day."

"Have you decided on a style you like?"

"No, I figured I had to stay open since I'm limiting the selection by choosing silver. I really hope I can find that. I know silver was done so many seasons ago but that's when I fell in love with the color and the idea."

"Who's all going?"

"Our group is gonna be pretty big. My mom of course. My sisters get in tomorrow night. My sister-in-law Amy, Amber, Sophia, and her daughter Sabrina, you, and Nicole. I'm debating about Sonya, I wasn't in her wedding so I don't think it will be a big deal that she's not in mine."

"Oh yea that's a nice size group. Ok well I'll be there."

"Oh wait Carina and Tanisha are coming, but they're gonna meet us there."

"Why are they coming?"

"Because my dress will determine a lot about the decor, so she needs to know which one I choose."

"That makes sense. You chose the design of your invitations right?"

"No."

"No? Why not?"

"Duh, we were gonna do that together. I'm waiting on you."

"Oh, yea!" She laughed, "girl I forgot. I can come over Friday or Saturday. Even Sunday if that works better."

"Sunday might be best."

"Let me go, my baby girl's crying."

"Ok, see you Saturday."

When I hung up the phone Yussef was walking past. He stopped in my cubical, "I need to talk to you."

"Ok" I said with a smile.

"Not here, I checked out a conference room."

"Ok," I grabbed a pen and paper. I know one of our internal teams has been dropping the ball. Yussef has been doing a good job of keeping them liable for their actions. Which has translated to meetings, etc. I followed Yussef into Bullwhip. He locked the door. That made me actually look at his face. "Mister cool like that" was falling apart. Instantly I got scared thinking something happened to Andrew or I was in danger some how.

He sat down, he folded his hands on the table, but his leg was shaking. He scooted back, adjusted in his chair by leaning back and then he scooted forward. He mumbled a few times, and then he inhaled and exhaled. "You know I always wondered something. How a girl like you even got mixed up with a guy like Andrew? It's like two different worlds colliding."

"You really think so? Andrew has been nothing but good to me. I know he grew up differently, but he's a good guy."

"Andrew is an excellent man! No doubt about that. You just didn't know about everything before you got together huh? You probably still don't."

"What's everything?"

He moved his hand to say drop it. "Never mind. My point!" He blew air and looked at the ceiling. "You know I liked you from the moment I met you. I've worked really hard to get where I am, and I myself am only going up from here."
"What are you saying?" I said now shaking my foot under the table.

"I applied for another position in the company. It's a promotion really. But it's in the Concord office."

The room started spinning. "WHY? Why would you do that?"
"It's time for me to move on."

"Why are you moving on? What about me?"

"Tracy you're gonna be fine. Honestly I don't see why you continue to work. Maybe once you start having babies you'll slow down."

"Why are you leaving all of the sudden?"

"I have to, and I'm not supposed to say anything to you." He looked me directly in my eyes. "But I couldn't up and leave without saying anything to you."

"Yussef we have become such good friends. You're like one of my best friends." I tried to think of a way out for him. "Applied doesn't mean you got the job yet. Couldn't you at least hang in here with me until the wedding?"

He sighed, "I can't sit here and pretend to be happy about your wedding anymore."

Tears started to well up in my eyes. "You're not happy for me? I thought you were."

He looked frustrated. "You never get it do you!" I was honestly confused. "Why do you think Andrew came by here that time?"

"To see me."

"Yes, but..." He was trying to think of the right wording. "The closer we get the more relaxed, if you will, my reporting has gotten. Honestly nothing has been jumping off here. But when others have very detailed reporting and mine lacks the reporting style it used to carry. Only a fool wouldn't come and investigate. And Andrew's no fool! I respect him, and it's not right for me to continue."

I felt frustrated like he was beating around the bush. "But you've been doing your job, so what's the problem?"

"Tracy, you're.... You can't...." He was searching for words. All kinds of thoughts were going through my mind. Then he said, "out of respect for Andrew I can't keep working with you."

I frowned, as I let the words sink in. Is he trying to tell me he likes me? Ok so let me get this straight. When I was a big girl and I needed someone to love me for me. No one stepped up. No one even looked in my direction. I decide to finally get healthy for me and still nobody's looking. I lose a little bit and I do mean a little bit and here comes Andrew. The only man to look at me and see me. But I guess even still my progress wasn't good enough cause he left me but now Steve wants me. No one wanted me before, but now that I'm a lot smaller Steve wanna kill me. Andrew act like he'll die without me. Strangers telling me I'm pretty. And now this, I've never flirted with Yussef or did anything as far as I know that would make him look at me like that. I don't get it, and this isn't fair. I've finally developed a friendship with him and that wasn't easy. Now who's it gonna be some weirdo, AND I LOSE ANOTHER FRIEND! "This is so unfair!"

He cocked his head to the side. "How is this unfair to you?"

"We're friends or at least that's what I thought. I have to lose a friend for nothing." I pouted

He looked me in my eyes again, "my feelings are nothing?" He said that too calm.

"That's not what I mean." I said shaking my head

"What do you mean?"

"I mean, my world has seemed to have gotten a lot smaller lately. I value the ones I can be close to. Can't we just be friends and forget everything else?"

"So you want to continue on as friends?" He sat up in his chair.

"Yes"

He stood up and walked to the chair directly next to me. He sat down and moved his chair as close to me as possible. He leaned in and his lips were about a inch from mine. I leaned back and he pulled my chair tipping it a little on its side. "But if I come at you like this, that's not ok right?"

My heart stopped and everything was betraying everything. Maybe I felt something but kept chalking it up to friendship. I don't know. "Right, I love Andrew." I said tearfully.

"I know you do. I wish someone loved me like you love him. I envy him for that."

"Yussef you're a great guy. You will have someone love you like that."

"I'm picky!" He sighed

"If you were looking at me, you can't be too picky."

"Stop putting yourself down like that. I hate when you do that."

I lowered my head, "sorry". I could smell the sour apple jolly rancher on his breath as he sat there breathing. Then he kissed me on my cheek. It shocked me; the feeling it sent up my leg shocked me too. It felt like someone was tickling me. A line of sweat burst across my forehead. "Please don't do that."

"I wanted you to know why I have to go." He said

"When are you leaving?"

"Probably end of next week. I've had

Three phone interviews. So now I'm waiting for the actual job offer. I asked Becca not to tell you about this change until it was official."

"How long has this been going on?"

"I started looking as soon as things started changing with me. I know it's not right how I feel."

"Why do you keep saying that? What's not right?"

"My feelings are my feelings. They're not Andrew's problem or yours for that matter."

"So why tell me if it's not my problem?"

"Guess the selfish part of me wanted you to know. I didn't want you wondering why I disappeared."

"But you're not disappearing. You're just going to another office. I'll be able to instant message you. We can still talk."

He smiled a knowing smile, "right."

"Will you come to my wedding?"

A pained look appeared on his face. "I don't know."

"I wanted you to be in my wedding. It would mean a lot to me if you were there."

"You may not see me, but I'll be there. I'll leave you a sign that I was there."

"Why wouldn't I see you there?"

"Didn't you say five hundred people?"

"Yes"

"It's gonna be impossible for you to see everyone personally. So you may not see me."

"Un huh," I said eyeing him suspiciously. Then the whole point flashed in my head. "What about Steve? If he got your number, he has mine. I didn't put my address, but what if he pops up?"

"There's already someone with you." Then his face turned serious. "I will handle it personally if he ever touches you again!"

I lowered my head again; I didn't want to know what that meant. You know how people say they'll do this and that, but you honestly don't believe them? I know there has to be a reason why Andrew trusted him with my life, with that said I don't ask questions. "Ok, will I know who this person is? Who ever is supposed to be watching me?"

"Andrew doesn't make the same mistake twice." He said with a serious face.

"I wish you would just tell me. Don't talk in code."

"Andrew is not stupid. He knows, that's why they took me out. Remember we didn't have this conversation."

"But we didn't do anything nor were we going to."

"Women don't think like men. If you see some female catching feelings for your man, how do you react?"

I laughed, "that's when Karen got slapped!"

He laughed too. "Oh yea, well Andrew's slaps hurt a lot more. You can't have that around your relationship."

"I get it." I said in defeat.

"I honestly didn't think this would ever be me. I'm gonna miss you." He said standing up.

"I'm gonna miss you too." I said

He put his arms out for a hug, so I hugged him. That's when I realized he's been sniffing me all along and I never paid attention. I let go first and then he reluctantly let go.

"Remember this conversation NEVER happened. I need you to promise Tracy!" His face was serious.

"I promise!" I said feeling a lump in my throat.

When I got back to my desk I composed myself. Then I called Andrew. "Bad news babe the St. Regis isn't available...."

CHAPTER 37

I tried my best to be as normal as possible last night, but there was so much I didn't understand. Andrew is definitely attentive. He did his best to Waite on me hand and foot. My man is the best, and I don't know where I'd be if it weren't for him. Probably struggling to hang on to this house, etc. but it's more than just financial. Andrew loved me when the world ignored me. He thought I was beautiful when most in the world said, "pass" so I'm not crazy. No one compares to Andrew, even with all his skeletons. But say if I wasn't with Andrew and Yussef came along. Would I have gone for him? Would I have gone out with him if he asked me? YES! But I have to know that everything is working out for the best. At least I have one more week with my best friend at work. I will savor everyday for what it is. I'll try to be strong, and I will be so surprised when Becca tells me next week that he's leaving. Yussef met me at the garage same as everyday. We had normal conversation. When I sat down I saw Becca rush past my cubical. She didn't tell me she was coming out, but she did that from time to time. I could hear her dropping everything in the commuter cube as she dialed into what I assumed was a conference call. A little while later I saw Enton chatting at Yussef's cube. Random, but again it could be a coincidence that he's here too. Oh wait there's Bill too. Still doesn't mean anything right? When I heard Shirley's voice I stood up like what's going on. But everyone was busy. I instant messaged Yussef:

Me: Y is every1 here

Yussef: (shrugs)

Me: u r a lot of help

Yussef: smiley face

The rest of the day flew by. At two o'clock Becca came over to my cube. "Can you join me in the conference room?" She said lowly.

"Of course" I followed her to the conference room Shirley, Enton, and Bill were sitting at the table. There was a cake on the table in the corner.

"Ok, Clara's on the phone. Tracy I know you might be wondering why everyone's here. Today's Yussef's last day with us. He asked me not to mention it to the team until we had a definite departure date. So we're gonna have cake in his honor this afternoon to say goodbye." I was devastated. I couldn't say anything. Everybody was quiet.

"Yay for Yussef!" Clara said over the phone, she was so sweet.

Everyone did a polite giggle but it felt like they were waiting for a reaction from me. Yussef worked with me. Shirley had a smirk on her face. "Ok so I'll go get Yussef." Becca said. No one said anything while she was gone. "Congratulations Yussef!" Becca said and everyone started clapping.

"Congratulations Yussef!"

"Thanks Clara" Yussef said leaning into the intercom.

"Congratulations!" Everyone said one by one. I didn't say anything I stayed seated.

"Thank you everybody." He said, "I know this maybe be a surprise to everybody. But I got a hold of some information that kind of forced my hand to speed things along. I won't say goodbye cause I know I'll see you all again very soon." He addressed the room but I knew he was talking to me.

"We'll save you a seat at our table for the next offsite in the city." Shirley said

"Thanks Shirley. But tell me something." She smiled, "can you please tell Tracy about your new boyfriend?"

"Oh dear!" She whimpered, "um, um I don't know what you're talking about."

"Oh come on Shirley, you know the same guy you were trying to get her to forgive and take back. Tell her how he lives with you! It's ok Shirley she doesn't want him. But you should ask him who Toya is. Ask him who's the father of her child? Ask him if she's pregnant again? Tell him to go on Maury." He started laughing. "You are the father!" Then he laughed some more. "You should really get to know the whole story before you run around this office spreading lies. And just so you all know the stuff she's been telling you about Tracy isn't true. How do you call yourself someone's friend treating them like you've treated her? More than once you've jeopardize her safety. All for what? So that, that twerp will see how much you have his back? You're too old to be acting like this! Grow up Shirley! Grow up! The only person who's told you the truth, you didn't want to believe. Oh and one more thing, he's also sleeping with your friend Pam, and the other one" he snapped his fingers, "what's her name oh yea Naomi! Don't ask me how I know but it's all true. He'll be staying with either one of them as soon as you kick him out."

"Yussef!" Becca said, Shirley was in tears.

"I wanted to set the record straight before I left. I know she's filled your ears with a bunch of lies about Tracy. Truth is Tracy's marrying a standup guy. She's finally getting what she deserves, the love of a good man. Shirley don't know anything about none of that. Instead of being happy for your friend you helped create more drama for her. Grow up!" Then he walked over to his cake and cut a slice. "Who wants some cake?" Bill and Enton raised their hands. I think Clara was afraid to make a sound. Shirley walked out the room in all out tears. A few tears rolled down my face, but they weren't for Shirley. Yussef was always protecting me down to the end. I'm sure Becca was supposed to stop Yussef from talking but you could tell Shirley filled all of their ears with things that weren't true. "Oh snap! Fresh strawberries!" Yussef exclaimed

"Only the best for you." Becca said, then she whispered to Yussef. "How do you know all that stuff?"

"Oh a little birdie told me." He said in a joking manner.

When he finally looked at me I mouthed "thank you" and he nodded his head.

At the end of the day he left his desk in tact as if he was coming back Monday. I wondered who was gonna be over my security now. Before we walked out Becca came over and hugged him. And then I did the same. I heard him sniff me again. We both walked kind of slow to the garage. I didn't know who was watching so I didn't want to say anything. We said goodbye as usual, and then I went home. Andrew wasn't home yet. So I spruced up the guest bedroom for my sisters and then I poured a glass of wine. I was sitting at the kitchen table almost in the dark. I had one candle burning in front of me. I didn't feel like showing my tears to the light. I had music playing throughout the house. Eve and Cain were at my feet. When Andrew came home I didn't move.

Instead of turning on lights he left them off. "You ok?" I shook my head no. He exhaled, "why do you have to take it this hard?"

"Why didn't you tell me?"

"You would've asked me not to. It had to be done."

"Imagine my surprise when my boss announces to the group that he's leaving! Now how am I supposed to feel safe?"

"You are safe."

"Andrew I don't want to argue about this. I'm disappointed and now I'm scared. And in kind, it's only fair that you fire Lisa."

He laughed, "what?"

"Need I remind you of what she said to me? Yussef never disrespected you or me. She disrespected me."

"This is California I can't just fire her."

"Fair is fair Andrew."

"Ok" he looked around the kitchen. "Moms gonna bring Andre in the morning. Can I interest you in a bath and more wine?"

I said a defeated, "ok"

"What time do the girls arrive?"

"9:30 but I have a car service picking them up. They'll call as soon as they're in transit."

He set the alarm and then he led me upstairs. He had two wine bottles under his arm. Eve and Cain sat by the door. He made bath water for me, lit candles, and poured two glasses of wine. "How you feeling?"

"I'm sad, we were friends. I didn't want him to leave the Oakland office but a promotion is a promotion."

Andrew stared at me for a few minutes reading my face. "Un huh!"

"What?"

He was staring me in my eyes, I hate when he does that. "What else Tracy?"

"Nothing!" I said as I stepped into the tub.

When I sat down he lifted my chin, "baby what?"

Realizing he could sense something I decided to go with what I thought was the lesser of two evils. "He told Shirley off today. He put her on blast."

His eyes lowered, "what did he say?"

"He told her to stop bad mouthing you and I. That you were a stand up guy, and that I finally got from you what I deserve, a good guy who loves me. Then he put her on blast about Steve. But you know he alluded to Steve being the father of Toya's son, and possibly the father of her new baby. I didn't know she was pregnant again. How far along is she?"

"I don't know. What else did he say?" He said focusing on my words.

"He told her that Steve is sleeping with two of her friends. He told her to grow up."

"How did that make you feel?"

"I didn't know she was bad mouthing us. Apparently it was true cause no one denied it. That hurt that she would do that. But I'm glad someone clued me in." He didn't say anything. "I wish you would tell me who's with me now. That way I won't feel vulnerable when I'm out there."

"It isn't necessary for you to know."

"But I still would like to know."

"Naw Tracy, you should be able to try to exist without depending directly on someone. Their job is to protect you. Not to fall in love with you." He kept his eyes on me.

I flinched when he said it. "What are you saying?"

"I'm not stupid! And I know he probably FINALLY said something to you. My question is do you feel the same about him?"

"Get real!"

"I'm being as real as I can be with you right now. You're sitting in the dark sulking cause this guy is gone. Do you share his feelings?"

"His feelings? What feelings?" I said trying to play dumb.

"Don't do that! Just answer the question." He was starting to get mad.

"Andrew! I'm in love with you! I don't want anybody else."

He eyed me real hard. "Ok now I feel confused!" He sat on the edge of the tub with his back to me. "It feels like I'm losing my ability to see clearly. Don't mess with my head Tracy. Just answer the question. Are you in love with him? Do you want to go be with him?"

"Andrew!" I said standing up. "Look at me!" He turned his head, his face looked pained. "Baby, I love you with my whole mind, body, and soul. I don't want to be with anyone but you! I just realized that Yussef felt anything for me. I've always only looked at him like he was a friend and a protector. I still only sing your praises. I wanna be your wife; I wanna have your babies. Yussef is a nice guy, but he's no you." Then I bent down and kissed him. He accepted my kiss, but his kiss lacked conviction. "Andrew! Kiss me!" He kissed me again, but it was the same. "Do you really have such little faith in me that you would believe that someone else could change the love I have for you?"

"This is just new territory for me. My mom loved David but she was always looking back at Malcolm. I don't want you looking back and regretting me." He stood up like he was irritated. "I feel so vulnerable right now."

"Welcome to my world. All you know is what I tell you. You're gonna have to trust me."

He looked at me then he smiled a wicked smile. "He better be happy I'm a changed man. Even still he needs to watch his back."

That made a chill come over me. Well that and the fact that I was still standing in the tub. "What does that mean?"

"He's gone, I don't know where he went. I'm not gonna look for him based on this conversation. But he needs to stay away. He knows it."

"Andrew!" I couldn't believe he said that.

"Hey you don't mess with the bosses wife! He should know that. He does know that."

"You say that like his life is in danger?" He smiled at me. "Hey! This ain't no down low video. Who you supposed to be? Mr. Big Deal?" We both laughed, "seriously though Andrew. He would never disrespect you, he always said you are the man, etc. he wouldn't hurt you."

"Yea, and I know if you stuck to Steve when I was at you! I'm pretty sure I know how it would've went down if he did come at you."

"Exactly!" I exhaled in relief. At least my track record showed I was trust worthy.

Then he eyed me. "You know when we said no more sex that's when I thought we were getting married right away. That was months ago, and now you're telling me seven more. Can we call off the engagement for a few? I need you!"

My body immediately responded to his request but I sat down. "Ok just give me a minute."

"I don't know why you'd get out when you're gonna get back in."

Then he undressed and got in the tub with me.

****

The girls got to the house around ten thirty. We introduced them to Eve & Cain. "Why are they named after the evil ones?" Tia asked

"Evil ones?"

"Yea Cain killed his brother, the Original murderer. And Eve, well she messed with Adam's head and now we're all condemned to death." Tia said

"Guess who's back into reading her bible." Tara said dryly.

"That's the names they came with. I really didn't think about it." I said

"While we're on the subject. Are you going to service Sunday? Cause we really need to go."

I wanted to say heck no! But I knew I needed to go. "Yes, I'll go." Then I clapped my hands together. "Ok so linens are in the closet. Remote controls are in the nightstand. I'm gonna set the alarm so please don't open any windows or doors until Andrew or I say its ok. " They agreed we hugged, I left Cain outside their door and I went back upstairs.

As soon as I got in the bed Andrew spooned me half awake. He fell asleep hard really fast. I could tell he was stressed by how quickly he fell asleep. We weren't asleep long when the dogs started going crazy. I let Eve out the door and she joined Cain downstairs running around barking like crazy. Someone was in the backyard. I followed Andrew down the stairs. The alarm outside had been tripped and the cameras were filming. Andrew shut off the alarm. He opened the sliding door and Eve and Cain took off. The person ran up the tree. I opened the girl's room. "Stay in here!" I said, and then I closed the door.

Andrew had a gun, and he approached the tree slowly. Suddenly there were four other guys with Andrew and they all had guns. I stood back in fear.

"Turn on the lights!" Andrew commanded, one of the guys with him reached in the door and hit the switch for the floodlights. "You've got to the count of three to come down or I'm lighting you up!" The kid slid down the tree. As soon as he hit the ground Eve

and Cain sunk their teeth in. He screamed. Andrew said something
in another language and the dogs let go but they sat there growling
at the kid. "What do you want?" Andrew said lowering his gun.
But his guys didn't. The kid was crying. I ran up to the bathroom I
grabbed a couple towels and some alcohol. I threw on my robe and
then I ran downstairs. As I walked out the door Andrew was asking
everyone there how this kid got past them? He was loud and he
looked so mean. Andrew looked at me like I was crazy, but I kept
going. I pulled up the kids pant legs and I put a towel around each
of his legs, I could see the puncture wounds from Eve & Cain's
bite. The kid grimaced. We heard sirens approaching. No one
moved. The police banged on the door. Andrew and his men stood
there putting their guns away. So I ran to the door to let them in.
"Berkeley Police Department" one of the officers said.

"Please come in he's back here." I said leaving the door open.
The officers followed me. I saw Tara peaking her eye out the
door.

Andrew told the officers what was happening. Eve and Cain
returned to loveable puppies. I took the puppies with me in the
room with the girls.

"What's going on?" Tara asked

"Some kid was in the yard. Andrew's talking to the police."

"Andrew means business!" Tia said

"Why do you say that?"

"We heard him, his voice was deeper but you could tell it was
him. He was MAD!"

"Oh yea! My baby don't play, especially when it comes to his
queen." We all laughed.

We ended up falling asleep. The last time I slept on that bed
was with Steve. I don't know what made me think of it. I hadn't
remembered that until I woke up. Andrew had all four guys in the
living room. He was going on a quiet tangent. I couldn't tell what
he was saying but I knew he wasn't happy. When he heard the door
open, he dismissed them. They shuffled out the door each going

their separate ways. I tried to get a good look at one of them. But I couldn't identify any of them.

"You've been up all night?" I asked. His face was stone; I could tell his mind was going a mile a minute. "Hey!" I said standing on my tiptoes. "A little attention here." I said.

His face softened when he looked at me. I loved seeing that reaction happen within him. "Good morning" he gave me a closed mouth kiss.

"Go get some rest the Anthony's and Andre will be here in a few hours. You need some rest." I said leading him up the stairs.

"Good morning Andrew!" The girls sang

"Good morning" he said blushing.

I tucked him into bed and then I showered and brushed my teeth.

My mom and Amy were super early. They wanted to see the girls as well. Tia was too excited to tell our mom that I agreed to go to service. And my mom got excited hearing it. Tara stood next to me as we blank stared at the three of them. Thankfully Joy and family arrived. They were such a cute family; they both had their little mini me's. Little Anthony was disappointed that Andre wasn't there yet. But it did give us a chance to hug like we used to when he was a baby. Nicole arrived next and she was so excited. She kept making everybody giggle it was like she was hopped up on extra silly juice. Andrew got up when he heard the sound of another male. He called Anthony up from the bottom of the stairs. As Anthony came up, he said, "man I'm so happy another male is here. With all these females I found myself giggling too." I thought to myself how nice it was that no one outside of Nicole views Andrew in any kind of dangerous way. It made me feel like I wasn't the only one. Amber, Sophia, Andre, and Sabrina arrived. I introduced Sophia and Sabrina to my sisters and Joy.

"Wow! You guys could be triplets!" Sabrina said

"Oh I wish I was as pretty as they are." I said

The girls both shot me looks. "You need to stop that right now!" My mother said from across the room. I put my hands up in

defeat, as I didn't want a scene. So I bowed out gracefully. Andrew
came down and greeted everyone then they proceeded to hurry us
out the door. They said they had man stuff to do and we needed to
be gone. It had started to rain so the party bus driver stood by the
door with an umbrella. After Joy strapped Veronica in her seat we
sat on either side of the seat. I couldn't believe she was six months
already. Funny when I estimated a year for our engagement
everyone said it was too long. By the time we actually tie the knot
it will be well over a year. Oh well I like not feeling rushed into
this final and permanent step in our lives. Plus we've both needed
the time to flip out, melt down, and drive each other crazy.

"Can I have everyone's attention!"? Everyone stopped to look
at Nicole. "I just want to give you a little preview to the reception
and take this time to gloat." She looked at me with a wicked smile.
"On the eve of my wedding Sonya and I had a heart to heart with
Ms. Tracy. And I wanna put emphasis on when I told her that she
was gonna MARRY Andrew. Honey child had a fit and cried. My
my my how times have changed." She smiled at me. "SEE I TOLD
YOU! True love never dies." Everyone started clapping for her. I
shooed her away. I was smiling now, but back then her saying that
hurt like hell!

We pulled up to the boutique "Cassondra's Bridals and
beyond". My mothers eyes got big, I could tell she liked the look
of the place. Our driver held an umbrella out and he assisted
everyone off the bus to the covering. I told him we would be here
for hours and that we would call him when we were ready. I was
the last person to enter, but I found myself oohing and awing with
everyone else. The main entrance had antique lounge chairs with
blue, gold, and silver designs. The carpet was a dark blue color.
The ceiling was really high, but you couldn't see beyond the first
three steps that led to the back. The receptionist was young and
very fashionable. She greeted us with a smile. "Welcome to
Cassondra's Bridal, how may I assist you?"

"Hello we're the Wallace party we have an appointment at
10:30."

"Wonderful, I'll page your consultant. You may have a seat and she'll be right with you."

The receptionist placed a call and in less than a minute our consultant was there. She was tall with long beautiful legs; her eyes captured your attention first. They were beautiful and almond shaped. As she smiled at us her dimples showed, I loved her free flowing locs. "Hello Wallace party, my name is..."

Before she could get it out Amber shouted, "NIHJIA!"

The consultant looked confused but she was still smiling. "Yes I am!"

"Oh my goodness girl look at you all grown up! How's your mom?"

Nihjia blushed "she's good, she's here."

Everyone looked at Amber waiting for her to explain. "I went to school with her mother. I had no idea she owned a shop. I'm sorry sweetheart I didn't mean to cut you off. Go ahead."

Nihjia laughed, "ok well I'm Nihjia, let me lead you to your show area. Part of your party is already here." She led us up the stairs and around the corner. There was a sea of white dresses. I could tell there was a pattern to the store. The main level was all bridal. There was an upstairs for bride's maids and a lower level for alterations, fittings, and tux rentals and purchases. Nihjia took us to the biggest and most private show area. Carina and Tanisha were already there waiting for us. They greeted everyone as we walked in. We all took our seats. "So who's my bride?" Nihjia asked taking out her clipboard.

"I am," I said raising my hand.

"Excellent," she said looking at her clipboard. "So you're Tracy," I agreed. "And then we're gonna have a mother of the bride and mother of the groom dress selection, brides maids, and then we're going over ideas for the groom and grooms men. Whew!" She smiled we've got a long day ahead of us. So before we get to the formalities. Lets decide on lunch, beverages, and snacks." She had a box full of clipboards. She passed one out to each person. "Now don't worry, it doesn't matter if you choose different cuisines we will make it happen. Over to the left we have coffee, tea, fresh fruit, and pastries just in case anyone skipped breakfast. I'm gonna go grab my mom so she can come say hello."

Everyone looked at the list of options. Some of them seemed really good. When I reached a decision, my mom asked, "what are you going to have?"

"I figure a sandwich is the best way to go. Otherwise, it may get cold. I can take my time with the sandwich."
Everyone nodded their heads in agreement.

Then Nihjia returned with her mother. Her mother was significantly shorter than her. It wasn't until they smiled that they favored. Nihjia had a lot of her mother's mannerisms, facial expressions, and manner of speaking. When Cassondra walked in Amber popped up and they ran to meet each other they both squeezed each other and started talking at the same time. "You look so good!" Amber said

"Oh my goodness! You look exactly the same!" Cassondra said

"Thank you." Amber blushed

Then Sophia cleared her throat. Cassondra looked over and they did the same thing. "Who's getting married?" Cassondra asked

"Andy!" Amber said all proud

"And this is his lovely bride?" She asked with complete excitement, and pointing at me.

"Yes, and this is her mother." Cassondra shook each person's hand and said hello as they were introduced. "Her sister-in-law Amy. Her sisters Tia and Tara, I'm sorry sweeties I can't tell you apart. This is Sophia's daughter Sabrina. Tracy's besties Joy & Nicole. Little mommas is Veronica. Do you remember Rosalind?"

Cassondra thought about it for a minute. "Of course!"

"This is her daughter Tanisha. Carina is the wedding planner, Tanisha helps Carina."

"Nice to meet you all. I hope you enjoy your visit here."

"Thanks girl, I can't get over how gorgeous Nihjia is." Amber said to Cassondra looking at Nihjia.

"Did you see my other daughter at the receptionist desk?"

"I didn't know that was your baby. What's her name?" Amber asked

"Dafina." Cassondra said proudly.

"Nihjia & Dafina, do you have anymore?"

"Yes, two sons Xavier & Jaeson. But they work with their father."

"I love the names." Sophia said

"Thank you. Sophia do you have anymore?" She asked

"Just Sasha, she lives in Southern Cali. But Sabrina's my baby." Sabrina blushed.

"She's lovely!" Cassondra said looking at Sabrina.

"Thank you." Sophia said

"Excuse me Cassondra, you have a call waiting." A different young lady said.

"Ok, I'll be back in a bit." Then she looked at Nihjia. "They get the Royal treatment!" Then she walked away.

Nihjia still had that beautiful smile. "Ok so, it's twelve o'clock somewhere, can I interest anyone in champagne or mimosas?" All of our hands went up. Nihjia laughed. "Sabrina I can bring you as much sparkling cider as you can drink. I'll put it in a champagne glass as well."

As she turned Dafina came in balancing a tray of both champagne and mimosas, and holding a glass of cider in another. She handed the cider to Sabrina. Nihjia thanked her sister for her assistance. Then she asked me what types of dresses I was interested in, while Dafina gave us each a glass and collected our lunch orders.

"I'm not a huge fan of the crumb catcher neckline. But I have one specification for the dress." I inhaled and exhaled. "I want a silver dress. In my mind I see a silver dress for me. My mom and Amber in pewter. Joy and Nicole in chrome. And the rest of the dresses in Royal Blue."

Nihjia didn't seem shocked or surprised by my request. She wrote it all down. "When is the wedding?" She asked

"In seven months" Carina said

"Do you have a venue?" She asked

"We just booked the Ritz" Carina said

"Ok, and do we have a budget? For the bridal gown."

"No, not really. Depending on the dress I may need a second dress. But I would prefer a dress that is beautiful for the ceremony, and light enough for the reception. I know it's so many seasons ago, but once upon a time I fell in love with a Margret Sutter dress." Carina handed Nihjia a picture. "I'm thinking something like this." I said

"Oh this is pretty." Nihjia said, "so you like satin, corset back, sweetheart neckline, asymmetrical rooshing on the bodice, small train, sexy knee high slit this is beautiful." She said

"Thank you."

"Ok so why don't you all go pick out a dress each. Lets have some fun. I'll pull dresses similar to this one that will come in silver." It was like she said go race. Everyone took off running.

Of course my mom picked up some monster of a princess dress. And although it was a totally different dress Amber picked a monster princess dress as well. Sophia's dress wasn't as bad but still a big puffy dress. Nicole's dress was sexy. Amy's dress was beautiful. Sabrina pulled a lovely lace dress. Tia picked a dress with lots of pick-ups in the skirt and the bodice was really simple. Tara picked a very whimsical dress it had an empire waistline. Joy pulled a beautiful and elegant dress. Nihjia brought all the dresses to the dressing room. Starting with my mother's pick I put the big heavy but beautiful dress on. Everyone laughed when I came out in Amber's. Hers was even heavier than my mom's. Complete thumbs down. I felt like a complete princess in Sophia's dress. But it was still too much dress for me. Amy's dress has a beautiful skirt. The ruffles were beautiful and almost delicate. But the top did nothing for my body. Everyone oohed when I came out in Sabrina's pick. It was very pretty on but it didn't fit me. Nihjia shared that this dress was the one she wore in her wedding. Then she brought us a couple pictures from her mother's desk. She was a beautiful bride, and then she shared pictures of her babies with us. She had two of the cutest little girls. Then I put on Nicole's sexy dress. I was almost too embarrassed to walk out in it. The bodice was lace and completely see thru. The cup area had lining, so from just beneath my breast down to my waistline it was completely see thru. Then the skirt began, but it was mainly ruffles with a huge split up the middle of the front of the skirt. Knowing that Nicole mainly selected this dress for kicks I told Nihjia I was going to pretend that I loved it. I put the biggest smile on, shoulders back, head up, and strut! My mom blushed when she saw me in it. Amber & Sophia were hysterical! They loved the dress, Nicole was smiling so big. I stood on the pedestal, I modeled in the mirror. "I LOVE IT!"

"WHAT?????" Everyone said in unison.

"Yes! I can see Andrew drooling as I walk down the aisle! Oh yes! I'm loving this!" I could tell Joy knew what I was doing she started cosigning. My mom, Amy, Tia were having a heart attack. "I really feel this is the dress!"

"Ok, but try on another dress." My mother said

I smiled and then she realized I was kidding. My mom almost deflated once she realized that I was kidding. She started sliding in her seat to almost say she was relieved. And I wonder where I get my dramatics. Tia's dress was pretty on but too simple. Tara's dress was beautiful on but it felt like a beach venue dress. Lastly I put on Joy's pick. It was beautiful! Classy, sexy, and not slutty. It hugged my body perfectly! It was almost perfect, but it didn't come in silver.

Ok so now on to Nihjia's picks. She had three dresses for me. She put them in the order that she wanted me to try them on. The first was somewhat of an A-line; it had a lot of details in the pattern and beading. It had a crumb catcher neckline, which I never thought I would like. Everyone liked the dress, but no one could say it was the dress. The next dress had a halter neckline. This dress had beading, and a trumpet silhouette. The train was a little heavy. But I've always loved halter necklines. I loved it I twirled in the dress in the dressing room. When I walked out in this dress everyone oohed. Before we set our hearts on this dress Nihjia wanted us to see the final dress. When she took it off the hanger I was in love. The dress had spaghetti straps, a subtle mermaid silhouette, it gently caressed my curves, just above the knee there was a split in the dress but it was very subtle. In fact I don't think my mother noticed it. The main striking feature of this dress was all the crystal beading. Drop dead gorgeous! The dress was silver but the bling took it over the top! When I walked out everyone stood up! Everybody was cheering my mother was crying. I cried! This was my dress!

CHAPTER 38

Tia, Tara, and I walked into service five minutes late. Tara was moving like molasses. I spotted Karen right away; she wasn't in her usual spot. She was sitting closer to the front. Her back was to us, so she had no idea we were there. Joy told me that since the accident Karen had calmed down a lot. She was a lot quieter, and her manner of dress was a lot simpler. Joy said Karen appeared to be drawing closer to God and letting go of her former ways. Sister Harris wasn't there. Cameron required a lot of care. Although he survived the accident he wasn't the same person either. He had a long road to recovery, and he had a lot of brain damage. They weren't sure how extensive yet, but his memory was all messed up. After service I was talking to Joy when I saw Karen see me. She had a bunch of scars on her face and neck as far as I could see. They looked like she had stitches all over and they were still healing internally. She stared at me but not in a mean way. At first she was shocked and then she looked nervous, even a little scared. I could tell she was looking for Andrew, when she didn't see him. I could see her debating. So I waved at her, and she slowly walked over. She approached with caution, and it was like if at any moment I showed any kind of rejection she would keep walking.

"Hello Karen" I said once she was in earshot.

"Hi" she said nervously, "so I hear the big days approaching."

"Yea, pretty soon." I said not wanting to mention the seven-month timeframe.

"Listen, I really owe you a huge apology. I don't blame you if you never forgive me, I've behaved so horribly." I smiled a courtesy smile, as I didn't know what to say to that. She looked at Joy and then back to me. "I know you have no reason to trust me but, I really need to talk to you about that night." Her eyes pleaded with me, and my gut didn't tell me to run.

"Sure, I'll walk you to your car." I said, then I turned to Joy, "can I leave my purse and jacket here?"

"Of course."

I started to follow Karen then she stopped and put her arm around mine. She waited until we walked out the door to speak. "There was a lot going on that night. Something told me to stay home, but when Cameron called and said he was in town and he wanted to go out, I suggested Elegant Affairs. I know Andrew owns the place, but I didn't think he'd be there. I hadn't seen him there in forever. Cameron spotted you guys when you walked in. Neither one of us were happy about you two."

"How do you know Andrew owns the place?"

"That's where I met him. I picked him up there." Then she huffed. "But that's when I formally met Toya. We were ranting about you guys, and she came over and introduced herself. We were bad mouthing you, and now that I look back on it, she was pumping us up. Alcohol and entitlement should never mix. She kept saying how she didn't like you, and all this stuff. How you thought you were better than everyone, etc. When we got kicked out of the club she was in my ear. I was so angry and pumped up when you guys came out the club." Then she paused, exhaled. "Well you were there. I was so shook up when that guy pulled a gun on me, and then he rattled off my address off the top of his head. I almost peed myself. So we went to the bakery on Merritt. Cameron was livid! But that's also when he let it slip that he never slept with you." She stopped our extremely slow pace. "I'm sorry!" She shook her head. "Toya was there. She kept trying to pump up the anger and I was trying to calm my nerves. After awhile Cameron walked her to her car. She kept trying to pump us up like there was something we needed to do to revenge ourselves. We hung out at the bakery for a couple more hours. Clowning with our friends, etc. when we left, we were on our way back to the 580 freeway when Cameron spotted Toya and Andrew on the street by the Grand Lake Theater." My heart sank; I didn't know he still talked to her at all. I waited for the Boom! "Cameron circled around the block. When we came back around we hopped out the car. It wasn't until we were on them that I realized they were arguing. Of course Cameron started in about sleeping with you.

Andrew was upset but he wasn't responding. Toya kept watching me. I wanted to talk to Andrew. I didn't know how he knew Toya. Andrew was ignoring me and that hurt too. So I told him I wanted to talk to him. Toya's neck whipped around at me. She started yelling telling me that I didn't need to talk to her baby daddy about anything. I asked him if he had another baby, but he ignored me. That really hurt! I started yelling about all the years wasted on him. Toya was quiet for a minute. Then she started connecting the timeline. She started screaming about me being the one! Andrew didn't confirm or deny when she asked him if I was the one he was cheating on her with when she was pregnant. She started looking crazy. I went and got back in the car. Cameron was stupid but not stupid enough to walk into Andrew's circle of fire. When Toya started acting crazy and hitting the car, Andrew got in his car and left. Cameron finally got in the car when Andrew left. We got on the freeway and Toya was on our tail. Cameron wasn't paying her any attention until she almost hit us. He tried to shake her by going up the 24 freeway through the Caldecott tunnel. We didn't see her again until we were on San Pablo Dam Rd." She took a deep breath, "she rammed us with her car. We flipped a few times and then we almost went over the edge."

"Did you tell the police?"

"I don't know her last name, I couldn't even tell you what kind of car she was driving. All this time I thought it was only you. Not that it makes what I've done any better. But I've had some time to think. I know you don't have to forgive me, but I am sorry. I know you have a huge plate dealing with the likes of the little things I saw that night. You don't need me adding to the madness. I'm thankful to be alive! I'm not wasting any more time on dumb things. But I wanted you to hear my side, heaven knows what Andrew told you about that night." I nodded my head. I was still in shock to know he still talked to Toya. What did that mean? Is she lying? I needed to talk to Andrew. I put Karen in the car with her friends that she rode with. As I walked back inside I noticed the white car on the corner that normally sat outside my house. When I walked back inside naturally Joy wanted to know what she said. I told her about the apology, but I couldn't tell her about the rest. I needed to talk to Andrew first. The Tompkins' invited all three of us and my parents to their house for lunch. I told Joy I would call her later so we could finish our design for the invitations. I told my parents I would catch up to them later at the Tompkins'. I had a missed call from Andrew. We got home so late last night I didn't have a chance to discuss this morning with him. I knew he was operating on minimal sleep all day yesterday. So when we got home, we said goodbye to everyone, and then we passed out. I drove home as fast as I could. Andre was watching cartoons when I walked in from the garage. I gave him a hug and kiss. Then I went up to the bedroom, Andrew was sitting on the edge of the bed watching TV. He was expressionless when I walked in the door. When he looked at my face he started shaking his head.

"Here we go!" He said

"What does that mean?"

"You got drama written all over your face. What now?"

"Why didn't you tell me?"

"It was a lot happening that night."

"How do you know what I'm talking about?"

"Come on! You know I know you were talking to Karen."

"Ok, but even if you didn't tell me that night why didn't you loop back around?" He blew air. "You're asking me fifty million questions about Yussef whom I've never even been involved with, but you're sneaking off having secret conversations with your ex-girlfriend? How is that right? How often do you see her?" I felt the emotions that I've been denying myself to have. I haven't questioned him about cheating on me or anything since that night when it felt like we broke up. I thought I had turned a blind eye to things like that. But here I am, still waiting for the boom to hit me. Was she having Andrew's baby? Would he tell me if she was? Why would she be so protective over him even after all this time?

"Tracy it wasn't like that."

"Then what was it like?"

He was completely annoyed. "Now is not the time. I needed to talk to you about Friday night anyways."

"Friday night?" I had no idea what he was talking about.

"When that fool was in the backyard!"

"Ok!"

His voice raised, "DON'T YOU EVER IN YOUR LIFE DO THAT AGAIN!" I waited for him to tell me what he was talking about. "WHEN IM HANDLING A SITUATION YOU DON'T EVER COME TRYING TO BE MOTHER TERESA OR WHOMEVER! YOU DON'T EVEN KNOW WHY THAT FOOL WAS HERE!"

"What?"

"The towels Tracy! Never do that! Stay back, let me handle it!"

"He was bleeding Andrew!"

"You let him bleed out if you have to. You don't go helping them! Especially when...." He turned his head.

"When what?"

"Nothing!" He said trying to fix his face.

"When what?"

"Nothing, just don't do it again!"

"When what Andrew?"

"NOTHING! Drop it " he barked

"Seriously, I'm not one of your employees. You can't boss me around and expect me to do it without knowing why. Tell me!"

He rolled his eyes. "What if he was sent here to hurt you? Did you ever think about that? Or you're too busy being a goody-goody, that you think you could be with me without people wanting to hurt you?"

"Why would someone want to hurt me just because I'm with you? Who would want that?" He looked at me like that was a stupid question. "You said people".

"Toya is people!"

"Speaking of Toya, have you...." I lost my air. I bent over, yes I was being dramatic I had to ask the question I've been wrestling with myself over. Andrew sat there looking at me, not amused by my dramatic scene. What was the point of asking? "Treat me the way you to be treated Andrew!"

"What does that mean?" Andrew asked with a ton of attitude.

"I could have secret meet ups. I could keep secrets from you. I could make you wonder if I was being faithful."

"Tracy! Stop it I can't do this right now!" He growled at me.

"What's going on with you? You keep closing off to me. The more time that passes the more you close off. Now I'm finding out about secret rendezvous with your ex, one whom you're informing me that wants to hurt me because I'm with you. You've shut down, but you expect it not to affect me! How is that possible?" He was mad, "what do you mean affect you? Affect you like what?"

"In every way Andrew!"

He stood up, "like what?" He said through his teeth.

"Whatever! You don't want to discuss it, we won't discuss it." I said giving up. I walked into the closet. I took a pair of jeans and a shirt off their hangers. I took off my dress and put it back on its hanger. When I walked back out the closet he was still standing there looking mad. I put my clothes on while he stood there looking at me. His mind was going fifty miles a minute. But I didn't have time to sit there and guess for him to still tell me nothing. My feelings were hurt, I felt betrayed, and I felt tired.

"Where are you going?"

"It doesn't matter. Your goons will tell you anyways." I said then I rolled my eyes. I put on my boots, and my pea coat. I slammed the bedroom door. Fortunately Andre was in the bathroom when I came down. I got in my car and I drove to the Tompkins'. I called my mom to tell her I was on my way. She told me that they left the gate to the driveway open for me. I pulled into the driveway; I pulled up to the garage, which was on the side of the house next to my parent's car. I walked inside the house through the sliding glass door on the side of the house; none of this was visible from the street. Everyone was in the kitchen. My mom was on her cellphone talking to one of her sisters. Tia was talking to Sister Hayes. Tara saw my face; she casually grabbed my hand and led me to the guest bathroom.

"What's wrong?"

debated on what to tell her. "I need to get away."

"Where do you want to go?"

"I have a weird request."

Tara watched me for a minute. "What?"

"We gotta switch cars with mom and dad."

"Ok?"

"And I gotta lay down in the back for awhile. You can't talk to me or act like anyone's in the car with you until I tell you the coast is clear." Tara frowned, "I'll explain once we're alone. Tia has to stay with mom and dad though."

"Oh God yes!" Tara exhaled.

So I asked daddy if he would switch cars with me. He was in the middle of a conversation so he handed me his keys as I gave him mine. I grabbed my jacket and purse. I gave Tara the keys and my purse. I laid on the floor in the back seat. She sang out as she was driving. "I need to fill up the car." I laughed and I told her to use my debit card. I told her my zip code. I stayed on the floor while she filled up the car. She said there was a white car following us until we got to the gas station. Once the driver realized she wasn't me they went back towards to the Tompkins'. Once we crossed the bridge, we pulled off the freeway. I got in the drivers seat. Tara stared at me until I started talking. So I told her the mildest version of my story, but even with that her mouth was hanging open. We went to Menlo Park. We ended up in a Good Friday's. We sat at the bar. We chatted about relationships, the wedding, and life. Then my phone rang; I was completely surprised to see Yussef on my caller ID.

"Hello?"

"What are you doing?"

"Talking to my sister, what are you doing?"

"Having lunch with my sister before I shove off."

"Are you here?" I said looking around.

"No, but I figured you were out and about. Curtis called me asking if I heard from you."

"They're looking for me?" I don't know why I played dumb. He knew better and so did I.

"I'd hate to be you tonight." Yussef laughed.

"Can I ask you something?"

"You just did." I could hear his smile

"Is Andrew sleeping with Toya?"

He was quiet for a long time. Tara was looking at me sitting on the edge of her seat waiting for my response. "Hold on." I heard him say something in the background. "I haven't been gone a full weekend and look at you. Why would you think that?"

"I just found out that they still talk."

"They have a son. What do you expect them to never talk?"

"Yes! Especially if he's saying she's a threat to my safety."

"They may not get together for Sunday dinners, but they're still gonna need to interact."

"You didn't answer my question."

"Not that I know of. Stop being so paranoid."

"What would you think if you're finding out months ago your fiancé was on the street talking to Satan?"

"I would think Andrew would tell you. He's always come to you. You've never had to find anything out about him." Yussef said matter of factly.

"True, but..."

"Butt is what you get beat on." He laughed

"True! However, something's troubling him and he's not talking to me about it. Of course my mind is gonna wonder all over the place."

"Is that the reason you ran away today? It's really not safe for you to be doing this. You are completely vulnerable right now. Anything could happen to you, while you're trying to teach him a lesson."

"It's not fair Yussef! What if I didn't have a crazy ex who wanted to hurt me? What if he and I were just not together? If I saw him, had secret conversations with him or whatever. Andrew couldn't handle it. Once when I painted a vivid picture of me with someone he almost lost it. He can't handle what he expects me to handle."

"Look at it this way. We may not have technically gone out or have a history, but the connection is there. He won't be happy."

I smiled, "you think we have a connection?"

I could hear his smile through the phone. "Stop it! If Andrew wasn't a good guy..."

"And I'm in love with him."

"Right, if it wasn't for all that." He sighed. "My point is you have that."

"Yea, but he ran you away." I said

"Hhmmmm, yea cause I'm on the phone with you right now."

"But you're leaving."

"I'll always be around." He said

My stomach fluttered, "you can't be. I would be devastated if something happened to you."

I could hear his smile through the phone. "I'll be ok." Then he exhaled pretty loud. "Go home to your man. Talk to him and be patient. He's going through a lot right now. He needs you." Then he hung up.

The suspense was killing Tara. "What's going on?" So I told her about the conversation. "You guys are like a freaking movie!"

"Is that a compliment?" I asked

"I don't know." We both laughed.

We got back into the car and we went to my parent's house. We chatted with them for a little while. Then all three of us went home. Andrew and Andre were sitting at the table eating an early dinner when we walked in.

"Hungry?" Andrew asked in a pleasant tone. "Pasta's on the stove."

Andre ran over and hugged me, then his father called him back to the table to finish his dinner. The girls went in the kitchen and fixed their selves plates. Andrew eyed me but he didn't say anything. He joked with them, he was completely hospitable. Tara kept flashing me looks when he wasn't looking since she knew what was going on. She even whispered to me that she was scared because he was too calm and nice. I had to admit I wasn't looking forward to going in that room. We watched a movie, I sat on one couch Andrew sat on another. He wasn't mean, but I was still nervous. All the sudden I felt guilty, and I was mad for feeling guilty. Andrew was reading me like a book and I hated it. At about seven-thirty Andrew took Andre upstairs for his bath and bedtime story. Tara and Tia had to go to bed too, they had an early flight in the morning. The car service would be at our house at five am. I killed as much time as I could with them. I left Eve with them, set the alarm, and then I made my way up the stairs. Andre was knocked out, Cain looked at me and then he went back to sleep. Andrew was getting out the shower when I walked in the room. He walked out the shower with only a towel wrapped around his waist. His hair and body glistened from the water. His face held no expression when he saw me. He didn't soften, but he didn't look mad. He just stood there looking at me. Since he didn't look mad, I was able to take in how good he looked. I rolled my eyes, and I walked into the closet. He hadn't spoken directly to me, so I wasn't gonna talk to him. I came out the closet in only my robe. Andrew looked at me, tried not to look again but he ended up looking again. While I was in the shower he walked up to the window. He watched me for a minute. Then he opened the shower door. He stepped in the shower still expressionless. He lifted my hair to look at my neck. He looked me over really good like he was looking for evidence, then he stepped out. Furious I got out the shower a few minutes later. "So what I'm a cheater now? Should I be inspecting you like that every time you come home?"

"If you want." He said very nonchalantly.

He makes me sick! "Why didn't you tell me you still talk to her? When you don't tell me stuff like that it makes me feel like you're hiding something. My imagination goes wild about what that something could be." He didn't say anything, he stared at me. "Andrew, please talk to me! What did I do? Why are you shutting me out?" He rolled his eyes, and got in the bed. I felt like I was going to explode! I went into the closet. I shut the door, turned off the light, and I went to the furthest corner behind my dresses. I sat on the floor, as I covered my mouth and cried. I didn't know what else to do and I was beyond frustrated. I sat in the dark crying for what seemed like forever, but it was really probably five minutes. Andrew opened the door and turned on the light. He walked to the middle of the closet then he looked around.

"Why are you in the closet behind your clothes?"

"Cause my sisters are downstairs, and I don't wanna alarm them by going downstairs." I said through my tears.

"You're crying?" He sound surprised

"NO!" I said through my tears.

"Listen, it honestly slipped my mind to tell you I talked to her. That night I was so angry with my father... I don't want to do, or allow to happen, what he was telling me has to happen. He says its only a matter of time."

"What's a matter of time?"

"When I'll have to choose between you two." He said leaning on the waist high dresser in the middle of the closet. There were three rows of four drawers on each side. My twelve were on the front And his on the back.

I moved from behind my clothes. I stood up and matched his lean towards him on the dressers. "What do you mean?" Tears were still pouring out of my eyes.

"Your friend Cameron told her about our engagement. I was on my way to get Andre when I saw her car. I was going to ignore her, but I figured why run from her. She was in tears asking me how I could marry you stuff like that. But I basically stopped to tell her that her shenanigans were on my father's radar. She knows he has very little tolerance and patience. But she's so far gone..."

"I still don't understand what that has to do with choosing?"

"She has always been out to hurt you. That much we know. But eventually she's gonna find someone better than a stupid kid to send over. She's Andre's mother, but you're my wife. I can't keep protecting her."

"Do you still love her?"

He looked at me. "What do you mean?"

"Like Steve is evil, but it hurts me how much he hates me. All I wanted to do was love him. I tried, and his reaction to discovering the pregnancy test was the straw that broke the camel's back. That time at National Burgers I was scared of him, but when I saw you making short work of him it killed me. As much as I don't wanna see him again, I still don't wanna see him hurt. I don't think I could've handled seeing what you did to him at the restaurant, even though his handprints were on my neck. You know what I mean?"

"Yes, I don't want to take Andre's mother away from him. But now my dad is getting involved. I can't protect anyone from him. Besides, we're getting married if she threatens you, she's threatening me. I warned her that night. She's the one who can't seem to pull it back."

"Why couldn't you tell me this?"

"Tracy, I was focused on a whole other level. This was a minor detail."

I grabbed his hands. "What was the major detail?"

He pulled his hands away, and instantly shut down. "I can't!" He visibly became depressed all at once.

His reaction surprised me. I looked at him. Then he turned on his heels and walked out the closet and got in the bed. I followed him out, and I picked up his wet towel. I tossed it in the bathroom. I got in the bed and I spooned him. "So is this what I have to look forward to? Whenever you don't understand something you run?" His tone was angry. I wasn't expecting that so I flinched. "I don't appreciate your little stunt today! I'm trying to be patient with you, but woman you are...." He moved his head and exhaled. I touched his face and it was wet. His breathing got faster; he threw his body to face me. "Do I have to convince you that it's not safe for you to go running around? I've never met someone I had to prove to them that they're in danger. Sometimes I wonder what planet you come from!"

I backed away from him. "Stop trying to turn this on me! I don't even know what you're really mad about."

He sat up, I could see the outline of his face in the dark, but I couldn't make out his expression. "You have fun today? You like living on the dangerous side?"

"What?"

"All you gotta do is say the word. I won't send anybody. Let your dumb behind dangle out there like fresh bait and then we'll see how long you like the fast life."

"Andrew we don't talk to each other like this! What's wrong with you?"

"You are what's wrong with me! Did you go see your boyfriend? All this fluff about Toya was just an excuse for you to go hook up with him huh!"

"What?"

"ANSWER ME!" He barked, "I LOOKED AT YOUR CELLPHONE! I SAW HIM IN YOUR CALL LOG! DID YOU GO TO HIM?"

"No"

"ARE YOU CHEATING ON ME?"

"No"

He turned on the light on the lamp stand next to him. "DON'T LIE TO ME!"

"That's not what happened at all."

"IS THIS SUPPOSED TO BE PAY BACK? YOU HAVE SOMETHING TO PROVE? SOME WILD OATS TO SOW!" He was mad, and extremely scary.

I started edging off the bed. He's never been this angry with me, and I didn't feel comfortable. I moved over to the couch. He watched me move. "Andrew I was with my sister. I did not cheat on you."

"I FIND IT REALLY FUNNY HOW SOMEONE TELLS YOU THAT TOYA TRIED TO KILL THEM, AND THE PART YOU FOCUS ON IS ME TALKING TO HER AND NOT TELLING YOU ABOUT IT! HOW DOES YOUR BRAIN WORK? YOU DON'T STOP TO THINK IF SHE TRIED THAT WITH THEM MAYBE SHE'LL TRY WORSE WITH ME. NO! YOU GO SLIP OUT TO MAKE YOURSELF AN OPEN TARGET! HOW DOES THAT MAKE SENSE???" He very angrily waited for my answer.

"It doesn't, but you wouldn't talk to me." I wish I could've thought of something more clever. I felt like he had me up against the ropes with nowhere to retreat to.

"I WOULDN'T TALK TO YOU?" He stood up! "YOU COULDN'T THINK OF NONE OF THIS ON YOUR OWN? I THOUGHT YOU WERE SMARTER THAN THIS!" My heart sank as he approached me. He's never been this mad at me before. "YOU GOTTA BE SMARTER THAN THIS! Even if I had a temporary lapse in judgment I gotta know that you're smart enough to not only have my back, but also figure it out. Every time you do something stupid like this you leave us open." He didn't grab me although I could see in his eyes that he wanted to. "The police are looking for Toya. They came and questioned me not long after the accident."

"But Karen said she didn't know Toya's last name or even what type of car she was driving." I said talking over my tears.

"She doesn't, but she knows my name. They came to my job to talk to me since she told them I knew Toya. I gave them her name, told them what I knew. I even told them about our restraining orders, etc. She knows it's only a matter of time before she's locked up. She's been striking at you left and right, you just don't know about it. Your little stunt today was bigger than you know. And you wanna pick now to play games." He shook his head.

"I'm not a child Andrew if I'm in danger and you know things got worse why wouldn't tell me?"

"Because you're dramatic, and I was really hoping they would've caught up to her by now. But she's even fallen off my radar. I don't know where she is, but by her little stunt Friday she's not far."

"She knows where we live." That hit me like a ton of bricks. "She knows where I work then too?" He looked at me like there was no point in answering my question. "What do I do?"

"Same thing you've been doing, go to work the whole nine, just be smart." Then he hugged me. He's never yelled at me like that before. I didn't like it, but he was right.

"I'm sorry," I said, crying into his arm.

CHAPTER 39

"I just wanna tell you that I'm sorry about that whole scene a couple weeks ago. I had no idea Yussef was going to do that. I did not have my manager's cap on." Becca said

"Thanks, I didn't know she was talking about me to the whole office."

"Off the record?"

"Of course" I said

"I thought you guys were friends. I thought something was odd about her sudden change up."

"She needs to be careful."

"To say the least." Then she exhaled. "How's the wedding planning coming?"

"It's coming along. There's so many decisions, and always so much to do."

"Don't forget you have the option to work from home when you need to. I remember how stressful it can be."

"Thanks Becca I appreciate it."

We finished up our meeting, and then I shut down my computer. I didn't sit because I needed to run to the potty. When I came back I sat on something hard. When I stood up there was a sour apple jolly rancher on my seat. I looked around my cubical there was only one. Then I went to what use to be Yussef's cubical. It was still empty. I don't know when he came back to clear it but when I came into work that following Monday, it was all cleared out. That kind of made me sad. I missed our friendship, talking to him everyday and all day. He was my best friend at work for sure.

It took Andrew a couple days to calm down. He was really upset with me. He kept hugging me and kissing my forehead. But then he'd walk away from me cause he was pissed. I didn't like the feeling of him being so angry with me. I would impulsively reach for a snicker or some other junk food. Then I'd hear Yussef's voice in my head telling me to put the junk food down. I grabbed my coat, purse, and laptop. I took a deep breath, told myself to man up and walk to my car. I had the same pep talk with myself every morning and every evening. Walking through the civic center there was always tons of people. It only made me nervous when I had to walk alone. A couple of times I would hear commotion behind me. But I would focus on the garage ahead of me, and then act as if I had blinders on.

In the car I couldn't remember what we had at home and what we didn't. So I picked up Andre from school and then we went home. Andre told me about his day as I decided what we needed and what we didn't from the store. As I wrote out my list Andrew walked in the door. He still wasn't excited about seeing me, which hurt my feelings. But what could I do? I apologized more times than I could count. So I decided to stop apologizing and let him have his space. "What are you doing?" He asked

"We need groceries, I was writing out a list."

"What store are you going to?"

"Berkeley Super Bowl," he was just kinda standing there. No real expression on his face. "You wanna go with us?" Andre got excited.

"Sure" he said. Andre was speaking my feelings with his excited display of his dad's acceptance to come with us. It felt like my baby was coming back to me. He gave me a huge hug unlike the courtesy hugs I had been getting for the past two weeks. So I kissed him, and I kissed him long and deep! Andre covered his eyes while he giggled at us. Andrew backed up slowly, and he grabbed the counter to steady himself. "Well ok!" He smiled

We loaded up the family in Andrew's car, puppies too. Andre held my hand while he told both of us about his day. His story was cute and full of energy. Andrew pushed the cart, and put the things on my list in. Andre grabbed a number for us for the butcher, while I got another wonderful hug. Then all the sudden, "Drew?"

We both looked over and it was some female I didn't recognize. When Andrew looked at her, his face completely lit up. "Jennay!" He said with the biggest smile.

She smiled at me, "hello" she said

"Hello." I said waiting for an explanation of who she was. She was pretty, average height, plus sized, and her hair was in a short haircut that framed her face nicely. His reaction to her wasn't making me feel great.

"How long has it been?" He asked

"Sophomore year" then she looked down at Andre. "Your son looks exactly like you! That's amazing!" Andrew blushed. "How have you been?" She looked at both of us.

So I couldn't be mad like she was disrespecting me. I didn't get the impression that she meant any harm by her hello and questions. I just didn't like the reaction I was seeing in Andrew. I thought he only responded to me like this. Yea, I wanted to cry, throw a fit, or something. But she had the nerve to be nice and respectful, so I would come off as the insecure jerk if I did anything. "Great! Nothing really new to write home about. How about you?" He said

"I'm good. I live in Chicago. My job brought me out here temporarily."

Good! All I could feel was relieved that she didn't live in the area. "Isn't that where you're from?" Andrew said

She smiled, "yes". Then she saw my ring. "How long have you been married?" She asked me.

"We'll be married in a few months." I said trying not to sound the way I felt.

"Congratulations! Drew I know your mother must be excited."

"Thank you, and she is. They went dress shopping a couple weeks ago. Mom's can't stop talking about her dress. Everyone's excited."

I flashed Andrew a look, "I'm Tracy by the way." I said stretching out my hand to shake hers.

"Oh I'm sorry. This is my wife Tracy, and this is Jennay we went to college together."

"Nice to meet you Tracy." Then she sighed. "Let me finish my shopping and get back to my room. "It was nice to meet you," she said to me.

"It was nice to meet you too." I said trying not to sound fake.

"Congratulations Drew, it was good to see you."

"You too, and thanks." Andrew said still all smiles. Then she walked away; Andrew caught himself, as he was getting ready to glance back after she walked past. Then he looked at me, I was pissed. "What?" He had the dumbest guiltiest smile on his face.

"Daddy who was that?" Andre asked

"Just an old friend from school." He said still smiling.

If I didn't think he'd run into her on another aisle I'd walk away and go get in the car. I reluctantly followed him around the rest of the store. Now all the sudden he was really happy. Now he and Andre were chatting up a storm. I followed them around the store feeling... I'm trying to find a nice way to express how jealous I was. I thought I was the only big girl in his life. Maybe she wasn't a big girl when they were in college. But that doesn't matter; he was in to her today. This fool didn't even introduce me! When she asked him what was new, why didn't he mention the wedding? Clearly I was an after thought. We passed Jennay a few more times in the store. Andrew kept grinning like, like... Anything that would piss me off! When we got home, Andrew volunteered to make dinner. Annoyed with him I walked upstairs and sat on my couch in my room. I was pouting and sulking. He was hugging me, digging me, until miss nice nice walked up. Now he's heck of happy and full of energy. I thought I wanted some affection from him tonight, but now all I want is to be left alone. So I showered and put my feet pajamas on. Carina called me; she needed my schedule so that she could schedule the cake tasting, floral appointment, meeting with hotel, photographer, etc. I turned on my work laptop so that I could see my schedule. We were going back and forth about dates and times when Andrew walked in the room. His smile dropped when he saw my pj's. "Dinner's ready."

"I'll be there in a minute." I said rolling my eyes. I finished my conversation with Carina, and then I reluctantly went down stairs. Andrew and Andre were waiting for me. "You didn't have to wait."

"But we always wait for you mommy." Andre said

I kissed his forehead and then I sat down. Andrew kept eyeing me, and I kept rolling my eyes at him. When dinner was finished I went to the sink to wash the dishes. "Leave them!" Andrew said probably not wanting to look at me in my pj's any longer.

So I went upstairs. It was early but why not get in the bed? Eve followed me up, it was our sisterhood. She looked at me like she understood my pain. I settled on the cooking channel, and the dishes being created entertained me. After a LONG time Andrew came in the room. He didn't look at me he went straight to the shower. After he brushed his teeth he came out of the bathroom in only a towel. I didn't wanna look, but I couldn't help it. I had to look every time he was naked. I thought he would follow my queue and put on pajama pants. But he got in the bed naked. I rolled my eyes. Then he laid there looking at me. "WHAT?" I said loudly.

"Why you let that girl steal your thunder?" He said grinning

"Wait until it's your turn and then I'll ask you the same." Then I rolled my eyes.

He blew air. "We dated in college. I really cared about her. But I broke her heart; remember I was mister big man on campus. We broke up, she eventually changed schools. Why are you tripping?" He said matter of factly.

"I saw your reaction to her." I huffed

"What about it?"

"You lit up when you saw her. You didn't introduce me, I had to mention the wedding." I huffed

He smiled, "I'm sorry!" Then he kissed me. I allowed his kiss but I wasn't feeling it. Dude check the pj's! Not feeling it!

When he came in for a third kiss I backed my face up. "I'm tired Andrew."

He looked disappointed, but I had to be honest. Besides even if I pushed my feelings aside, I'd be wondering if he was with her or me tonight.

In the middle of the night he had me in a bear hug and he was moaning. I looked at his face and he was knocked out. He kept mumbling something, and then he'd moan. This fool is having a sex dream! HE BETTER BE DREAMING ABOUT ME! I turned to face him. His eyes were fluttering and he was into whatever was happening. His grip got tighter, he was hurting me a little but I didn't say anything. I guess it was over cause he relaxed. His eyes became still, and his breathing was heavy again. I didn't want to jump to conclusions, but since this has never happened before, I doubt he was dreaming about me. Pissed off again, it took me awhile to fall back asleep. When I finally did, to my surprise I dreamt that I was walking towards the office when I saw Yussef like I used to. When I saw him I got really excited. I ran to hug him, but he kissed me instead. Even though I was dreaming I felt guilty. Chaos broke out in the civic center. He took me away to a "safe" place where we were secluded. He wanted to make love to me, but I couldn't go through with it because I'm in love with Andrew. Then a siren started going off. I jumped awake, as it was my alarm, so I thought. When I opened my eyes Andrew was staring at me. He looked mad; he kept trying to read my face. I put the sheet over my mouth. "Good morning?"

"What were you dreaming about?"

"I should be asking you the same thing!"

"What?"

"You dang near had me in a choke hold. You were mumbling and moaning. Who were you dreaming about?"

A guilty look flashed on his face. Then he looked at me. "But you were calling Yussef in yours!"

"I wasn't having sex in my dream." No need to tell him about the convincing.

He huffed, "you deny me, but then you calling out some other nigga's name in your sleep!"

"Who were you having sex with in your dream?" I shot back with just as much attitude.

He tried to hold onto his angry face but he had a busted look on his face. Then he said, "ok truce!" We both laughed. "I know how we can settle this..." He kissed me but I wouldn't open my mouth. He grabbed my hair, "give me my tongue!" He pulled me in close and squeezed me tight. He wouldn't take no for an answer. I let him kiss me, and he had already brushed his teeth. He always cheats! "I hate these pajamas! Take them off!"

"No, I like them. They're very warm!" I said caressing them.

"You have me, you don't need them. I'll keep you warm!" He started pulling at my pajamas. As I was opening my mouth to say stop before you rip them, they tore. "Oops!" He said with the biggest grin.

"You did that on purpose!" I pouted.

He started laughing, "honestly I didn't. But forgive me!" He said as he continued to rip them.

I grabbed the post on the bed to pull myself up. I stood up, my poor pajamas were shredded that fast. We laughed at how ridiculous I looked. He started coming after me again. "Wait a minute! I gotta pee!" I said hopping off the bed and running to the bathroom.

He growled at me. "If you take too long I will come in there after you."

I grabbed my diaphragm, and then I had a feeling in my gut. This morning's session wasn't about me. That made me a little sad, but at least it was gonna be with me. I guess that was the silver lining right? As soon as I opened the door he was standing there ready. I pushed past him in my ripped up pajamas and washed my hands. He didn't even let me dry my hands. He picked me up and threw me over his shoulder. He was beating his chest like he was Tarzan or something. This clown of a man was acting so crazy. He laid me on the bed, Eve's head popped up.

"I think she needs to go out."

He groaned, "not right now!"

"Just put them both out. I'm not going anywhere." I said.

He huffed, and then he got up. He turned the alarm off, grabbed his robe and took Eve out. I heard the door, close, the alarm arming and him running up the stairs, I laughed. You couldn't say he wasn't eager. Before the door closed he had that robe back off. He was so eager that he didn't remember to reach for the condom. Once he entered it was a wrap. There was no point in telling him. He was in a zone. It was GOOD! But the whole time I kept telling myself it wasn't for me. When we were done, I felt weird. I didn't feel my normal satisfied and loved self. I felt, hhmmmm, used and dirty. He fell back asleep, and I got up. It was really early but I didn't care. I took all my clothes and I showered in André's bathroom. I turned off the alarm and then I reset it. I went to work. Civic center was barely hopping. I sat at my desk at 5:45 am. Knowing that I was alone I put my face in my hands, and I let all my tears out. I was sobbing for a good ten minutes when someone touched my shoulder. I screamed, as I heard no one come through the glass door or anything. I wasn't crying that loud where I wouldn't hear them. I turned around, and to my delight it was Yussef. "Wait a minute am I dreaming?" I said out loud

He laughed. "Why are you here so early?"

"Couldn't sleep, so I came in. I'll probably knock off early though. What are you doing here?"

"I told you I'd be around."

I stood up and gave him a hug, he sniffed me. "I'm so happy to see you. I thought I'd never see you again."

"I told you, I'd be around." Then he sat down. "Come on spill it, why are you crying?"

"It's stupid, and I wouldn't know how to explain it so that you understood me."

He got comfortable in his chair, "try me". He said smiling. So I went all the way to our last conversation up until he came to my desk, leaving out the part about me saying his name in my sleep.

He didn't need to know about that. "So you feel bad, because you feel like even though he didn't cheat on you. He cheated?"

"Kind of, like I said its stupid." I said feeling really stupid.

"So what are you going to do?"

"Nothing, what is there for me to do? He didn't cheat on me technically."

"Come on, I know you. Even if you don't say anything your passive aggressive nature will have you leaving the house in the middle of the night to go to work. Leaving like that speaks volumes. What do you think he's gonna think when he wakes up and you're gone? Why not try talking to the man?"

"He doesn't talk to me anymore." I started crying again. "Ever since the topic of his stepfather came up, he's shut down a lot. I'm waiting for him to talk to me, but now he keeps getting mad at me."

"Keeps?"

"Or I should say he's not in the mood for my drama, as he calls it."

"He did tell you who the lady was. That's progress though, right?"

"Yes, but still. He'd have a fit if I did that to him."

"Men don't think the same way women do. A man wouldn't get all pushed out of shape, behind one time. Shoot I wouldn't care, you served me up. And I didn't have to work for it that one time. It's fine." Then he shook his head like he didn't like the visual. He took a jolly rancher out of his pocket.

As he unwrapped it I said, "you know yesterday I found one of those. I thought I was tripping."

He smiled, "is that right?"

"Yea, it was...." Then I got it. "You were here yesterday?" He smiled at me. I don't know what you're talking about. "I thought you were going away?"

"I am gone, you don't even see me now." He smiled

"Ok, whatever you say." I said turning around

"Oh by the way, I like the final dress you chose. That dress gets the nod." He had the cheesiest grin.

I spun back around. "How did you?" Why am I surprised anymore? "You liked it?"

"YES!"

"Do you think Andrew will like it?"

His smile slightly dropped, "he would be a fool not to."

"Thank you! I was wondering about that." Then I thought about it. "How did you get in here?"

"I still have my badge." He flashed a badge at me.

"How? I thought they took them when you leave?"

He shook his head. "Not mine." Then he looked at his watch. "It's almost seven. People will be here soon, I'm gonna get moving. Just talk to the man." He said standing up.

I stood up and I initiated a hug. "I wish you were still here."

He sniffed me again, while holding on a little longer to the hug. "I miss you too." He kissed my cheek, and then he walked in the opposite direction of the glass door.

I wanted to know where he went. I stood up, and then my desk phone rang. It was Andrew calling from the house phone. "This is Tracy."

"When did you leave?"

"I couldn't sleep so I decided to come in early."

"Since when do you leave without saying goodbye?"

"I didn't want to wake you."

"Right!" Then he blew air. "What did I do wrong?"

This was my chance. Although I didn't want to I opened my mouth. "I'm not mad, but it didn't feel right. Were you with me this morning?"

He was quiet for a minute. "I was all over the place this morning. You're right, it was different. A little wreck-less huh?"

"Yea" I said feeling relieved that he didn't get defensive.

"I almost didn't pull out. I know you had your thingy in but I don't trust that thing. I'm always knocking it around."

"You can feel it?"

"I feel everything! When I hit your G spot, you react immediately. The Beast knows his home." We both laughed. "I'm sorry Tracy."

"Thank you, I'm sorry too."

"Can we have a do over?"

I didn't want to remind him about how were supposed to be pulling back, and only giving in if we have to. "Sure."

"How long will you be there?"

"No later than two o'clock." I said

"Ok see you then. I love you!"

"I love you!"

CHAPTER 40

"I'm sorry I forgot to mention yesterday that Yussef's replacement starts today. His name is Neil Damanti; the receptionist will call you when he gets there. It was virtually impossible to get someone before Yussef left, especially with everything happening so suddenly." Becca said

My second line beeped. "There's my second line right now. Hold on." It was Danielle calling to tell me Neil was waiting for me. I went back to Becca, "that's him. But I'm gonna knock off at twelve."

"That's fine, tell him to call me if he needs anything." Becca said

Still shaking off my emotional state from this morning. I inhaled deeply, and then exhaled as I pushed through the door. His back was to me when I walked through the door. Danielle was grinning from ear to ear. When he turned to face me, we locked eyes. Oh lord why???? Why is he FINE!!!!! I had on heels and he was a tad bit taller than me. He had dirty blonde hair, hazel eyes that sparkled like gems, his ears stuck out slightly. But the way his eyes locked on mine told me this is gonna be trouble. His eyes swept over me, but he locked on my eyes. "Neil?"

"Yes"

I stuck out my hand, "Tracy".

He smiled, "nice to meet you."

"And you as well. This is our receptionist Danielle. She will get your picture for your badge, and get your parking pass setup." He turned and waved at Danielle. "Follow me, I'll show you where your desk will be." When I turned around I saw his eyes go straight to my butt in the glass door. So Neil likes Sistahs, I exhaled. "This is where you'll sit. I'm sure the IT department needs to reconfigure this station. While they're working on that you can come shadow me." I said leading him to my cubical. "Go ahead and have a seat." I gave him basic information, as I didn't want to overload him with too much information without his computer. The IT person came and started working on his computer right away. Every time our eyes met I looked away. I told myself I was tripping, and that this guy wasn't digging me like that. The IT person got Neil's computer up and running rather fast, THANK GOODNESS! We went over to his station, got him logged in. I gave him Becca's number and a simple enough task that would keep him busy for the next couple of days. "So you have Becca's number, and Danielle is just outside or you can dial #6200 to reach her by phone. I'm gonna take off for the rest of the day. I will see you bright and early at eight tomorrow morning."

"Ok, see you then." He said

When I walked out the glass door, Danielle asked for info on Neil. I told her I didn't have any yet. She looked disappointed. As I hurried through civic center I had the wonderful idea to surprise Andrew and take him to lunch. I was praying he hadn't left yet. I tickled myself with how surprised he'd be when I walked into his office.

There was no parking by the door; I had to park in the far corner of the parking lot. Right after I locked the door to my car and took four steps the door to the building opened. I stopped in my tracks, as I didn't want anyone to see me and spoil the surprise. Out walks Jennay and two steps behind her was Andrew. They were both smiling. I felt frozen and suspended in air. They walked to his car; he opened the door for her. I got back in my car. I instantly broke out in a sweat. "I've got to be dreaming!" I said out loud in the car. I waited until they made a left out of the parking lot to follow. When I came to the stop sign I saw them make a right at the light up San Pablo. I waited four Mississippi's then I turned and followed. There were about four cars between us. As soon as they descended into Pinole they made a left at the light and a quick right into the parking lot for the Apple Street Bistro. I continued straight, and made a left on Pinole Valley Rd. I saw them walking towards the restaurant. I pulled into the parking lot and parked next to his car, I don't know why I needed a close up look at the car as if it could've been someone else's car. I walked the long way around the building and I crossed the street in the intersection. When I looked back they were sitting in a table by the window perfect for me to watch. They were all smiles. At one point he had his hand resting on the table, she reached out to cover his hand with hers. He jumped and moved his hand. They were a little awkward, but they found a way to keep talking. His hand ended up back on the table; this time when she touched it he didn't jump. He sat there and allowed it. Tears ran down my face as I sat there watching this horrible scene. I tried to think of what to do, but nothing was coming to me. They had cocktails, they ate. After one o'clock he started looking at his watch. That's when I realized no one was following me. I guess since I told him two he felt the coast was clear. I walked back across the street. I got back in my car, and I drove back to the office. I parked in the back again. He parked in his reserved parking space then they both walked inside. I counted to ten Mississippi's then I called his desk.

"Hello beautiful!"

"Hey babe, I was wondering what we should have for dinner tonight?" I said as I walked across the parking lot.

"I don't know maybe something light like salads. I had a big lunch."

I walked past the receptionist, "really what did you have?" My heart was pounding as I walked towards his office and the door was closed.

"A big ole burger." He said emphatically.

"Oh really?" I said turning the handle to his office. "How was the Apple Street burger?"

I opened the door just in time to see that busted look on his face. Jennay was sitting in one of the chairs facing him, and he was sitting on the corner of his desk. They both turned white for a second when they saw me. Jennay looked good, she looked like she was on a mission to change his mind. I looked at him and then back at her as I closed the door behind me. Andrew was dumb founded, his mouth was open but nothing was coming out. "So Jennay girl how was lunch?" She swallowed hard and looked at Andrew. I looked at Andrew, "Seriously? For real? Really?" His eyes followed me but he didn't move. "I'm paranoid! I'm over exaggerating! I'm dramatic!" I punched him in his chest. Although you could hear it I knew it didn't hurt him. "AND WHAT KIND OF FEMALE ARE YOU? You know good and well we have a family! What are you doing?" She didn't say anything either. She kept her eyes to the floor.

"Tracy!"

I looked at him and waited for him to say something else. "What Andrew? You're gonna tell me how you only had lunch? How it was nothing? Or were you gonna wait for someone else to tell me, and then deflect by telling me how I don't think about things?" I walked to the door. "I'm cool!" Then I walked out the door. I had a smile plastered on my face for people who saw me go in and waited for me to come out. They had no idea who she was, and they weren't gonna know because of me. I sat in my car crying my eyes out. About twenty minutes later Jennay walked out of the building. Andrew didn't even walk her out. My mind told me to let her go. But my heart wanted to cause her pain just like she caused me. To my delight she unknowingly was walking towards my car. I took my shoes off and I stepped out of the car. When she saw me she exhaled. She let her purse hit the ground, and she squared off. I wasn't gonna waste time walking around in circles like it looked like she thought I would do. I punched her straight in her mouth. She swung at me and hit me in my arm. It hurt but my adrenaline was kicking in. As she recoiled from her punch I punched her in the face again and I kicked her leg at the same time. She stumbled backwards, and I kept coming for her. She tore my blouse, my pencil skirt ripped from all the movement. I stayed on her face. Then someone grabbed me. They picked me up effortlessly. I was trying my best to get back to her, but he had me good. When he threw me in the passenger seat, I realized it was Yussef. He hurried over to the driver's side. Jennay was bent over holding her face. Andrew walked out the door as we drove away. I couldn't tell if he knew who was driving, but he knew it wasn't me cause I was screaming all kinds of obscenities out the passenger side window.

Yussef hopped straight on the freeway towards Vallejo. Once I calmed down some my hand was throbbing. I was crying and trying to massage my hand. When we passed Fairfield I wondered where we were going. Yussef didn't say anything he just drove. We got off the freeway in Dixon and he drove for a long time down a two-lane street. Pretty soon we passed the veteran's graveyard, and then there were farms and then there were trees. We pulled up to a run down looking house with a barn. He parked in the barn. Still not saying a word he got out of the car and waited for me to join him. I put my shoes on, grabbed my purse and I got out the car. When I stood beside him he took my purse and pulled out my phone. He turned it off and then he took the battery out. He put them both back in my purse. Then he put his hand in the small of my back to guide me out of the barn. He shut the door and locked it. Then he opened the front door. This house was really nice inside. All the furniture and decorations were older but still very nice.

He gestured towards the couch. "Have a seat." Then he went in the kitchen. I could hear ice, etc. he came back with a towel, which he laid across my lap. Then he set the bowl of ice on the towel. There was a little water in the bowl. It was freezing cold which felt like heaven on my hand that was throbbing and on fire. He walked away; he came back with a white t-shirt and sweats. He put the t-shirt around me, "put this on once your hand starts to feel a little numb." Then he sat in the rocking chair across from me. He had a wide smile on his face. "You can take the girl out of Richmond, but you can't take the Richmond out of the girl!" I sat there. I knew I looked a hot mess. Clothes all tore up, hair all wild, eyes swollen and red, snot running down my face. I started crying again. He came and sat next to me. He rubbed my back and tried to comfort me.

"You shouldn't have come. He's gonna get you."

"So what was I supposed to do? Let someone see you? You go to jail for assault? He'll make sure everything is cool on that end. I needed to get you out of there."

"Yea but when I go back..." I heard the words as soon as they came out my mouth. I started crying again.

Yussef started rubbing my back again. "It's ok."

I put my head on his shoulder. "Your replacement started today."

"He or she?" He asked still rubbing my back.

"He"

"He any good?"

"He's a FINE white boy!"

We started laughing. "They gonna have to learn to stop putting guys around you. I give him a year max before he starts losing his mind." He laughed

"Am I that horrible?"

"No, you're that irresistible! I pity the poor guy. He doesn't stand a chance."

"How could you tease me right now?"

"I'm dead serious! I told you I liked you from the moment I met you. At first I thought, 'oh she cool'. Then I thought, 'oh she's heck of cool'. Then that changed to, 'she's cool folks'. Then I started thinking about you all the time. Then desire set in, and I knew it was time to go. Then it started burning inside me." He shook his head, "that poor guy don't stand a chance.

I smiled, "I don't know why you say stuff like that but thank you for the ego boost."

He exhaled. "So you think he slept with her?"

"No, by the way he jumped when she touched his hand. They hadn't touched before. But given the space and more time it could've gone there." I exhaled, "he told me they dated in college, but he broke her heart. Maybe they never had closure, but that's not my problem."

"So why were you fighting her?"

"Cause she knew exactly what she was doing. It would've been different if she didn't know about me. But she knew exactly what she was doing. She knew we have a family. She knew!"

"So does he."

"And that's why I'm not protesting to being here."

He was quiet for a minute. "Go change your clothes then come help me make dinner." He got up and walked into the kitchen.

"Where's the bathroom?"

"Go change in that bedroom." I went in the bedroom and shut the door. There was a brass bed, cushy carpet on the floor, and a wooden dresser. I put on the sweats and the t-shirt. Everything was four sizes too big. I was swimming in these clothes, which also made them extremely comfortable. When I walked back in the kitchen he laughed. "Not your normal attire, but it works." Then he gave me two bowls, a cutting board, and a knife. "Wash, chop, dice" he said pointing at new potatoes and the white onion. He prepared the chicken breast and put them in the oven. Once I was finished chopping he roasted the potatoes. Then took some frozen spinach out and cooked it. The chicken was boneless and skinless just the way I liked it. He took out two bottles of chardonnay wine. It was delicious, and kind of strong. It helped me relax quite a bit.

"It's getting late." I said looking out the top of the window where the curtains left a small peak of nightlight in.

"You ready to go home?"

"No" then I moved closer to the window. "The moon is huge!"

"Have you ever looked at a starry sky outside of city lights?" I shook my head no. "Come on, it's almost like you can see God when you do." He led me by the hand. We stepped out on the back porch. He was right there were so many stars in the sky. It made me think of the bible story when God promised Abraham that he would multiply his seed like the stars in the sky. I sat in the chair on the porch and stared up. I prayed, I asked God what to do. I really didn't know what to do. I asked for a sign cause I was really confused. We sat out there for what seemed like forever. "Come on. I'll sleep on the couch." He took blankets out of the closet.

"Do you live here?"

"No, but I come here every so often. If anyone comes here I'll know it's because you brought them." He smiled at me. Then he closed the door. I heard him making up the couch. Then he went in the kitchen to clean up. I couldn't fall asleep so I went in the kitchen. He was standing at the sink washing dishes. I walked up to him and put my arms around his waist while laying my head against his back. I could hear his heart and it was beating overtime. He inhaled deeply, "what are you doing?"

"Thank you for always protecting me. Setting me straight, when I know that can't always be easy. You've always been a gentleman to me. You are very precious to me. I want to say thank you, cause I don't think I ever have."

He inhaled and then he exhaled. He turned to face me. "I mean.... I know you're in love with your man. I know you're going back to him. But... Can I ask a favor?"

I asked a leery, "what?"

He smiled, "I just remembered that couch is not the most comfortable. I'd rather sleep on the carpet in the bedroom. The hardwood in the living room will get too cold."

"Are you asking to sleep with me?" I asked still holding him.

"Sleep on the floor. There's a difference."

"This is your house, you can do what you want." Then I walked back to the bed.

He stood there for a few minutes silently. Then he finished washing. When he finished, he brought his blankets in the room and he laid on the floor. "So say you never met Andrew, and we were two lowly employees, would you..."

"YES!"

He hesitated, "you know what I was gonna ask you?"

"If I would've been into you, or something along those lines. And the answer is yes."

"Really?" He sounded like he was thinking about it.

"My turn"

"Ok"

"If I was still a big girl, would you have looked at me?"

"How big we talking?" He said laughing.

I hit him with my pillow. "I showed you a picture."

"Honestly, you still would've been you. When you first see you, yes you're pretty, but so are fifty million other girls. It's the talking to you that did it for me."

"What do I say?"

"It's hard to explain, but when you become passionate about something it's intriguing. You're good to people, unless they've messed with your man obviously. When I talk you listen, a lot of the time people only listen enough to think of what they're going to say next. There are so many attributes that combine to make you who you are. It's hard to explain."

"Wow! I think you just did."

"That wasn't even the half."

"Yussef why don't you have a girl friend?"

"It's kind of hard when you're stalking someone." He laughed. "I've been a little distracted. But recently I did meet someone. So far she seems cool, but it's kind of hard to get you out of my head. But if I thought Andrew was a bad guy, I wouldn't care. You'd be mine. It's just that I know he's a good guy. I can't tell you what today was about. It's like that man suddenly became a amateur or something."

"Even after today, you still think he's a good guy?"

"He's human Tracy! We all mess up. He saw ole girl, started reminiscing about the old days. I don't know who reached out to who. But he had lunch with the broad. She was willing to hurt his family, how far do you think she would've gotten? I've seen him turn down bad females! Bad! I really think he would've been smart enough to leave her alone." Then he started laughing. "But you busting in on him like that. I think that was enough to get his attention. They messed up today. Heads will roll!" He laughed.

"I guess you're right."

"Can I kiss you?" He said real fast

"What?" I sat up real quick.

"I'll never ask again, but I know this is the only time if ever that you would say yes. I PROMISE it won't go any further!" He put his hands up.

"Ok" I said

"Ok? Really?" His voice cracked.

"Yes" I was as nervous as he was. I couldn't believe I said yes either.

He sat on the edge of the bed. He was still nervous. He slowly leaned in and I did the same. His lips were a lot softer than I imagined. He didn't kiss like Andrew, but his kiss was still good and full of emotion. He suddenly broke free from our kiss, and he laid on the floor. "Ok! I'm good! Gotta stop there!" We laughed. I laid down. "I SHOULD'VE NEVER DONE THAT!" He yelled. We laughed again.

"Good night Yussef!"

"Good night my love!"

CHAPTER 41

"Don't put your battery back in your phone until you hit Concord." Yussef said as he unlocked the barn.

"Is my phone bugged or something?" I asked

"I don't know, but I'd rather not find out the hard way." He said

We stood there looking at each other. "You be good to that girl. She deserves to get the best you." I said barely smiling

"Yea," he exhaled. "Try not to give my man such a hard time. I think last night was pay back enough." He said looking at the ground.

"Ok well stop being silly, give me a kiss goodbye."

We kissed our last kiss goodbye. It was very passionate and emotional, Yussef held me so tight. It almost felt like he didn't want to let me go.

Although we said good night last night, we kept talking. Eventually Yussef got up on the bed and we kept talking. We even talked about the new possibility in his life. It was REALLY new, but so far he liked her. He asked me how I met Andrew, what makes me feel like Andrew is the man for me. He told me why he respects Andrew so much, in a way he looks up to him. It was nice to hear someone else sing my man's praises. We talked about our first loves, first heartaches. We laughed a lot, some awkward pauses. I don't remember falling asleep, but when I woke up his arms were around me and he was awake. When I asked him if he slept at all he smiled at me. He made us breakfast, I was dying for a shower but I refused to put on dirty underwear, and I wasn't about to go commando, poor Yussef's head might pop off. I did use my finger as a brush and put toothpaste in my mouth. I gotta stop running away! I told myself as I rinsed my mouth.

I got in the car, when I pulled out of the barn he shut the door and then he walked back to the house. As soon as I hit Concord I called Becca and told her I had a family emergency and I needed to take the day off. She was very understanding. When we hung up, I got an alert that I had a voicemail message. I listened to it:

"Tracy please call me as soon as you get this message." It was Amber

"Tracy! Are you alright?"

"I'm ok." I said doing a horrible job of holding back tears

"Sweetheart where are you?"

"I'm on the freeway, coming through Walnut Creek."

"Please come over."

"I need a shower."

"You can shower here."

I wasn't in a hurry to go home and possibly breakup with Andrew. "Ok, I'm on my way." I bypassed my exit and went to Oakland. When I got to Amber's house she had me put my car in the garage then she squeezed me so tight.

"I knew you were ok." She said, "Andrew was so worried about you."

That made me cry all over again. She rubbed my back. Once I calmed down she took me to her bedroom. She had a few pairs of brand new jeans that she laid out on the bed. She laid out shirt options for me. She even had brand new underwear with the tags still on them. The only thing she couldn't give me was a bra. We did not wear the same size. I picked out an outfit and she gave me towels for the shower. She told me that body wash, etc. was in the shower and to help myself. I let the water beat me in the face while I cried my eyes out some more. I washed my hair with her expensive products, which smelled, like heaven. I pulled my wet hair all back into a ponytail. Amber had the good stuff, her lotion made my skin feel like silk. I knew I'd have to ask her later where she got all this stuff. When I came out her bathroom she was walking back into the room.

"I was coming to check on you." She put her hands on her hips as she gave me a nervous smile. "I'll get you a bag for your things." She hurried out, and she came back with a tote.

"Thank you" I said

She gestured for me to sit on her bed. So I did, and then I folded my t-shirt and sweat pants. I wanted to keep them forever.

"I hope you don't mind. I told Andrew you were here. But only after I made him promise not to come over."

"Thanks!" I said relaxing a little bit.

"He came over in such a panic yesterday. I knew he had to be at his whit's end to come to me." Then she sighed. "I know my son isn't perfect. He's got a lot of his father in him." Then she touched my leg. "Never tell him I said that he would die." Then she sighed again. "So Jennay resurfaced? Ain't it funny how old flames pop up out of the blue? Did he tell you the story?"

"Kind of."

"Do you want to hear it?" I shook my head yes. She sat next to me on the bed and she brought her knees into her chest like she was gonna tell me something good. "So you know Andrew has been dealing with that biscuit head Toya for forever. When they were in College they were forever breaking up and getting back together. I don't know when he met Jennay, but when I met her I was happy he had found a nice girl, even though at the time he wasn't exactly ready to be a nice guy. I really hoped that he would slow down. But we both know he didn't. When Jennay found out about them that was a turning point for him. He felt horrible for hurting her like he did. They were kind of back and forth as well. He couldn't seem to get it together relationship wise. Then Toya was pregnant, so he proposed to her. Jennay found out about the baby and the proposal and she left. Even though Toya turned Andrew down, it was too much for her to deal with. She didn't say goodbye, she packed up and left. Until you, I think he always felt like she was the one who got away."

"So you're telling me they needed closure?"

"I guess so."

I shook my head. "Seeing him light up when he saw her made me so jealous. He played it down like it was something from the past over and done. Just to see him out with her! I guess she was worth risking my feelings.... My anger!"

"Your anger! Girl I was popping him all upside his head. These boys know everything I've been through and then to watch them turn around and be like those guys." She shook her head. "Besides, how he gonna have us all excited about a wedding and then jeopardize it?" Then she thought about it. "You can tell him you came here late last night. I was the only one here all night." She had sad eyes.

"Why would I do that?"

"Unless you've got some extremely obese friends that I haven't met, I don't know a girl who wears crisp white t-shirts and baggy navy blue sweats. Besides I could smell another man on you when I hugged you." She said sadly

"I didn't sleep with anyone if that's what you're thinking." She was searching my eyes like Andrew does. "Ok sweetheart." She said patting my hands.

"Amber?" I inhaled. "Do you REALLY think your son loves me? I keep looking at this ring. I don't want to take it off, but there's the other part of me that's telling me to run. I don't want to live the rest of my life like this. Crazy baby momma, girlfriends and lovers popping up out of nowhere, ex boyfriend wanting me dead. On the drive I was thinking about moving away and starting over. Love shouldn't be this hard."

"Oh sweetheart please tell me where you're gonna go that doesn't have that? No matter where you go, who you see, there's gonna be an element of drama involved."

"But why does it have to be so complicated?" I asked

"What is life if it isn't complicated?"

"Happiness for one!" We both laughed.

"So" she blew air. "You think you want to throw in the towel?"

"I don't know", tears came to my eyes again.

"Do you still love him?"

"Of course I do! I hate feeling like this! I don't want to be rolled over the rest of my life. When Andrew is good, there's nobody better! But this stuff! It wasn't like this before. We had little dramas here and there, but why does it have to be so traumatic the closer we get to this major milestone?"

"Oh sweetheart, every couple goes through something right before they marry, and you're gonna keep going through things afterwards but you gotta stick together. You gotta work it out." Then she exhaled. "I loved David so much! No man wanted me to be his forever before then! He was my prince! But we couldn't handle the stresses. I handled a lot of things wrong. So did he, I lost him a long time before he died. But I'm glad I had some good times with him before he lost it. I've dated some since then, but ole biscuit head Malcolm is always blocking!"

"Do you still see Malcolm?"

"From time to time. I guess that stops me from having someone for me huh?"

"Whatever makes you happy."

She started staring off, "I haven't been truly happy in a long time." Then she shook it off. "Guess the only way you'll truly know for sure which way to go is to talk to Andrew."

"Yea" then the thought of telling him about where I was last night flashed in my head. "I'm scared!"

"Why?"

"I just am." I couldn't tell him where I was last night, and I wasn't gonna have his mom lie for me. I started praying, and I felt guilty for coming to God with drama, and staying away when things were "good". But I prayed anyways. I didn't know what to do and I was afraid to go home. Even more afraid that he wouldn't be there. He could rightly say, I bring him too much drama. And say he wanted to be with Jennay. She was worth risking our relationship for, maybe she gives him something I can't or don't. We went downstairs; we sat on the couch talking. Every time I thought I even had the courage to say I was going home I'd bust out crying. I sat on that couch for hours crying and talking. Darryl came home, when he saw me he nodded to say hey. Then he left. It was like he came in to inspect the place or something.

Then Andrew and Andre walked in the door. Andre was so happy to see me. He ran to me and threw his arms around my neck. He was so happy to see me, and I him. But my heart was pounding as Andrew eyed me as he stood by the door. Amber took Andre to the backyard, he didn't really want to go, but his father flashed him a look. Andrew stood by the door trying to read me, so I eyed him back. We were having a stare down.

"So, how come you didn't know I was coming?" I asked

He cocked his head to the side. Then he sat down in the recliner across from me. "You normally do things a certain way. My man is used to having Yussef as a back up. He slipped up. He's been dealt with."

"What does that mean?" Andrew blank stared at me. "Was that really the first time you saw her at Berkeley?"

"Yes"

"How did you end up Hooking up for lunch?"

"She called my office. I figured lunch would be harmless."

"In what way?"

He blew air, "in what way what Tracy?"

Through clinched lips I said, "in what way was lunch supposed to be harmless Andrew?"

Andrew was reading my face. He wasn't gonna bully me out of my feelings. "It was the easiest option." He said like he wasn't interested in talking to me.

"So it was the easiest way to hurt me." I huffed

Then he leaned forward, "so your staying out all night wasn't to hurt me?"

"Of course it was." I blurted out.

He wasn't expecting me to admit that. I could tell I caught him off guard. He squirmed in his seat. Then he sat back, and released a little chuckle. "So what about fighting her?"

"She knew exactly what she was doing. She was just as guilty."

His smile got bigger, "you hit me."

I had to think about it. Everything was happening so fast. "Yes I did. I apologize for doing that."

"Where did you go?"

"I don't know where I was exactly."

His smile went away. "Who were you with?" I swallowed hard, but I didn't say anything. "Tracy! So help me God I'm not playing with you! Who were you with?" I stared at him. He got up very angry. He picked up the recliner effortlessly, and then he put it down. He started getting really big, and tears started pouring out of my eyes. He stood over me with his hands flexing and unflexing. "ANSWER ME WOMAN!" He looked really scary and huge. I kept staring at his eyes. If he was gonna hit me I wasn't gonna close my eyes. "YOU'RE CHEATING ON ME!"

"NO IM NOT!" I said standing up on the couch to match his growl. "IM NOT THE CHEATER YOU ARE!"

"I DIDN'T CHEAT ON YOU! I WASN'T GOING TO CHEAT ON YOU! I JUST HAD LUNCH!!" He yelled "I SAW YOU! I WAS THERE!"

"What?" He backed down

"I left the office even earlier then I said, cause I wanted to surprise you and take you out to lunch. Imagine my surprise when I see you holding the door open for her. You opened your car door for her. I followed you, I saw everything! You're so used to following me, you forget it can go both ways." He sat down. "I saw the cocktails, saw the touching, I saw everything!"

"Just like I saw Yussef driving your car." His expression was full of pain. I looked at him. "I wasn't sure if that was him. But when no one had you, I knew it was him. Did you call him?" I shook my head no. He got angry.

"Andrew, Yussef has nothing but respect for you. He looks up to you. He admires you."

His expression changed multiple times. "He wants to be me you mean?"

"No!"

"Yes!"

"No! Andrew stop trying to assign some kind of evil plot to him."

"Stop defending him!" He barked
"Ok!" I said

"Are you in love with him?"

I looked at him, "how could you ask me that?"

"Answer the question!"

"No! Are you in love with Jennay?" He blew air. I mimicked him and blew air too.

"No!"

It was silent for a few minutes. "Do you think we should be together?"

My question wounded him; as soon as I saw the affect I wanted to take it back. "You want to break up?"

"That's not what I meant."

"Then please tell me, what do you mean?" He sat back in the chair waiting for me to speak.

"I mean we've had one drama after another. I liked us when this drama didn't exist. I liked us when it was simpler to be together." I said

"The deeper in you get the more that has to be settled. You told me you were with me until death do us part. You told me as long as I didn't cheat or hit you, we'd work it out. Now you want out!" He was getting big again. "You wanna go run after Yussef? I'll kill him! That's not a threat! He's a dead man!"

"Andrew! Please! That's not what I meant." I started crying again.

"Oh so now you're gonna cry because he's a dead man!" Andrew said hitting his fist into his hand. The sound of the hit echoed

"Andrew!" I tried to talk through my tears. "That's not what I meant!"

Tears started running down his face. "THEN TELL ME WHAT YOU MEAN! CAUSE IT SOUNDS TO ME LIKE YOU'RE CHOOSING SOMEONE ELSE OVER ME!" He was screaming in my face.

I tried to talk over the tears, but I could barely talk. I touched his face. He was furious! "Andrew!" I could barely get his name out my mouth. I kept shaking my head no. "I love you!" I tried to calm down so that I could speak. "I don't want to break up! I figured you didn't want me anymore. You stopped talking to me." He looked confused. "You have been shutting me out. Every time I ask you questions you tell me not now. Then the other morning didn't help. I figured you wanted out but didn't know how to tell me."

"I'm gonna ask you one more time. Did you cheat on me? Tell me the truth!"

"No, I've never slept with anyone other than you since we've been together."

Then he stood me up, I didn't want to. But I dare not deny him in this state. I thought I was about to be hit so many times. "STOP! Stop running from me! It hurts me when you do that. Make me feel like you're not a flight risk."

"What do you mean?" I asked

"You want me to open up to you, but every time something happens you run away from me. Stuff like this doesn't make you the most trust worthy in my book."

"Ok" I said

Then he hugged me. More like squeezed the life out of me. I hugged him back, we both stood there crying our eyes out. Then he checked my hand, "NEVER take this off!"

"Ok" I said feeling relieved that he said that. I had him sit down and then I took my favorite seat, on his lap. I laid my head on his chest. His heart was beating so fast. I know it's stupid but it did feel good to know he was jealous about me. I wasn't the only person looking stupid.

"You smell like my mom." He said taking me in.

I thought about what Amber said about me smelling like a man earlier. I was happy I didn't go straight home. That could've been a death warrant for Yussef. "I used her stuff". Then I inhaled and exhaled, "so you still want to be with me?"
His heart started speeding up. "Yes"

"Why?" I asked

"Because I love you! I don't want to be without you. No, I can't be without you!" Then he squeezed my thigh. "You still want to be with me?"

"Yes" I said

"Why?" He asked

"Because no one has ever made me feel loved like you do. Outside of today you've never scared me, although I get it. You're a scary guy, you've never been that to me."

"I scared you?"

I blew air. "Yea right! You know you were being scary! Picking up chairs, and screaming in my face."

"I was going crazy yesterday and all last night. I couldn't find you; I knew you were mad at me. Then to know you were here and not coming home. I know I promised mom's, but you were stalling and probably would've stayed gone another night if I didn't come over."

"I was scared."

"You never have to be afraid of me." He said kissing my forehead.

I got butterflies in my stomach. "On that note, can you do something for me?"

"ANYTHING!" He said as he squeezed my thigh again.

"Leave Yussef alone."

In one quick move I was on the couch and he was on his feet. "You gotta be kidding me! He's dead!"

"Andrew! Please! What did he do?"

"HE KNOWS EXACTLY WHAT HE'S DONE!" He started pacing. "YOU DONT MESS WITH YOUR BOSS'S GIRL!"

"Andrew! I'm still here, and it's not like that. He knows I love you, he encourages it. He has your back."

"Yea my way back!" He said visibly unraveled. "I can't Tracy! He knows better!"

"Please Andrew!"

"I was going to leave him alone as long as he stayed out of my way. But he crossed the line yesterday!"

"What did he do?"

Still pacing, "I'm over here trying to calm down. And you're stirring things up again! I don't want to talk about this. You can't change my mind!"

"Please Andrew! He's my friend! You know how many of those I have these days. Please!"

He gave me a evil look. "I bet he's your friend alright!" He started to walk away. Then he turned towards me. "If I ever find out you slept with him!" He said pointing his finger at me. "I'm not responsible for what happens next!"

I flew off the couch. "So if you cheat basically you want me to deal with it. Get over it and keep loving you. But if I cheat on you you're threatening me?" He didn't say anything, his face was stone. "That doesn't work for me!"

"It is what it is!"

"Then I don't want this! I have no intentions of sleeping with anyone other than you. But you will not threaten me. You will not impose double standards on me. I will not live like this!" Then I walked past him to go upstairs to get my purse.

As I was on about to go up the stairs he grabbed my shoulder but it spun me. My back hit the wall, he grabbed me and put me in another bear hug. It happened so fast that I screamed. "Ok! Ok! Ok!" He said holding me. "I'll kill both of us, ok?"

I laughed, "you'll kill both of us?"

"Yea you first then me. But only after I'm sure you're dead. Then I'll kill myself." He said laughing

"How about no one dies, including my friend?"

He squeezed tighter. "I can't promise you he won't die. I can't. Tell him he needs to stay away."

"Andrew!"

He squeezed tighter, "Ssshhhh! I don't want to talk about him anymore."

"But.."

He squeezed tighter, "no more".

"Can't! Breathe!" I said turning red

431

"Oh my bad!" He said loosening his grip. We stood there hugging so long that we were swaying. Then my stomach grumbled. "Are you hungry?"

"I haven't eaten since breakfast." I said

"Lets go eat." He invited his mother to come with us.

She hugged both of us so tight. Then she said, "if I didn't get to wear my dress, heads were gonna roll!" Then she smacked the back of Andrew's head. He rolled his eyes.

Andre chose Mexican food so Andrew took us to Gonzalez's, a mom and pop restaurant. I got butterflies when Amber said they've been coming here since the boys were little. Two more cars pulled up at the same time we did. Andrew nodded at them they nodded at him. I calmed a little when we walked in the restaurant. The hostess showed us to a booth in the far left corner. Andrew and Amber sat on the side facing the door. Andre and I sat on the opposite side. Andre and I were cuddling and catching up on the hugs we've missed. Our waiter came and took our orders. He brought water chips and salsa right away.

"When do we come pick out our tux's?" Andrew asked

"We already picked them out." Amber said

He looked at his mother, "what am I five? I know how to pick out a tux."

"But baby you don't know our dress styles. So we picked them out and all you have to do is get measured." I said trying to smooth out his roughness. He was on a short fuse.

"But I don't want to rent, I want to buy mine."

"Well excuse me!" Amber said rolling her eyes

"Ok, I don't know if that requires more time. I'll call Cassondra's and ask." I said taking out my phone.

"You probably don't remember her, but Cassondra and I go way back. She was around a lot when you were a baby." Amber said smiling

"So how are we positioning that?" Andrew asked

"What do you mean?" Amber asked

"Any business we give her is a commission for her right?"

"Right." She said

"You're getting all your dresses there?" He asked

"Yes"

"Ok, we'll buy all the tux's there too. I'll pay for it."

"Really?" I asked

"Sure, it'll be one of many groom's men gifts."

"It doesn't make sense to buy Andre and Anthony's tux's. They're still growing and will probably only wear them this one time." Amber said

"The point is that we're giving your friend our business. I'm not concerned."

"All of this will put a huge dent in our budget." I said

"Then we won't put it in. I'll pay for the dresses too." He said

"I'm paying for my dress, but I was gonna pay for my mom's, sister-in-law, and sisters. You can cover those?"

"Sure. Why are you paying for your dress?"

"I just want to."

"Suit yourself." He said drumming his fingers. "Come on Andre lets go to the men's room."

As soon as they turned the corner, Amber said. "He's still pretty up tight." Then she looked up. "Ooh! And this isn't gonna help."

I looked around the side of the booth. Toya was walking in with her Hubby, baby on hip, and pregnant belly. She was a lot further than I expected her to be, but I didn't get a good look at her that night at the club. She looked tired and her hair was down. She didn't see me, so I scooted to the wall in the booth, Amber did the same. She shot me a look like crap! I put my hands up. Our waiter brought our food. Toya and family were sitting in the middle of the floor; it was only a matter of time before she saw us. I peaked out the booth, my heart wanted to see the baby. I felt like someone punched me, he had Steve's eyes. I wanted to cry as soon as I saw the little boy. He was beautiful just like Andre. She definitely made beautiful babies. Her husband's back was to me so I couldn't see his face. Maybe that wasn't Steve's child, but looking at him my heart said it was. When Andrew came out the hallway from the bathroom, surprise was all over his face. Toya saw him and she looked surprised as well. Then her eyes locked on Andre. Her face looked pained, Andre was oblivious to what was happening. Andrew held his hand and walked over to our booth. Toya's eyes followed him.

"Mommy smell my hands!" He sniffed his hands. "I like this soap." He said holding his hands out to me.

Toya grabbed her stomach when she heard him say that. She was pissed but not saying anything. Andrew smiled at her, he pulled out his phone and he texted someone, and then he started eating. Eventually her husband started looking to see who she was looking at. When he saw Andrew he asked her who he was. She said lowly that he was her ex. She was too pregnant to pull anything herself. Her husband didn't seem concerned. Then Andrew stood up, my heart sank again. He walked over to the table and introduced himself. Her husband was fine with meeting Andrew. He didn't seem bothered at all. Toya looked nervous all the same. Andre looked over, and I watched his face as he recognized Toya. He didn't say anything he, stared at her. His face looked sad.

"Did you want to say hi to Andre?" Andrew asked since Toya was staring at him. "Andre come here." Andre walked over slowly, he had the saddest face. He grabbed his daddy's hand. "Do you remember her?" Andre shook his head yes.
Tears flew out of Toya's eyes. "It's been a long time." She said looking at Andre.
"How you doing little man, I'm Will." He said sticking his hand out for a shake. Looking at his face I knew the baby wasn't his. Then he looked at Toya, then back at Andrew. "These pregnancy hormones got her acting so crazy." Will attempted to explain.

"Is that right?" Andrew smiled a knowing smile.

Then Darryl walked in. "Look who's here!" He announced to the restaurant. Toya hissed!

Then she looked at Will, "we need to go!"

"Why you wanna leave so soon? Do I offend?" Darryl said sniffing himself. Toya attempted to stand up, and Darryl shoved her back down.

"A! Man! That's my wife." Will said in an authoritative tone.

"Andre go sit with your mommy and nana." Andrew said.

Toya sucked his teeth. "You have him calling her mommy?"

"Yea, she takes care of him. Loves him like a mother should love her son. You have a problem with that?" Andrew said

"Why would you have a problem with that?" Will asked Toya. She shook her head and put her eyes on the floor.

"Ask her again!" Darryl said with a smile

She turned her voice really sweet. "Baby can we discuss this later? Lets go!"

"Un huh! Naw! It's about to get interesting in 5, 4, 3, 2," Darryl said right as Derrick walked in.

Toya started crying. I looked at Amber, her face was sad but she stayed back in her corner.

"What is going on here?" Will said not understanding any of this.

Derrick looked Will up and down then he turned to Toya. "We been looking for you." Toya pleaded with her eyes. "Malcolm wants you. You know you messed up right! You sent a boy to do a man's job!"

"I don't know what you're talking about." Toya said staring at the wall with her face all twisted.

"You don't know what I'm talking about?" Then he grabbed her arm.

Will attempted to get up. Andrew pushed him back down in his seat. "Naw man, you need to hear this. Be cool and we won't have any problems." Will looked confused and scared. He gestured to say he was cool.

The baby started crying. Toya reached for the baby, Derrick squeezed her arm tighter. He looked at Will, "you better get your baby!"

"His baby?" Darryl laughed

"What?" Will asked angry

"I don't know why you would be stupid enough to come here! You were doing well for a minute. Didn't nobody know where you were."

"What's going on LaToya?" Will yelled at her.

"Ooh! You hear how he called her LaToya? Who does that?" Darryl said laughing. He laughed like he was in the middle of a comedy skit.

In a sweet tone she said, "baby, I..."

Darryl cut her off. "Psshh! She's about to lie to you again." He said as he sat down at the other end of the table. "She used to go with my brother." Darryl said pointing at Andrew who was still standing behind him.

"I know that, she told me he was her ex." Will said

"Did she tell you about their son?" Darryl asked

Toya started crying, and Will looked at her with a betrayed look. "That's your son? That's why you don't want him calling her momma?"

"Oh but wait! There's more." Darryl said with a smile. Then he said to her. "I CAN'T STAND YOU! I'VE NEVER LIKED YOU! YOU ARE GETTING EVERYTHING YOU DESERVE RIGHT NOW!" Toya kept her head down. "That baby you're holding, yea that's not even your baby." Darryl said matter of factly.

"Whose baby is this?" He said still caressing the baby.

Toya didn't look up. "I doubt this one is yours either." Darryl said pointing at her stomach.

"Who's the father?" He yelled at Toya. The baby started crying again.

"Steve" she said very lowly

"Your cousin?" Will said. All the guys looked at him like he was the stupidest person in the room. "Is that my baby?"

"I don't know." She said through tears.

"Oh and the police is looking for her. She got two counts of attempted murder hanging over her head." Darryl said

"What?"

"Get this, she flew into a jealous rage over my brother and some girl he used to toss. She tried to run them off the road over in Orinda."

"The hit and run you told me about?" Will asked putting it altogether. "This is why we're moving? You're running from the police?"

"Ok so check it meanwhile, she keeps trying to put people up to hurting my sister-in-law. Why, because if she can't have Drew nobody can. Now I know you don't know who Malcolm is, but he don't play. She knows this, but ask me why she messing with him? I guess she's hoping to plea bargain her way out of a possible life sentence because she knows she messed up. The question is, does she walk out of here?"

Will's face was so hurt while he held the baby. He kept staring at Toya. "This is all true, isn't it?" Toya kept her head to the ground. The front of her shirt was wet from all the tears.

The owner of the restaurant came out; he shook Andrew's hand. "I just wanted to let you know, we did call the police. This is Oakland, but they should be here soon." The owner said

"Alright man, thanks." Andrew said

Derrick pulled Toya in to him. "You better pray the police get here before Malcolm does."

"LaToya what did I do to deserve this? I love you!"

I felt bad for Will. He believed everything she told him. Why wouldn't he? Another man messed up by a scandalous female in the world.

"Where's Steve?" Darryl asked

"I don't know!" She said

"Why do you like that fool? He's an idiot who thinks he knows so much." Darryl asked

Toya started breathing. "I think my water just broke!" Derrick released her arm and she stood up. Water gushed on the floor, her pants were wet.

"Did you throw your water on your pants?" Darryl said

"Naw man, there's no ice. I think it did, Eeewwllll!" Derrick said backing up.

"Please let me take her to the hospital." Will pleaded.

Andrew stepped back. "Go!"

Andre was eating his quesadilla not really paying attention. Will and Toya hurried out the door. Will was calling someone as they got in the car. He strapped the baby in, and then he got in the driver's seat. You could tell he was yelling at Toya. Of course the police showed up five minutes later. Darryl told them to check the hospitals. Amber and I didn't say a word as Andrew, Derrick, and Darryl came back to our table and proceeded to eat like nothing happened.

That night when we went home Andrew and I were both really quiet. While Andrew bathed Andre, I took the bag with Yussef's clothes out of the car. I put the bag at the top of my closet in the far back corner. Then I took a bath, in the tub all I could think about was what Steve's reaction was to Toya telling him she was pregnant. Again I asked myself why was it ok for her to have his child and it was the end of the world that I was pregnant? Maybe he was in love with her, and only liked me. Or only tolerated me. But if that were true I don't know how he would justify all that he's done to me. He had to have more than like for me. I couldn't understand it at all, but not understanding had me feeling hurt. I try not to think about how old my child would be right now. I'm thankful that I'm not forever tied to Steve, but I'm devastated that my child had to die before I got away from him.

CHAPTER 42

"Welcome back!" Dafina said as Nicole, Joy, Veronica, and I walked in the door.

"Thank you" we all said

"So where's my men?"

"They're on their way. They had to have a party bus because we had one." I said rolling my eyes.

Nihjia came down with Cassondra. "Hello! Hello!" Cassondra said

We all hugged and said our hellos. Then the party bus arrived. The men were all pumped up when they came in. Amber and Sophia rode with the men. "This is little Andy?" Cassondra said putting her hands on his face and pulling his forehead to hers.

You could see the light bulb go off for Andrew. "Oh snap! I do remember you!" He said laughing, "you always put my forehead on yours. I remember, you used to always sing a silly song too." Andrew was searching his brain to remember.

"I got a dimple in my knee and it's just for me, and I like it. Oh yes I like it!" Cassondra sang.

"Yea! That's it!" Andrew said, he was blushing so hard; if he turned anymore red he'd burst.

"And here are my other sons. This is Derrick my no nonsense son. And Darryl my jokester." Cassondra hugged and kissed them.

"Who else do we have?" Cassondra asked

"This is my brother Terrence," I said

"My cousins Jeff and Joseph. This little man is AJ, Anthony junior. And this is my son Andre."

"Oh Andy! He looks EXACTLY like you! Hello Andre."

"Hi!" Andre said blushing like his father. Cassondra hugged Lil Anthony, Terrence, Joseph, and Jeff.

"This is my soon to be father-in-law, my best friend Hubby, and last but definitely not least my boy Anthony. He's been helping me grow up a lot." Andrew said.

Cassondra hugged everyone then she placed us in Nihjia's capable hands. This time we went downstairs. Nihjia showed

Andrew the tux's we picked previously. The problem with that particular style was it wasn't available for purchase. I told him I didn't want the colors to change, but I was curious to see what style he chose. I thought the men were uninterested in their fashion and would go along with what we said. Wrong! Again Nihjia had us pick out our lunch orders, champagne was opened and our men modeled the styles they picked. Darryl said he had to be able to tootsie roll in the tux. We all fell out laughing. Andrew actually did an impressive job picking out the tuxes, shirts, vest, ties, and shoes. While everyone was eating Andrew picked silver flask for his groom's men. He wanted them engraved with each person's initials. I tiptoed away to Dafina's desk to schedule an appointment to come back tomorrow without my girls to find something special for them. Even though picking out tux's for the guys was a lot easier, it still took a long time. The guys were dancing and carrying on. They were a lot of fun nonetheless. When we finally finished the guys went bowling. They had it all setup as part of their male bonding experience. Amber and Sophia hitched a ride with us to the Cheesecake House in Union Square. It only took us thirty minutes to get a table, and I said only thirty minutes cause this place can sometimes have a two-hour wait at least on the weekend. The place was crowded, full of tables. Veronica was such a little lady even as a baby. I found myself all day finding comfort in spending time with her. I know it's stupid, but seeing Steve's son only made my belly feel empty. So spending the day with Veronica was just what the doctor ordered. When I realized I spaced out again, I excused myself and went to the bathroom. Why am I tripping in five months I was gonna be married and working on my own pregnancy. Finally I'd feel full and complete myself. In the mirror I tried to stick my stomach out to see what I would look like. There's nothing like doing something stupid and complete strangers walk in on you for you to feel stupid. As I washed my hands I remembered talking to Shirley in here. How she couldn't understand what I was trying to tell her. When I walked back to the table I pulled out my chair and a apple jolly rancher rolled around in the middle. I looked around, but I didn't see any one who looked familiar. "Did someone move my chair?"

"Other than you? Not that I know, what's wrong?" Amber asked as everyone looked at me.

"Nothing, I was wondering." I said as I grabbed the candy and then I sat down. I felt nervous; Yussef can't be following me around. It's too dangerous for him to do that now. Even if I don't see him doesn't mean others don't. I haven't brought him up since the day I came home, but it didn't go unnoticed that Andrew wouldn't promise me that Yussef would be fine. And especially since I've been sad he looks at me. I can tell he wants to ask, but doesn't. I'd normally volunteer my sad thoughts, but since he's been keeping his all bottled up, I don't say anything. I know my sadness will go away once I'm pregnant; it's hard to wait. We're so close! I looked up at Joy; she mouthed, "are you ok"?

I nodded yes, but I knew she wasn't convinced. I ordered another Tokyo iced tea. After my fourth tea, I felt a little numb which is what I was shooting for. Outside of Joy I don't think anyone noticed how many drinks I had. I sat there debating whether to have another. Our waitress came out to clear out the dinner dishes.

"Can I interest you all in some cheesecake?"

"Of course! We need menus though!" Amber volunteered.

Then the waitress looked at me, "would you like another?"

My tipsy state said, "YES!"

She brought my drink out and then she said, "this is Jeremy, he's gonna serve you for the rest of the night. Please let him know if you need anything. I didn't turn to look at him I was staring at my drink. He put menus down in front of each person. But when he put mine down he put a apple jolly rancher underneath it. When I saw I the candy my head popped up. It was Yussef and he winked at me, but she said Jeremy. Suddenly I wished I was sober so I could take it all in. Then I wondered if I was hallucinating. I put my hand in my face, I don't know why.

"Excuse me, what's your name?"

He touched his nametag, "Jeremy" he smiled again. "Can I bring you something?"

I shook my head no. I looked at everybody at the table; they were all looking at me.

"What's wrong? You look like you saw a ghost!" Sophia said

"Oh" I tried to think of something quick. "I think my teas are getting to me." I said as I took another sip.

Everyone went back to their menus except for Joy. She was eyeing me, so I pretended not to notice. I was trying to figure out where Yussef went.

Knowing if I didn't say something she'd follow me, I asked Joy to order a slice of snickers cheesecake for me while I ran to the bathroom. She gave me a look, but she agreed. I really did have to pee, so I hurried. I put a cold paper towel on my face in hopes to wake me up. Maybe I was tripping maybe I was imagining that the guy was Yussef. When I exited the bathroom I expected to see Yussef somewhere along the way, but I made it back to the table without a hitch, I realized my mind was playing tricks on me. My cheesecake was waiting for me. So I dug in.

"Can I get anything else for you ladies?" Yussef I mean Jeremy was back.

"Yes, I would like to order a cake for home." Amber said still looking at her menu

"Me too" Sophia said

"Me three, well maybe not a whole cake, a couple slices for the road." Nicole said

Yussef walked over and one by one he took their orders, no one looked at him. I stared at him to make sure I was seeing straight, and then I started looking around the restaurant. I still didn't know who was following me if anyone at all.

"And for you?" he said standing besides me.
I shot him a look like what are you doing. Joy shot me a look like what's going on. Yussef smiled at me. "My son likes Oreo so I will take one for him. Amber would you agree that Andrew likes the lemon raspberry or lemon cello?"

"Hhmmmm, girl I don't know. Get him both, he's always liked lemon." She said still looking down.

"As his mother you should know best." I said, and then I looked at Yussef. "My mother-in-law knows best."

Still smiling he said, "and for you?"

"Snickers and Reese's"

He eyed me, "both?"

"Yes, I'm a little stressed, both." I said

"As you wish, would you like another?" He said pointing to my drink.

"One more." He flashed me a look, "one more and I'm done! Promise!" I could barely see straight as it was. All the sudden I didn't want to feel anything.

"How many of those have you had?" Nicole asked, she realized she hadn't been paying attention.

Suddenly all conversation at our table stopped and all eyes were on me. Yussef sat the fresh drink in front of me. I picked up the drink rolled my eyes and drank. Yussef gave everyone their take home bags. Then he set the bill in the middle of the table. I snatched the billfold first so no one could look for my drinks. I took out Andrew's Amex black card and put it in the billfold. I didn't even look at the total. Everyone was eyeing me. "What?" I said looking around the table not really feeling my lips.

"You've been acting weird all day!" Nicole said

"I thought it was just me, but she has, hasn't she." Sophia said

"What?" I blew air, "no I haven't!" Amber and Joy looked at me. "Honey, what's going on?" Sophia said in a tender tone.

"It's Toya isn't it?" Amber said

I wasn't gonna do it. I wasn't gonna melt down right in the middle of the restaurant. "You guys really know how to kill a buzz!" I said picking up my drink. When the card and bill came back the gratuity was already included. I signed the receipt and finished my drink. I wanted to carry the now sleeping Veronica out, but in my drunken state I knew better so I grabbed Joy's purse and diaper bag. Everyone was quiet as we walked out the restaurant. I didn't even look for Yussef, but I was starting to see double anyways. Funny how when I was seeing double I clearly saw two guys following us. They looked familiar, but maybe normally I look too hard and I don't see them. We piled into Joy's SUV. Joy turned the radio off. "Ok Tracy, what's going on?"

"I thought we were supposed to be having fun." Everybody was quiet. "Guys please! I'm having a hard time right now. No big deal. It's life."

Everybody remained quiet; eventually Joy turned the radio on. When we got to my house Amber took me in the guest room and shut the door. "Spill it!"
I thought about holding back but I was about to explode, plus the alcohol was making it difficult to be quiet. "I don't want to put you in the middle of my stupid life drama."

"Spill it!"

"Andrew left me to get back with Toya. I never really came to terms with that. But then I got back with my ex."

"Ok" Amber said following me.

"Steve"

She gasped! She put her hand up to her mouth, "NO!"

"Yes, we didn't end on good terms." Tears started pouring out of my eyes. "I was pregnant and he was acting like a nightmare. I needed him to be kind to me, hold me, something. But no he treated me like I was a Toya, stressed me out until I miscarried. I sent him a letter about it and moved on. I don't know when they got together. I come back and find out she had Andrew's baby ok. Then when I see her pregnant my gut told me it was Steve's baby. So she gets to have my man, and ex? It's stupid to think about such things, I know. But why does that heifer get to have all the babies, and I have none?"

"Sweetheart you're about to marry the man of your dreams. You can have as many babies as you want. Plus you have the love of a good man. All her scheming will not end well for her. That girl is wildly unhappy, and constantly starting drama just because she's unhappy." Then she thought about it for a minute. "Did you ever reach out for help with the loss of your child?"

"Why, women lose babies all the time. Truth be told I was devastated when I found out. I didn't want to have Steve's baby, I was just coming to terms with the fact that I needed to break up with him. Then I found out about the baby. Amber he was so horrible! It just hurts that a part of me had to die because of him." I said

"What if it wasn't because of him? A lot of women miscarry in the first trimester without any reason or anyone's fault."

"Then it would be about the way he treated me."

"Do you want to be with him?" Amber asked

"NO!"

"Then why are you looking back?"

"The woman who keeps causing me heartache has given birth to a son by both of the men I've loved at one time or another. I'm sorry but that hurts me. I don't want to be with Steve, I wish he'd leave me alone."

"But here's what I'm trying to get you to see. You're letting her games and ridiculousness cause you to hurt yourself. She wants what you have! She don't want any of those kids she got."

"I know, and I love Andre! I couldn't imagine Andrew and I without him. I'm not saying that I wish he wasn't here or anything like that. I LOVE that little boy!" The tea had me balling out of control. "I'm tired. I want her to go away."

"You and Malcolm feel the same way. But I have a feeling your answers to the Toya problem are totally different."

"What's the deal with him? I don't even understand how you two were ever together."

"What do you mean?" Amber asked

"I don't exactly understand the family dynamics over here. You guys have so many unspoken things."

She started to say something when we heard the once again very pumped up men come in the door. We stood there trying to listen to all the noise, there was laughter and silliness. Amber stuck her head out, seconds later Andrew, Derrick, and Darryl came rushing in the room and shutting the door. They were all just as wasted as I was if not more. Their eyes were red and sleepy looking. "Where's Tracy's dad?" Amber asked

"We dropped him off at his house." Derrick said laughing

"Then we made a stop." Darryl said cracking up.

"Where's my grand baby?" Amber asked

"Him and AJ knocked out on the bus before we left the city." Amber opened the door and sloppy intoxicated men were everywhere. Andre and AJ were sleeping on the couch. Joy was shaking her head at Anthony as he professed his undying love for her. Hubby was all hands as Nicole led him out the door. Jeff and Joseph agreed to help Joy out the door. Joy lovingly tended to her man; Sophia carried the sleeping Veronica out the door while AJ sleep walked to the car. Amber carried Andre upstairs while all three of her boys had the most hilarious conversation that I couldn't follow. When Sophia and her brothers came back inside the conversation became even more hilarious. They told me stories about when they were growing up and all the fun they had together. They kept forgetting parts of their stories, which would cause more laughter. Eventually Sophia and Amber loaded up their boys to go. Andrew went upstairs and I set the alarm. Cain was in his usual spot, and Eve was by my side. When we walked in the room Andrew turned on soft music. He was waiting for me. He gently but firmly took me in his arms. We slow danced forever, I melted in his arms.

****

The next day I was back at Cassondra's by myself. I used Andrew's card to pay for my bridesmaids and mother of the bride & groom dresses, shoes, jewelry, and accessories. I told Nihjia about the office party I was attending next Saturday with Andrew. She showed me a few dresses. I decided on a gold colored dress. It was long and elegant with just a touch of sexy. Since it was a work function I didn't want to shoot for outright sexy. The shoes Nihjia paired with my dress were completely gorgeous. Her husband

Jaden and little girls stopped by. Her little family was lovely. I paid extra to have the alterations completed in a few hours. At the Powell street mall my watchers stood out like sore thumbs. For their sakes I pretended not to notice them. I walked around Norm's, when you have the money to buy anything you want in the store, buying takes on a whole new experience. I used to look at the clothes and shoes and wish I could afford them. Now I look at most of them as a waste. Why spend so much on stuff you would rarely wear because they cost so much. Plus I never want Andrew to feel like I'm going crazy with his money. I walked around Bloomies; I found the most beautiful clutch to complete my ensemble. It was small and covered in rhinestones and sequins. I left Bloomies after I bought it for fear I might find something else I needed. I went down to the food court and got the largest sized gelato they had. It still looked small to me; I paid eight dollars for it, huffed, and walked out the Mall onto Market street. I stumbled upon my old home Old Sailor. I walked around the store remembering this place as my home. Finally it was time to pick up my dress. As I walked back towards the garage, I glanced back to see if my followers were still there. When I looked forward I saw a guy with a brown leather jacket on and dreads. He didn't walk like Yussef, but I still wondered if it was him. My pace quickened. The guy walked at a quick but strolling pace. He took the stairs, so I took the stairs. On the fourth level where I parked he came out of the stairway as well. I was on his heels; my followers were still coming up the stairs. "Yussef?" I said lowly.

The guy turned around it wasn't him. I felt disappointed, but relieved all at the same time.

He smiled, "no" then looked me up and down.

"I'm sorry I thought you were someone else."

"No problem, but I wish I was him."

"Have a good day." I said as I hurried away. My followers were coming out the stairway when I went in the opposite direction of the guy.

One of the guys continued after me, and the other went after the guy. I got in my car and he got in his. I drove around the corner and the guy looked spooked! He had his hands up and he was breathing deeply. The other guy was hopping in the car that was following me. I felt bad for the leather jacket guy. But I drove on and I went back to Cassondra's. I parked in the garage across the street from her boutique, as there was no more parking in front of the boutique any more. I grabbed the last spot on the second level. As I entered the elevator I noticed my followers driving past my car. Inside the boutique I tipped everyone very handsomely for all of their efforts. I even tipped Dafina for waiting with her sister and the tailor. Everyone was all smiles as we left the boutique. Nihjia and Dafina watched as I crossed the street. I stepped into the elevator, and there was Yussef.

"WHAT ARE YOU DOING???" I screamed.

"Ssshhhh!" He said as he pushed the button to close the doors.

"Yussef! You can't pop up anymore, I don't know what Andrew will do."

"What is the dress for?" He asked disregarding my excitement.

"Are you listening to me? I'm serious!"

"I know you are."

"Then why are you here?"

"You didn't look good, I wanted to check on you, and see how you are."

"I'm fine!"

"No you're not." He said looking me in my eyes. Then he stopped the elevator.

My heart was pounding. "Yussef, you're always hinting that Andrew is dangerous. Why do you keep risking your life just to freak me out!"?

"I told you I will always be around."

"Yea, but please not at the risk of your life."

He blew air. "This is truly a thankless job."

"It's not your job to protect me any more."

He stared at me. I know I was being mean, but I was scared for his life. I was happy to see him and know that he was ok. But to even think about what he was risking just to see me, didn't seem worth it. "I can't leave until I know you're gonna be ok. I know things have been really tense."

"How do you know it's been tense?"

"I know about Toya and Malcolm. I've known for some time."

"Ok..." Then I asked, "where's Steve?" He gave me a weird look. "Andrew said he's her weak spot."

"Ok so he's hers, what's his?" Yussef said

"I don't know." I said

"Ok so while those wild cards are still out there I can't sit back in good conscience not knowing whether you're ok or not."

"Yussef if I don't go there's gonna be problems. I'm ok, please let me go."

"Ok" he released the elevator. Then he pressed the fifth floor button as well.

I fixed my face and stepped off the elevator. I got in the car, my heart was racing and I felt horrible for seeming so unthankful. But in that moment I couldn't show anything but fear. If anyone knew who they were looking at last night, it could've been major drama. Andrew kept asking me if I was in love with Yussef. I'm in love with Andrew! Everyone knows it, but do I have love for Yussef? Let me be honest and say yes. It's hard to explain, but I've only ever felt safe with the two of them. Steve has only shown real heart about hurting me, never about protecting me. And why would Steve be her weakness? Unless she fell in love with him.

When I got home that fancy car was outside. I parked in the garage, when I walked in the house Andre was watching a movie. When he saw me with all my bags and garment bag he hopped off the couch and grabbed my two bags. He is such a little gentleman. As we walked past the living room Andrew and Malcolm were talking both of their tones were serious. We went upstairs and put my things in the closet. I gave him a big hug and kiss thanking him for helping me. He happily hopped down the stairs and back to his movie. I walked into the living room I hugged and kissed Andrew and then I gave Malcolm a hug. He was awkward about me hugging him but he didn't reject it. Andrew was grinning wide about his father's fumble. Then I went back in the family room with Andre. Andre was watching some show that he was totally into. When Andrew and Malcolm were finished Malcolm came to say goodbye to us. Andrew was thoughtful for the rest of the evening. I told him I got a dress for Saturday night. That made him smile, but only for a moment. He went back to his thoughts. I went to bed long before he did, when he got in the bed I slightly woke to him telling me how much he loved me just above a whisper. He kept kissing me and hugging me. He was troubled about something, but if I asked I knew he wouldn't answer me. At work all week I made sure conversation stayed short and sweet with Neil. Every time conversation would get light hearted and off the work topic I would hear Yussef's voice telling me that the poor guy only stood to last a year. That actually made me feel bad. So this time around I'm being really careful.

Wednesday night my brother called he wanted to take Andre to a forty-niner game. Although Andrew was grooming him to be a Raider fan he said it was ok. Then he spent the rest of the week highlighting the Raiders and saying why he thought they ruled. We made arrangements with Amber to take Andre when the game was over.

Friday I went to Jovance salon in Hilltop to get a facial, manicure, and pedicure. After I was done I dropped by Andrew's office. He was deep into work, but he was so happy to see me. Since the office was just about empty we made out for a while. Then I left to pick up Andre, Andrew said he'd be home later. Andre and I went out to dinner and then we went to the movies. When we got home Andrew was running on the treadmill. He seemed disturbed all week but he wouldn't talk about it. I put Andre to sleep, and then I stood in the doorway watching Andrew's body as he worked out. He was in a zone and he was really intense. I stood there watching his muscles tighten and release. He was glistening, and his curls loosened with all the sweat. His shirt was drenched, and he kept going and going. I could tell he was in pain, but he kept pushing through. I wished he would tell me what was going on.

I got up in the morning and I went back to Jovance this time to get my hair done. This time for a complete change of pace I had them straighten my hair, which beautifully fell down my back. Then I had Michelle put the front up in a roll and left the back down. Loving the look, I kept looking at my hair in the mirror. Then I made my way to the Makeup Store on fourth street in Berkeley. Paul did my makeup. He did a fabulous job. I got his information after I told him about my upcoming wedding. Andrew called me to check on my progress and to let me know he was getting his hair cut. Which meant he'd be home a lot later but that was perfect cause it gave plenty of time to get ready in a leisurely manner. I showered and made sure I was ready to walk out the door by five pm. I hung out in the guest room so that I could make a grand entrance when Andrew was ready. I stood in the mirror admiring myself. Eve stood at my side as if she was cosigning that I looked nice. We heard Andrew come through the garage. "I'm late!" He yelled

"I know!" I replied

"I'll be ready in a minute!" He said as I heard him rushing up the stairs. He quickly hopped in the shower. In thirty minutes he was showered, lotioned, and dressed. He knocked on the door, "ok I'm ready". I could hear the smile in his voice.

I stood in the middle of the floor. "Come in!" I said

I stood there slightly posing but trying not to look like I was posing. He slowly opened the door, and then he gasped when he saw me. "You are beautiful!" He said almost breathless.

"Thank you! You look good yourself!" Oh my goodness did he, but he always does. He had on a black suit, crisp white shirt, black tie, white handkerchief, and a fresh haircut. Black and white never looked so good.

He kissed me like it was killing him not to. Then we got in his car and headed to the Blackhawk museum in Danville. He held my hand the whole way there. He seemed a little nervous which was unlike him especially for work events, but I didn't really pay it too much attention. When we got there the cars in the parking lot were either fancy like Malcolm's car, car service, or limos. We were definitely in the big leagues, especially when Andrew's car was the hoopty of the parking lot. He opened my door, and then he put my arm around his. He kissed me on the cheek, "stay close ok." Yea he definitely looked nervous when he said that.
I kissed him on his cheek, and I said "ok".

Everyone was dressed up, some even wore tuxes. Andrew found our nametags on the table. Then we found our assigned seats. Andrew introduced me to his colleagues at the table. Most of them were older and white. I know shouldn't have, but I scanned the room to see how many other black couples were there. There were a few interracial couples, but only one other sister there with a brother and they were older. There were maybe two other couples there about our age. Dinner was served and the ambiance was nice. The classic cars all around the museum added a classy touch to the evening. While we ate dinner the host of the evening went over the financials, I didn't understand anything they were talking about. But since I appeared to be the only one who didn't, I tried my best to look like I followed the information. At one point they showed a chart reflecting growth performance and they said it was all due to Andrew Wallace! Everyone erupted into applause, and Andrew stood and took a bow. I couldn't stop smiling at him; my baby was truly the man. Once they moved the spotlight off of him, I looked up at the curtains on top it looked like someone was up there. I assumed it was the personnel handling the lighting. Once the presentation was finished they encouraged us to take advantage of the full bars and to make use of the dance floor. Almost immediately people came over to congratulate Andrew on

his success. He graciously accepted their praise and then he made sure to introduce me to everyone. When the crowd dissipated for a moment he grabbed my hand and led me to the dance floor.
"So you really are the man I see." I said into his ear.

I could hear his smile. "I do my job very very well." Then he stopped dancing, "here comes my boss."

I turned to see a middle aged gentleman. "I'm so sorry sweetheart, I need to steal your fiancé for a moment."

Then Todd a colleague he introduced me to earlier asked, "Andrew would it be ok with you if I danced with your lovely fiancé until you come back?"
I could tell Andrew wanted to say no, but his boss wanted him to go, and made it clear he didn't want him to bring me with him. In defeat he agreed. Todd talked more than he danced. He was singing Andrew's praises the entire time, which made me relax a little. Someone came over to Todd, and our dance was over.
As I walked to our table, someone grabbed my wrist. It wasn't Andrew's touch, my heart dropped when I saw that it was Steve. He had on a suit; he looked like he belonged here. Not wanting to cause a scene I tried to pull my hand away, but his grip was firm. I noticed a few people looking so I let him lead me to the dance floor. He had the biggest smile on his face. "You look beautiful!" He said taking me in his arms. My body was stiff and uninviting; he acted as though he didn't notice. "Why do you look so surprised to see me? You had to know I was gonna pop up sooner or later. Besides I saw you look at me when I was upstairs."

"Steve if you leave now you may still live to see tomorrow."

"Who cares about tomorrow when I have you right now? Your man ain't gonna do nothing with all these people here."

"Please let me go." I said

"Why do you act like you're scared of me? I don't know how we got here? You were supposed to be my wife, not engaged to mister mafia."

"You told me you were going to kill me."

"That was after you started acting scared of me. You up and abandoned me. Why did you leave me like that?"

"Like what?"

"You tell me you're pregnant then you disappear. You sent me a letter telling me you miscarried, but then I see you with a baby. The next time I see you, I wanna talk to you and you have mister mafia beat me up. I thought we were in love, I thought you were the one."

"That's how you treat someone you're in love with?"

"Used to be, you never told me anything different. I've had some time to soul search, and now I get how that was messed up. But why didn't you say anything."

"Steve you and I are not a good mix. You lack the patience or commitment to be the man I need you to be. I don't want you pretending to be someone you're not." I said

"You hurt me when you left me like that. And then your scared act hurt me too. Why don't you understand how much I love you?"

"You don't love me Steve. You loved the crap I used to take off you, but you don't love me."

He squeezed my wrist. "How you gonna tell me? I always came to you first whenever something was going on in my life! I could show you all my weaknesses and not feel like I was open to be hurt. You used to be there for me." His voice cracked a little. "I know my reaction to the baby was less than ideal. But I wasn't ready."

"Then suddenly you became ready with Toya?"

He smiled, "why miss Tracy you sound a little jealous."

"You traumatized me! I was your woman, not some hoe you met at the club. Or one of your one night stands, and you..." I grabbed my composure. I wasn't gonna give him the satisfaction of one tear.

"So disappearing was pay back for the way I treated you? You never gave me a chance to make it right. I know you miss me. Mister mafia can't possibly put it down like me." I didn't say anything, why dignify such ridiculousness with an answer. He laughed, "Toya told me a lot about him. She told me how you were begging him at your friend's wedding to get back with you. How when you were supposed to be at the gym you were trying to push up on him. She told me how you would call him all hours of the night when she was pregnant. She told me the truth about you and how you always put on airs like you're a good girl, but you're no better than her. At least she's honest."

"You mean honest with you, her husband thought both of those babies were his."

"That's not my fault. I told her I wasn't getting married and I couldn't afford no babies. So she married him, didn't change anything between us. I know her past is sketchy, but once she led me to you I couldn't cut her off." Then he closed his eyes "you feel so good."

I looked around the room, I didn't see Andrew anywhere, but I saw Yussef. He was over in a corner watching. He nodded at me when I saw him. "Steve, I gotta pee." I said trying to walk away. My heart was still pounding extremely hard.

"Yea right! I know this is probably the last time I'll get to hold you in my arms. Your mafia dude gonna have you surrounded like you're Michael Jackson. I want this moment to last as long as it can." He opened his eyes. "I got an idea. Why don't you put down the good girl routine for one night? I'll put it on you one last time for old times sake."

He couldn't be serious. "You disgust me!" I said

Then Andrew walked into the room. His pace slowed once he realized that Steve had me. He looked around the room. He saw Yussef first, and then his eyes danced around the room some more. He walked over to the table and grabbed my clutch and wrap. I could tell he was trying to think his thoughts through. He calmly walked over to us on the dance floor where I was being held against my will. Steve's grip on my wrist got tighter, my hand was turning white. Andrew walked up to us, "you are the stupidest somebody I've ever met in my life! I know you realize you are dead don't you!" His face was stone.

"Ah nigga what you gonna do? All these white people here, we're in the middle of San Ramon! They don't play your Oakland games out here."

Andrew grabbed the pressure point under his arm. "Let her go!" Steve's grip released immediately like it was an involuntary reaction to Andrew's touch. Andrew put his arm around me. "The only reason you're still alive is because you're so stupid! But you might as well start counting the moments left cause they're limited." I looked back at Yussef but he was gone. "Lets go." He said to me holding my hand. A few people glanced our way but for the most part no one was even looking. My heart was pounding out of my chest. Steve's face was furious, I guess he wasn't finished. As we walked towards the door, Andrew's boss asked him if we were leaving. Andrew chatted with him as if nothing was wrong. I stood there with the fakest smile plastered on my face. Steve walked outside ahead of us. As we walked towards the door Andrew took out his cellphone and he texted someone. He grabbed my hand to lead me out the door and I hesitated. He stopped and looked at me. "Andrew I'm afraid to go out there!" A tear ran down my face.

He wiped my tear away. "It's gonna be ok, trust me!" He said looking me in my eyes. He kissed me on the forehead, and then he opened the door. I let him lead me although I was scared like you wouldn't believe. The walk way seemed long and cold. When we reached the parking lot a black car pulled up. A guy got out and he walked over to the trunk. He waited for Andrew to walk over. He brought me with him then the guy opened the trunk. Steve had a little blood on his temple probably from where someone hit him, and he was knocked out. He was breathing so I knew he wasn't dead.

"The stupidest somebody I know!" The guy said

"Call Malcolm, let him know. And Jeremy is around here somewhere find him!"

That was the name Yussef used at cheesecake last week. I looked at Andrew, he was beyond angry. Tears came to my eyes, what was he gonna do to him. Andrew slammed the trunk shut. The guy got back in his car, and drove off. Andrew already knew what my face looked like so he didn't even look at me. He just held my hand. When he opened the car door for me I looked him in his eyes, "please!" He closed his eyes and shook his head no.

When he got in the car, he put out his hand for me to hold it. But I didn't give him my hand. He started up his car, he looked at me, he was completely annoyed. He started driving, he drove really slowly. Minutes after we were on the freeway his cellphone rang. He put it on speaker, "we don't have him" my heart sang a cheer. "But I think we know what car he was in. We should have him by morning." I wanted to scream.

"You've said this before! Don't fail me!" Then Andrew hung up.

"Andrew PLEASE! Let him go!" I pleaded

He ignored me and turned on the radio. He turned it up just enough so that he didn't have to listen to my tears. Then he turned the music down. "How did you end up on the dance floor with Steve?"

"Todd was called away, as I walked to our table Steve grabbed me before I made it off the dance floor. I don't even know where he came from. Please Andrew!"

"Who are you pleading for?"

"Yussef"

"I thought so. I've tried to be patient with him, but he knows better and he keeps popping up anyways. He knows if I'm laying off him he needs to lay low. But he's not doing that either. These fools are ridiculous!" He grumbled

"I'm sorry I'm such a problem for you!" I said through tears. "I'm sorry I make your already complicated life a more complicated one. Maybe if I go away then you can get back to your simple life with a new female every week!"

"Are you kidding me! Seriously the drama right now!" He yelled! "Think about it Tracy! This isn't really about you!" He switched to the 680 freeway to Sacramento instead of using the 24 to Oakland and San Francisco freeway at the junction. "Regardless if you were here or not, I'm done with Toya! I've been done with her. She would be causing these problems no matter who I was with. My father wants her head! I can't and I won't protect her anymore! For whatever reason she's weak when it comes to that fool. And he's stupid enough to have a weakness for you, when you don't want him. Having him she's gonna come out of hiding. I'm out of it, I can't protect her. The mother of my son is just about dead. And you're sitting over there thinking this is all about you!" He was fuming!

"So you used me as bait?" He didn't say anything. We crossed the Benicia-Martinez bridge. "Andrew!" I said

"Yes" He said

I sat there quiet waiting for more detail, but I guess he already gave it to me. "That's why you were nervous?" He didn't answer me; pretty soon we were on interstate 80 headed towards Sacramento. I sat there not knowing how to feel about that. "But why does anything have to happen to Yussef?"

"Why do you advocate for him?"

"Because he's my friend. I told you that."

"You should tell your friend to stay away. If you knew what was good for him."

"I have!"

His neck whipped at me, "WHEN?"

"Last time I saw him."

"When was that Tracy?" I couldn't tell him about Sunday. "Did you talk to him tonight?"

"No"

"So when then?"

"Where are we going?"

"Answer me!" He demanded. I sat there quiet cause I never confirmed or denied that I was with him that night, so I couldn't say that either. He growled in frustration, then his foot got heavy and we were flying down the interstate. Pretty soon I saw the Arco Arena to my right. He got off the freeway and we drove through the Natomas suburbs of beautiful new homes. We pulled up to a gate, he entered a code and he drove to a house with a ton of cars outside. Joseph came to the car. He got two suitcases out the trunk. "Hey Tracy!" He said giving me a kiss on the cheek. "Come on in the party is still in full swing." Andrew stood next to the driver's door; he had his head on the car. I felt bad for him. As much as he was trying to put on a brave face I knew he was torn up about what was happening with Toya. I walked over to him and I rubbed his back. I didn't know if he would accept me touching him or not. He grabbed me and hugged me super tight. "I'll take these to the guest room you guys come on in when you're ready." Joseph said then he disappeared into the house.

Andrew was crying harder than I've ever seen him cry before. I cried with him, we were outside for a while.

Then as if he appeared out of nowhere Malcolm put his hand on Andrew's shoulder. Both of us jumped cause we thought we were alone. He hugged over me, so now I was in the middle of their huddle. It was very dark in the middle and I saw no light. I was feeling claustrophobic, but my fear of Malcolm was greater so I suffered in silence. Andrew kept crying and I could feel the vibration from Malcolm patting Andrew's back with his big powerful hands.

"It's done!" Malcolm said, which made Andrew cry harder. I was crying too, partly because Andrew was crying so hard, and the other part because I needed air and I was too scared to say anything. "No son, not like that." Andrew's head popped up. Which gave me air! I wiggled from between them afraid that they were going to embrace again, I was afraid my hair was about to go back. "She has nothing! We turned her in, and him too for aiding and abetting. They're going away!" Malcolm said. And sure enough they hugged again, I was so happy I wasn't in the middle of that.

"Malcolm?" I said scared to ask, "what does that mean?"

"She's up for attempted double murder. She could spend the rest of her life in jail. Since Steve was stupid enough to take her in after she left the hospital knowing what she was up against, he's considered an accomplice to her crime. Whatever sentence she gets, he gets."

"They're gone?" I said smelling the air so much clearer.

He nodded. "Son, I know how messed up you were about this whole thing. I couldn't mess up twice." Then they hugged again.

That's when I heard Andrew tell his father he loved him. It shocked all of us, and that brought Malcolm to tears. I wanted to run, seeing big ole Malcolm breakdown was scary. But his big ole hand grabbed me and pulled me into their hug. At least this time I wasn't stuck in the middle.

Eventually Amber came outside. "What are you guys..."She stopped in her tracks, then she hurried over. "Oh my goodness! Malcolm are you crying?" Amber said in disbelief.

"Yes woman! Come here!" She came and he pulled her into our hug circle.

Then he let go. Andrew grabbed my hand. "Malcolm will you come to our wedding?"

Malcolm stood up tall and proud. "I would love to!"

"What's going on?" Amber asked

Seizing the opportunity to get away from those emotional men. I took Amber by the hand I explained the entire night to her. But I told her the way I had experienced it. By the end of the story she was exhausted. "You could've just said they got arrested." Amber said

"Now, where's the fun in that?" I said.

Surprisingly my makeup held up, and we went inside. Amber introduced me to her Aunt and Uncle, Sophia's parents. It was their anniversary party. All of Amber's siblings were there, and their children. They all kept telling me how excited they were about the wedding. When Andre saw me he jumped into my arms. He whispered to me that he wanted to be a Niners fan. I told him I think his father had all the heartache he could muster for one night.

CHAPTER 43

"Tracy, where are you?" Carina said her voice was panicked

"I'm picking up Joy and then we'll be on our way." I said completely annoyed. I knew things were going too well. Nihjia called to tell me everything had arrived. Carina was in the city inspecting for the ceremony. She called me frantic because the dresses came in the wrong color. She said they were powder blue instead of Royal Blue like I specifically said. I was almost in tears when I called Joy. She asked me to pick her up and we'd go together. I called her to tell her I was outside, but AJ answered the phone. He said she was in the bathroom. In my dramatics I parked my car and walked to the door while talking to AJ on the phone. He opened the door with a goofy look on his face. I walked in the door and everyone yelled "SURPRISE!!!!!!" I ran out the door. As I was running I realized that they said surprise and that there were bridal shower decorations everywhere. Everybody was hooting and hollering about my reaction to the surprise. I composed myself then I walked back in the house. People were literally on the floor laughing at me. And then to make matters worse they were video taping my reaction. As soon as the laughter calmed down they'd play it again. The house was decorated nicely, but when I went in the backyard it was beautiful. There were so many people there. Tara and Tia were even there. There were a lot of people from Amber's family there, she even had Cassondra, Nihjia & her daughters, and Dafina there (who hit it off nicely with Tia & Tara). A lot of my aunts and cousins as well. It was amazing that they all fit in Joy's house. I thought I had been keeping Joy and Carina plenty busy, I don't know when they found the time to do this. As I was still taking everything in Sister Harris, who I didn't even realize was there, came up to me. She gave me the biggest hug. "I understand that I have you to thank for the arrest of that girl." Sister Harris said softly to me with tears in her eyes. I couldn't say anything, I smiled. She hugged me again and thanked me over and over again. Then Nicole rescued me, she took me back to the middle of the party. We played games, the food was delicious, and it was really nice. The afternoon was lovely. Then it was gift opening time. Since I already had a furnished house everyone stuck to lingerie. I got some really nice things, none of the hardcore stuff. My mom bought us personalized champagne glasses. The day was really lovely; it was six weeks until the wedding, crunch time for real. While everyone chatted and finished eating I found myself in the corner watching everyone. I was excited to finally almost be Mrs. Andrew Wallace! But still I worried about Yussef; I hadn't seen him since that night. He said as long as I was in danger he was gonna be around. The last few months I hadn't been in danger. The last few months my life had returned to some normalcy. No more strangers posted outside my house, no more followers. I actually started running outside again. I still took one or both of the puppies with me when I ran, but it felt ok again. Andrew actually called me more often to check-in and see where I was. From time to time when I knew Andrew wouldn't be home for a while I'd go in the top back of the closet and pull out my t-shirt and sweats. I'd smell them and take in Yussef's smell. I wanted to know he was ok, but I dare not ask Andrew. It didn't seem fair to me that he could plead for Toya's life, and she disrespected everyone because she wasn't getting her way. But Yussef who wasn't trying to cause ripples has to pay for seeing what he sees in me. I didn't get it, but at the end of the day it didn't stop me from loving Andrew. I guess it was one of those things.

Carina was very prepared. At the end of the party she had a cleaning crew come in and clean up. They returned Joy's house to normal in less than an hour. It was amazing. A few of us hung around after the shower talking and enjoying each other's company. When I came home I had a back seat full of boxes. Andrew and Andre were in the garage tinkering around with the garage door open.

Andrew came to the car and kissed me. "How was the shower?"

"You knew?"

"Of course!"

"Get this, they yell surprise and I ran back out the door." I said cracking up.

Andrew laughed, "a little jumpy huh?"

"Joy has it on video."

"What's all that?" He said pointing to the back seat.

"Gifts" I said with a big smile.

"You gonna model for me?"

I looked at Andre who was in his own world looking for something to hammer. "Not until we exchange vows."

"I have been a good boy can't I get time off for good behavior?" He fake pouted

"Not when we're six weeks away from the finish line. We went over a year without indulging we can wait six weeks?" I said

"Yea, but that was before you and The Beast connected."

"Seriously? Andre is right there." I said

Andrew sucked his teeth. "Now that you said his name he'll be paying attention."

I got out of the car and started grabbing boxes. "You need help?" Andre asked coming to help me.

Andrew was standing watching me bend over.

"Yes, thank you sweetheart." When we got up into the room, I told Andre to put the boxes on top of the dressers in the closet. Everything from the top shelves of the closet had been taken down. Andrew was reorganizing his side of the closet. He was taking his personal items from his loft, and only leaving the furniture for Darryl who was going to be renting it. Andre and I finished taking the boxes out of the car. Andrew told me to leave my car in the driveway, and he'd put it away once they were finished. So I went back up to the closet. The things I kept at the top of the closet were mostly keepsakes and things like that. I had things spread out over the tops of the closet; I needed to decide what I was keeping and what was going to Goodwill, and what was trash. I looked around the closet trying to figure where to start. So I walked over to Andrew's suits and smelled them. His smell was weaved all

463

through them. As I was smelling his suits and getting lost in their aroma I remembered my t-shirt and sweats. Panic entered my mind as Andrew walked in the closet.

He had a smile on his face. "What are you doing?"

I tried to compose myself. "Oh, just smelling you." I said dropping my eyes because I was embarrassed that he busted me.

"Have I told you how weird you are?" We laughed.

"So weird that you want to spend your life with me? Yea, you have."

"So that side is my side right? I figured we should reorganize the top shelf. I've got knick knacks I need to store."

"Right, that side is officially yours. I need to downsize my side."

"I didn't realize you were so sentimental."

Butterflies hit my stomach. "What do you mean?"

"You've got all kinds of mementos in your boxes. Some I don't think you realize you still have." He walked over to a box. "You've got old diaries, poems, love letters, all kinds of stuff."

"Of course I am. I hold on to things like you wouldn't believe."

I looked at his face and his smile dropped. "What about this?"

My heart was beating out of my chest as he reached down picked up a envelope. Then he handed it to me. "It's a old letter from Steve. Do you think you should keep it?" He didn't look mad, but I'm sure depending on my answer that could change.

"I didn't know I still had anything from him. I'll throw it away."

"You don't want to keep it?" He said searching my eyes. "It's part of your past. I can handle it.... I think." He smiled.

"Everything I thought he was turned out to be all in my head. The way I saw things. I don't need to hold on to him."

"Hhmmmm" he said. Then he picked up the brown tote. My heart dropped, busted was all over my face. "What about this one?" He held up the bag with a knowing expression on his face.

"What about it?" I said taking the bag out of his hand.

He sat on top of the dressers, knocking a few of the boxes to the floor. I bent down to pick them up. "What is it about?"

"It's just sweats and a t-shirt."

"Yea, but what's the story? That bag is from that new store in Rockridge, I thought there would be something good in there. But a pair of sweats and a plain white t-shirt? It peaked my curiosity." He watched my face.

I couldn't lie; if I lied he'd know it right away he studies my face too much. I sat there feeling busted! I opened my mouth and closed it. He wasn't getting mad he was watching me. He was patiently waiting for me to speak.

"It's just a t-shirt and sweats, what's the big deal?"

"No big deal" he said still searching my face. "But your reaction is very telling. Who's is it?"

"Why would you go through my things? Is this what's going to happen from now on? I'll have no privacy anymore." I was trying my hardest to get off topic.

"Hey I was enjoying the stuff I was seeing. I'm not even sorry. It was like I had access to your little sick twisted world. But for some reason this one felt alarming. And your reaction isn't helping. Obviously this stuff belongs to a guy. Who? And who would be so special that you would hold on to it with the rest of this crap?"

"Why are you making such a big deal out of this?"

"I'm not. I wanna hear you tell me who these things belong to?"

"Andrew!" I pleaded with my eyes.

His face turned cold. "Who's are they?"

I walked out the closet. I threw myself on the bed. I didn't want to talk about this. He was pissed when he walked out of the closet. He stood in the middle of the floor. "Is he dead Andrew?" The question made tears pour out of my eyes.

"WHAT????" He hollered, "let me get this right! Explain to me how you have his clothes!"

"Where's Andre? I don't want to scare him." I said

Andrew threw his hands up as he went to sit on the couch. "He's in the backyard with the dogs." He inhaled and exhaled. "I knew things were going too good with us!"

"Is he dead?"

He turned to me with the evilest look on his face. "What do you think!"

I lost it. "What did he do that was so terrible?" I was in full tears. Andrew was looking at me in disbelief but he didn't say anything. "He managed to see in me the same light you do. The difference between him and you, he never tried to change my mind about you, or even push up on me like you did. He knows I have a good man, and he's not trying to interfere."

"Oh yea that's clear. He kidnaps you, and then keeps showing up where you are. He was really standing down." Andrew blew air.

I cried harder. "He was trying to make sure I was ok. Apparently I was in danger, and he was trying to protect me." I caught my breath, "did you kill him?"

"You were not HIS TO PROTECT!" Andrew yelled

"Is that a yes?" I couldn't even look at him anymore my heart hurt.

He stood up and went to the closet. "Good thing I asked you. We can't have stuff like this around the house. I'll burn it in the fireplace. Do you have anything else?"

I couldn't even answer him. My heart hurt so badly. I cried so hard I fell asleep. When I woke up it was dark in the room, and I could hear that someone was downstairs. I went to the bathroom to splash water on my face. My eyes were swollen, it was clear that I had been crying. There was a log burning in the fireplace and a ton of ashes. Derrick was in the family room with Andrew. They were sipping on Hennessy and playing chess.

"Where's Andre?"

Andrew didn't even turn to look at me. "Anthony came and picked him up. They're having a sleepover."

"Hey Tracy how you doing?" Derrick said without looking at me.

"Fine" I said dryly

He glanced up at me, and he jumped really hard. "What happened to your face?"

Andrew looked at me, and then he rolled his eyes. "Nothing man, she been up there crying."

Derrick gathered his composure. "What she crying about?"

"That punk Jeremy!" Andrew said as he made his next move.

Derrick screwed up his face while studying the board. "Why?"

"Cause he's gone!" Andrew said half way angry.

Derrick looked at Andrew, and then he looked at me. "Is that right!" Then he made his next move.

I went back upstairs crying all over again. I wanted to run away! Where was I gonna go? I told him I would stop running away from him, but I didn't want to stay here. I sat on the bed and wrote myself a letter. Telling myself how I felt about the whole thing. One thing was for sure, Andrew's jealousy was not to be mocked or ignored. Like I always told Yussef and anyone who would listen I was in love with Andrew, no one has ever loved me and accepted me like he has. He always makes sure I know how much he loves me, and needs me in his life. I didn't like him very much right now. But I guess this too shall pass. I kept seeing Yussef in my mind, remembering our conversations, hearing his laugh, and seeing him look at me like I was crazy. No one could take my memories and throw them in a fire. Needing something to do I straightened up the closet. I consolidated my lingerie to three boxes and I put all the like pieces in the corresponding boxes. Once the closet was back to its normal neatness, I still needed something to do. Even though it was dark out I decided to go for a run. The fresh air would do me some good. Besides I needed to run off that delicious Nelson's cake from earlier. I got dressed, and then I put a leash on Eve. This run was for the girls. Eve was so happy to be getting out of the house. Andrew watched me walk out the door, but he didn't say anything. Eve and I ran all the way down to Ashby Bart. I remembered Yussef laughing with Andrew after he tazed Steve. I cried all the way back to the house. When I came back in the door Andrew and Derrick were putting the chess pieces away. I guess Andrew knew I was coming back he didn't even come after me.

"Hey sis come hang out with us." Derrick said.

Covered in sweat I walked into the kitchen and made sure Eve had a good amount of water, as I chugged on a bottle myself.

"What's up Derrick?" I said like nothing was wrong.

"What's going on with you? How you doing?"

"I've been better, but oh well. How you been?"

"Look, I'm not gonna beat around the bush. Just cut it out! Were you going to be with Jeremy or something?"

"No."

"Then why all the drama?"

"He was my friend. He didn't do anything wrong. He didn't have to die."

Derrick looked at Andrew, "what did he do?" Andrew held up one finger. Derrick blew air. "Baby girl, that's the luck of the draw. He knew better!" He shook his head. "He knew better!"

I exhaled. "I gotta go shower. Good night Derrick!" I said as I walked out of the kitchen and down the hallway.

As I walked up the stairs I could hear them talking but I couldn't make out what they were saying. I got in the shower and I let the water beat me in the face. I cried some more, my heart was heavy. I put on lotion and pajamas. I sat on the couch and turned on the TV. They were showing a Rosey marathon. I was watching funny episode after funny episode, it helped lighten my mood. Andrew walked in the room; he made both of the puppies sleep outside the door. He looked at me and then he went and got in the shower. He put on pajamas and then he sat on the bed. I could feel him staring at me, but I didn't move.

"What made him so special?" He asked

"He was my friend." I said not looking at him.

"Tracy come here, lets have a real conversation."

"Funny how the only time you'll be honest with me about Toya is when you're drunk, but you want me to spill the beans with you." I said wiggling my neck.

He frowned, "Toya and I were in a relationship for the lack of a better word. You're telling me you and Yussef were in a relationship?"

"No" I had to catch myself. "But I cared about him."

"Come talk to me."

"But Rosey is making me feel better." I whined

"Well HELL! That's what I'm trying to do too. Get your butt over here woman." He patted his lap.

I reluctantly turned off the TV and I whined the whole way over to the bed. I sat on his lap but I crossed my arms. "So you cared about him huh?"

"Yes" I said feeling like a little girl admitting the unthinkable to her father.

"Did you love him?"

"Yes, but like a friend! I was not in love with him."

"What's the difference?"

"I'm in love with you. I want to be with you. I loved our friendship, and when I would go off on the deep end about you, he'd always set me straight. Joy and Nicole would do the same thing, but a male point of view is always different. Besides Nicole doesn't know everything about you, and Joy really doesn't. I could be completely honest with him, and I could relax with him and know that at the end of the day he knew I was in love with you, and that felt wonderful to me."

"So tell me what happened that day."

"He pulled me off Jennay. She ripped my blouse, and my skirt got torn during the fight. He put me in the car and drove off. He said she could've tried to press charges or something. He took me to a house I honestly don't know where we were. He gave me those sweats and that t-shirt to change into. He made dinner, we talked, and in the morning I came home."

"What else Tracy?"

"What?" I said opening my hands.

"I know there's more."

"He showed me the stars." I lowered my voice, "I kissed him." I said real fast.

His body jerked and he closed his eyes. My heart was pounding I didn't know what he would do and it was too late to run. "I know!" He said with his eyes closed.

"You know what?"

"I knew something happened." Then he looked at me with all seriousness in his eyes. I was scared. "I know you, and you had that guilty look plastered on your face. Besides, what you didn't see was when Jennay kissed me." He looked me in my eyes.

"Did you want to be with her?"

"I'll be honest, the thought crossed my mind. Until she did that. She saw my family, didn't care. She was going for hers." He frowned his face, "I didn't return the kiss. But I knew it was my fault for accepting her invitation to lunch thinking nothing was gonna happen."

I put my face on his forehead. "I wasn't trying to hurt you by keeping his stuff. Even the way he cared about me was different than you. I've never had someone care, but be willing to put it aside because they want what's best for me. That has never happened to me before."

He kissed my neck, "I have to have you! All of you. How he did that I don't know. Can you stop moping around about this? He's gone, act like he's on vacation or something."

Tears started pouring out of my eyes. "I'll try, but you balled like a baby when you thought Toya was dead, and you don't even like her."

He chuckled, "I did not!"

"Did too, ask Malcolm."

He laughed, "yea but that's over. Her behind is in jail where she belongs and Steve too."

"What happened to her kids?"

"Will has them. He's a good guy. He kept the kids and he kicked her out. The little girl is his, and he bonded with Will J. So mom's sends him a little something each month to help out. We agreed that the kids should know each other, but he's not gonna take them to see her."

"Funny how everybody gets to live but Yussef. That's not fair!" I said as tears rolled down my face.

"Ssshhhh!" He said rocking me.

CHAPTER 44

"If you don't stop it!" Joy said

"I got this!" I said

"No you don't!" Nicole said snatching my purse from me.

"Why do you have to be like that? I really appreciate all that you've done. I don't want anyone eating noodles for the next couple of weeks because of today." I said

Nicole scoffed at me. "My man may not have Andrew's money, but we are far from broke." Nicole said

"Right! My man does pretty well himself." Joy said, "and yea we work too. Stop worrying about the bill and enjoy the night."

My bridal party rented out a King Suite at the Court Hotel in Emeryville. But they also reserved a conference room to host our pleasure party and stripper show. We started drinking in the room then we went downstairs for the party and show. Although my mother would NEVER attend anything like this Amber and Sophia were there, even Sophia's other daughter Sasha was up for the wedding. My sisters brought Dafina; I made her promise not to tell her mother. I didn't want to be in trouble as the bad influence. Even Becca was there. Sonya was still a little pouty about not being asked to be in my wedding. "I was there for the beginning. But it's too late now anyways." First thing she said when she saw me. Even Marie was disappointed about not being in the wedding, but she got over it.

I was happy to see so many people show up for the Party. A lot of Amber's family was there. She was definitely closer to her father's family than she was to her mother's. Then a bunch of my cousins were there. There were about forty women at least at my party. We had a blast. I couldn't tell if the host for our pleasure party or the group was having more fun. She made a hefty commission on our party. Plus she and her assistant were tipped handsomely. The stripper show was off the hook! There was a main guy but he had two other guys with him. My oh my, can you say embarrassing? Even with all their tricks and flips I told Joy "they still ain't got nothing on Andrew!" She cracked up but I don't think she realized I was serious. When the party downstairs was over they all piled into their cars and of course Amber had a party bus for her folks and they went their ways. Nicole, Joy, Sonya, Tia, Tara, Sasha, Marie, and I went upstairs for our more intimate party. Sasha was our age and really cool. She told us stories about her and Andrew growing up together. She said even as a little girl that Malcolm was scary to her. It's funny how across the board he was a scary guy. Eventually one by one everyone started falling asleep. Lastly Joy and I were the last two awake.

"I can't believe it's almost here. In one week I'll be Mrs. Wallace! It felt like he was never gonna propose even though he told me he was going to."

"Girl, I told you how Anthony completely surprised me. Seems like we were dating, engaged, and married all in one week. But when a man has a plan for you, how do you fight it?"

"I guess. I can't believe it's happening. And all the drama is gone. I feel normal again. It's been like when we first got together. It's been great. I'm so ready to get pregnant and start popping out babies."

"How soon do you plan to start trying?"

"Wedding night!" I said with the biggest smile.

"Ooh girl I wish I had your enthusiasm, how many?"

"As many as we can logically handle. We don't have a limit though."

"How long you gonna work?"

"As long as I can handle it. Becca said the company would be willing to let me work from home if need be."

"That's so good." Joy said happy for me.

We eventually fell asleep. I was awaken to Andrew's call. We agreed not to see each other until the rehearsal dinner. The passion between us was getting so intense. I was ready to throw it out the window. I was begging him to give in. He was the strong one telling me that we needed to stay strong etc. I cried, I tried my hardest to break him down, but my baby held out for the greater good. I admire his strength cause strong wasn't what I wanted. It has been six months and I don't know how we've done this. He asked how my girl's night went. I gave him a high level overview of the evening. He laughed at me and mimicked my report. I laughed telling him I could fill in the blanks. It was nice chatting with him, all those feelings I used to get whenever he would call before came back over me. We both went on and on about how much we missed each other.

We spent the rest of the weekend taking the out of town family site seeing. On Tuesday we picked up our dresses and accessories. Everyone except Amber (but only because she was there) was surprised to get their deposits back and know that Andrew paid for everything. He even bought a dress for Carina.

Carina was working so hard on our wedding. She negotiated everywhere she could to get the best prices. Although our wedding was not cheap, she was coming in at less than half our overall budget of 500K. We had a block of booked rooms at the hotel even. She did a good job of documenting all the events she assisted us with to put in her portfolio. She even had a few much smaller parties in between our events. She was a go-getter, professional, and the whole nine.

Wednesday afternoon Andre and I stole away a few minutes alone. So we went to Park Yogurt by the college for frozen yogurt. We sat on a bench eating our yogurt. He kept telling me how excited he was about the wedding. He was happy that we would finally have the same last name. There were students running around saying their last goodbyes on this lovely June afternoon.

Ms. Berry, a teacher from Andre's school spotted us, and chatted with us. She wanted to show Andre something inside the Phoebe Hearst Museum of Anthropology. She asked if it was ok to take him. I agreed, I guess it's hard to take the teacher hat off once it's on. I sat on the bench still debating about the final style of my hair for Saturday. A group walked by and something hit my lap and bounced off into the grass. I looked at the group walking past. They were all involved in their conversation. Clearly someone dropped something without realizing it. The group crossed the street and I looked down to see what fell. But I couldn't find it. I went back to daydreaming about my upcoming day. Then I heard something hit the grass next to me. I looked up expecting to see a tree dropping nuts or something. But there was no tree, as I turned to my right something hard tapped me on the cheek and fell on the ground. I looked down at the grass, and I saw a bunch of green candies in the grass. My heart stopped and tears instantly poured out of my eyes as I realized they were sour apple jolly ranchers. I popped up on my feet. I spun around looking up and all around. "WHERE ARE YOU????" I screamed out. Students passing by smirked, some even laughed. Andre and Ms. Berry came skipping out of the museum. I pulled myself together quickly, and then I thought about picking up the candy. I wanted to send them away, but Ms. Berry needed to get to her meeting. I couldn't think of anything to postpone our departure. I slowly walked to the garage. I was looking at every person. But we were in Berkeley every black man had dreads. Feeling defeated I loaded Andre into the car. I drove down the street slowly. Andre recited for me all that Ms. Berry had shown him. I didn't think they were gone long enough, but this boy was like a sponge he soaked everything up, he was definitely his father's child. I dropped him off at the loft to his father. Andrew waved at me from the courtyard. When I got home Tia was in the hammock in the backyard, Tara was in the kitchen making dinner. I walked up to her and put my lips on her ear. "I think Yussef is alive!" I whispered. She dropped her knife and led me by the hand to the toilet area in the master suite. She closed the door. Then she whispered, "why do you think he's alive?"

"Why are we whispering in the bathroom?" I asked

"Just in case this house is bugged, I don't think what happens in here is monitored." We laughed

I told her what happened at the college. She smiled, "what does it mean if he is alive?"

Feeling a little deflated by her lack of enthusiasm. "It means that my friend is still breathing and I won't carry the guilt of costing someone their life by being their friend." She looked at me without an expression. "What?"

"You sure?"

"Um yes! I love Andrew with my heart and soul."

"Why would Andrew lie though? How did he tell you Yussef was dead?"

I thought about it, he didn't outright say he was dead. He said he was gone, that doesn't mean dead though. "But if he wasn't dead, why did he burn his clothes?" We shrugged. "Maybe I really want him to be alive so I'm imagining things." I said feeling disappointed

Carina called and went over all the last minute details. The plan was for our honeymoon to be a surprise so I had no idea where we were going. Not knowing how to pack, I packed essentials for the honeymoon. And a separate bag of essentials for our wedding night.

Friday a limo came to pick my sisters and I up and take us to the hotel in the city. It was and interesting feeling locking the house up for the last time as an unmarried woman. Andrew sent Curtis earlier to pick up the dogs. Curtis was a man of very little words, he creeped Tia out. When we arrived and checked into our suite Carina had all of our dresses and everything we needed for tomorrow in the room waiting for us. Our suite was a two-bedroom suite with a king sized bed in the master and double beds in the other room, it had a pullout sleeper, and a few rollaway beds set up as well. I took my rehearsal dress out and threw it on the bed, and then Sylvia my stylist from Jovance came to fix my hair for the rehearsal. As she worked on my hair the rest of the bridal party arrived. The out of town family and friends that arrived today were being escorted by car service to the hotel according to their flight information. In their rooms would be a simple itinerary reflecting what time the limo bus would be downstairs to take them to the rehearsal dinner. If they were not there when it was time to leave it would be assumed that they did not want to attend the optional dinner. The wedding wasn't scheduled until four pm on Saturday. I had butterflies all day. Once Sylvia finished my hair I did the barely there make up look. The bridal party had arrived and was ready to go. Our rehearsal was at five. Everyone was giddy with excitement. I excused myself to go put on my dress. It was cream colored with a square neckline; the back had crisscrossed straps and was completely open down to my waistline. It had a gold skinny belt. I put on simple gold earrings, a simple necklace, bangles, cream and gold strappy heels, and a cream floral clutch with gold hardware. I looked at myself in the mirror pleased with my appearance then I saw the green candy in the middle of my decorative pillow on the silver duvet behind me in the mirror. My heart stopped, I went over to the pillow and picked up the candy. Ok, I'm not crazy. I squeezed the candy in my hand to convince myself that it was real. Yussef is alive, my body temp sped up. Then my mother knocked on the door.

"Come in"

She smiled so proudly when she saw me. She closed the door behind her. She came and gave me the biggest hug. We cried which gave me a lovely cover for my now red eyes. I put the candy in my clutch and then I told her I was ready to go. Everyone looked so nice. I really appreciated that everyone stepped up and wore something nice to the rehearsal. They could've come in jeans and t-shirts, but everyone was dressed up which made me smile. When we walked out on to the atrium where the ceremony was going to be held the men were excited that we had finally arrived. Although we were on time Andrew made all of them come early. Andrew stood three feet taller when he saw me. Knowing that he approved of my appearance always made me feel light as a feather. He gave me the biggest hug as he gently kissed my neck. "You are stunning!" He said in my ear.

I threw my arms around his neck. "Thank you! I could eat you up right now!" Then I kissed him. My baby looked good! And all the love in his eyes made me want to bite him.

"Alright you guys, you got one more night. Try to keep it together." Tara said.

I stuck my tongue at her. On either side of the atrium I noticed Andrew's watchers. My smile dropped, "what's going on?"

He smiled at me, "nothing" then he grabbed my hand. "You ready?"

Carina explained the marching orders to everyone. I was a little distracted looking up at the sky and seeing all the beautiful stars. I could feel it in my heart Yussef was here. Everyone was so happy and full of excitement for us. Derrick kept watching me, which also confirmed for me what I felt to be true. I smiled at him, but when he kept watching me I started making faces at him. His very serious demeanor relaxed. At the start of the ceremony Andrew walks down the aisle. Then Andre escorts my mother to her seat then he joins his father where they stand waiting. Then Malcolm and Amber walk down the aisle together. Then Sophia and Derrick walk down. Sophia waits on my side Derrick waits on Andrew's. Then Sabrina and Darryl. Then Terrence and Amy. Then Tia and Joshua. Then Tara and Jeff. Then AJ walks down as our ring bearer. Then Nicole and Hubby. Then Joy and Anthony. Then everyone rises for my dad and I. We practiced a couple times, and then it was time to eat. Andrew held my hand as we made our way to the party bus. Derrick and Darryl were stone faced looking around and at everyone as we walked to the bus. They were the last two to get on. Andrew's watchers followed the bus in two cars. To my surprise Malcolm was all smiles all evening nothing like his normal strictly business self. My mother asked me where he came from cause she thought he wasn't around. I quickly explained that he and Amber weren't together, and so he was always in the background until recently. "They're both very young!" My mom said as she observed them. I let that comment ride on the air. Who knew Malcolm was so charming, at one point I realized all the women were blushing and all the men looked like they needed to step up their game. Maybe if I wasn't so busy looking out the window for a sign from Yussef I would've known what was going on.

"I can't believe our son is getting married tomorrow, " he said reaching for Amber's hand. Then he looked her in her eyes. "You raised a man!" Everyone got choked up, but Amber lost it. She went into the ugly face cry and everything. Then she laid her head on his shoulder and said, "Thank You!" There were a couple other party buses in the parking lot when we arrived at "Sophia's" and a few cars. The bridal party entered the restaurant in the marching order, everyone cheered as we all entered. Then they stood up and went crazy for Andrew and I. As a gift to us Sophia closed her restaurant for the evening to host our rehearsal dinner. When Andrew told me, I had mixed emotions about going there. Nothing good had happened there. But I got over myself and decided to go with the flow. Seeing the restaurant full of our family and friends definitely changed the vibe for me. So many people made me blush all night long by telling me how good I looked. A lot of my family members hadn't seen me since I was heavier and none of them had seen my face when I was in love. All of our parents were so proud, it was nice to see how much happiness our love brought everyone. I had a stomach full of butterflies, so I ate very little at the table. Plus different ones were coming over to congratulate us and say their hellos. The evening went off without a hitch; I really prayed that Yussef didn't show up at the restaurant anyways. I saw someone from the kitchen take the watchers a box full of food to go. Slowly the guest got in their cars and the buses back to the hotel took off. Sophia thanked her staff for covering so beautifully, and as a special thank you from Andrew and I Carina provided each employee with an envelope. We tipped each person $500 in cash as a thank you for everything. There were tears and lots of hugs in the kitchen. Andrew was being so bashful, but his generosity was greatly appreciated by the staff. "Tonight is a very special night for us, and we wanted each of you to not only know, but understand how much we appreciate everything you did to make it special." Everyone applauded him including me. My baby was always the man. Sophia left the close up in her manager's hands and then we were back on the bus.

I laid my head on Andrew's shoulder. "You know you answered someone's prayer in there. Did you see all the tears? They really needed that." I said kissing his cheek. "You are always the MAN! And I love you so much it hurts!" He blushed as he kissed my forehead. When we got to the hotel, I didn't want to leave Andrew right away I was feeling very sentimental. So Terrence and Amy took Andre and AJ with them to their room, the boys were tired. Once Andrew and I went our separate ways he would come get them to stay in his room with him.

We went to the bar area. "Can you believe we're getting married tomorrow?" I asked so excited.

"I don't think I'll be able to sleep too well tonight. I can't wait for tomorrow to get here." He said

We held hands at our table and gave each other goofy looks. "I guess you really do love me." I said

He blew air. "You love me more."

"No way! It's been you this whole time." We laughed then we sat quietly with no words.

Then Andrew swallowed hard. "I love you and trust you so much that I'm going to do something this one time out of my norm." His face turned serious.

My hands started sweating, "what?" I honestly had no clue what he was going to say.

"I'm gonna call it a night. But you're gonna stay here. I know Yussef is here. Go ahead and talk to him, clear the air. But make sure you explain to him after this..." He squeezed my hands. "After this if he doesn't go away...."

"Ok" I said in disbelief. I leaned over the table and kissed him deeply. "I LOVE YOU SO MUCH!"

"I'm gonna see you tomorrow, four o'clock! Don't be late!" He said looking me in my eyes.

"Bet I beat you there!" I said with tears in my eyes.

He smiled, inhaled deeply and then he stood up. He kissed me on my forehead, and then he walked away. One by one the watchers went away. I sat there feeling stupid after awhile. Then I heard footsteps in the lobby coming towards the bar. I watched the corner as the steps got closer and closer. Yussef came around the corner with the biggest smile on his face. When he got close to the table I stood up and I gave him the biggest hug. Then I saw Derrick sitting in the far corner watching. Andrew trusts me, but he ain't stupid. Yussef squeezed me tight! "I thought you were dead!" I whispered.

"Nope, I'm alive and well!" He said through a smile. We sat down, "the big day is tomorrow are you ready?"

"Yes!" I shouted! "I'm so ready! I can't believe it's finally here."

"I know," he said smiling and taking me in. "You are a glowing bride." Then he tilted his head. "Are you pregnant?" He teased.

"No! You clown! I'm so happy right now. I was so worried about you."

"Once I knew you were ok, there was no need for me to hover."

"I want to apologize for how rude I was the last time I saw you. I was so scared!"

"I know! What you were saying was right. I needed to make sure you knew I was there. I wasn't gonna show myself that night, but when I saw Steve, and Andrew was in the other room, I wanted you to know it was ok and that you were protected. It was important to me that you felt safe."

"Thank you! But did they find you that night?" My eyes were wide.

He closed his eyes and then he looked at me. "It was a crazy night. I thought I was gonna die at one point, but as you see." He smiled again. "You have a good man."

"I know! He's the best!"

Then I remembered my burning question. "Who is Jeremy?"

He laughed. "That's an alias that Andrew gave me. Depending on the job I have quite a few. Jeremy is the lowly servant, my quick give name."

"So Jeremy the waiter?" I asked

"Yea, Jeremy the waiter, Jeremy the car wash attendant, Jeremy the chef."

"What did your mother name you?" I asked

"Yussef, very few know me by that name. Angela knows me as Jeremy."

"That's right, how's things going?"

He blushed, "they're going really good. Especially since I'm not running around behind a drama queen anymore."

"Do you have a picture?"

"I do actually." He showed me a picture of them on his phone. She was a beautifully average looking full figured female, in my book that made her gorgeous. "Yussef! She's gorgeous!"

He blushed, "thank you. She's a really good woman. A thinker!"

"I'm so happy for you. When will she meet Yussef?"

"Things keep going like they're going very soon. I might even have a baby or two." He said still blushing.

"That's so good!" I was so happy for him. And I was so happy to be able to talk to my friend again. I told him what Andrew said. He assured me that he understood. We hung out for about and hour and then I thanked him for everything he has done for me from the bottom of my heart. He told me that he still loved me, and that he was truly happy for me. Derrick looked at his watch when I hugged Yussef goodbye. Then he came over.

"So you shoving off?" Derrick said reaching out his hand for a shake.

"Oh yea, got a long drive ahead of me."

"We got the number in case we need you in the future right?" Derrick asked

"Yep, you know it stays on."

"Alright man!" Derrick said

"Alright!" Yussef said

Then he walked away, and I walked with Derrick. I was cheesing so hard at Derrick. He looked at me, rolled his eyes, and shook his head. "I'll never understand women."

"What's to understand? He's my friend! Nothing more!" I said still smiling

"I guess!" He said shaking his head.

Derrick walked me to my room where everyone was still awake and waiting for me. I hugged him goodnight, and he stood there frozen like I threw ice on him, he fumbled through that hug just like Malcolm. "You're weird!" He said and then he walked away shaking his head.

In the morning we all had breakfast and massages in the room. They sent estheticians up to do our facials, manicures, and pedicures. Carina had the rotation running so smoothly. I showered then Sylvia styled my hair. Then Paul from the Makeup Store did my makeup. He brought a team with him, everyone was beautiful! The photographer captured wonderful shots of us all day and as we got ready. I was last to put on my dress. It was beautiful and it fit perfectly. There was nothing left to do other than marry my prince. My father came to get us. He got teary eyed when he saw me. We walked through the lobby in the order of our procession. Carina had my father and I stand in a room over to the side. When it was time she handed me my beautiful bouquet of Casablanca lilies and silver sash. When we stepped into the doorway it seemed like a million people were standing. They were all smiling at me. A lot of people cried. I even saw Andrew's lip quiver when he saw me. He grabbed the railing and Anthony steadied him. A few people laughed. His reaction to me was priceless and everything I envisioned. When my dad gave my hand to Andrew he said, "this is not a loan" loud enough for only us to hear. Andrew shook his head and whispered, "yes sir". Our ceremony was short but sweet. My mother asked a Brother from her congregation to officiate, he told her he would be honored to do it. It seemed like I floated outside myself to watch us exchange our vows. Andrew stared into my eyes as he vowed to love me forever in sickness and health.

After the ceremony the guest were asked to go to the appetizer room while we took pictures. Andrew and I couldn't stop kissing. Most of our pictures contained Andrew, Andre, and I. But we did manage to sneak a few of just the two of us. Joy and Anthony signed as our witnesses. Then Carina showed us the reception hall before anyone entered. It was beautiful! Everything I dreamed of. She captured everything I said I wanted and more. Andrew and I hugged her and thanked her so much. Then we told her in addition to her commission, we wanted her to keep the surplus from our budget. Now she cried. She told us that she was going to use the money to lease her office space. I reminded Andrew again, that he was making miracles happen. Then we returned to our pictures. The guest were shown to their assigned seating, and then the wedding party was announced. It sounded like thunder when the applause erupted when we entered. We danced our first dance as husband and wife.

"I love you!" Andrew said

"I love you!" I said

MORE FROM THE AUTHOR

Thank you for allowing me to entertain you. I hope you have enjoyed reading my current release. If you have not read Volumes I – VIII of the Wallace Family Affairs series, please do so. Click here for a list of all the background stories. Once you have read the background stories, please checkout the current date series Together We Are Strong. Stay tune for more to come shortly.

Wallace Family Affairs

At Last (Click here)
Volume I Tracy's Complications
Distorted Mirrors (Click here)
Sometimes Love Isn't Enough (Click here)
Love Is Just Enough (Click here)
Just A Friend (Click here)
Invisible (Click here)
Look Beyond Your Eyes (Click here)
No Regrets (Click here)
First You Laugh Then You Cry (Click here)
A Heart That's Taken (Click here)
Abandoned (Click here)
 Last Words (Click here)

Together We Are Strong

Season 1 Present (Click here)
Beyond The Wallace's ~ I Knew You When (**TBD**)
Season 2 What Comes Next (Release **TBD**)

Standalones

Secrets & Lies ~ (**TBD late 2016 release**)
Anthology **Short** Story (Where Love May Find You Collection) ~ (Click here)
Waiting (**TBD**)
Hopefully you've enjoyed all of the background stories for our lovely Wallace's and Latour's. Please tune in for more from the "Together We Are Strong" Wallace & Latour Family Episodes on Amazon.